Honeymoon for One

Honeymoon for One

Rachel Bowdler

embla books

First published in Great Britain in 2022 by

Bonnier Books UK Limited
4th Floor, Victoria House, Bloomsbury Square, London, WC1B 4DA
Owned by Bonnier Books
Sveavägen 56, Stockholm, Sweden

A CIP catalogue record for this book is available from the British Library.

ISBN: 9781471415487

This book is typeset using Atomik ePublisher

Embla Books is an imprint of Bonnier Books UK
www.bonnierbooks.co.uk

For Leah,
The first person who wanted to listen to me
ramble about the worlds and people in my head.
But, most importantly, my best friend.

Chapter One

'How could you *forget* to cancel a *honeymoon*?'

A valid enough question. Still, it didn't make Robin feel any better about the discovery she had made this morning when an email notification from Delta Airlines requested that she confirm her details before her flight to Canada in two days. Worse was that it had arrived on the very day she would have been getting married had the engagement not ended in many tears, quite a lot of shouting, and Robin having to move back into her mum's house eight months ago.

It had also woken her from a well-deserved lie-in. After a fortnight of working endless overtime shifts at the restaurant, she hadn't been too impressed. It turned out that the holidays were neither merry *nor* bright for a flustered, exhausted pastry chef trying to neatly spoon out quick-melting black cherry sorbet in a hectic, red-hot kitchen. As much as Robin loved her job – and loved all things sweet – she would be glad not to see another profiterole for the next two weeks.

'I suppose I was too busy being jilted and heartbroken,' she bit back now, scowling at her sister and snatching an untouched waffle from Wren's plate. She made sure to avoid the healthy portion of strawberries on the side.

'Okay, but . . . a *honeymoon*.' Wren scanned the email on Robin's phone again, disbelief twisting across her features as though she hadn't read it just two minutes ago.

'You can keep saying it,' Robin said through an extra-large mouthful of food, 'but it will still be true.'

'But it's like forgetting to cancel your wedding! Oh, God. You did cancel the wedding, didn't you?'

1

She sighed. 'Yes. I cancelled the wedding. And the cake. And the reception. And the flowers.'

'Does Lexi know?'

'About the cancelled wedding? If she doesn't, she's not very perceptive. I did flush my engagement ring down her toilet.' That sharp pang of hurt, betrayal, hopelessness, still sliced through her chest when talking about her ex-fiancée, even after all this time. The email felt like an ill-timed prank; a gift better left at home. As though Robin needed the blatant reminder of the plans she and Lexi had made together this time last year when she'd been happily swathed in blissful ignorance.

Well, *Lexi* had made the plans. Robin had gone along with them. Paid for them. She would have agreed to anything if Lexi had asked: even that weekend-long yoga retreat that had almost cost Robin the use of her knees, or cleaning the guttering because the council wouldn't come out for them when it had been blocked by a dead pigeon. And, apparently, even a honeymoon spent freezing in the snow.

As though living in the north of England hadn't already granted them a lifetime of crappy weather.

Robin had complained at first. She'd wanted to go somewhere hot and relaxing. Somewhere she could lounge by a pool and eat a lot of cheese and crisps. But Lexi had always wanted to go skiing. It would be fun, she'd claimed. They'd learn a new hobby together and enjoy romantic nights by a log fire. Robin had caved only when Lexi had said, 'Think of the poutine. And the toasted marshmallows. And the cakes and mulled wine from the Christmas markets.'

Comfort food was Robin's weakness – and so was Lexi, until Robin had found her cheating not six months into their engagement, and just four months after booking the wedding.

Wren tutted. 'I mean does she know about the honeymoon, idiot.'

'No, I doubt it.' Robin's voice was strained, chest tight.

'Everything was booked in my name, surprise surprise. It was my job to cancel it all.'

'Okay . . .' Wren finally placed the phone down, pensively chewing on her lip. 'So go.'

The orange juice that Robin had been sipping almost sputtered out of her nostrils. 'Excuse me? *What?*'

'*Go.*' Wren shrugged. 'You deserve a break. The trip is booked. I doubt you'll get a refund now, and you already have the time off work.'

'I can't go to *Canada* on my own!'

'Why not?'

It was easy for Wren to suggest taking a transatlantic trip; she hadn't been cheated on and dumped on the same day, for starters, and with those sharp cheekbones and her glowing, blemish-free skin, she probably never would be. Besides, she was in a stable relationship with perhaps the most reliable man on earth, a cardigan-wearing primary school teacher named Tom.

Robin would never be as comfortable in herself as her sister was. She would always feel out of place, would always say the wrong thing and embarrass herself just to make it worse. Verbal diarrhoea had become a permanent affliction, and so had frequently tripping over her own feet.

Not that she *wanted* to change. Not that she *minded* being awkward and loud. But that didn't mean she wanted to take that awkward loudness to Canada alone. Especially not as it was probably one of the reasons her fiancée had decided to cheat on her in the first place.

No, going on her honeymoon on her own was out of the question. Robin would be lucky if she even made it to the airport without some sort of trauma. It was Wren who was the sensible, independent one; Wren who was brave enough to put herself out there. Lexi had been the one to pull Robin out of her shell. Now that it was over, Robin would probably never move out of Mum's house again or do anything exciting with her life, and maybe she was okay with that. She would *have* to be okay with that. Besides, Mum would throw a fit at the idea of Robin going away.

Unable to say any of these things aloud, she simply stuttered, 'Because!'

Wren rolled her eyes and tightened her ponytail. She was already dressed in her nylon workout gear – a fact that made Robin feel quite nauseous, wrapped in her cosiest pink robe as she was. '"Because" what?'

Robin searched for the first excuse she could find. 'I hate skiing.'

'You've never *been* skiing. Wasn't that the whole point of going? To learn? Be more adventurous?'

'That was Lexi's idea. Not mine.' Curse their mother for bringing life to such a rational human being. Robin might not have been skiing before, but she had surfed her way down a hill on a dustbin lid as a teenager and almost lost her two front teeth, and that was proof enough that she shouldn't involve herself in any sort of sports reliant on . . . well, moving. 'I hate snow.'

'More than you hate Mum's Christmas Eve Eve Eve fish pie?'

The protest died on Robin's lips. She *did* hate that fish pie. She hated Mum's annual Christmas Eve Eve nut roast and her Christmas Eve seafood stir-fry, too – made from fish pie leftovers. More than any of that, she hated spending the short time she had off work amongst her crowded family, and she didn't doubt that this year would be much worse. She was single again. That meant offers of blind dates with friends of friends and pitying glances and Nanna Bessie reminding Robin with a waggling, bony finger every five minutes, 'You know, my neighbour is one of those bisexuals,' in order to prove her dedication to the LGBTQ+ alliance. It was very nice and very progressive of a ninety-year-old, but also a little bit repetitive to hear after the fifteenth time.

'Don't bring the fish pie into this.' Robin crossed her arms over her chest, pouting with the knowledge that Wren had weakened her defences. 'I'm not going.'

'*Robin*,' Wren scolded, snatching the plate of waffles away so that Robin was forced to look at her. Robin glowered and tried to grab it back, but her sister was four inches taller than her even when Robin was perched on a stool. 'I really think you should go. I think it will be good for you.'

'You think that *spinach* is good for me,' Robin retorted. 'Am I supposed to trust your judgement? Besides, Mum wouldn't let me go even if I wanted to!'

'You're twenty-six years old, dear. You don't need Mum's permission.' Wren threw the plate down and popped her earbuds back into her ears, hands lifted in surrender. 'But, y'know, stay here moping around all Christmas while Aunty Joan updates you on all of her stamp-collecting endeavours if you want. You're only wasting – how much was it? A grand?'

It was closer to two grand, actually, and had drained Robin's savings account. Easy to ignore as long as she didn't open her mobile banking app too often. Less so when Wren reminded her.

'*Ugh!* Why are you even here, anyway? You don't live here anymore.'

'I came to get *my* earphones. The ones you stole from me in the hopes I wouldn't notice.'

Robin grunted dramatically again, throwing a waffle at her sister's back before she left. It flopped to the floor pathetically and was then devoured by their mum's severely overweight chihuahua a second later. Wren only flashed her middle finger and slammed the front door, leaving Robin to wallow in a silence that was broken all too quickly.

Mum bumbled into the kitchen with a laundry basket, singing one of those old Elvis Presley Christmas songs that Robin had always despised. She stopped to pet a happy-looking Cleo around the ears – and then stilled, brows furrowing. 'You haven't been feeding Cleopawtra waffles again, have you?'

'No,' Robin lied, only to bow her head guiltily when her mum rose with the corner of a waffle in her hand. It was difficult to slip anything past the woman, especially when it came to her beloved not-so-furry fur baby, who, due to her sheer elegance, smooth black coat, and long lashes, was also believed to be the reincarnation of her namesake. Mum had gone through a documentaries phase when she'd gotten bored of watching *Loose Women* while ironing, and the showings on Egyptology had coincided with Cleo's adoption.

She tutted now and began to load the washing machine, still whistling. 'Your Nanna Bessie called this morning. She'll be here a few days early for Christmas. You'll never *believe* the gift she bought you this year.'

Robin's mother was never one to keep secrets – a blessing and a curse depending on the circumstance. Robin couldn't be sure which of them it would be in this case, though she supposed that when it came to her grandmother, she needed a forewarning to practise her "*I'm so chuffed with this gift I have absolutely no use for!*" face. 'What?'

'A new girlfriend!'

Robin choked on her strawberry. She knew that fruit was a bad idea. '*What?*'

'She made it out of pillows and blankets, apparently. Please pretend to like it when you open it.'

Robin groaned again, reaching the end of her tether. She couldn't spend the entire Christmas here, single and subjected to her bizarre family. With work not as enjoyable as it used to be, the date of her non-wedding, and Britain's weather as miserable and rainy as ever, she was burned out enough as it was. Perhaps if she *did* go on the already booked holiday (she refused to keep calling it a honeymoon), it wouldn't be *so* bad. It would be difficult without Lexi, but there would be a hot tub in her room, and she could take a few books to read by the log fire to distract herself. She wouldn't have to *actually* ski – or even leave the lodge. A secluded cabin holiday, free of fish pies and pillow blanket girlfriends. People went on those all the time, didn't they?

The more Robin thought about it, the more appealing it sounded, even if she wasn't too keen on the idea of a fifteen-hour flight. But that was fifteen hours she might have otherwise spent trying to avoid Nanna Bessie, and at least the space next to her would be free for her to put her feet up. Plus, Lexi had made her book fancy business-class seats. Robin had always wanted to see if the squishy cushions and footrests were worth the extra hundreds of pounds they cost. She'd paid for them now. Might as well test them out. She could even smuggle one home for future use.

Her mind was made up, but that wasn't really the hard part. *This* was the hard part. She hadn't missed a Christmas here since birth. Even when she'd taken a gap year to travel – with friends, thank goodness, and not on her own – Mum had forced Robin to come home five days before Christmas Day or else face the consequences of skipping her countdown eve feasts, and those usually included month-long silent treatments and all of Robin's recordings of *I'm a Celebrity . . . Get Me Out of Here!* deleted from the Sky planner.

Mum's need to keep her children close had only worsened since Robin's father had passed away three years ago in a car accident on the way back from a fishing trip. It had happened just after Wren had moved out, leaving Mum to rattle around in a three-bedroom house with only Cleopawtra and a grieving Robin for company. Losing Dad so suddenly had been awful enough, but Robin could only imagine how difficult it had been for Mum to lose her husband.

Robin had certainly tried to break free once before, when she'd moved into Lexi's flat in the centre of Manchester, an entire train ride away from home. Mum hadn't spoken to her for a month afterwards. In her post-engagement, pre-break-up haze, Robin had never actually gotten around to telling her about the honeymoon booked for Clement Falls, Alberta, scheduled for the ninth until the day before Christmas Eve. Another thing she'd argued about with Lexi and lost. If Robin wanted a peaceful couple of weeks, she was going to have to break the news – *now*.

'You know what, Mum?' Guilt turned her voice small, her stomach churning as aggressively as the washing machine on speed rinse. 'I don't think I'll be here this year. Not until Christmas Eve, anyway.'

Mum dropped her bundle of laundry, and all hell broke loose.

'*Excuse me?*' The question came out so high-pitched that Cleopawtra had a better chance of translating for Robin.

'Well . . . I forgot to cancel the honeymoon . . .' she swallowed the word down bitterly '. . . I booked with Lexi, and Wren thinks I should go alone—'

'*No*,' Mum protested. 'Absolutely bloody not. Christmas is *family* time, Robin. You never even mentioned a honeymoon before!'

Because I knew you'd react like this, Robin almost said, but then thought better of it. 'Mum—'

'Where were you even going to go?'

She paused nervously. 'A ski resort in Canada.'

'Canada!' Mum scoffed as though Robin had said the Bermuda Triangle. 'I can't believe you would even *suggest* such a thing. And to spring it on me now!' She cupped her freckled hands to her face. 'I can't believe you would want to abandon us over the holidays. Honestly, after everything this family has been through . . .'

When Robin caught a glimpse of the golden band curling around Mum's ring finger, her resolve weakened slightly.

'You make it sound as though you'd be here all alone. The house is always full over Christmas. You wouldn't even notice I'm gone.'

It was wishful thinking and, judging by Mum's clenched jaw and blazing blue eyes, the wrong thing to say. 'Of *course* I would notice, and so would everybody else. You're my *daughter*!'

'But I'd be back on Christmas Eve. I'd still be here for the important stuff.' Robin was no longer sure why she was putting so much energy into arguing. She hadn't even wanted to go on the bloody trip an hour ago, and now she was risking exile for it. Still, her gaze slipped to a photograph of Dad on Mount Everest, which was pinned to the fridge with a magnet. She used to fall asleep listening to his tales of travelling. He was always telling Robin she needed a nice holiday, and how important a change of scenery or learning a new skill was. He'd want this for her. The victorious smile in the photo felt like him saying so.

'It's *all* "important stuff".' Mum's chin wobbled with the rest of her head. 'What about Christmas Eve Eve, and Christmas Eve Eve Eve, and—'

'I get it,' Robin interjected with a wince. 'But, Mum . . . I'm *tired*. It's been an awful year, and work is rubbish at the minute, and I'm just not in the mood to be trapped in a crowded house. I really do think this would be good for me. Dad always wanted me to travel, didn't he?'

With her slippered foot stamping out an imaginary mini-Robin into the kitchen tiles, Mum placed her hands on her hips.

And that was the crux of it, wasn't it? Robin would always have to make her decisions based on what everyone else needed from her: when she'd moved in with Lexi, she had to come back every weekend to make sure Mum was all right. When she'd been left devastated by the break-up and moved back home, she hadn't been allowed to show her pain because Mum couldn't have any more moping in the house. When she'd begun to realise that maybe the restaurant wasn't a good fit for her anymore, she hadn't been allowed to quit because, with just the two of them living in the old family house now, Mum needed any contribution to the bills that Robin could give her.

Her entire life had been a heart monitor flatlining, her energy and time and offerings saved for everyone else. Her *love* saved for everyone else, until there was nothing left for herself. There was the occasional blip, the occasional pulse – the gap year spent travelling, which her dad had encouraged her to do; dropping out of university to enrol in a catering course, also Dad's idea; moving in with Lexi – but they were few and far between, especially since Dad died and she had nobody to push her forward.

Maybe Robin didn't want to go skiing or get snowed into a cabin or travel halfway across the world, but she *did* want a little bit of peace, some time to remember who she was when she wasn't a daughter without a dad or a pastry chef rushed off her feet or a fiancée who'd never made it to the altar. Everything was weighing on her, and *God*, she was tired – of herself, of it all.

So yes. Yes, she would fight for the trip, even if it meant her mother looking at her as she did now, heartbroken and rejected and furious.

'You'll have Wren,' Robin said. 'And Cleopawtra. And Nanna Bessie.'

'And what if you don't come back? Hmm?' Mum said sternly.

Robin's heart faltered. 'Mum . . .' Her sinuses burned with oncoming tears, grief a familiar flame in her gut.

'No.' Mum cut her protest off with a wave of her hand. 'No. What if you get stuck up a ski slope or slip on black ice and break your neck? What if the plane crashes or your cab slides off the road? What then? What happens to me then, Robin?'

It was ridiculous. This entire conversation was ridiculous. Mum only ever brought the loss up as a warning, a way of throwing it in their faces when they wanted to branch out. *You might not come home. Everything outside of this house is out to get you.* Was Robin supposed to spend the rest of her life walking on eggshells?

Mum did. She barely left the house anymore, and only dared if Wren offered to take her shopping or out for a coffee. It had been worrying at first, but she was stubborn and claimed to be fine. So they all just got on with it. Made it their new normal. Is that what Robin wanted for herself? To be stuck at home, stagnant as their old, neglected fishless fishpond in the backyard, growing algae and having only the blue bottle flies for company?

The idea made her nauseous. Restless. She couldn't find herself in the same place she'd become lost.

'What if I get run over by a tram on my way to work tomorrow? What if I have an allergic reaction to my shampoo? What if I get salmonella from those dodgy eggs you bought from Dave up the road?' Robin spat out finally, more bitterly than she'd intended. Maybe a part of her blamed Mum for not having a life of her own, and she'd only realised it now. But that wasn't right. She had to start making her own choices. Softer, she said: 'I'll be fine, Mum. Promise.'

She reached for her mum's hand, but Mum snatched it away, face red and blotchy with distress. 'Honestly, Robin. This is the most ridiculous idea you've ever had. You can't even *ski*.'

Defeated, Robin sighed and pushed away from the bar stool, avoiding the chihuahua hovering around her feet for more breakfast scraps. 'Apparently that's why you go on a ski trip. To *learn*.'

'Don't walk away from me, Robin Louise Ellis—'

But Robin Louise Ellis did walk away, because her mother's shouting was giving her a headache and so was everything else. A seed of doubt still threatened to bloom in her stomach. She didn't know if she was making the right decision, but she did know that, despite what she'd said, she trusted Wren's judgement more than she trusted her mum's. She couldn't keep doing this. She couldn't keep feeling guilty for wanting to *live* again.

So, before Robin could talk herself out of it, she printed off the plane tickets, rootled through her wardrobe for a suitcase, and threw in her warmest clothes.

It was the first thing she'd chosen for herself in years, and it was freeing. Frightening, but freeing.

Chapter Two

The first benefit of going on a one-woman honeymoon was the empty seat beside Robin on the plane. The first drawback was . . . well, the empty seat beside Robin on the plane.

No matter how she tried, she couldn't stop imagining how different things would have been if she were with Lexi now, in a state of post-marital bliss. Robin was so used to being constantly surrounded by family that it was an effort not to say every thought that popped into her head aloud, forgetting that – for the first time in her life – she was completely and utterly alone. The other passengers probably wouldn't want to hear her intermittent bursts of internal monologue, usually about whether she had chosen the right bra that morning – she hadn't, because the wire was digging into her ribs – or if it was socially acceptable to take off one's shoes on an aeroplane. If it wasn't, it should have been; fifteen hours was a long time to suffocate one's feet with the stiff snow boots she'd borrowed (stolen) from Wren's wardrobe.

To distract herself from the stifling solitude, Robin popped on her headphones to watch a film. The sour-cream-and-onion-flavoured pretzels offered by the flight attendants were repeating on her, and she had to swallow down her belches. An elderly man in the next row seemed to be having the same problem, only he was quite happy to set his gas free. If Lexi had been here, they would have laughed about it.

No. No more thinking about Lexi.

Growing fidgety, Robin glanced out of the window. Solid ground was a mere memory against the bright, cloudy blue skies yawning out behind the small windows. It was surreal. A dream: the anxiety-inducing sort that made her feel as though she was floating, about to fall, and when she finally would, when her stomach would plunge with the realisation that there was nothing to catch her, she'd wake up.

Only Robin didn't wake up, and there was nothing to catch her now, and this wasn't a dream at all.

Panic roiled through her, sharp and icy. She was untethered. She could fall out of the sky at any moment. The only thing stopping her was this cage of metal, weighed down by hundreds of passengers and gravity and luggage and . . .

Oh, God. What was she doing?

No. No, she was fine. She would just focus on the film – which worked for the first hour or so, because Renée Zellweger's posh British accent in *Bridget Jones's Diary* always seemed to calm Robin down on a bad day. She could imagine herself tucked up watching it in bed with Wren, pigging out on chocolate while Wren ate yoghurt-covered cranberries or grapes. But then Mark Darcy told Bridget that he liked her, just the way she was, and Robin thought about the fact that Lexi had never said that to her in any capacity. She'd told her to shush when she got a bit loud and drunk at parties, or tutted when Robin burned her hand on the oven – *again* – but she'd never given her that smouldering, moon-eyed Colin Firth look.

Maybe Lexi had never loved her. Maybe their whole relationship had just been Robin imagining something that hadn't existed.

Maybe Robin was Bridget Jones without the Mark Darcy part, on her honeymoon alone, ready for two weeks of wine and pyjamas and moping while singing "All By Myself" because nobody *wanted* her or *needed* her.

She hadn't realised she'd started crying until a hand on her shoulder startled her. Robin swiped her damp cheeks with the sleeve of her jumper, removing her headphones to find a middle-aged, dark-haired flight attendant with an annoyingly perfect smile hovering in the aisle. Her brows knitted with concern. 'Is everything okay, ma'am?'

'Oh, wonderful.' Robin sniffled into her empty pretzel packet and then smiled appreciatively when the flight attendant swapped it for a tissue. 'Sorry. Thank you.'

The woman glanced both ways as though making sure nobody was watching and then sidled into the empty seat beside Robin. Lexi's seat.

'Colin Firth always makes me cry, too,' she whispered. Robin searched for a name badge and found one pinned onto the lapel of her pristine red uniform. Stefanie.

'Oh . . .' Drained and mortified, Robin didn't have the energy to point out that it wasn't the film that had set her off. Well, not really. She hid her embarrassment behind a sip of her water. 'Yeah.'

'Are you a nervous flyer? Can I get you something stronger?' Stefanie nodded to the plastic cup in Robin's trembling hands.

She almost said yes. Almost. But getting drunk now was not a good idea. Robin was a weepy, embarrassing, loud drunk and the other passengers didn't deserve to have her slobbering all over them while she told them how pathetic she was.

'No. No, thank you. I'm just . . . I'm emotional. It's my first holiday alone and I'm freaking out a bit. Not that I can do anything about it now. Can't get the pilot to turn back, can I?' She laughed, but the more she thought of it, the better the idea sounded. 'I *can't* get the pilot to turn back, can I?'

'Unfortunately not.' Stefanie smiled politely and patted Robin's hand. Her perfume was pungent, expensive, and Robin fought back a sneeze with its growing proximity. 'You know, I think you'll be okay once you get there. I grew up in Calgary, and it's a beautiful place. There's so much to do that you won't even notice the nerves soon.'

'Yeah.' Robin wasn't convinced as she dabbed at her eyes again, trying not to look outside, where there was still nothing to break her fall but wispy clouds. Nothing to catch her, nobody to hold her up. She had no idea how flight attendants managed it, stuck in vast and endless skies every day. It was just an in-between: a void. Easy to forget that there would ever be a way out again.

'How long are you staying?'

'Two weeks. I fly back the night before Christmas Eve.' If she managed to survive until then.

Maybe her mum had been right. Maybe this was too risky, too stupid. Anything could happen to her, and what would she do if it did? She didn't have Wren to hide behind, or her mum to talk to. She didn't have Cleopawtra to yap aggressively like she did at the postman. She didn't have Lexi.

'See!' Stefanie's green eyes twinkled with reassurance. 'You'll be home in no time. You want my advice? Enjoy the vacation while you can. And drink your water.'

Robin obeyed with a wavering smile, but it was lukewarm and only made her more nauseous. 'You must think I'm a mess.'

'*Pfft*,' Stefanie dismissed, batting a tanned hand. 'I've been doing this for twenty years. I've seen far, far worse. I have to ask, though, if you don't like being alone . . . why are you? Why the empty seat?'

There went pretending. Robin pressed herself further into her cushioned chair – not worth the extra hundred pounds, by the way – in the hopes it might collapse and swallow her whole. When it didn't, she sucked in a jagged breath. 'You're going to think I'm pathetic. Like, worse than Bridget Jones when she sings "All by Myself" at the beginning of the film. Worse than when she trusts Hugh Grant and then finds out he's cheating on her.' Come to think of it, that was practically the plot of Robin's life. She just had to age six years and make blue soup.

'Try me.'

'Okay. Challenge accepted. I'm on my honeymoon alone.'

15

Stefanie gasped, her French-manicured fingers falling to her mouth. '*No*. Did you have a runaway groom?'

'No, just a cheating fiancée and a terrible memory. Anyway, my sister convinced me I should take the holiday anyway, even though I hate snow and can't ski, so I gave in, but now my mum hates me because she thinks I'm going to break my neck on black ice, and I'm all alone and I don't know why I'm here and—'

'Water,' Stefanie ordered, and thank God. Robin was about to spiral again. She gulped down the water, trying to steady her breaths as Stefanie continued. 'Look, travelling alone is scary, and getting cheated on is one of the worst things you can experience, but look at you. You're here, on a plane, with . . .' Stefanie checked an expensive-looking rose gold wristwatch '. . . nine hours and thirteen minutes left to go. And then you're going to feel solid ground beneath your feet, and you're going to pick up your suitcase and get in a cab to your hotel or resort or whatever, and you're going to call your mom, and she's going to tell you how proud she is of you. Does that sound so bad?'

'No,' Robin said weakly. It wasn't a lie. She quite liked waiting for her luggage to appear on the conveyor belt. It still filled her with the same childlike wonder it had when she'd gone on her first family holiday to Ibiza and airport security had shouted at her for climbing onto it. Besides, it was only an hour's drive to Clement Falls from the airport. Once she got into her cabin, she could freak out and break down and then get in her pyjamas and drink herself silly if she wanted. She'd be alone, but there would at least be wine and, with any luck, a comfy bed. She could call Wren. Wren would know what to say.

Robin only had to make it through the flight. She could do that. She'd made it through worse: health and safety training at work, for example, or that time she'd gotten food poisoning just before a Katy Perry concert.

Nine hours. That's all it was. Nine hours with an empty

seat on one side of her and a complete abyss on the other. That was nothing.

'You've done the hard part,' Stefanie said. 'You got through customs.'

That was true, too. A wrinkly old man had patted her down with a stale baked bean stuck to his chin. He mustn't have looked in the mirror since breakfast, and Robin didn't have the heart to tell him.

'Is there some secret talent to being good at travelling?' she asked. 'You must move around a lot. How do you keep from panicking or feeling homesick?'

Stefanie smiled and stood from the chair. Apparently, her break was over. 'There's no talent. You just have to find the things meant for you – did you find them at home?'

'No.' Not unless the things meant for Robin were a frustrating job, a life of perpetual loneliness, and an overweight chihuahua. 'But don't you feel a bit lost when you're always . . . floating around in here? What about your family?'

She tilted her head as though considering, her green eyes glistening with something wistful and far away. 'I never thought of it as floating. I guess it is a little lonely sometimes, but it's the choice I made. Besides, I'm going home for the holidays this year. Finally get to spend Christmas with my kids. I miss being a mom.'

It felt strange to be doing the opposite. Robin looked around at the other passengers – an old lady who slept with her mouth agape, dribbling; a boy who didn't look to be out of his teens with his nose in one of those books Robin always said she would read but never got around to; a middle-aged woman with a child napping across her lap. How many of them were going home for Christmas? How many of them would be welcomed into Canada with family and friends and loved ones while Robin went to a resort in a new place, alone?

'How old are they?' Robin asked, more out of politeness than anything else.

'Oh, they're adults now.' Stefanie batted her away. 'What about you? What's your family like?'

She shrugged. 'Chaotic. Irritating.'

Tears pricked her eyes as she thought of Mum, Wren, Nanna Bessie. They might have been those things, but they were still the most familiar people in the world. They were home. And she couldn't forget the look on her mum's face before she'd gotten into the taxi this morning. She had snatched Robin's suitcase from her room and hidden it in the linen closet while she'd showered, so Robin had almost missed her flight. It was Wren who had resolved the situation with her level-headedness, but Mum hadn't said so much as a goodbye to Robin before her departure. The fact made her feel queasy, and she still wasn't sure if she'd made the right decision. No matter how old she was, she couldn't help but feel achingly lost and hurt when Mum was upset with her.

'My mum didn't want me to come,' she continued. 'But my dad . . . he'd want me to try new things. Do something exciting for a change.'

'I think I'd like your dad.' Stefanie squeezed Robin's shoulder gently. 'Problem is, if you keep worrying so much, you'll forget to enjoy it. Calgary is a great place at Christmastime. You'll fall in love with it, I'm certain. Besides, maybe you'll meet new people. Come out of your shell.'

Robin wasn't sure, but it was worth a try. At the very least, she'd already found a bravery in herself she didn't know she had. She just had to keep going. Keep floating.

She gave the flight attendant a final, appreciative smile and settled back into her seat.

'By the way, it's their loss. The ex, I mean,' Stefanie added. 'You deserve better.'

Robin hadn't really believed it until then. Wren had told her so plenty of times, of course, but . . . Lexi was Lexi. She was beautiful and charismatic and everybody loved her. But Stefanie was right. Robin deserved better. She deserved to enjoy herself. She deserved to love herself.

So she set herself at ease and slipped her headphones back on. No more rom-coms this time, though.

Somehow, she made it to Canada without losing or breaking anything.

Unlike the Canadian customs officer, who had given one-word answers to Robin's questions, the cab driver who picked her up at Calgary International Airport quite appreciated her rambling – or, at least, he seemed to. He smiled and nodded when the situation warranted it as she told him the story of how she had gotten here, including the tantrum her mother had thrown.

But there was no going back now.

A jolt of anxiety rushed through Robin when, after a sickeningly bumpy journey up steep, icy roads, through the fairy-lit high street of Clement Falls, they pulled up to the lodge. She grimaced when she stepped out, the awful, cold snow dampening her jeans. Every step was made twice as difficult, until Robin had to kick up her feet just to avoid having to drag them through the thick sludge.

She only realised when she reached the door that she could have just taken the well-gritted footpath that had been cleared for guests.

The receptionist behind the front desk didn't appear too pleased when Robin brought the snow and ice into the lobby with her, her boots flattening it onto wooden floorboards and vintage rugs. An Elvis Presley song droned out from a crackling old-fashioned radio on the desk. "Blue Christmas", Mum's favourite. Somehow, she'd followed Robin to Canada after all.

Robin wheeled her suitcase through the cosy lobby, glancing around apprehensively. It was a miracle in itself that she'd even stepped foot on the plane, but here she was: alone in Canada, tasting the peace she had so desperately hungered for. She wasn't sure if she liked it yet; the foreign, frayed surroundings were eerie and made Robin feel uneasy.

On her way to the desk, she passed a roaring fire and a

taxidermied moose head whose mammoth antlers almost impaled her.

'*Oof*, safety hazard,' she pointed out, only half-joking. Another short-haired brunette woman already stood at the desk, but she didn't so much as look up when Robin let out a sigh of relief and hunched over to recover from the snowy hike. 'Are you waiting?'

'Nope,' the woman said without tearing her focus from the pamphlets she was organising. She probably worked there and thought Robin was a fool for asking. Robin tried not to scold herself for her own stupidity as she pasted on a false smile for the sour-faced receptionist.

'Hello.'

'Hello.' The receptionist's forced enthusiasm turned bitter. 'Can I help you?'

'I have a booking under the name Ellis.' Robin riffled through her purse and pulled out her ID and the booking information Wren had printed for her in a hurry yesterday. She was surprised Mum hadn't shredded it.

The receptionist – the badge pinned to her breast pocket named her Helen – typed something into the computer with long, manicured nails that looked almost as capable of poking out Robin's eye as the moose antlers.

'Does he have a name?' Robin asked, if only because she was waiting for the inevitable: having to explain that she would not be needing the honeymoon cabin she had booked, obviously for two, now that she was here alone. Anxiety made her ramble. Then again, everything made her ramble.

'Excuse me?' Helen's narrowed gaze rose lazily back to Robin. The other woman had lifted her head, too, as though Robin had just pointed out that Mariah Carey had walked through the door.

'The moose.' Robin motioned to it. 'Does he have a name?'

Helen frowned, bewildered. 'If there was a christening ceremony, I must have missed it.'

'You should name him Elk-on John. Or Moose-olini.'

If Helen understood the joke, she didn't bother to laugh. Maybe it was Robin's accent. From the corner of her eye, though, Robin was certain she spotted the pamphlet woman clamping down a grin. That would have to be enough until Robin recited the conversation to her sister tonight and got all of the laughter and praise she deserved. Her comedic talents were wasted here.

'All right.' Helen sighed, placing a key on the desk and sliding Robin's ID back with it. 'You're in the honeymoon cabin. Will your husband need a copy of the key?'

'Wife,' Robin corrected, and then realised it didn't matter either way. There were no husbands or wives here. There was only her, in the honeymoon suite alone. The more she thought about it, the sadder it became. 'Is there, er, any chance that I can downgrade my cabin to a basic, normal, standard thing? The honeymoon part didn't really happen, you see.'

'Sorry?'

Oh, God. She was going to have to spell it out and risk looking even more pathetic. Luckily, the pamphlet woman was heading out, but a few other guests had arrived and idled by the armchairs, and a cleaner was mopping up the puddles of snow Robin had left only a few metres away.

She lowered her voice to a whisper and hoped it would be enough. 'I'm here alone.'

Helen raised a perfectly plucked brow. 'Can you repeat that? I didn't quite catch it.'

Robin gave up. The entire resort was bound to learn how pathetic she was sooner or later, anyway. 'I'm here alone,' she repeated, louder. 'I'm asking if I could downgrade my cabin, since I'm no longer on my honeymoon and, ergo, won't be needing the honeymoon cabin.'

Helen, at least, did not deign to show sympathy. 'All of our other cabins are booked, ma'am. This is the only one available.'

'Okay.' Robin sucked in a deep breath, preparing herself for rose petals and champagne and a dozen other reminders of her tragic love life. 'No problem. Thanks anyway.'

21

'Here are a few flyers to help you get settled in. You'll find a guidebook, a schedule of upcoming activities, a list of ski instructors and rental stores, et cetera, et cetera.'

'Ooh, the et cetera sounds *very* interesting.'

Another blank expression was the only response Robin received.

'Tough crowd.' She huffed in despair and took the pamphlet. 'Thank you, Helen. You've been a pleasure.'

'Enjoy your stay.'

Robin had a feeling she would do no such thing.

The honeymoon cabin was as sickeningly romantic as Robin had dreaded. Rose petals had, in fact, been scattered on the fleecy bed sheets as predicted and, worse, cross-stitched tapestries of brides and grooms with the word "congratulations" hung on every wall. The resort had at least made it inclusive, with a picture of two brides labelled "Mrs. & Mrs." above the roaring fireplace. Robin had half a mind to burn it, if only because the dark-haired wife on the left looked too much like Lexi, wonky and frayed as she was.

She turned away before bitterness got the better of her, glad to find that there was at least a bucket of complimentary champagne on the table. She popped the cork, nearly busting her nose in the process, and drank it straight from the bottle before shucking off her snow-dusted coat and boots. The bristling of her damp, socked feet against the old carpet seemed to send a slash of reality through her, as though she hadn't really thought about what she was doing until now, with the crackling log fire her only company.

She was on her honeymoon. Alone. At Christmas.

What the hell was she going to do here for the next two weeks? If she stayed locked up, she'd think too much. If she didn't, she'd be frozen and soggy all day. Neither of those options sounded much better than being trapped at home with Nanna Bessie's pillow girlfriend and Cleopawtra slavering all over her new penguin-patterned pyjamas, so she wandered out onto the patio in search of the hot tub that had been promised in the brochure.

It was miniature. Almost as though they'd known that Robin would be sitting in it alone. Sighing, she got it running anyway, laying down her suitcase and searching for her bikini. At least she had an excuse to wear the two-piece she'd gotten in the Black Friday sales in very early anticipation of next summer.

But the swimwear was forgotten in her hands when something else caught her eye. An envelope she didn't remember packing had been tucked neatly between the spines of the tattered romance novels she'd brought with her. Robin's name was scrawled on it in familiar handwriting not so different from her own, though perhaps slightly – fine, *a lot* – neater.

Wren.

Robin tutted and pulled the letter out, unable to keep from grinning when she read what was inside:

Robin,
  This is your reminder, should you need it, to
STOP MOPING!

That part had been underlined three times in red ink.

I know you. You'll probably spend the entire
holiday locked away in your room, reading or
watching telly because you hate snow and
you're all on your own. As your sister, it's my
responsibility to say: Don't. You. Dare. I forbid
it! You're halfway across the world, alone! If you
don't come back with stories of good holiday
sex, new cake recipes, and a set of skis you can
at least put on without falling over, I'll send you
straight back to the airport. After the year you've

had, you deserve to have fun. So get out of that cabin, go for a drink at the bar, and book yourself some ski lessons. Explore. Find new things (and maybe people) to fall in love with. The world is yours, and it's been waiting. I expect to see photographic evidence of you enjoying yourself when you get back. That's an order.

Oh, and don't worry about Mum. By the time you're home, she'll have missed you so much that she'll have forgotten all about your little argument. Just put yourself first, Robin. And HAVE FUN! Dad would have wanted you to.

Love, Wren x

It was just like her sister to find a way to lecture her even with an ocean between them. But the handwritten, looping letters warmed Robin all the same, and she pinned the letter to the noticeboard below the fire evacuation protocol as a reminder. She *would* need it.

Wren was right, though. Robin was untethered, somewhere new. She could choose to feel sorry for herself, or she could choose to make the most of it. Dad had always encouraged her to do more, *be* more; to travel and live without regrets.

So, Robin turned off the bubbling hot tub, changed into fresh, warmer clothes, and left the cabin before she could talk herself out of it again.

Her first ski lessons were booked for noon, both the next day and the one after, because apparently only suffering once was not an option and the resort offered a "buy one get one free" deal. Helen had not taken Robin's, 'No, really, just the one is fine, thank you,' for an answer. As a reward for her bravery, Robin treated herself to a mulled wine before she could regret it – and then another for good measure.

The bar was as rustic and lived-in as the rest of the resort, with sagging, tattered couches dotted around and more poor Elk-on Johns on the wall. She groaned when a man dressed incongruously in a Hawaiian shirt and cargo shorts announced that karaoke night had begun, and the first to go up on stage was a group of men not much older than her singing "Last Christmas" by Wham!

'Drinking on your own tonight?' the bartender questioned, swiping his cloth around a pint glass. It took Robin more than a few seconds to realise that he was talking to her, and she ceased stabbing her straw into a wine-drowned slice of orange to nod.

'And every night,' she murmured, loneliness already beginning to seep back into her chest. Nobody else sat alone here, she noticed. Nobody but her.

The bartender raised a thick, dark eyebrow. From the lines bracketing his mouth and the dark stubble on his chin, Robin guessed he was in his mid-thirties, and she supposed he was attractive to those who might have been interested. Still, he seemed friendly enough, with warm dark eyes and a friendly curve to his lips. 'You're vacationing here alone?'

'Yep.' She guzzled the last sour dregs of her wine and slid the snowflake-patterned mug back over to him. 'Same again, please.'

'Do you ski, then?' He ladled the wine into Robin's mug, wiping the excess down with a napkin before serving it to her. Curiosity glistened in his eyes, and Robin supposed she knew why. People didn't often come to a resort like this alone, especially around the holidays, unless for the winter sports.

'God, no,' she snorted. 'Well, not yet. I booked lessons that I'm already planning to bail on.' She faked a cough. 'Think I'm coming down with something.'

He smirked, bracing his palms against the bar. 'Oh, come on. Skiing's fun. If you don't like it, why are you here – alone?'

'My fiancée liked to ski.' Robin wrinkled her nose and then corrected herself quickly. '*Oops. Ex*-fiancée. I sort of forgot to cancel our honeymoon after the break-up and, well . . . here I am.'

'Ouch.' He winced.

'*Big* ouch,' she agreed, glugging the wine now. She needed it to deal with the ear-piercing singers on the stage behind her, who were now butchering a rendition of "All I Want for Christmas is You". 'So, Mr Bartender . . . what else is there to do around here for a sad little singleton who hates snow?'

'Well, if you're in the honeymoon cabin, you can probably get a free massage.'

At the thought of being oiled up and touched by strangers – and turning up alone, no less – Robin shuddered. The couples' massages offered in the brochure hadn't even sounded appealing with Lexi there to talk her into it, never mind now. 'I truly couldn't think of anything worse.'

'Okay.' He pondered for a moment. 'What's your stance on Christmas markets?'

Robin brightened at that. She would have to buy her family's Christmas presents at some point, since she hadn't had time between work and packing for the trip. And, in Manchester at least, there were always delicious desserts on offer that inspired her baking.

'Worth the chaos for the cakes.'

When a shrill scream crackled through the microphone, she finished the last of her wine and slid off the stool onto wobbly feet.

'That's my cue to leave. Thanks.'

'I'm here almost every evening if you need company.' He shrugged, slipping the tip she'd offered him into his breast pocket. Wren had reminded her three times that everyone expected them here, but she had no idea if three Canadian dollars were too much or too little. 'The name's Nick, by the way.'

'I think every bartender's name is Nick,' she replied. 'But it's nice to meet you. I'm Robin.'

'I'll see you around then, Robin.' His eyes crinkled when he smiled, and unlike most men she'd chatted to in bars over the years, there didn't seem to be any hidden flirtation there.

Good. She needed a friend, and Nick seemed decent enough to talk to if the only alternative was having a conversation with the four panelled walls of her cabin. If all else failed, at least she had *somewhere* to go.

She stumbled out of the bar feeling slightly lighter, packed snow and grit crunching beneath her feet. Nightfall had dissolved the resort into nothing more than clustered specks of gold and shadows, the mountains and luminous ski lane markers just visible behind the chalets and shops.

And Robin supposed that, with the stars guttering above her and the frosty night stealing her breath, there were worse places to be in the world. Perhaps that was just the wine still warming her belly, though. Either way, she decided to take a detour, following the pathway into a copse of towering pines if only to avoid the empty cabin waiting not too far away. At least she could tell her sister that she'd gone to a bar, perhaps even making a friend in the process, and explored the resort. It was better than nothing; better than what she'd planned – and certainly better than Mum's fish pie.

The ground became uneven, the woods wreathed in darkness and low-lying mist as Robin continued on, until a rationality that seldom surfaced when Robin needed it to drove her to turn back.

But she couldn't.

As she whirled on her heel, she found pale eyes staring back at her, a long tongue lolling across the pointed canines of a gaping maw.

Oh. No.

This was the end. She was going to be killed by a wolf in the middle of the Albertan woods. No one would find her body. She would die honeymooning alone, sad and desperate and ravaged by a wild animal. This was it.

Heart racketing against her ribs, she stretched out her hands in caution.

'Please don't eat me, Mr Wolf. I . . . I don't taste nice, promise.'

Robin dared a step sideways, the grey wolf watching her every move with pointed ears and a cocked head.

'Nobody warned me that there were wolves here,' she muttered to herself. 'It definitely wasn't in the brochure, sir. You should really fix that.'

Perhaps it had strayed from the mountains. Perhaps it had scented her pathetic loneliness on the wind and come to put her out of her misery. She took another step, wincing when the wolf's tail curled. It was going to pounce. She could sense it.

Robin glanced around desperately and found a long stick by her boot. If it was the only weapon she had to defend herself with, it would have to do. When the wolf shifted again, she panicked.

'Shoo!' she warned before launching the stick. It sent the wolf scuttling back just slightly and then caught in one of the trees behind. 'Go on. Shoo!'

'What are you doing?' The voice came from a short-haired woman who had emerged from the shadows.

'*Bollocks!*' Robin screamed, startled.

The wolf jumped up at the woman and . . . *licked* her hands. Her hands, where a lead dangled. Because it wasn't a wolf, Robin realised far too late, but just a dog. The collar around its neck proved it. Had it been wearing that a minute ago?

She smoothed herself down, cheeks blazing with embarrassment. Hopefully, her blush wouldn't be too obvious in the dark. 'Nothing. Just taking a walk.'

'You were trying to hit my dog with a stick.' Her features were narrow, stern, and Robin began to worry that she was about to get arrested on account of attempted animal abuse on her first night in Canada. 'You said something about a wolf.'

'Nope.' Robin shook her head nonchalantly. 'Nope, I was just playing a very gentle game of fetch with this animal here, which is very clearly a dog.'

The woman frowned as she stepped into a shaft of moonlight, the fresh snow glistening by her boots. Now,

Robin recognised her. She'd been standing by the front desk when Robin had checked in. The woman sorting through the pamphlets.

'Do you really think there are wolves around here? On a ski resort?'

'Of course not,' Robin lied again, and then, beneath the woman's doubtful gaze, sagged in resignation. 'Okay, fine. But your dog *looks* like a wolf. You shouldn't let it just wander around. It might scare the tourists.'

'Well, maybe the *tourists* shouldn't be in the woods in the dark if they're paranoid enough to mistake a husky for a wolf.' Her eyes narrowed as she clipped the lead onto the dog's collar, ruffling its snow-dusted fur as she did. The husky reached the woman's waist, which only left Robin more uneasy. 'Juniper is harmless. You're just lucky you have terrible aim.'

Robin glanced warily at the dog. She only noticed then that it had one unnaturally blue eye, and it sparkled with mischief. 'She has a glint in her eye. I think she's about to turn. You never can tell, you know. One of my friends had a bearded dragon that tried to eat her in the middle of the night.'

'Hmm, yeah, I've heard reptiles and dogs *are* very similar *and* very deadly creatures. Or, y'know, maybe they can just sense something off about *you*. I'd sleep with one eye open tonight just in case.'

She gasped at the insult. 'There's nothing *off* about me, thank you very much.'

The woman only raised her brows, unconvinced. Robin took it as her cue to leave, glancing around in an effort to remember which way she had come. Any sense of direction was muddled by the tall trees shrouding her, and the not-so-near-death experience had thrown her completely off track.

'Lost?' The woman sounded irritatingly pleased at the suggestion.

'*No.*' Robin glared. And then, weakly: 'Maybe. Only because you distracted me.'

'And I suppose the fact that you stink of wine even from here has absolutely nothing to do with it.' Wrapping the lead tighter around her knuckles, the woman inclined her head to something behind her. 'The resort is back this way. Where are you staying?'

'I'm in Cabin 301.'

She whistled, guiding Robin forward with Juniper at her heels. Robin was still convinced that there was something savagely wolfish in the way the dog eyed her and she made sure to keep a safe distance.

'Right. The honeymoon cabin. Congrats.'

Robin winced, not needing the reminder. Apparently, the woman hadn't heard her mention her perpetual singleness in the lobby earlier, or she had and was mocking her.

She only hummed as the lights of the resort came back into view, feeling silly when she realised they hadn't even been that deep into the forest. If she hadn't been fearing for her life, she might have easily found her way out alone and saved herself the embarrassment. 'I'm good from here.'

'You sure?' Laughter still danced on the woman's lips.

In an effort to dismiss it, to act more confident than she felt just as Wren would, Robin nodded. 'Positive. Thanks. And thank you, Juniper.' She dared extend her hand to the husky – and snatched it back a moment later when Juniper howled at her and left her startled. A puff of breath curled from her mouth. Robin hadn't known that dogs could cast dirty looks until Juniper stared at her again, her barbed intensity never wavering.

'Are you *sure* she's not a wolf?' asked Robin a final time before wandering back onto the footpath.

'Who knows?'

The sound of the woman laughing and praising Juniper followed Robin back to the lodge.

Chapter Three

Neve didn't like to be kept waiting – and she was, by her midday appointment, who had only signed up the previous day. She sighed, her breath a wispy cloud in front of her as she peeled off her ski goggles to rest them on her helmet. The slopes were jam-packed today, families soaring through the blinding-white snow and lone, confident pros zigzagging between obstacles on the next lanes over. She'd been one of them not too long ago, but here she was now on the green slope, waiting for an amateur who probably wouldn't even show.

Neve hated working at the resort over the holidays. It got too busy, too noisy. Skiing was supposed to be a way to escape all that, but there was no way of escaping anything when the screams of kids hurtling down the hills in their sleds pierced her eardrums.

And she had nothing to do but listen to it as the minutes ticked by. *Time-waster.* Since no cancellation had been made, she'd still get her money, but it pissed her off nonetheless. She had better things to do than stand here, freezing her ass off. Grab lunch, for example.

Her stomach grumbled at the thought of that. She hadn't eaten since six a.m., just an hour before she'd made her way here to check her schedule and start her first lesson at eight. Her next break was an hour and a half from now – but she promised herself that if she were still waiting here in fifteen minutes, she'd give up and leave.

The world had other plans.

A short woman shrouded by the furry hood of her parka

stumbled towards her, leaving behind a trail of snow that seeped into the too-long cuffs of her trousers. *Give me strength*. The skis rattling in her hands were the chipped, rented ones that even Neve was no longer brave enough to use. A beginner if she had ever seen one.

And if first impressions were anything to go by, it was going to be a long, *long* session. Neve could say goodbye to dreams of hot soup or mac 'n' cheese.

'Are you here for the lesson?'

Neve barely made out the woman's nod beneath the floppy hood as she gasped out breathlessly, 'Are you the ski instructor?'

'That's me. Neve.'

'Sorry I'm late. I had an . . . *ordeal* with the ski lift.'

Neve almost snorted – but any reaction was lost when the woman pulled down her hood to slip on her goggles. She was familiar. *Too* familiar, with shoulder-length blonde hair and pale eyes that looked almost silver against the bright snow. The British woman from last night. The fool who had thought Juniper, Neve's husky, was a damn wolf. The one who had plagued Helen, the receptionist, with terrible – but, okay, surprisingly funny – puns as she'd checked in not a few hours before that.

No. Neve trapped the groan rising from her throat at the same time the woman's – *Robin's*, according to the name given on the sign-up sheet – pink lips parted in surprise.

'*You*,' Robin said.

'*Me*.' Neve's eyes narrowed to slits. 'What are the chances?'

A rosy blush smattered Robin's cheeks, as vibrant as her neon jacket. 'You know, I'm not feeling too well. I think we'll save this for another day.'

'I don't think so.' Neve pinched the cuff of Robin's jacket before she made to leave. 'Do you want to learn how to ski or not?'

'*Not*,' Robin deadpanned. 'Look, you already probably think I'm an idiot after last night – and you would be right – so imagine how dangerous it would be for me to *ski*. On a big hill. With . . . *skis*. This is a big, big mistake.'

'*You* signed up, and this is a beginner's slope,' Neve pointed out, jabbing her ski pole into the snow impatiently. 'Why are you here if you don't want to be?'

'It's a long story.'

She gritted her teeth impatiently. 'Then shorten it.'

Robin's features – elfin and round and freckled in the daylight – flattened into a glare. 'Do you talk to all of your clients this way?'

'When they're wasting my time, yes.' It wasn't a lie. Neve wasn't known for her sparkling charm when it came to giving lessons. She did it for the money, not because she enjoyed working with unskilled skiers who weren't serious about the sport. If she had it her way, she would never work with, or for, another living soul again – and a second run-in with the woman dithering in front of her only reminded her why. 'If you want to go, wolf girl, go. Just make sure you pay me first.'

'*Pay* you?' Robin repeated, voice rising incredulously as she blinked a dusting of snow from her lashes. 'You haven't taught me anything!'

'Not true. I taught you the difference between a wolf and a dog,' Neve bit back. 'If you're not going to take the lesson, you still owe me for the time I could have spent with somebody competent. We have a policy.'

'A "two lessons for the price of one" policy, which means technically, I don't owe you anything until my second lesson. What's your problem?' Robin went to thrust her arms across her chest – and then decided against it when she found her stiff thermals made it difficult. 'You've been nothing but rude to me since last night.'

Neve blew out an impatient breath, fingers flexing in her warm gloves. 'My problem is that I don't have expendable time. Just make up your mind. Do you want the lessons or not?'

The corners of Robin's mouth sank into a petulant pout, but she threw down her skis and slid her feet into them with more than a few huffs and puffs. 'Fine. But if I end up in A&E, that's on you.'

'And here I was thinking you'd be an excellent skier,' Neve retorted under her breath, tightening the straps of her skis before she pulled her poles from the snow and readjusted her goggles. 'I assume this is your first time, then?'

Robin only gave her a look that Neve read as "*no shit*" before pulling her own goggles down.

'We'll start over here on the green slope.' Snow crunched beneath Neve's skis as she guided Robin towards the smallest slope – nothing more than a gentle incline that even Juniper could have cleared. 'All right. Let's start with stance. I want you to strap your hands into your poles and bend your knees like so. You only need to lean forward slight—'

An almighty shriek cut Neve off, and a moment later, the bright pink of Robin's jacket whipped past her, streaking down the slope. The skis wobbled unsteadily beneath Robin's boots, gathering lumps of snow as her knees knocked together and then fell apart. Neve could only watch, somewhere between annoyed and amused, as Robin's flailing legs finally fell out from under her and she landed on her rear end.

With a roll of her eyes, Neve glided down the slope to meet her, smooth and steady as ever. After over a decade of practice, skiing was second nature to her. 'What are you doing? I didn't tell you to go.'

Robin scowled and stretched her skis out in front of her as though the blame was all theirs. 'I'm fine, though. Thanks for asking.'

Neve freed one of her hands and extended it with an exasperated sigh. 'Well, perhaps if you'd *listened*.'

'I *did* listen,' Robin snapped, clutching Neve's hand to pull herself up before dusting the snow from her clothes. 'I leaned forward like you said and ended up on my arse.'

'You were supposed to stand still until I said so.'

'I was standing at the top of a *hill*. How was I supposed to defy the laws of gravity?'

'By keeping *still*. And with these.' Neve waved her poles upwards before digging them into the ground. 'I would have explained that if you'd have waited. Come on. Let's try again.'

The huff that left Robin's mouth might as well have been from a grouchy teenager asked to tidy their room. Patience fraying, Neve shot her another glare and dragged herself back up the mini slope. 'Where's your partner, anyway?'

'What?' Robin asked from behind her, breaths leaving her in ragged gusts. The sound of her poles cutting through the snow followed Neve up the hill.

'Your partner. You said you were on your honeymoon. Usually, couples do these things together,' Neve pointed out. 'Then again, if you're this difficult, I'd hang back from coming with you, too.'

'Ha,' Robin laughed humourlessly. 'I'm not on my honeymoon. Well . . . I am, but not really.'

'You're on your honeymoon but not really,' Neve quipped without a hint of interest. She turned back and squinted to find Robin crawling up the last few steps of the hill. 'Okay.'

'I'm on my honeymoon alone.' Lines wrinkled across Robin's forehead as she caught her breath at the top. Beneath the goggles, Neve couldn't spot any other emotion on her face, though a flicker of guilt guttered in her chest.

'You're not one of those people who married themselves, are you? I'm all for self-love, but . . .'

'No.' Robin snorted. 'No. I never actually got to the marriage bit. My fiancée – *ex*-fiancée – and I broke up, and on top of all the other wedding things I had to cancel, I forgot all about the honeymoon.' Her throat bobbed, the only sign of her pain.

The flicker of guilt turned into a flame that Neve tried to snuff out quickly. She couldn't imagine how heartbreaking it must have been, planning what was probably supposed to be the most special day of her life only to have to cancel it all instead. For it to end in Robin coming here alone. Most people wouldn't have been brave enough to do that, Neve included. 'I see.'

'I know it's sad and pathetic, but . . .' Robin shrugged as though that explained it. 'Might as well put it to some use. I paid for it all, anyway.'

'So why here?' Neve couldn't help but ask. 'Why not somewhere hot and sunny?'

Robin shrugged. 'She liked snow.' As though it was that simple. As though Robin would do anything for her. *God*.

Neve wished she hadn't asked. She cast her gaze back down the slope, voice softening just slightly, though she hadn't meant it to. 'Want to try again? This time without the falling?'

Robin's lips quirked into a smirk, brief enough that Neve almost missed it. *Almost*.

'I'll do my best, but no promises.'

'Don't open Instagram,' were the first words out of Wren's mouth when Robin called her not long after the ski lesson had finished. 'Or Facebook.'

'Why?' Robin sat on the bed – and winced. Her backside hurt more than the rest of her strained muscles combined from the number of times she'd fallen in the end. Neve's already scant patience had only dwindled the more Robin had tumbled, until they were barely talking to one another at all by the end. She'd basically paid to embarrass herself for an hour and a half – a new low, even for her. Not to mention that she'd have to do it all again tomorrow and she was still mortified about the wolf-dog incident.

'Just don't.'

Naturally, her sister's cryptic instruction only made Robin want to know why. She put Wren on speaker and opened her Instagram app, frowning. 'Has Aunty Joan been posting selfies without her teeth again?'

'Yes, and I'm trying to save you the trauma of seeing it.'

Wren's voice shook with uncertainty – a lie. Her sister had never been able to lie in her life, especially not to Robin.

It didn't matter. Robin scrolled through pictures of Starbucks cups and elves on shelves, her thumb freezing when she came to a familiar, beaming face.

She didn't even know why she still followed Lexi on social media. Robin's ex barely ever posted, though she still left a like on Robin's pictures of cakes now and again, as though reminding Robin she was still there, still a part of her, even when Robin no longer wanted her to be. If Robin had possessed an ounce of dignity, she might have blocked Lexi after she'd cheated, but perhaps a little bit of her was reluctant to let go.

But any semblance of that ebbed now. Because Lexi was not alone in the picture. She was curled up on a couch with a man Robin had only ever seen in passing – passing through their old bedroom, for example, and finding him on Robin's side of the bed without clothes, curled around her then-fiancée. An old friend, Lexi had introduced Shawn as at their engagement party six months before. Apparently, the criteria for "old friend" included "sex pal". And now that Robin was out of the picture, they clearly *weren't* just friends anymore. The diamond ring sparkling on Lexi's left hand confirmed that.

The caption read, "I said yes!" with an emoji of a ring and a brunette bride. They were getting married. Robin hadn't even known they were still dating – but why would she? She didn't know Lexi anymore. Their lives were no longer entwined. Robin was just a background character in their story, just as she was in everyone else's.

Something aching and tight yanked through Robin's chest, leaving her eyes stinging and her lip trembling. For just a heart-wrenching second, it hurt just as badly as the day she'd come home early from work and found them together. The day they'd called the wedding off and Lexi had admitted she wasn't sure she loved Robin anymore.

'Rob?' Wren was saying, somewhere distant; somewhere miles away from the bubble of pain and loneliness and betrayal trapping Robin. 'Oh, God. You're looking, aren't you? I told you not to.'

'Of course I'm bloody looking!' Robin snapped without thinking. 'What else would I do?'

A sigh whistled down the line. 'I'm sorry. You're right. Look, don't let this ruin your holiday. She isn't worth it.'

Robin scoffed at that. It wasn't a holiday. It was a honeymoon. And while she stayed alone in the cabin booked for the both of them, Lexi had moved on with the person she'd chosen over Robin. She probably didn't think of Robin at all. Why would she? She certainly hadn't when it had mattered.

'Robin?' Wren asked again.

'I'm going to go. I'll talk to you later, okay?'

'Oh, wait—'

But Robin didn't want to hear any more of her sister's pep talks. It was easy for Wren. She'd already found the person she was going to spend the rest of her life with, and Tom worshipped the ground Wren walked on. Robin had thought she'd found her person once, too, but it had all been a lie. A delusion. And even if she ever found someone else, she couldn't take care of a succulent without killing it, let alone maintain a healthy relationship.

She didn't know what to do now, still perched on her bed in her ski pants, melted snow puddling on the rug. She'd had no plans past this – not beyond moping by the fire or drowning herself in the hot tub, at least.

The second idea didn't sound so bad. She hadn't gotten to try it out the night before. Her limbs felt heavy as she dragged herself up, opening the patio doors to turn on the tub. She watched the bubbles surface absently for a while, snow-topped pines and the light flurry eddying from the clouds her only friends. And then when the cold bit her fingers, she dug out her romance book from the suitcase, slipped into her bikini, and marinated in the hot water until her skin pruned and the steam made her dizzy.

If she was going to stay here alone tonight, she thought afterwards, she would need a drink. Something stronger than mulled wine this time.

'Rough day?' Nick questioned, ruffling Neve's hair before he went back to polishing his pint glasses. Juniper sat at Neve's feet, an oversized mass of grey and white fur beneath the bar stool's footrest. The managers of the resort had long since stopped caring about the husky wandering around the place. The guests loved her and she was usually well behaved.

Neve tucked into the tray of sweet potato fries she'd picked up from the resort's cafeteria – not before dousing them in ketchup.

'Uh-huh.' The agreement came out muffled through the mouthful of food. She didn't have the energy for manners tonight. 'All of my students were beginners today. One of them spent more time on the ground than on her feet.'

And yet Neve hadn't been able to stop thinking about Robin since last night. The peculiar woman irritated her to no end, but . . . she was quite entertaining, to say the least. Neve wondered how she'd managed to get through life in one piece, so clumsy and naive, with those huge doe eyes that were definitely *not* beautiful in a Zooey Deschanel sort of way.

Nope. Definitely not. And if they were, Neve hadn't noticed. Clearly.

It was as though her non-thoughts had summoned the woman. A short, blonde figure slumped into a stool three seats away, burying her head in her hands and sighing.

Robin.

Neve tensed and munched on her fries, pretending she hadn't noticed – until she caught Robin turning to her from the corner of her eye.

'*You*,' Robin said, just as she had on the slopes.

'Me,' Neve echoed with a crooked, smarmy grin she already hated herself for.

'Nick,' Nick intervened, resting against the bar between them. 'You two know each other?'

'No,' Neve said at the same time that Robin said, 'Yes.'

Nick arched an eyebrow, amusement dancing across his lips.

'I paid her to watch me fall on my arse today,' Robin waved off. 'And I checked, by the way. They won't refund the lesson booked for tomorrow. Terms and conditions and all that. I need something very strong tonight, Nick. Something very, *very* strong.'

'*Oof.*' Nick winced. 'What did you do to the poor girl, Neve?'

'I did nothing.' Neve frowned at her brother as he poured a dangerous amount of vodka into a glass of eggnog and plopped in a candy cane for good measure. 'I take it you won't be signing up for more lessons while you're here?'

'No, I do not loathe myself that much yet, thank you.'

Robin perked up when her drink was set in front of her, and then seemed to notice Juniper at Neve's feet for the first time. She eyed her warily before wiggling her fingers in front of the husky's snout. Unlike last night, Juniper melted into Robin's touch, tongue lapping at her hand until the ghost of a smile curved across Robin's face. It was gone just as quickly. She returned to the eggnog, sipping and then flinching.

'Nick. There is too much eggnog in this vodka.'

Nick snorted at the joke. 'You're my kinda girl, Robin.'

Neve glowered at her brother's shameless flirting, but Robin seemed too busy trying to suck a cherry through her straw to even notice. Anybody with a pulse was Nick's kinda girl. The problem was that he was terrible at asking them out, and thank the heavens. Neve couldn't think of anything worse than Robin becoming his next fling.

Another round of customers had crowded around the bar, and Nick patted the counter once to bid Neve farewell. 'Still want a lift home later?'

'Please.'

He nodded and tended to the new guests, leaving Neve and Robin to settle in a thick silence. Only the three stools between them and the tinkling instrumental of "Let It Snow" drifting from the stereo kept it from being completely, unbearably awkward.

'So are you two married or something?' Robin's eyes flitted from Neve to Nick in question.

Neve gagged on her fry at the suggestion. 'No. Absolutely not. Nick is my older brother.'

'You're brother and sister?' Robin's brows rose in surprise.

'Is that so hard to believe?' With a frown, Neve threw a fry down to Juniper. Most people could tell from first glance that she and Nick were related, with the same hazel eyes and dark hair. They practically had the same haircut, too, for God's sake – unintentionally, of course, and Neve's was slightly longer now. She'd been too lazy and too broke to visit the hairdresser's recently.

'Well, yes. You're so different.'

'In what way?' She cocked her head – a challenge.

One that Robin rose to without censoring herself. 'Nick is nice, for starters.'

Neve scoffed at that. Her brother's charms had already worked on her, it seemed. 'Right. And I'm . . . ?'

'Mean?' Robin tried. 'Hostile? Condescending?'

'Well, maybe I should be more like you. Walk around with my head in the clouds, making moose puns, getting lost in the woods, and attacking dogs with sticks.'

'That was one colossal misunderstanding, and I didn't *attack* your dog.'

Neve only hummed, unconvinced, her glower scathing.

'Wow, yeah.' Robin's voice flattened, shadows darkening her features. 'I see I was wrong about you. How could I ever think you were awful?'

Neve could only roll her eyes, venom rising in her throat. She tried to suppress it – but it was too late. 'I can't imagine why you're spending the holidays all alone.'

The lack of reply was how Neve knew she had gone too far. She was good at that. Good at saying things without thinking, knowing that she would regret them afterwards. It was probably why her brother and her grandpa were her only friends.

'Nick! I need another.' Robin's shrill call cleaved through the silence.

Neve had a feeling she would need something just as strong if she was going to sit here for another hour, waiting for her brother's shift to end while Robin drowned herself in spiked eggnog.

Chapter Four

Robin probably shouldn't have accepted the last two vodka shots offered to her by a group of Scouse men who had been entertaining her for the last hour . . . or the two cranberry sauce margaritas before that . . . or the three vodka-doused eggnogs before *that*. She realised that at about the same time she got up on stage to sing an extra-solemn karaoke version of her favourite Christmas song, "River" by Joni Mitchell, and had to fight to suppress both tears and vomit. The creamy cocktails churned in her gut, made all the more unsettled by the reason she had started drinking in the first place.

Lexi. Getting married. To the person she'd given Robin up for.

It wasn't that she still loved Lexi, she had slurred out to her new friends at the bar earlier. It was just the way Lexi had made her feel so small, so unimportant, and she had to watch her move on while Robin . . . didn't. It was a kick in the gut more than a kick in the heart. It was her own insecure brain that did the real damage. She hadn't been good enough. She never seemed to be good enough.

And apparently the only way to combat the fact was to wail out how badly she wished she had a river she could skate away on, completely out of time with the backing track, while her new friends cheered from the sidelines. Beneath the purple spotlights, she could just make out the stand-offish ski instructor, Neve, still sitting at the bar, wincing at Robin's high notes while Juniper remained curled around her feet.

Maybe Robin should get a dog. Cleopawtra was her mother's, and they had never really seen eye to eye unless

Robin was feeding her waffles. Maybe a dog of her own would solve her problems. Or a cat.

The song came to an end, and Robin just about fell off the stage, her head spinning and throat burning. She'd *definitely* had too much to drink. It didn't stop her from dancing her way back to the bar, tripping over a stool as she searched for Nick. He had returned to talk to Neve – Robin was still processing the fact that they were *siblings* – and halted untying the green apron at his waist to cast a thumbs-up.

'Great singing, Robin.'

'Thanks, Nick. I'll have another one of those eggnog thingies. With extra cherries.'

Neve and Nick scoffed in perfect synchronisation.

'I think you've had enough, don't you?' Nick asked.

'Are you cutting me off?' Robin crossed her arms over her chest, well aware that she was unintentionally swaying.

''Fraid so,' he said. 'You need help getting back to your cabin?'

'I'll take her,' Neve volunteered – and if Robin wasn't distracted by the bile slowly rising up her throat, she would have passed out from shock alone. 'Take Juniper. I'll meet you in the car.'

'But the night is so young!' Robin protested dramatically. 'We should sing a duet, Nicholas. How are you with "Fairytale of New York"?'

'Maybe tomorrow.' Nick smirked and took Juniper's lead from Neve as he shrugged on his coat. Neve collected Robin's coat and the purse she'd left draped across the stool.

Though she knew it was childish, Robin pouted. She didn't want to go back to the cabin, where she would be left alone with her own thoughts. She wanted to keep singing and talking to her new friends. But Neve had grabbed her by the hand and was dragging her away.

'Come on, boozy.'

'But I want to stay!'

'Tough luck. Put your coat on.'

They stopped by the door, where red and green lights danced and tangled with garland. The group of "lads", as they had called themselves in a loud chant earlier, had taken to singing "Mr Brightside" without the use of the karaoke machine, much to the distaste of the woman trying to belt out "White Christmas" on stage. Robin wanted to join in, but Neve held her coat out like a mother preparing for the school run.

'I don't need a coat. I'm sweaty.' The Christmas ballad had really taken it out of Robin.

'If you'd rather freeze to death out there, that's fine by me.'

After sticking out her tongue, Robin stepped into the night – and regretted being stubborn instantly. The cold bit into her, turning her bones to ice and her breath to vapour. She wrapped her arms around herself as Neve followed her out.

The fresh air did nothing to clear Robin's head, instead only drawing attention to just how intoxicated she was. Even so, she realised that she was embarrassing herself in front of Neve for the *third* time in a row, and pride got the better of her. 'You don't have to walk me back. I can make my own way . . . wait . . .' she paused '. . . isn't that a song?' She sang 'I can make my own waaaay,' to the tune by Fleetwood Mac.

'That's "Go Your Own Way". And given that you couldn't even find your cabin *sober* last night, I think I'll stay and help.' Neve raised her eyebrows and offered the coat again, burying her chin into her own tartan scarf. Defeated, Robin slid her arms into the parka, finding herself too unfocused to zip it up.

'Nick would have taken me.'

'Come here.' Neve sighed, nudging Robin's fingers away from the coat's hem to replace them with her own. They were nimble, gentle, as they slotted the zip together and drew it up so that Robin was shielded from the cold. 'Nick does anything anyone asks him to.'

'That's not a bad thing.' Robin waited for Neve to draw away, to keep walking, but neither of them had moved. Neve hadn't even dropped her hands from the zip, though she lifted her eyes now. Robin had noticed green rings around her pupils earlier, on the slopes. Now, they were full of gleaming shadows.

'It is when he puts everyone else first.' Neve's brows knitted together, and Robin had a strange urge to smooth them with her fingers. With their proximity, she hoped to God that Neve couldn't smell the sour eggnog on her tongue. 'You two seem to like each other.'

'I don't know him.' Robin shrugged – and then, at the quirked eyebrow, she understood what Neve was really asking. She thought they *liked* each other. 'Don't worry. I'm not going to be your new sister-in-law.'

Neve stepped back at that, a lopsided smirk gracing her features as she shoved her free hand in her pocket. 'No?'

Shaking her head, Robin waded through the snow. She didn't even know which direction she was supposed to be going anymore. 'Nope.'

Silence fell between them, broken only by the crunching beneath their boots. Neve was the one to break it. 'Still hooked on your ex?'

The mention of Lexi here, where nobody really knew her, drew the wind from Robin.

'No. No, that's not the reason.' She was surprised to find that it felt like the truth. And then, quieter, because her stomach was aching and she just needed to say it out loud: 'She got engaged today. Again. Not with me this time.'

'Oh . . .'

Yeah, oh. Robin didn't know what she'd expected. Neve was a stranger who didn't need to know about her tragic love life, but it felt freeing, somehow, to get it off her chest. Just once. Maybe now she could sweep the broken pieces of herself back under the rug and continue having a mediocre holiday.

She nearly fell on her arse – *again* – when they began to make their way uphill towards the cabins, but something stopped her: Neve's hand, supporting her lower back as she stumbled.

'I'm fine.'

Neve tutted, unconvinced, but let go all the same. 'So is she why you're drinking yourself into a state tonight?'

'I am *not* drinking myself into a state,' Robin scoffed – though it came out with little conviction. Mostly because she was thinking about Lexi and feeling nauseous again. 'Can't a girl enjoy herself on a one-woman honeymoon?'

'You didn't look like you were enjoying yourself when you were blubbering into the microphone singing Joni Mitchell.'

'It's a sad song!' she defended.

They reached the lodge, and Robin stopped at the bottom of the steps. From here, they might as well have been Mount Everest. She gripped on to the wooden railing as she took the first step – and lost her balance immediately. Neve was there to catch her, her hands wrapping lightly around Robin's waist.

'I can't do it,' she whispered, and she wasn't sure whether she was talking about the five steps up to her door or the rest of the honeymoon entirely. She couldn't stop wondering why she was here; why she'd thought it had been a good idea. All she'd done so far was make a fool of herself and bask in complete and utter loneliness.

'Well, you don't have much of a choice. I'm not carrying you.' Neve pushed her up again, and Robin used the force to get a grip on the railings as she climbed the stairs. She stumbled only once more on a slippery patch of snow before reaching the top still wrapped in Neve's support. 'Where's the key?'

Robin dug around her pockets, finding the cabin key at the very bottom of her coat. She didn't even attempt to slot it in herself, instead passing it over for Neve to handle. She did, too easily, and ushered Robin inside with a blank expression.

The effort it had taken to crawl up the stairs left Robin's chest straining and her stomach twisting with sickness. She could still taste the eggnog, still feel the heavy creaminess of it lying on her stomach.

Her mouth watered in warning. She was going to puke.

She had no time to explain. If she didn't go now, she was going to throw up all over the wooden floorboards and the vintage rug. All over *herself*. So, she scurried to the bathroom without a word – and got there just in time. The cocktail of liquids heaved itself out of her stomach as she gagged on cherries and candy cane shards she hadn't digested properly.

And then that hand was on her back again, rubbing soothing circles through her thick coat. The other brushed her snow-dampened hair from her face.

Neve said nothing. Just stayed behind Robin until she was done, empty, hollow, and so embarrassed that she wished she could flush herself down the toilet with the rest of the gross things that had just left her. Her throat felt raw and blistered from the acid, and she splashed water into her mouth before wiping herself down, still not daring to look at Neve.

'I'm really sorry,' she rasped behind a paper towel. 'I'm not usually like this.'

With the exception of every party or night out she'd ever been forced to go to, that was. Robin couldn't handle wine at the best of times, let alone all of the heavy, rich things she'd guzzled down tonight.

'You can go. I mean, thank you for getting me home, but I won't be looking you in the eye ever again. I'm sure you understand. I think it's best for us both.'

A sigh followed, and then a shuffle. But Neve didn't leave. Not the cabin, anyway. Her boots squelched as she trudged out of the bathroom, and then a clatter of pots and slamming cupboard doors sounded and the boiling kettle began to whistle. Unable to so much as look at herself in the mirror, Robin screwed her eyes shut as she rose up on legs that felt like jelly.

Pathetic. She was pathetic. She made an early New Year's resolution then and there to stop drinking and unfollow Lexi on all social media to avoid ever putting herself in a situation like this one again. Never again.

Sucking in a deep breath, she staggered out of the bathroom. In the small kitchen, Neve waited by the steaming kettle with a mug set out on the counter in front of her.

'You need to settle your stomach. Hot water should do the trick until you can get your hands on ginger tea.'

'You really don't have to do that,' Robin muttered quietly, pulling off her coat and boots as exhaustion began to weigh on her.

Neve seemed not to have heard her. When the water shrieked to a boil, she poured it into the mug. She could have left then, but she didn't. Robin couldn't fathom why.

'I was out of line before,' Neve said finally, worrying at her lip, 'with what I said to you at the bar.'

'About my moose puns?' Robin pulled at her frumpy cream sweater as though stretching it across herself might protect her from this conversation; from those piercing hazel eyes she'd all but gotten lost in earlier, even with the barbed words directed at her. She couldn't figure Neve out, couldn't decide if she found Robin funny or silly or annoying or all of the above, but Robin wanted to, even if it was just a hint. She didn't know why, but she did.

Neve snorted. 'Among other things.'

'I vaguely recall you trying not to laugh at Elk-on John,' Robin admitted. 'Don't worry. I didn't take it personally. You don't owe me an apology.'

'Oh, I wasn't apologising. Just saying. And I definitely *wasn't* laughing. It was a terrible joke.'

'So is this pity, then, because you just saw me puke?'

'God, no. You brought that on yourself.'

The Neve of two minutes ago, Robin hadn't known at all. Kind, nurturing, gentle. But this present Neve was familiar. This one was easier to deal with, even if it felt harder to reach her.

Robin's lips quirked up, and she could only nod. Most of the things in her life she had brought on herself. It didn't seem to stop her from making the same mistakes over and over again. 'Won't Nick be waiting for you?'

'I guess.' Neve wandered out of the kitchen, pausing when she reached Robin. Her high cheekbones caught the shadows, hazel eyes locking away the golden light. She might have been hostile, with a bite as venomous as a cobra's, but up close she was all soft lines and pretty edges, all of them only highlighted by her cropped brown hair. She looked younger than she'd seemed, too. She couldn't have been all that much older or younger than Robin's twenty-six years.

Something warm and unsure spread in Robin's belly. She pushed it down, away, waiting to be freed from Neve's stifling, all-consuming presence.

'I still expect to see you on the slopes tomorrow. Don't be late this time.'

The thought of risking the uneven slopes and even riding the ski lift again made Robin want to rush back to the bathroom, but she pursed her lips. 'Okay.'

'Make sure you drink the water.'

'I will. Thanks again. And . . . sorry, again.' Robin followed Neve to the door, where Neve paused and turned to cast half a smile. It was still half a smile more than Robin had expected.

'See you tomorrow.'

It was about as close to kindness as Robin knew she would get, and when the door closed, she couldn't help but feel an unfamiliar warmth spread through her.

And then nausea hit, and she grabbed the hot water to purge herself of everything she'd done and felt and drunk tonight.

'How is she?' Nick asked as Neve climbed into his car and slipped on her seatbelt. Having forgotten her gloves in the chaos of . . . well, Robin, she warmed her frostbitten fingers by the heater.

'Better, I think. She threw up, but that's probably just the effect of your disgustingly sour eggnogs.' Neve left out the part about making her hot water and holding her hair back while she puked. It was usually Nick's job to be so caring, a role that had always come naturally to him as the doting older brother in a mostly parentless family. And yet she had jumped to attention when he had tried tonight. She'd wanted to make sure that Robin got home okay. Maybe it was the guilt that had spurred her. She'd been harsh. Unfair. It most certainly wasn't the fact that she'd thought Nick was interested in her, anyway. Not at all.

The truth was, though, that despite all of her criticism towards Nick and his perpetual role as the pushover, taking care of Robin in her own vaguely aggressive Neve way had been instinct. She was used to it – from years of helping her grandpa when he was sick. She even still did it on the odd occasion that Nick stumbled in drunk at three a.m. No matter how guarded she had become over the years, that incessant need to make things better remained, an earthworm wriggling constantly in her chest. Maybe beneath their different masks and their eight-year age gap, she and Nick were the same after all.

She told herself *that* was the only reason she'd helped Robin tonight. It wasn't that she'd cared or felt bad. She'd have done it for anybody.

As though reading her thoughts, Nick raised an eyebrow. 'Is something going on between you two? There was some definite . . . what do kids call it these days? *Flanter?*'

Puzzled, Neve replied, 'What the hell is "*flanter*"? One of your cocktails?'

'It's short for flirty banter, I believe.' Nick shrugged. 'Seemed like there was a spark, is all. She got you all riled up. Haven't seen you like that for a while.'

'She's annoying.'

'She's cute. Not your usual type, but she's gotten under your skin.'

Neve rolled her eyes and feigned a nonchalant yawn, though heat prickled along the tips of her ears. She didn't *have* a usual type. All of her "relationships" – more like flings – had been fleeting, either because Neve checked out early or their commitment level ability was even worse than hers. Some woman she'd only just met would have to do more than get a little drunk and ski badly to get under her skin. Her skin was . . . gated. Sealed shut. Better left alone. 'I don't know what you're talking about.'

He hummed disbelievingly, amusement simmering in the sound. From the back seat, Juniper panted, ready to get home, and Nick took it as his cue to start the engine. *Thank God.* They reversed out of the parking lot and onto the winding road leading into town. The radio crackled to life soon after, the same Mariah Carey song Neve had already heard four times today drifting from the tinny speakers. Nick hated having a moment's peace from anything. He was always restless, always keeping himself busy. It had been that way since he'd broken up with his ex-fiancée, Molly, but his need to take care of people had started long before that. Probably around the time Mom began leaving them on a not-so-regular basis for the sake of "work" when Neve was just eight. Sixteen-year-old Nick had become more like her parent than her big brother after that. Her grandparents, too.

'Are *you* okay?' Neve questioned when Nick began to drum his fingers across the steering wheel.

'Yeah, I'm okay.' A red headlight passed across his face like a failed lie detector test.

'Once more with feeling?'

Nick huffed, hazel eyes remaining fixed on the winding road ahead. A muscle in his jaw ticked along to the radio. 'I'm okay, Neve. I am.'

'But . . . ?' This was always how it was. If Neve wanted to know how Nick was, she had to coax it out of him word by word. It was frustrating, but she supposed she wasn't much more forthcoming herself.

'There's no "but".' He shook his head. 'Just . . . y'know. It's Christmas.'

'Yep. The crappiest time of year.'

'Do you think we'll hear from her this year?'

The question sank like a stone in Neve's gut, and she averted her attention to the window, to the unblemished shadows of the things she didn't want to face. If she didn't acknowledge them, she'd never have to. 'No, I don't.'

Of course they wouldn't hear from her. Mom was probably getting a tan in Hawaii or refurbishing the apartment she owned in Toronto, or maybe she would find a smaller excuse like she had the year before last, when she'd had to stay in the city for her cat's vet appointment. She hadn't spent a Christmas with them in at least five years. Hadn't been home for more than a flying visit for a lot longer.

The truth of it was that she didn't care, and Neve had stopped expecting her to a long time ago. But Nick had the right to more bitterness. It had been him who had taken Neve to the movies on the weekend and helped her with homework. He joined Gran and Grandpa at every parent-teacher conference and went to every ski competition. He hadn't gone to college like most people his age, and though he never admitted it, Neve knew it was because he didn't want to leave her the way Mom had.

Yet every year he expected it to be different; expected that, this year, it wouldn't just be the three of them celebrating together with a turkey made for twelve. Almost as though their roles had reversed and he was the younger, more naive sibling with more hope, less to lose.

'Have you heard from her recently?' Nick asked.

Neve scraped at her chipped red nail polish: her one and only attempt at festivity this year. 'Not since August.' Her birthday. The fact Mom had remembered this year had been surprising enough, though the phone call had lasted all of five minutes. 'You need to let go, Nick.'

'I've let go.'

He wasn't a good liar, but Neve didn't say so, instead

pursing her lips as they crossed the speed bump and weaved back into the fairy-lit centre of Clement Falls. Silhouetted markets and stores closing their barriers for the day greeted them: the only home Neve had ever really known, even if it *was* overrun with tourists half the year.

'Besides,' he continued, 'you're one to talk.'

'I don't wait for her to come back.' Her defences rose at the accusation, and her voice with it.

'No, you've just given up on everybody altogether, and that's worse. When was the last time you had a conversation with someone who wasn't me, Juniper, Grandpa, or one of your students?'

'I keep myself to myself,' she muttered, venom seeping into her tone. 'That's not a bad thing.'

'Neither is giving people a chance. And what about skiing? You given up on that, too?'

Anger burned in Neve's gut. Nick knew exactly why Neve had stopped skiing competitively, even if she never said it out loud. Besides, she would rather be alone than be taken advantage of the way Nick was. It was one of the reasons his last relationship had ended: Molly had used him until there was nothing left of him, and then she'd given him an ultimatum when she'd decided out of the blue to move to New York and start a new life. Nick hadn't been able to leave his family, not so soon after Grandpa Artie had lost his wife, and Molly had left him broken. If that was love, if that was giving people a chance, Neve didn't want it.

'This isn't about skiing. This is about Mom. How many chances should she get before we accept she doesn't give a shit about us?'

'As many as it takes.' Nick raked a hand through his feathery hair and then scratched the stubble around his jaw. 'She's our mom, Neve. She's flaky and distant and difficult, but she's just about the only family we have left besides Grandpa. That means something to me.'

Neve's breath caught in her throat, and she swallowed

it back down, glaring out of the window at the snowflakes beginning to drift from the heavy clouds. They left streetlamps smudged and the shadows smeared. A world out of focus, just how Neve liked it. She supposed that's why skiing had been her calling. It snatched all clarity away, leaving nothing but biting wind and white hills unravelling around her. That didn't change, regardless of whether she was in Clement Falls or on Alpine Canada's national team halfway across the world.

'She's never coming back,' she said. 'Not this Christmas or the next or the one after.'

Nick only shook his head before flicking on his indicator. 'People can always surprise you. She can change.'

Maybe it was cynical, but Neve had long since stopped hoping for her mom to change. It had never gotten her anywhere. Still, she let the conversation drop, let the silence carry them home, just like she always did when things felt strained.

It was easier that way. She didn't care if her brother thought otherwise.

Chapter Five

Robin was absolutely certain that she should not have been riding a ski chairlift with a stomach-curdling, head-splintering hangover. She was even more certain that she had put her boots on the wrong feet this morning, and now examined them as the lift slowly hauled her up the blindingly white mountains, where the skiers and snowboarders looked like ants.

Looking at the snow moving beneath her feet and the battered, rented skis made her dizzy, and she swallowed the rising bile down, forcing herself to gaze straight ahead. She clutched her ski poles so tightly she was surprised they didn't break in her hands, feeling both hot and cold as her stomach swooped. She was too high, and she couldn't help but imagine her bench detaching from the lift, sending her plummeting down the Rockies.

Her knuckles turned white around the safety bar, feeling too small on the long bench. And she couldn't help it. She imagined Lexi sitting beside her, probably laughing at Robin's fears and storing anecdotes to tell their – well, *her* – friends just how many times Robin had embarrassed herself over the honeymoon. She would have had a field day with the drunken karaoke and the throwing up, not to mention Robin's terrible skiing abilities.

It only occurred to her then just how often Lexi had made fun of her. Robin had always been the butt of the joke at their fancy-schmancy dinner parties. 'Robin tripped over a *frog* yesterday,' or 'Robin still sobs her little heart out at *Finding Nemo*, you know,' or 'Robin spilled wine all over her blouse on our date last week and everybody could see her lacy, coral bra.'

Robin frowned now, wondering how things would be if she'd never found out about Lexi. If they'd actually gotten married and come on this honeymoon together. Would they have had fun, or would it just be another instance where Robin was completely out of her depth, stumbling and making an oaf of herself while Lexi skied smoothly over the slopes?

And then she wondered how many times it had been like that before, and Robin just hadn't seen it. The yoga retreat, for example, where Robin had not taken well to being turned into a pretzel, or the time they'd gone to a roller rink and Robin had spent most of the time on her arse. The time they'd gone to a petting farm and Robin had been bitten by a goat. They'd all been plans Lexi had made, Lexi had enjoyed, while Robin suffered through them because she'd just been grateful to be with her. To be in love.

It hadn't been reciprocated. Robin had ended up at a couples' cooking class alone because Lexi had called her five minutes prior claiming she couldn't make it. She'd never wanted to go to concerts with Robin or take the European city break she'd dreamed of. The relationship had been on her terms. It still was, even now. Robin was on their bloody honeymoon alone while Lexi moved on. Got engaged. Lived her life without her.

What the hell was she doing?

She didn't have time to work it out. The peak of the slope was quickly approaching, and she lifted the safety bar with trembling hands. A dark figure waited at the top: Neve, looking as unshakeable as ever in her helmet and goggles.

Stomach fluttering, Robin gave a small wave and prepared herself for landing. It had not gone well yesterday. She'd almost ended up stuck on the lift, too afraid to get off. Now, she tried to avoid the same problem by jumping as soon as solid ground came into sight.

Not a good idea. With a high squeal, she landed in the snow, her limbs sprawled like a starfish's and her face sinking into the cold damp.

'So elegant,' Neve commented.

Robin groaned and struggled to pull herself up, until eventually, Neve grabbed her arm and yanked.

'Ow!' she complained. Snow covered her face, and she brushed it away, cringing against the icy numbness it left behind. To think she could have been getting a suntan – well, sun*burn*, since she was too pasty for a nice golden glow – in somewhere like Malta if she hadn't been in love with an adventurous, snow-loving cheater. It made her sick.

'You're chipper today,' she commented. 'Nick's eggnog will do that to you.'

'Please don't mention eggnog,' Robin grumbled, finally standing upright. Her stomach lurched at the very thought of those heavy, milky cocktails she'd all but guzzled last night. 'Not unless you want to see my vomit again.'

Neve grimaced. 'No, thank you. Let's just ski, shall we?'

Skiing did not sound much more appealing than the alternative, but Robin nodded weakly and waded through the snow behind Neve until they reached a quiet spot on top of the beginner's slope. She clenched her teeth when a child who couldn't have been much older than ten mastered it on the first go. Why couldn't she have booked a baking honeymoon? Then *she* could have shown off like that.

'Not too much enthusiasm, please.' Sarcasm dripped from Neve's words, though the corner of her mouth curled with a smile. A slight improvement from yesterday, perhaps.

'What if I just . . . walk down the slope in my skis? Wouldn't that count? Like that man over there.' She pointed with her pole at an elderly man who was crawling down the slope on his hands and knees while his partner took photographs with a disposable camera. A perfect representation of what it would have been like if Lexi was here.

'That man will be there for the rest of the day,' Neve said.

'In fact, I'm pretty sure he called mountain rescue last week because he went off-piste and got lost.'

'Oh dear,' Robin murmured.

'Shall we try it on two legs before we resort to all fours?' She sighed, readying herself on bent knees and strapping her hands into her poles. Neve raised her eyebrows as though surprised Robin remembered even the basics.

'This time, please don't set off before I tell you to, okay?'

Another, more determined, nod. Robin wouldn't be the butt of the joke today. She wouldn't make a fool of herself again. She'd prove to herself, to Lexi, to everyone, that she was more than just a clumsy idiot to laugh at.

'Bend your knees a little more,' Neve instructed. 'Is your weight equal on both feet?'

Robin glanced down at her strapped-in boots, puzzled. 'I don't know. I've always had one knee that's slightly bigger than the other.'

Neve blinked patiently. 'Okay . . . oddly large knee aside, does it *feel* equal?'

'I suppose.'

'Your arms should be wide to help you with balance.'

Robin outstretched her arms, almost knocking Neve out in the process, and Neve scoffed, pushing the one closest back in. 'Not *that* wide.' She positioned Robin's arm, her gloved hands heavy against Robin's tensed elbow. 'Here.'

'Okay.'

Neve's eyes seemed to snag on Robin for a moment, her lashes a stark black against the white mountains and her cheeks rosy from the cold. 'Okay,' she echoed, her hand lingering before she finally stepped away.

Robin barely felt it between so many layers of thick clothes, yet she was sure her skin tingled with warmth.

Neve cleared her throat. 'Now, a lot of control comes from your legs. You need to turn in your skis at the front slightly when you want to slow down.' She demonstrated, turning in her toes so that the skis formed a triangle. 'The wider the skis are, the slower you'll go, but make sure they don't overlap at the front.'

A veil of focus fell across Robin as she tried to mimic Neve's position, gathering snow between her skis as she formed a wedge. 'Like this?'

'Exactly.' It was about the closest to a compliment Robin had ever gotten from her. 'I want you to try to stay in that position when you set off, and try to widen your skis when you slow. If you can do that, you won't have nearly as many tumbles.'

'You underestimate my clumsiness,' Robin pointed out.

Neve shrugged. 'Guess we'll soon see. Do you think you're ready to attempt it?'

'No,' she deadpanned, sucking in a long, cold breath. The air was heavy and sharp with snowdrift. 'But I can't be any worse than yesterday, can I?'

'Watch me first.' Neve got into position, bending her legs and turning the tops of her skis in as she slid steadily down a tiny, almost flat lump of snow. 'Watch how I slow when the triangle widens,' she called over her shoulder and, sure enough, came to a stop only a few metres away.

She made it look so bloody easy. Robin tightened her fingers around her poles and looked at her feet for a few moments, mustering her courage. And then she pushed off, her toes turned in slightly as ordered.

It worked, somehow. She didn't tumble or go too fast, only coasted as Neve had over the smooth snow.

'That's right. Now widen to slow,' Neve ordered as she approached.

Robin did – too much. Her skis overlapped at the top, and as she tried to correct them, she passed Neve and began to panic.

'It's okay. Just—' Neve was cut off by a shout coming their way. Robin looked over her shoulder and screamed, too. One of the Scouse lads she'd met in the bar last night barrelled towards her on a snowboard, right on her path. She flailed as she tried to get out of his way.

'Watch out!' he yelled, but it was too late. He zoomed into her like a speeding car, his heavy weight pushing her down the hill until she was certain she'd never stop falling. She clutched on to the man's arms for all they were worth, Neve's figure fading in the distance.

Their skis and snowboard collided in a spray of snow, and then Robin was falling to the ground, still refusing to let him go. They tumbled and tumbled until there was nothing but goggle-tinted white and crashing and their mingling cries.

And then, with a twinge of pain shooting from Robin's wrist, they finally came to a stop.

Robin heaved, instantly regretting the pancakes she'd had for breakfast this morning.

'Sorry, love!' The man winced, glancing at their tangled legs and equipment. 'Think I'm still a bit pissed from last night, like.'

She glared at him between stifling her dry retches, swiping her mouth with the sleeve of her jacket. 'I was doing it right then, too. Sort of.'

As her shock ebbed, the pain rolled in, and she squeezed her throbbing wrist as she searched for a sign of Neve. She was gliding towards them on her skis, her lips pursed and face a mask of hardened stone.

'Are you all right?' she asked as she came to a stop in the perfect wedge position Robin had almost achieved.

'Just a bit drunk, like,' the man answered.

'Not *you*,' Neve ground out, her gaze fixing on Robin.

'I'm not sure,' Robin answered weakly, patting herself down. 'How do you know if you're dead?'

'You can't usually speak,' she answered, scowling at the man once. '*You*' – she jabbed a hand and then seemed to realise it was covered in a mitten, disguising what must have been an aggressive point – 'should not be on the slopes. You could have seriously hurt someone.'

'Sorry, love.' He winced.

'Don't "love" me,' she growled before holding out her hand to Robin. 'Come on. We should get you checked out in first aid. We have an on-site nurse.'

'Oh, I'm really okay,' she lied, letting Neve help her up nonetheless. And if she did feel a little wobbly-kneed, she did her best not to show it. Which didn't work out very well when she tripped over her skis again and fell into Neve.

Neve held her up. 'Take your damn skis off.'

Robin did, numbly ejecting both feet from the grips. Neve did the same, picking up both hers and Robin's before her stormy eyes raked up and down Robin's frame again. 'Are you sure you can walk?'

'It really wasn't that bad.' It wasn't . . . she didn't think. She wore a helmet, so the dizziness was more likely from the hangover. Only her wrists and ribs felt a little strained and painful.

'Still, better to check,' Neve murmured. She perched the skis on her shoulder and then guided Robin down the hill. Robin didn't miss the final glower she threw the snowboarder's way.

'At least it wasn't technically my fault this time,' Robin commented. 'Still, I, er, don't think I'm meant for the slopes.'

Neve hummed, her hand finding the small of Robin's back when she almost stumbled into the path of another skier. These slopes were worse than trying to cross a motorway at peak time.

'Trouble does seem to follow you, doesn't it?' She narrowed her eyes, mirth sparkling in them.

Robin only shrugged and said, 'Apparently so.'

'Water,' Neve instructed, extending the cup she'd filled from the water dispenser on the way in. 'You need to stay hydrated, especially since you were drinking last night.'

'Thanks.' With frail, trembling fingers, a pale-faced Robin took the drink and sipped. 'Note to self: don't go skiing with a hangover.'

'Believe me, I've learned that the hard way myself.' Neve

collapsed onto the plastic chair and checked the clock impatiently. Her next lesson began in an hour, but the resort's first aid nurse, Amy, had disappeared, most likely on her lunch break.

'Am I keeping you?' Robin quipped, her tone light as she rested her wrist in her lap. She still wore her helmet, though she'd unzipped her coat.

Her gloves were still on, too. Neve sighed and beckoned with her finger. 'Let me see your wrist. Probably just need an ice pack and a bandage anyway.'

Hesitantly, Robin tugged her right glove off and rolled up her sleeves. Neve took her hand as gently as possible, squeezing around the joint the way her old ski instructor used to whenever she ended up with a strain. It didn't feel swollen or hot, thank goodness, and Robin only winced a little. 'How's it feel?'

'Just tender.'

'Where?'

She sucked in a breath when Neve prodded the knobbly, jutting bone harder. '*Ow*. There.'

'What about your hand?' Neve furrowed her brows in concentration, squeezing Robin's hand between her fingers. Her palm was soft, well-cushioned against her rough thumb, if a little bit clammy. Still, she felt the fine bones jolt beneath when Robin straightened.

'Sore,' she murmured. 'It's not broken, is it? I don't think I bought travel insurance. Lexi said we wouldn't need it.'

'Did Lexi *know* you?'

She pursed her lips, a line burrowing between her brows. She didn't lift her gaze, didn't laugh at the joke, and it left Neve uneasy. Again.

'Maybe not,' she said finally.

Neve wanted so badly to ask more. A million questions clogged her throat, but she had no idea how to voice them without making it seem as though she cared. And she wasn't good at caring.

Still, the ex – Lexi, she assumed – must have done some damage, no matter how good Robin was at shaking it off with liquor and sad karaoke songs.

So Neve allowed herself one question, just for good measure. A careful, surprisingly soft question. 'What made you come here without her? Other than the money, I mean.'

Robin shrugged. 'I like making myself look as pathetic as humanly possible. Going on my honeymoon alone seemed like a good way to get there.' A pause, and then finally she locked eyes with Neve. 'I think maybe I'm tired of being the boring singleton who sits at home with her mum and her dog while everyone else lives their lives. And my dad . . . he liked to travel. He never wasted a minute. He was always out and about somewhere, learning something new. I s'pose I wanted to see what all the fuss was about.'

Liked. Was. All past tense. Like he was no longer around. It made Neve think of Gran. Neve certainly hadn't lived up to her legacy the way Robin had followed her dad's. She'd done the opposite. Used Gran's death as a sign that she was better off staying with Grandpa in Clement Falls, because she'd been too far away when Gran had passed, and it had filled her with so much guilt and grief she hadn't known where to put it. So she'd stored it in cardboard boxes with her old ski team uniforms, her gold medals, her photographs, and she'd locked herself up with them. Now, they all collected dust together because she didn't know how to open herself up again after a loss like that. Not when Nick and Grandpa were all she had left.

She swallowed and pushed the thoughts away, standing from her chair. 'I'm going to hunt down an ice pack for you while we wait.'

'Okay,' Robin agreed quietly. She blew out a heavy breath, fanning herself with her good hand. 'Whew, it's warm in here.'

'Is it?' Neve asked, despite the fact her own cheeks had been burning since the moment she'd touched Robin's hand.

Behind the closed green curtain where Amy's handwritten "Out for lunch!" sign was pinned, she searched through the medical supplies. Luckily, the ice packs were still where Neve remembered from countless ACL sprains in her training days. She squeezed one to activate it and then—

'Knock, knock!' A familiar, slightly accented voice echoed around the first-aid room, and then the sound of a door clicking shut. 'Oh, hello.'

'Are you the first-aid nurse?' Robin asked.

Neve sighed and mustered the courage to open the curtain, unsurprised to find Irina, her old ski instructor, standing with a bag of supplies by the door. She placed them down on the chair closest when she saw Neve, her brows rising and that usual disappointment thinning her features. These days, Neve had been avoiding her like the plague.

'Hello, Neve. Injured another student?' Irina smirked smugly as though glad she'd finally cornered Neve.

'Not on purpose . . . this time.' Neve feigned lightness, though her heart was anything but. She passed the ice pack to Robin, and Robin wrapped it around her wrist. It was about the quietest she'd been since Neve had met her.

Irina's lips twitched with amusement. 'I didn't think I'd see you here for the second winter in a row. Isn't it time to get back to the real world?'

Neve clenched her jaw. *This* was why she'd avoided her. Irina had been the most heartbroken of all when Neve had quit the team to stay in Clement Falls. She'd gone easy on her at first, while she grieved Gran, but after the first year, it was always: 'Why aren't you back on the team, yet? They need you, you know.'

Neve didn't want to hear it anymore. She didn't need to be reminded of the things she'd given up, nor the reasons why. She didn't need to be treated as though she no longer belonged here, just because she'd once been young and able to travel around the world for competitions. That was over. She had bigger things to worry about now.

'I'm sure that's not true.' Neve's smile was so strained her cheeks ached.

Irina glanced at Robin and whispered, not very discreetly, 'She was supposed to be an Olympian, you know.'

Robin's eyes widened. 'Oh?'

'Well, I'm not,' Neve snapped, crossing her arms stiffly.

Irina looked at Neve, her brown eyes steady and searching. Probing. She was always good at making sure Neve knew exactly what she was thinking without having to say a word. Even as a kid, she'd known when her landings hadn't been controlled enough from a single look, her speed too slow from a tapping foot. A good instructor, but a stubborn, slightly terrifying one, too.

And the disappointment she'd radiated constantly since Neve quit had been a million times worse than the discipline she'd once enforced. Neve had spent half her life trying to make Irina proud only to ruin it all in a day. Everything they'd worked on together. Neve couldn't imagine how it must have felt. She didn't have many long-term students, most of them beginners on vacation like Robin. She couldn't imagine pouring so much time into teaching somebody how to be the best only for them to walk away.

But Neve had her reasons. It was her choice, in the end. And she told herself that often enough to believe it was the right one.

'What happened to your student?' Irina asked finally.

'Sprained wrist, I think. We were waiting for Amy to make sure.'

She nodded, batting the words away. 'No need. I'm trained in first aid, too. I can take a look.'

Sinking down into the chair beside Robin, she held her hands out expectantly.

Robin glanced sheepishly at Neve before offering her wrist, removing the ice pack to reveal reddened skin. 'Has she always been so moody?' Robin whispered.

Irina smirked. 'Yes. I don't know where she gets it from.'

Neve scowled. 'I'm not moody. You're both just highly annoying.'

'Uh-huh,' Irina said. 'You know, Lara was asking about you just the other day. She still hopes you'll try out for the team again soon.'

Rolling her eyes, Neve decided to busy herself by searching for bandages or a wrist support. She refused to get into this now; refused to think about how her trainer had held Neve's place in the national team until Neve decided she wasn't coming back. Even then, Lara had been understanding. She'd told Neve she was welcome to return when she was ready, though if she left it too long, she'd have to try out again.

Of course, Lara was also good friends with Irina, which was how she'd managed to get the spot in the first place. And also how Irina managed to guilt-trip Neve whenever they bumped into each other on the resort.

Neve listened as Irina asked Robin about the sprain, how sore it was, whether she could bend her wrist, as she took a moment behind the curtain to regather her composure. But a curtain wasn't enough to stop Irina from continuing: 'If I were you, I'd be snatching up any opportunity I could get. You don't stay young forever, you know. I found that out the hard way.'

'Oh, cry me a river. You're, what, forty-five?' Neve retorted. 'That's not old.'

'It is in the sporting world. First, your knees start going, and then you get one too many concussions, and before you know it, your body tells you it's time to give it up.'

That's what annoyed Neve the most. When Irina's body had told her to stop skiing, she'd had to listen, but when Neve's mind, her grief, had done the same, she was just a young idiot who'd thrown it all away, taken it for granted.

She knew what she'd given up, and she stood by her choices. For Grandpa, she had to.

'I think I'm already there,' Robin admitted dryly.

Neve almost laughed. Almost.

Irina did. 'How many lessons have you had?'

'Two. And I've spent most of them on my arse. I can't even use the chairlift properly.'

'It's not for everyone. Pass the bandages, Neve?'

Neve did, her stomach sinking just slightly. She wasn't sure why. Not until she watched Irina wind the bandage around Robin's wrist. She wanted to feel the softness of Robin's skin again, the warmth. Wanted to go back to talking about Robin and how she'd been brave enough to come here rather than Neve's abandoned sporting career.

She bit the inside of her cheek, tension rolling through her. She checked the clock again. There was still half an hour before her next lesson, but she had no reason to stick around – and she didn't particularly want to. 'I should get going. I have a student waiting.'

'Oh.' Robin's brows furrowed as though disappointed. 'Of course. Thanks for . . . everything.'

Neve couldn't help but falter. It hadn't occurred to her that this might be goodbye. Robin hadn't booked any more ski lessons with her, and it was unlikely she would. She would only see her around the resort or in town in passing, if at all.

'No worries,' she said as nonchalantly as she could.

She made to leave, Irina's mutter following behind her like a second set of feet. 'She's very good at avoiding things.'

Robin's silence spoke volumes. Neve just hoped Irina wouldn't tell her everything. It was none of her business – and it might be nice if just one person in town didn't pick apart her choices; judge them without understanding them.

It would be nice if Robin didn't realise that, no matter how pathetic she felt for going on her honeymoon alone, Neve's failures would always be deemed far worse.

Chapter Six

'I don't know what I'm doing here, Wren,' Robin confessed down the phone. She'd taken to sprawling on the couch in her cosiest pyjamas, a pillow propping up her hand while she iced it. Irina had bandaged it tight, but most of the pain had ebbed over the afternoon. Which meant she had no real reason to be sitting in her cabin at six p.m. like an old lady, but if the alternative was potentially getting hammered in the bar for the second night in a row or colliding with drunk snowboarders, she wasn't sure she wanted to venture outside again.

'You're enjoying new experiences,' Wren replied firmly. She could hear Tom shouting in the background at their house cat, Sally, for urinating on the TV remote again. Robin missed that. Not cats weeing on electronic devices. Just . . . home. Being comfortable among people she knew. Her mum wouldn't reply to her texts or answer her calls, so Wren was the only connection she had left until she flew back in – she checked the time and date on her phone – ten days, twenty hours, and fifty-six seconds.

It might as well have been an eternity.

'"Enjoying" isn't the word I'd use,' she said. '"Barely surviving" would perhaps be more accurate.'

'Well . . . is your instructor at least hot?'

Her face flamed without warning, and she groaned. 'Don't.'

'I'm only asking,' Wren retorted with all the feigned innocence of Sally's background meows. 'Is she?'

'Doesn't matter. She thinks I'm a right plank, just like everyone else.'

'You are not a *plank*, Robin. Your clumsiness will be endearing to the right person.'

Robin didn't care about the right person. As far as she was concerned, they didn't exist anymore. She hauled herself up off the couch and began to pace, boredom settling into her bones. How did non-pastry chefs with free time and small families manage? It was unending torture, having this much time to think and do nothing.

Her fingers slid across the small table by the kitchen area, sifting through her passport and boarding passes and the leaflet she'd been given from the receptionist. Happy, smiling people filled the cover – families petting reindeer and snowboarders looking suave in the sun and snow. She turned the page to find more awful resort activities: couples' massages as Nick had mentioned; evening entertainment provided by Clement Falls' most renowned musician, Sheldon the Scootering Snowman, along with special guest, Robert the Roller-skating Reindeer; a "crochet your own Christmas decorations" class.

None of these things sounded like her cup of tea. Where were the biscuit baking competitions like in those Hallmark films she sometimes caught Mum watching, or mulled wine tasting? Where were the things she would enjoy?

Then again, she'd brought it on herself. This honeymoon hadn't been made for Robin. It had been made for Lexi and her fun-loving adventurousness.

'*Robiiiiin?*' Wren sang, and only then did Robin realise she hadn't replied. 'Are you still with me, or have you tripped over your own feet again?'

She hummed in reply, turning the page again and finding information about the town beyond the resort. There were plenty of hiking trails. Maybe she'd sign up for a guided one tomorrow – that way she wouldn't risk getting lost. It would mean she'd be able to get some pictures for Instagram at least.

Beyond that, market stalls were pictured surrounded by Christmas trees and fairy lights. She'd been meaning to go into town, buy some presents, but she'd only found out about the cable cars that would get her there on her way back from the first-aid room this afternoon. She could do that, too, she supposed. Maybe it would make her feel more at home, since she always visited Manchester's markets around this time of year.

'I think I'll go on one of these guided hike things tomorrow. Get the obligatory exercise stuff over with. And maybe on Tuesday, I'll do the markets. See if I can avoid near-death experiences there instead.'

'That's good. Just take it day by day.' A yawn. Robin had forgotten that it was late for her sister. 'I know it's weird when you're so far away and all on your own, but you're doing your best. Dad would be proud of you.'

'Yeah.' She smiled softly at that. 'What about Mum?'

'Mum has banned your name from the house until further notice.' She could practically hear Wren's flinch. 'I'll talk to her before you get home. Don't worry. She didn't talk to me for a month when Tom and I went camping last summer, remember?'

Exhausted, Robin closed her eyes and tried not to imagine the wrath that awaited her back home. She tried not to think about Mum at all, now. It only brought tears to her eyes.

'Yeah. Thanks, Wren. I should probably leave you to it, anyway. Things sound hectic there.' Tom was now shouting about the fact he had found cat poo in his slipper. Sally was surely in big, big trouble.

'I told him we should have gotten a dog,' Wren muttered. 'I'll see you soon. Let me know how you get on tomorrow.'

'I will. Ba-bye.' Robin hung up and took a deep breath, glancing at the leaflet a final time. Hopefully, her experience of the rest of Clement Falls would be far better than the resort.

Stepping out of the cable car – which was much safer and easier to use than the ski chairlift, thank goodness – and onto the cobbles of Clement Falls was a little bit more nerve-racking than Robin had expected. She'd been secluded from the rest of the world up at the resort, and there had only been a few other couples on her guided hike yesterday – more difficult than she'd expected, even though the trails had been cleared and the route was supposed to be "beginner-friendly", which, after her third slip, she'd learned was not quite the same as "Robin-friendly".

But the town itself teemed with people, life.

It was small and charming, fairy-lit roofs sagging under heavy piles of snow, and the buildings were crooked, leaning against one another for support like drunken friends coming home from a night out. The shop windows overflowed with tinsel and garlands, baubles and nutcrackers, all of them independent businesses Robin had never heard of before, and pretty red bows were tied on every lamp post.

She hadn't even reached the markets yet, and already she carried three bags from the candle and soap shop, whose rich, cinnamon-spiced scent still clung to her clothes halfway down the high street, and one filled with cashmere socks – gifts of course. Unless her feet got cold tonight. Maybe then a pair might mysteriously go missing.

It was magical, really; finally like stepping into one of those romantic, festive films, with carols drifting from every store and snow lining the kerbs. She just wished she had someone to share it with.

A pang of loneliness weaved its way into her thoughts. Wren would have loved it here. Everyone else walked arm in arm or clustered in groups, chatting and laughing and sharing their hot chocolate. But Robin caught her solitary reflection in every window, and it left her feeling hollow.

Her spirits lifted when she found a bakery named Clement's Cakes on the corner. The high street opened up onto a huge square, where the wood-panelled market stalls glowed golden in the dwindling afternoon light. Colourful bobble hats were all she could see for miles, much like her own, which was half-chewed because Cleopawtra had thought the pom-pom was one of her tennis balls the first few times she'd worn it.

Robin couldn't help but smile eagerly, soaking in the first few notes of "White Christmas". She couldn't tell if it was playing somewhere nearby, or just in her head. Either way, it was the most festive she'd ever felt, and the most comfortable she'd been since arriving here. The smoky smell of sizzling hog roasts hung in the air, reminding her of Christmases in Manchester: pulled pork and apple sauce on a usually quite stale bun from the markets. Her stomach grumbled, but her feet didn't take her towards the square yet.

Her priority was, as always, cake.

She fought her way through the narrow door of Clement's Cakes – no easy feat with half a dozen brimming shopping bags – and paused to take it in. A tree collapsing under the weight of its planet-sized baubles wilted in one corner, dropping its pine needles onto a tartan skirt scattered with gold-foil-wrapped presents, and each table had been decorated with poinsettias and faux snow. Paper chains dangled from the ceiling and the cheerful melody of "Sleigh Ride" by The Ronettes could be heard beneath the chatter of the customers.

The bakery was jam-packed. So much so that if not for the rich, earthy scent of coffee and the sweet smell of what must have been lemon drizzle, she might have turned around and tried the markets instead. But at the very least, she needed a snack and a hot drink to keep her warm while the sun waned behind the smoking chimneys.

She slipped into the queue, loosening her scarf as the bakery's warmth began to curl around her. Eyeing the menu and display of pastries at the front presented her with the toughest decision since choosing to come here at all: what did she want to eat? There were so many options she began to sweat, a common occurrence when it came to dessert. What if she chose the wrong one? What was she in the mood for?

The answer to the latter was all of them, really. Chocolate fudge cake would probably be too sickly for her and would leave her wanting to go home, get her pyjamas on, and have a post-dessert nap, so that was out of the question. There wasn't much room to sit, meaning she'd have to eat on the go, so she couldn't choose anything with too much frosting or crumbs.

The doughnuts were calling her name. So loudly, in fact, she didn't notice that she was now at the front of the queue. And the person behind the till had vanished.

'Hello?' Robin frowned and stepped on her tiptoes to peer over the counter.

A hunched figure with a head of pale brown curls greeted her. She swiped a puddle of coffee furiously with a tea towel. 'Just a minute!'

Robin waited patiently until she popped up again, blowing her mussed fringe out of her eyes and chucking the drenched tea towel somewhere behind the counter. 'Hello. So sorry for the wait.'

'Oh, don't worry,' Robin replied. She knew well how awful it was to have to rush around in a kitchen, even if she was usually hidden from impatient customers at work. 'I think I'll have the apple and maple crumble doughnut and a hot chocolate to go, please.'

The flustered woman – Hazel, her name tag read – nodded and grabbed the tongs, opening the door into the cake display. She manoeuvred past the shelf of doughnuts completely and landed on a toffee apple cinnamon roll instead, pulling it out and placing it in a pastel-green box.

Robin didn't have the heart to tell her it wasn't what she'd asked for, aggressively British as she was. Polite phrases such as "no worries", "oh, sorry, terribly sorry", and "please, thank you, lovely jubbly" were the staples of her culture, and she couldn't very well betray them by pointing out a mistake with her order, could she?

'I bet us tourists are the bane of your existence,' she said conversationally, shouting to be heard over the blitzing hot chocolate machine Hazel had just turned on. At least, she hoped it was hot chocolate. She couldn't abide coffee, and Hazel had already established that she wasn't too concerned about fulfilling customers' orders.

Still, she smiled over her shoulder as she steamed the milk. 'We love tourists. It can just get a little overwhelming this time of year, and half of my seasonal temps are off sick with the flu. I'm all on my own.'

'Well, you're doing a good job,' Robin lied with a bright smile. She threw a handful of pennies and notes into the tip jar just to be on the safe side, still not accustomed to giving out tips. Hazel looked like perhaps she needed them.

'Thank you. You know, you're the only person who's actually treated me like a human being today.' Hazel was all large brown doe eyes as she poured the frothy milk into the to-go cup and fixed on the lid. 'Christmas makes people loopy.' And then, whispered with a hand beside her mouth: 'And a little bit rude.'

She slid along the box with the cake Robin hadn't asked for and then punched the numbers into the till. 'Nine dollars and forty-nine cents.'

Robin offered a ten-dollar bill and took the cake box and drink appreciatively. 'Thank you. I'm going to devour this cinnamon roll.' Even if it was not the doughnut she'd had her heart set on.

Hazel's freckled cheeks dimpled as she counted the change. 'Are you going to the carolling concert by the big Christmas tree later on?'

'Er . . .' Robin hadn't seen that listed in the leaflet. Then again, she hadn't bothered to read the rest lest the sheer number of things to do – or, in her case, not do – left her overwhelmed. 'I don't know. Should I?'

'My niece is playing in the band.' Hazel shrugged. 'It's mostly locals who sing carols or play their instruments, but tourists seem to enjoy watching too. If you can stand out in the cold for that long, that is.'

Robin wasn't the biggest fan of carols and whatnot, but she supposed it was better than moping in her cabin or subjecting herself to Sheldon the Scootering Snowman or whoever was performing at the resort tonight.

'I'm British. I'm used to standing in the cold,' she said. 'When does it start?'

Hazel checked her watch, eyes widening. 'Is it that late already? Jesus, I don't think I've peed since, like, nine a.m.'

Raising her brows, Robin searched for an appropriate response to the confession, and found none. 'Oh.'

'Sorry.' Hazel shook her head, her curls rippling with her. 'The concert starts in just under two hours, but the shops stay open till late tonight if you need to camp out somewhere warm until then.'

'Great. I'll be there.' Robin smiled, not quite sure if she was telling the truth yet. She only knew that she wanted to trawl the Christmas markets next, and that could very well take her two hours alone.

'Good. I'll keep an eye out for you, then.'

Warmth spread through Robin. Was she . . . making friends? With people who were not moody, albeit attractive, ski instructors or bartenders paid to get her drunk and listen to her whine? Or maybe Hazel was being polite because Robin had tipped her generously, which she supposed would make this a PG, platonic version of *Pretty Woman*. Either way, it was easy to like Hazel and her gap-toothed smile, sparkly eyes, rosy cheeks, and sheer obliviousness to managing a bakery, and Robin wouldn't mind having her as company if it meant not spending the rest of the evening on her own.

'See you soon, then.' Robin beamed and then waved before gathering her things and leaving the bakery. Suddenly, Clement Falls didn't seem half as big and scary.

Robin went a little bit overboard at the markets, adding to the gifts she'd already picked up on the high street. Every stall had drawn her attention one way or another, until she'd bought three different cross-stitching kits for her mum, two scarves and a selection box of vegan chocolate truffles for her sister, and all sorts of knitted sweaters, ornaments, and jewellery for her extended family. She'd even bought

Cleopawtra a new collar and a snazzy, Santa-themed bandana to wear on Christmas Day while filling herself up first with the cinnamon roll, then apple strudels.

Maybe shopping had been a bad idea.

It was too late now. Robin weaved through the other shoppers, *still* pausing again when she saw something she liked at a little pastel-themed stall.

No. You're not supposed to be buying for yourself, she scolded herself after her sights settled on a cupcake-patterned apron.

And then again on a personalised chopping board.

And a set of decorative wooden spoons that would look lovely in her kitchen. Or her *mum's* kitchen, as she so often liked to remind her whenever Robin got carried away with baking.

But she *had* stained her old apron with cherries and food dye that not even baking soda and lemon juice could scrub out. Would it be so terrible if she treated herself to a new, necessary one?

'Robin!' a voice called above the din of Christmas cheer. She turned to find Nick waving at her. Something snagged in her chest when she found Neve beside him, offering what seemed to be more of a grimace than a smile. Behind them stood an elderly man she didn't recognise. Juniper wagged her tail at his feet, her lead clutched in his hand.

She stepped away from the apron with a silent vow of her return and freed herself from the bodies pressing around her to meet the bartender on the cobbled stones.

'Hello.' The greeting was mostly for Juniper, who seemed happier than usual to see her. She nudged Robin's palm with her cold, wet nose, desperate to be petted, and Robin was happy to comply.

'How's the wrist?' Nick asked.

Robin cringed. Her wrist had been fine until bearing the weight of all her new purchases. Now, it was throbbing a bit, though Irina's tightly wound bandages kept it well supported. 'Better. But you're not supposed to know about that.' She shot a glare Neve's way.

The corner of Neve's mouth curled into a dry smirk then, and she linked her arm through the older man's. 'This is our Grandpa Artie. He's been dragging us out here every year since we could walk.'

Robin smiled sweetly, her chest swelling. To think her own grandparents only ever tried to set her up with their neighbours or else make her fake pillow girlfriends as a last resort. She would like them a bit more if they took her shopping instead. 'It's lovely to meet you.'

Artie flashed Robin a pleasant grin. Though he was freckled by liver spots and had only a few wisps of silver hair creeping out of his woolly hat, his misty eyes still sparkled brightly as he shook Robin's hand. 'And you, my dear. Why don't I leave you all to it? You don't need an old man like me trailing behind you. Besides, Juniper is pestering everybody. I think she's hungry.'

Indeed, Juniper had stepped away from Robin's hand to sniff somebody's onion-topped hot dog.

'Oh, no,' Robin argued. 'That's not necessary. I was just finishing up, anyway.' She shifted from foot to foot, not fancying another night of burdening Neve with her presence. She might have been desperate for company, but not quite *that* desperate.

'You can't leave now. The carolling concert is in an hour,' Nick said, tugging her closer by the sleeve of her coat before she could escape. 'And we're about to go ice skating. You're more than welcome to join us. Right, Neve?'

'Oh, are we pretending I have a choice in the matter now?' Neve rolled her eyes as though Nick inviting Robin had caused her great hardship.

'Go, go.' Their grandfather ushered them away. 'Juniper and I will meet you back at home later on.'

Robin opened her mouth to argue, but Nick was already dragging both her and Neve away with a quick goodbye over his shoulder. Juniper panted with both ears flopping down sadly as they walked away.

'I really don't think I should ice skate. Neve can attest to the fact that I will probably end up breaking a bone, and I've already needed first aid once this week.'

'For once, something I can agree with,' Neve chimed in helpfully.

Nick only tutted. 'You can use one of those penguin supports. It'll be fine.'

Robin groaned, expecting Neve to back her up – but Neve did no such thing.

'Great,' she muttered, wondering if she could get away with flying home a week early. Even her mother's cooking was surely better than this.

Robin hadn't been lying when she'd said she shouldn't ice skate. Even hunched over her penguin aid, she slid and wobbled all over the place. Neve could only watch with faint amusement from the side of the rink as she slowly made her way over. Nick had already abandoned them to flirt with the pretty supervisor who had taken their shoes, and now she caught him trying to impress her every so often by whirling skilfully around the ice. Where Neve had chosen skiing, Nick's first love had always been skating.

Robin clearly was not adept at either of these things. Neve had to catch her when she almost tumbled over again, securing her hand tightly to the railing.

'I give up,' she pouted breathlessly, knuckles turning white as she gripped on to the support for dear life.

'But you've only fallen five times,' Neve observed dryly, mirth bubbling beneath the words. Robin might have been irritating and her polar opposite, but Neve was finding herself starting to enjoy all the chaotic clumsiness and light-hearted humour. Not that she would ever admit it. Besides, something about the night of too many eggnogs had made her wonder if perhaps she'd judged too quickly. There were cracks in

Robin's jokes and puns; shadows behind those glittering, pale eyes. Something Neve saw in the mirror each morning herself. The ex's doing, maybe, or the loss of her father, perhaps.

'That ten-year-old over there was making fun of me.' Robin stuck her tongue out at the group of kids huddled on the other side of the rink. One of them shot back a vulgar gesture that made Neve think perhaps they were a little older than ten.

She clamped down her laughter, working hard to keep a straight face as Robin turned back to her. 'Kids these days, huh?'

'I told you this was a bad idea!'

Neve lifted her hands in surrender. 'It wasn't my idea to invite you. Blame my brother.'

As she said it, Nick whipped past them, a dark, weaving figure cutting through the light and colour.

'Show-off,' Robin scoffed, then her features sobered. 'So . . . what was the thing with the scary first-aid lady about yesterday?'

Neve stiffened, though she should have seen it coming. Irina hadn't exactly been subtle. Still, she wasn't ready to spill all of her troubles to a virtual stranger. 'Nothing.'

'Really?' Robin narrowed her eyes. 'You've seen me drunk and vulnerable. Which I'm still completely mortified about, by the way. I swear I'm not usually this . . . *this*,' she seemed to settle on, motioning to herself as though it made things clearer.

Neve's eyes narrowed. Robin had said the same thing the night it happened, that she wasn't usually "like this". 'What are you usually like?' she couldn't help but ask, curiosity shimmering beneath her ribs.

Robin hesitated, gloved fingers swiping the fair strands of hair from her face. They fell flat beneath her bobble hat, ruffled only slightly by the open, frosty air. The rink's twinkling lights and the bright white ice painted every part of her silver – and perhaps if Neve was to admit it to herself, she found Robin beautiful.

She shouldn't. She knew that. But she couldn't get rid of that annoying little flutter in her chest; the one that had been chasing her since the first god-awful pun had left Robin's lips in the resort's lobby; the one that had caught up to her now.

It didn't mean anything. Just that Neve was bored and single and perhaps a little bit lonely. It had been a while since she'd met someone new, someone attractive in an unexpected sort of way. Besides, Robin was clearly still hung up on her ex. It was nothing. It would pass. Neve would just have to ignore the attraction until it did.

She'd forgotten that she'd even asked the question until Robin cocked her head and said, 'Probably as idiotic and annoying, just with fewer alcohol and snowboarder collisions involved. Which reminds me. I should probably thank you – again – for taking me to first aid. I'm sure it was a massive inconvenience.'

'Maybe, but it was an expected one, too. Bound to happen,' Neve couldn't help but quip. 'Don't worry about it. It was nothing.'

'No, it wasn't. I would probably be lying dead in a ditch somewhere by now if it wasn't for you.'

She didn't know what to say to that, so she only smiled through tight lips and shifted her gaze to the tall Christmas tree in the heart of the rink. Her brother whizzed past again, waving. She rolled her eyes.

'Can you skate like that, too?' Robin asked. 'Are you all just annoyingly talented Olympians?'

She stiffened at the mention of the Olympics, gritting her teeth as tension sliced through her. *Damn Irina*. 'No. Definitely not. My brother is the skater. I'm the skier.' She didn't dare mention that she wasn't an Olympian, either, too afraid the pain would seep through and betray her composure, and then she'd have to tell Robin everything that Irina hopefully hadn't.

Robin must have sensed it. Her eyes rested intently on Neve for a moment before she replied, 'You haven't fallen yet, though. Seems like you're good at everything. It's the worst.'

'Well . . .' Neve smirked '. . . we *have* been coming here every year since we were kids. I might have picked up a thing or two. What about you? What do you do?' It was strange. Neve knew next to nothing about Robin, and yet somehow still felt as though she knew everything she needed to: her favourite Christmas song, her aversion to winter sports, the way she always smiled but rarely laughed, the fact she should have been here with her wife but wasn't.

'I'm a pastry chef.' Robin shrugged. 'I work at a restaurant in Manchester.'

Neve's brows arched. 'Fancy.'

'Definitely not. It's very dull. I do miss Owen though.'

'Who's Owen? Another ex?'

Robin snorted. 'No. Owen is my oven and I love him very much.'

'Of course Owen is an oven.' Neve nodded as though she should have guessed as much. 'Well, I guess Daniel the dishwasher will keep him company while you're gone?'

Robin snapped her eyes to Neve with a cool, even stare — and then a chuckle burbled from her, as light and smooth as running water. It left Neve with a flicker of pleasant surprise. 'It's *Delilah* the dishwasher, actually.'

'Forgive me. I should have known.'

'You should've. I'll let you off this time, though.' As she worried at her bottom lip, Robin's eyes turned glassy and she braced her spine against the railings. The fact that she had been standing on the ice for so long without falling was a feat in itself. 'I think this is the longest I've gone without baking, though. The first thing I usually do when I'm sad or stressed is make a batch of biscuits or cupcakes. It's silly, really.'

'You know, there's an oven at my grandpa's place that hasn't been used in months. You're welcome to it.' Neve didn't know why she was offering. The words spilled from her without warning, her mouth working quicker than her brain. 'It hasn't been christened with a name, though, so you'll have to excuse it for that.'

Robin's features brightened, and she straightened – too quickly. Neve clutched her hand before her feet could slip from under her, unable to keep her laughter from escaping. 'Easy. No more first-aid trips, please.'

'Artie wouldn't mind?'

'Nah. If you don't have plans, we usually get takeout on a Wednesday night, so tomorrow we're pretty much free as birds. You're welcome to stick around for dinner, too. Nick usually orders way too much anyway.'

'I wouldn't want to impose . . .'

Disappointment tugged at Neve's stomach, but she wasn't about to beg.

She didn't have to, anyway. A moment later, Robin said: 'Then again, you *do* have an oven in need of a name. I suppose as long as I'm welcome . . .'

Neve rolled her eyes, secretly pleased as she was. 'I'll pick you up at four tomorrow afternoon.'

Robin's white, slightly gapped teeth flashed against the lights as she grinned, and Neve couldn't help but offer a gentle smile in return. Their eyes met, Neve's getting caught in that bottomless, moonlight grey – until Robin blinked, a look of determination hardening the set of her jaw.

'Right. I refuse to leave Clement Falls without acquiring at least one new skill. Show me how the hell you can stand on the ice without falling.'

Without protest, Neve held her hand out for Robin to take. She did, keeping the other one planted firmly on the penguin aid as Neve pulled her back onto the ice. 'Don't look at your feet. Look straight ahead.'

Robin obeyed, lifting her chin as she steadied herself. Her grip was so solid that Neve could feel the tendons in her hands being crushed, but she didn't mind. Their skates glided waveringly; out of sync, but they were doing it. They were skating together.

'Think you can let the penguin go?' Neve dared when they had made it halfway around the rink. A moment later, the penguin aid was pushed away, left to float sadly on the edge of the rink.

'Oh no.' Robin wobbled. 'This was a mistake. Bring Percy back.'

Neve assumed Percy was the penguin. 'You're okay. Keep going.'

She wasn't okay. Robin's balance lasted all of three seconds, and then they were on the floor before Neve could even register that she was falling.

No. Not falling. Being pulled down.

She almost cursed, but Robin was giggling beneath Neve's frame. They'd landed not just together, but with Neve on top of Robin. Instinctively, Neve had planted her wrist down, and it had landed beside Robin's head, their faces only inches apart.

'I'm beginning to think that you're not a very good teacher.' They were so close that Neve could feel Robin's cool breath feathering across her lips, her skin. Robin's citrusy perfume clung to them both now, a sharp, tangy scent that reminded Neve of lunchtimes at elementary school in scorching summer heat, biting into sliced oranges.

Heart sparking, Neve hauled herself up before she could lose herself; before she could think too much about the fluttering in her belly. 'I'm beginning to think that you really like the floor.'

Another laugh as Neve pulled Robin to her feet with both hands, making sure that she stayed upright this time. Perhaps losing the penguin aid *had* been a little premature.

'Sorry for taking you down with me.' Robin didn't seem sorry at all. She was still beaming, a tendril of hair falling across her lips and rising and falling with her ragged breaths. Without thinking, Neve reached out and tucked it away, wishing that she wasn't wearing gloves; that she could have felt the warm swell of her rosy cheek.

She should have taken her hand away then, but it lingered for a few moments, until Robin blinked and Neve's face blazed with the realisation of what she'd done. She threw her hands in her pockets. Looked away. Tried not to cringe at her own forwardness. What was she *doing*? 'We should go before we miss the concert.'

'Okay.' Robin's voice was quiet; not her own. She scoured the rink, and then her face fell. 'My penguin has been rehomed.'

Neve turned to find a girl wearing an elf hat skating away with the penguin, her colourful tights shimmering with glitter beneath the lights. With a sigh, she held her hand out and tried not to shiver when Robin took it. 'One last try to the door?'

'Just don't let go of me,' Robin whispered.

Neve couldn't even if she wanted to. Not until ice turned to soft foam mats and they returned to the harsh fluorescents and sturdy soles of the real world.

The town square was jam-packed, and Robin found herself being hauled through crowds by the hand. Apparently, Neve didn't mess about when it came to getting a decent view. Robin stumbled – over her own feet or someone else's, she didn't know – her shoulder burning with the threat of it being pulled from its socket and her shopping bags jiggling uncontrollably. Just as she was about to complain, something heavy collided with her.

'*Oof!*' The initial impact was winding, but what followed was a hot, sticky damp seeping through her scarf and coat into the sweater beneath. The smell was overwhelmingly chocolatey, just like everything else Robin had passed by tonight.

She looked down to find the cause and saw it was a young girl, eyes wide though half-concealed behind a thick, brown fringe and an elf hat perched on her head. In her hands, a now half-empty mug of creamy hot chocolate. The other half covered Robin's favourite powder-blue teddy bear coat, melting pink marshmallows included. And below the mug . . .

sparkly tights. It was the girl who had stolen Robin's penguin support on the ice rink.

'Oops . . .' The girl winced, wiping down Robin's coat with her fluffy gloves.

Oops was a little bit of an understatement, and Robin was about to say so when Neve came back into view. She must have realised that Robin was no longer following her.

'Come on. Nick found a great . . . Oh.' Neve's dark brows furrowed as she noticed Robin's ruined coat, her gaze flickering to the girl. 'Hey, Margo. What happened?'

'It was an accident . . .' she stuttered out – and then had the audacity to *sip* the rest of her hot chocolate. If she didn't look so young, perhaps about twelve or thirteen, Robin would have made a smart retort about whether she'd like to throw the rest of the drink over her, too.

A shrill call distracted Robin from her frustration, seeming to have been shrieked right beside her ear. 'Margo!'

'I'm here,' the girl grumbled with a roll of her eyes, gulping down the last dregs of her drink and leaving behind a hot chocolate moustache.

'Oh!'

Robin was nudged forward again as whoever had been yelling in her ear brushed past her. It turned out to be a familiar woman with wild, brown curls that bounced when she walked and beauty spots splashed in clusters across her cheeks. Hazel, the woman from the bakery.

'There you are!' she said. And then, glancing at Robin and Neve: 'Neve! Oh my goodness, you met my new favourite customer!'

'I didn't realise you knew each other.' Neve's cheeks dimpled with a smile as she waved. It was a new side of her that Robin was seeing tonight; that she had been *allowed* to see tonight. All of her sarcastic quips and judgemental frowns seemed to have dissipated in the light-dotted darkness, though after Robin's skating, she had deserved them all the same. Was this who she was without Robin here to annoy her?

Robin hoped so. She liked Neve like this, smiley and flushed and painted golden by the streetlamps.

'I didn't realise *you* had friends,' Robin taunted, nudging Neve playfully.

'Neve and I were in the same classes through high school.' Hazel chewed her lip. 'I thought I saw you at the rink earlier. And wasn't your brother there, too?'

'Oh, yeah. He's over there.' Neve pointed to Nick, who stood by the grand Christmas tree in the centre of the square, hands in his pockets and chin dipped into his scarf. When he saw everybody looking, he waved and motioned them to join him.

Apparently, they seemed to have forgotten Robin's poor coat, because they wove their way towards Nick, leaving her to trail behind with Margo.

She shifted sheepishly when Robin cast her a sidelong stare. 'Sorry about your coat.'

'That's okay,' Robin lied. It was only thirty pounds from Primark, anyway, but that wasn't the point. It had been on sale last year. She wouldn't be able to replace it now. It was like losing a child – she'd even been so enamoured by it that she'd named it Cara.

'Hi, Hazel,' Nick greeted, sporting his usual friendly smile.

It might have been the reflection from a luminous red Santa hat plonked on the head of the person behind them, but Robin could have sworn Hazel blushed as she replied. 'Hey, Nick.'

'You must be Margo, right?' He nodded to Margo, and Robin found it an apt moment to remind them all of her presence.

'Yes. Margo throws her hot chocolate on people's coats and steals penguins.'

Margo frowned, but Robin didn't have time to explain.

'And *Margo* needs to go warm up her flute.' Hazel offered a black leather case, swapping it for Margo's empty mug. Margo only puffed out her cheeks as though she'd been asked to commit an elaborate heist, before wandering off to join a band setting up on a small stage at the front of the square.

'She's the niece I mentioned earlier. I'm taking care of her for a while,' Hazel explained, worrying at her lip again as she eyed Robin's coat. 'I'm so sorry about your coat. Was it expensive?'

'No.' The low price didn't remove the sting of losing Cara the Coat, though. 'It's fine. Neve will buy me a new one for Christmas. Won't you, Neve?'

'Ha,' Neve deadpanned. 'You can use our washing machine tomorrow. It'll be fine.'

'Wait . . .' Hazel's soft features crumpled with confusion. 'How *do* you two know each other? Neve doesn't hang out with anybody but Nick and Grandpa Artie. Everyone in town knows that.'

'She also hangs out with Juniper the dog,' Robin added helpfully.

Neve narrowed her eyes. 'Thanks for that. She's staying at the resort. Unfortunately, it seems that until she leaves, we can't get rid of her.'

'Please. They *begged* me to join them tonight. Wouldn't take no for an answer.' Robin rolled her eyes and elbowed Neve again. Though it was brief, they never quite seemed to pull away. Robin remained shoulder to shoulder with her, sharing her warmth. Close enough to smell the frosty night air on her clothes.

'So you're taking care of Margo again?' Neve asked, concern pinching her features.

Hazel nodded, pursing her lips and bouncing her knees to stay warm. 'Catherine found someone new. I told her I could look after Margo permanently, but . . . she's still pretending it's just temporary.'

Robin looked at Neve in question, wondering if she should step away from what sounded like a personal conversation, but Hazel quickly explained, 'My sister is a little flaky when it comes to Margo. I've been taking care of her on and off for a while now.'

'Ah. That sounds difficult. You must be the cool aunt, though, what with all your yummy desserts.' It was Robin's dream to be the same if Wren ever took that step with Tom. She'd already planned which recipes to pass along to the next generation of Ellises, especially considering she didn't see herself having kids of her own.

She was about to compliment Hazel's mouth-wateringly delicious cinnamon roll, which had been all soft dough and strong, caramelised flavours, but a low, quivering note erupted from the band before she could. The tuba it had fallen from was played by a boy half the instrument's size. A stilted melody that could have been either "Jingle Bells" or "Let It Snow" followed. Robin couldn't tell even after the first verse. Either way, it pierced Robin's ears and synchronised with the loud grumbling of her stomach, which despite many desserts, was still not satisfied. She turned to Neve, raising her voice to be heard over the racket. 'Are you hungry?'

Neve seemed to sink with relief. 'Yes. Yes, please.'

After Neve told Nick that they were grabbing something to eat, Robin followed her away from the huddled crowd. The cold had a sharper bite to it now, leaving her nose and earlobes numb, but she didn't want to go home yet. It might not have been the peace she'd hoped for, but with the terrible band playing and the festivity fizzing through the crowd, the meaty smell of pork wafting through the air and the warm nutmeg from the strudels still on her tongue, it was the most festive she'd felt in years.

'Oh my God.' Robin came to a halt at the sight of a man scooping out roasted chestnuts into a paper bag. The next stall sold chocolate-covered marshmallows and gingerbread. 'Can we go to all of them?'

Neve snorted. 'Do you want a repeat of the other night, hunched over the toilet?'

She did have a point, and the memory curbed Robin's

appetite . . . briefly. Very briefly. She went back to being starving and craving all things sweet and savoury a moment later. 'I would gladly risk it for chestnuts.'

'You get those; I'll get *real* food.' Neve patted Robin on the shoulder and then sauntered away, slipping into a queue. From here, Robin couldn't tell what food they were serving.

Taste buds tingling, Robin cupped her hands over her mouth to yell: 'What sort of food is it?'

A thumbs-up was Robin's only reply, then Neve pretended to be interested in the chalkboard menu as though she didn't want people to know they were friends. Fair, Robin thought, since she was in a food-induced frenzy and almost ended up spilling all of her chestnuts across the cobbled stones when the warm bag was handed to her a few moments later.

Were they friends? They felt like friends. Neve hadn't mocked her once tonight unless regarding Robin's terrible ice skating, and she *had* half-taken care of her sprained wrist before Irina had taken over yesterday. Maybe they *were* friends. Robin didn't know why the thought lifted something in her chest, as though the string of a helium balloon had been tied to her ribcage, sending her floating into the vast, starry night.

Either way, Neve returned with two paper plates holding what looked to be meat pies, cranberry sauce dolloped on the sides. She gave one to Robin, wooden fork included.

Robin examined it warily. It was mostly just pale pastry and brown meat. Not the appetising dish she'd been hoping for, but rather something she could buy from her local chippy. 'Er . . . what is it?'

'It's called tourtière. Basically a meat pie, but tastier. It's a big holiday dish here.' Neve shovelled a bite into her mouth and hummed appreciatively. 'Yum. Tastes like Christmas.'

Robin's upper lip curled. 'It's like something my mum would try to feed me.' Still, she gave it a go, making sure to pick up more cranberry sauce than meat, just in case.

She was pleasantly surprised. The pastry was buttery and

warm, the pork tender and packed with flavour: cinnamon, cloves, and a hint of onion and thyme. Not the best pie she'd ever eaten in the world, but certainly not the worst.

'Well?' Neve asked.

Robin nodded, swallowing her mouthful and going in for seconds. 'I'll allow it. Not as bad as it looks.'

Neve tutted but seemed to accept it.

'Hazel has a ginormous crush on Nick, by the way,' Robin pointed out, savouring the sweetness of the cranberries by licking her fork's tines.

'Oh, I know. But Nick is a man,' Neve replied. 'He only notices women he has absolutely no chance at happiness with.'

Robin snorted and ended up dripping her sauce onto Cara the Coat, too. Chances of survival were becoming slimmer by the minute. 'Oh, bloody hell. Will you hold my chestnuts?'

'That's very forward of you.' Neve took the bag of chestnuts with a dry smirk that might have set Robin into a fit of surprised laughter had she not been trying to resuscitate her beautiful, precious, sullied coat with a napkin that was already on the brink of tearing.

She dabbed, dabbed, dabbed, willing the deep red stain to fade – but it didn't, and when the napkin began to leave white fluff all over her, doing more damage than good, she sighed and slumped her shoulders in defeat. 'Time of death . . .' a glance at the clock above one of the stalls '. . . two-fifteen p.m.'

'That's not a real clock, and if you really thought it was two o'clock in the afternoon, your grasp of time is frightening,' Neve pointed out. 'Anyway, there's still a chance we can save it in the washing machine.'

'*Her.*' Robin sniffed and focused on the comfort her food provided instead. 'Her name is Cara and though she hasn't been in my life long, she's very dear to me.'

She waited for the retort, but it never came – and the fact was peculiar enough that Robin's attention drifted back to

Neve, wondering if perhaps she was eating all of her chestnuts while Robin wasn't looking.

But Neve wasn't eating at all. She was staring . . . at Robin. Not in a *"you're completely bizarre and we'll never be friends"* sort of way, but more the way Robin looked at her filo pastries when they had emerged from the oven golden and buttery and perfectly flaky, just as she'd hoped.

Then Neve's eyes shuttered and she motioned to something on Robin's face. 'You have cranberry sauce on your chin.'

'Oh . . .' Robin used her napkin to wipe it off and then closed her eyes and smiled the least attractive smile in the world. It was a default to act ridiculous, to remind Neve of all of her flaws: puffy cheeks and gapped teeth and the fact she had all the dining etiquette of a toothless infant. It was a miracle she'd ever been engaged at all, and for some reason, it felt important to keep showing Neve the worst parts of herself. To show Neve that she was well aware of them, too, maybe. To mock herself so that nobody else could.

'Gone?' she asked.

'Gone.'

A static-heavy squeal of a microphone put an end to their conversation, the market stalls emptying as everybody flocked towards the town square's grand Christmas tree. A moment later, it sounded like someone was announcing the beginning of the carolling concert.

'Want to go back and sing really badly?' Neve offered.

Robin shook her head. She wanted to stay here, in this silly, easy space with Neve, where they could laugh and where Neve accepted her as she was. 'I'm okay here if you are.'

The ghost of a smile curled across Neve's lips. 'Then let's stay here.'

The sound of bells tinkled across the square, and then the trumpets joined in. Robin mouthed the words to "O Holy Night" with the rest of the crowd. The Christmas lights bled into the night, all green and red bulbs curling around the tree, and the fairy lights embedded in garlands around the lamp posts twinkled until there wasn't so much as a corner in Clement Falls kissed by shadows or silence.

Robin had never felt anything like it before. Her breath hitched as the world sang, hundreds of different voices blending into one.

Robin didn't believe in miracles, but tonight might have been close. Because she was here, so far from home, choosing new experiences and new friends, and Neve . . . Neve was looking at her like she was flaky, golden filo pastry again.

So Robin smiled, not to be silly and unattractive and to chase Neve away this time, but just because. Because she was happy.

Because she was here.

Chapter Seven

The following morning was the first one where Robin woke up without a weight pinning her down. She didn't feel the immediate urge to check her phone or go back to sleep or hope the day would pass quickly. She was glad to have her eyes open, glad to see thick flakes of snow drifting down outside the window.

Last night was the most fun she'd had in a long time. As much as Robin despised snow, and as little as she cared for the holidays, she couldn't deny that she was glad she'd taken the trip in the end. Even if it was the one and only night spent away from the resort, out of her pyjamas, and even if her mother never spoke to her again, she had done it, lived it. She'd chosen herself for once.

She spent the day in the cabin, wrapping her family's presents by the roaring fire, until Neve picked her up at four o'clock on the dot, as promised. Things were strange – *light* – between them. They talked and joked with ease as they shopped for baking ingredients in a little supermarket on the corner of town, falling into new habits and new ways of seeing one another. They were so different, but Robin was okay with that. She was okay with the sheet of ice that remained between them, a guard Neve seemed to keep up always. Robin would have been just as okay if they didn't talk at all.

It wasn't just Neve, though. As she sauntered down the aisle of cleaning products to find something to wash the stains from her coat, humming along with the Christmas instrumental drifting through the store, it occurred to Robin that she was beginning to enjoy her own company again.

She couldn't remember the last time she'd felt comfortable in her own solitude, and it left her warm. Proud, even. She was half the world away from home, alone, and she was okay.

By five o'clock that evening, she stood in Neve's kitchen, hands – and everything else in the near vicinity – caked in flour and icing as she rolled out the second batch of gingerbread dough. Neve hovered uncertainly behind, flinching every time Robin threatened to ruin her floor tiles with food dye.

'Do you live here with your grandpa?' Robin questioned carefully as she cut through the spiced dough with tree- and snowflake-shaped cutters. She'd been wanting to ask since Artie had welcomed her in earlier, and all signs pointed to the answer being yes. All of Juniper's bowls and leads were scattered around, and indeed, Juniper had been waiting for Neve when they'd arrived with their hands full of shopping bags. Neve's pair of skis were propped in the hall. This was their home, and it was written not just in the furniture, but in the ease with which Neve sashayed around.

'I do,' Neve replied, dropping a handful of cinnamon gumdrops into her mouth. It was a tiny – but cosy – little house on the edge of town. Old lace curtains were draped across the window with green garland and gold tinsel, the living-room furniture worn in and well used. Artie lounged on a brown leather couch in the midst of it all, his slippered feet resting on the coffee table as he flicked through the classic movies playing on the television. He, at least, seemed not to care that Robin had infiltrated his kitchen.

Robin slapped Neve's hand away from her biscuit toppings with the spatula now. 'Excuse you. Those are Mr Gingerbread Man's buttons.' She'd already made a batch of gingerbread men and women, which were naked and ready to be decorated on the cooling rack now. 'What about Nick?'

'Nick moved out a few years ago.' Despite Robin's glare, Neve continued to feast on the sweets. 'He bought an apartment with his fiancée after they got engaged.'

'Are they still together?'

'Nope. They split up last year. She decided she wanted a taste of city life in New York, but Nick is too set in his ways here. He decided to stay without her.'

'Ah. That's rough. My fiancée decided she just wanted a taste of other people.' Only silence and the whirring of the washing machine followed Robin's confession, and she wanted to shrink. Her cheeks blazed as she sorted the cut dough onto the greased baking tray and placed it into the oven, wondering if there was enough room to lock herself in there, too. 'Too much information. Sorry.'

'How long ago did the two of you split up?'

'Back in April this year.' She didn't dare gauge Neve's expression now, instead wiping her sticky hands down the cupcake-patterned apron she had, in fact, returned to the markets for after the concert.

While Robin no longer yearned to have someone like Lexi back in her life, she did long for the blissful ignorance she'd been cocooned in before it had all gone wrong. She would always be the woman who hadn't been good enough to marry, or even be honest with, and she'd always question her trust in people because of it.

'So she cheated?' Neve asked.

'Yep. And now she's engaged to the guy I caught her with.' Sighing, Robin tucked her hair behind her ear. Sweat was beginning to bead at the nape of her neck – from the heat of the kitchen or the weight of Neve's stare, she didn't know.

'Jesus. I'm . . .' Neve shifted, placing her hands on the counter beside Robin's. Her pinkie finger twitched, grazing against Robin's carefully. 'I'm sorry.'

Robin didn't like the way her stomach swooped. It had been too long, and the last time . . .

She cleared her throat then retied her apron nervously, otherwise she would overthink the small action and come to the wrong conclusion. A conclusion that might leave her no better off than the last time she'd felt this jittery. 'Do you like orange chocolate? I was thinking of making brownies too.'

She made to pick up the bag of flour – but her hands were held hostage halfway across the messy countertop.

Neve squeezed Robin's fingers lightly. When Robin finally dared to meet her gaze, she found sympathy and questions and something unfamiliar, something indecipherable, swimming in her hazel eyes.

'It can't have been easy, coming here alone after all of that.'

'I'm ready to move on.' Robin shrugged, but she still wasn't brave enough to pull away. Not until Neve did. She would savour this, would let the tingles crawling from her knuckles, across her skin, comfort her as long as Neve was willing. She had been thinking about her touch all day; how Robin's skin had burned last night when Neve had reached out and tucked away that disobedient strand of hair, even with gloves on and surrounded by a rink full of people. And afterwards, how they had laughed as the world turned to song.

But if Neve kept looking at her like that, with so much sympathy, Robin wasn't sure she could handle it. A lump rose in her throat; an old pain returning with new scars.

'I think that we should name the oven "Stoven",' she erupted before the tears came. 'You know, like Steven.'

Confusion flickered across Neve's features, and then she drew back, leaving Robin cold – as though she hadn't practically asked for it with her stupid jokes. Maybe she had her own wall of ice up, too, and just hadn't realised it before now.

'Stoven,' Neve repeated. 'I'll run it past Grandpa later.'

Robin forced a smile, clearing her throat so it didn't feel so raw. 'So? Orange chocolate?'

'Sounds good to me.' The reply was too soft, too gentle, as though Neve could sense how brittle Robin felt. Robin didn't want her to. She'd rather Neve see her as the hare-brained, bumbling idiot who fell over her own feet than the poor, sad, lonely woman who had been cheated on. She'd rather bicker with Neve again than be drenched in her pity.

So Robin pressed her lips together, gathering her

composure – and then a saviour appeared in the form of Nick. Juniper howled as he burst through the front door, drawing his family's attention.

Without Neve's piercing eyes on her, Robin could breathe again.

'So, Robin,' Grandpa began as Neve finished setting the table. She had a feeling she already knew what was coming. 'Tell me about you. It's not often we get a new face in this house. In fact, I was beginning to wonder if Neve had any friends at all.'

'Thanks, Grandpa,' she muttered, sitting down beside Robin and grabbing the first takeout box she came to. Though her stomach was in inexplicable knots, she filled her plate with soy-sauce-coated noodles and stir-fried veg then passed the rest to Robin.

Robin took it, meeting her eye for a moment. Concern flickered across her features, but she soon fell into one of those toothy Robin smiles as she forked her noodles onto her plate. 'Well, I'm only here on my hon—on holiday,' she corrected quickly, 'but Neve and I met because I signed up for ski lessons.'

'Actually, we met because she threw a stick at Juniper,' Neve said, pouring herself a glass of water and then doing the same for Robin.

Robin glared at her, kicking her shin under the table. As though it mattered what Grandpa thought of her, what her family thought of her. Neve didn't dare contemplate why that might be. '*Technically*, I met her in the lobby when I checked in. Sort of.'

Grandpa's white brows furrowed as his gaze flitted between them, and then searched Nick, probably hoping for a clearer response.

Nick only shrugged, mumbling through a mouthful of sweet and sour chicken, 'Don't ask me. I can't keep up with them either.'

'And what brings you to Clement Falls?' Grandpa asked.

Robin twirled her fork around her plate as though contemplating. Neve almost wanted to reach for her hand again. She hadn't known just how burned Robin had been from her ex. Just how much pain she must have gone through. One benefit of being eternally guarded was that Neve was lucky enough to never have been hurt that way. Her relationships were few and far between and had barely lasted weeks, let alone long enough to warrant an engagement. She didn't have any room in her life for more pain or abandonment, and she made sure it stayed that way, never getting too attached in the rare instances she was attracted to someone. It was easier to keep it casual. Easier not to get too invested.

'Well,' Robin began finally, 'a change of scenery, I suppose.'

He smiled knowingly. 'I came for a change of scenery once too. Never ended up leaving.'

Neve stopped mid-chew, melancholy washing over her because she knew what came next.

'Really?' Robin asked. 'Why not?'

'Met a girl. Isn't that how it always goes?' His wink at Neve left her cheeks burning. Did Grandpa think there was something between *them*?

Fine, Robin might have been growing on her, and she might have been Christmas-card-level pretty in the dim fairy lights, all rosy cheeks and sparkling smiles; and fine, Neve might have found her funny sometimes, but that was all. It wasn't like anything could come of it. It wasn't like Neve *wanted* something to.

She didn't think.

Of course, Neve knew she was lucky to have a grandfather as supportive of her pansexuality as Artie was; lucky that, should she have *chosen* to be more than friends with Robin, her family would have been happy for her. But she didn't want to scare Robin away. Besides, Robin wasn't over Lexi.

'Gran was the Clement Falls native. Grandpa moved from Portland to be with her,' Nick explained with a soft smile Neve knew too well. His "missing Gran" smile. His "remembering Gran" smile. There were an awful lot of those around this house.

Neve couldn't help but look at the empty fifth chair beside Grandpa. They wouldn't have been eating takeaway if Gran was here now. It was hearty home-cooked meals or nothing – to watch Grandpa's cholesterol and make sure Neve maintained enough energy for skiing. The patterned place mats and plates had been here longer than Neve had. The cross-stitches and photographs across the walls were all hers, too. Neve wished more than anything she was still here, nagging Nick about the fact he hadn't gotten out of bartending for something better, or asking Neve how her day was while she spooned her an extra helping of mashed potatoes. It had been so much easier then. Now, that empty chair was like a black hole, and Neve felt that void in her chest.

'We were married sixty years before she passed,' Grandpa said, tears sparkling in his eyes. Still, he took a deep breath and grinned, twirling his wedding band around his wrinkled finger. 'She would have loved you. Would have been glad to have somebody else make dessert for a change.'

Robin laughed softly. 'I'm sorry you lost her. My mum . . . she lost my dad, too. We miss him all the time. I still expect him to be waiting downstairs in the morning, ready for work, sometimes. It never really goes away, does it?' She extended her hand across the table, and Artie took it, squeezing.

'No, my dear,' he said quietly, 'it doesn't.'

Neve could only watch, a lump lodged in her throat. She had to blink back tears as she glanced at that empty chair a final time, and then at Robin. In the kitchen earlier, Robin had seemed so desperate not to talk about her pain. And all the times before, when she'd made jokes and acted silly . . . Neve hadn't understood her. Not until she saw her now, holding Grandpa's hand like she'd lost Gran, too. Like she truly cared.

Warmth curled around Neve's hand. Robin held it with her free one under the table, as though she could sense Neve's pain as well as Grandpa's. It took her aback, but she couldn't pull away. It had been too long since she'd felt seen, understood, cared for, and she wanted to cling to it for an eternity. It eased her grief, her guilt, just for a moment; made her grateful for the people around her who were still here. Grateful for the surprise of Robin and all of the strange newness she'd brought with her.

'How did you meet your wife?' Robin asked, easing away finally. But her hand stayed firmly in Neve's as she chewed on an egg roll. 'I'm a sucker for love stories.'

Grandpa beamed, and it made Neve wonder: when was the last time they'd talked about Gran so openly? Most days, she was an unacknowledged ghost haunting the house because it felt easier to miss her in private. But maybe she'd been wrong to keep it to herself. Even Nick looked eager to hear the story, though Grandpa had told it a million times before.

It made her feel like she was alive again – and Gran deserved that. Neve made a silent vow to talk about her more rather than leave her a shadow. She deserved that. They all did. They were allowed to miss her out loud. It shouldn't have taken Robin's encouragement to figure that out.

'My car broke down when I was passing through. I was taking a year out after college, travelling with a few friends,' Grandpa said, eyes turning glassy as he remembered. 'She was the mechanic, of all things. Anyway, I only meant to stay for as long as it took to fix the car, but one smile and I just *had* to ask her out for dinner. For some reason, she said yes. We decided to stay another couple days after that to see the Northern Lights, and she took us to the best spot – our very own tour guide. I was lost until that day. I think that's why I travelled so much. I was looking for something. And I found it.'

'That's really beautiful,' Robin whispered.

It was too beautiful. Neve loved the story, but she couldn't imagine one like that for herself. She couldn't imagine meeting someone worth dropping everything to be with. Her eyes snagged on Robin without warning, but she hadn't noticed, too rapt in Grandpa's tale. Something hitched in Neve at the sight. It felt like Robin had been here before. Like she'd sat at this kitchen table with them every night for years.

Like she belonged. Like Neve belonged here with her.

Grandpa shrugged. 'When you know, you know.'

'Not always,' Nick murmured.

Grandpa patted him on the back. 'Sometimes you have to make a few wrong turns first. That's all.'

'That's how I ended up here,' agreed Robin, finally pulling her hand away to sip her drink.

'Who knows? Maybe there's a reason for it all.' Another wink from Grandpa. Neve rolled her eyes but didn't have it in her to argue. Grandpa was just lucky he'd found somebody to share a long, happy life with – but that didn't mean everybody else had that luxury. Neve sure as hell made certain that nobody ever got close enough to try, though not always intentionally. She just hadn't found anybody she wanted to open up to completely, anybody she loved more than her independence. All of her friendships had dwindled after leaving the ski team, built only on the fact they'd had to travel together so often, and she'd never felt particularly . . . *close* to anyone.

Even her friendship with Hazel wasn't as strong anymore, mainly because Neve had always been away for competitions and then had cooped herself up in a little grief bubble after Gran's death. She was always on the edge of it all – not on purpose, but just because. Because being on her own came naturally. Because she felt out of place with most people. She just wasn't made for relationships or intimacy, and she was okay with that.

But she didn't feel that innate distance with Robin, somehow. Not now, holding her hand beneath the table. Robin was too easy to talk to, too easy to understand. She wore her heart on her sleeve and she made Neve laugh and, though soft, she didn't shy away from Neve's sharp edges. In fact, she only seemed to pull Neve closer, and Neve was letting her. She couldn't help but let her.

'Maybe.' Robin smiled politely, but her gaze still flickered across Neve as she said it, and that inextinguishable fire in her gut returned threefold.

'Erm, Neve?' Robin's voice drifted from the kitchen, more a question than a call.

'Hmm?' Neve's reply was more of a grumble. She had stuffed herself with way too much of Robin's gingerbread after dinner, and now she could barely move from her comfortable spot on the couch. *Home Alone* flickered on the TV – watched even by Juniper, who lazed by the lit fireplace – and the Christmas tree danced with golden light. Neve had decorated it all herself a few weeks ago. The only flaw was that the baubles were sparse; Juniper thought they were tennis balls and liked to play with them.

Grandpa had retired to bed before Kevin McCallister had even discovered he was, in fact, home alone, and Nick had left not long after. He'd asked Robin if she wanted a lift back to the lodge on his way. Neve hadn't known why she'd been so quick to tell him that she would take Robin home herself after the movie finished. She only knew that she wasn't ready for the night to end yet.

Robin hadn't seemed to mind staying. In fact, she got on with Neve's family like a house on fire. She and Grandpa had bonded over their shared affinity for cheesecake and jigsaw puzzles after dessert.

She had made herself at home, too, by disappearing into the kitchen five minutes ago without yet emerging.

Probably not a good sign.

'Robin?' Neve pulled herself up from the couch and paused the movie, waiting for a loud explosion to decimate the kitchen. Or maybe Neve had already missed the bang; maybe Robin – clumsy, directionally challenged Robin – had slipped on a patch of butter and already knocked herself out.

Or perhaps she had discovered something awful in the washing machine. Something like a powder-blue coat that had shrunk to a size that would have better luck fitting a five-year-old.

Robin stood in the threshold with Cara's remains, her lower lip jutting out in a pout that Neve tried – and failed – not to find heart-meltingly adorable. 'It's ruined.'

'Well . . .' Neve frowned and examined the front of the coat, just above the marble-grey buttons. 'At least the stains came out.'

'How can this happen?' Robin's grumble was muffled by the fact that she had buried her head into the coat. 'I put the right amount of detergent in, didn't I? There's no limit to detergent?'

'I think you have the answer to that already.'

Another stifled groan. Neve couldn't help but trap a laugh. She'd known Robin for less than a week and had already seen more absurd chaos than the rest of her life put together. She never knew what would come next, and she liked that. Liked the constant surprise that knowing Robin brought.

'Why can't I do anything right? Why?' The crack in Robin's voice drained Neve of any amusement. '*Whywhywhy?* Why?'

'Robin.' Neve tutted and prised Robin's hands from her face. It didn't work. Her head followed, remaining firmly smothered by the ruined coat. It was quite impressive, actually, since she had almost bent in half to touch her toes.

'No. Don't look at me. I'm a failure.' She sank onto the floor, earning the attention of Juniper, who begrudgingly rose from her spot in front of the fire to lick Robin's hands. 'No, Juniper. I can't give you cuddles. I'm going through something at the moment.'

Neve could no longer tell how much of it was a self-deprecating charade and how much Robin really meant it. Worry gnawing at her, she lowered to her knees and said again, 'Robin?'

'She's not here. She's died of patheticness. She's gone.'

'Oh, come on.' Neve took hold of Robin's wrists this time and used all of her strength to pull Robin's hands away from her face. When she did, she found Robin's face flushed, eyelashes damp, tears threatening to spill over. 'It's just a coat. You can get a new one.'

'It's not *just* a coat, Neve. If I can't even wash my clothes without a disaster, how am I supposed to be a *person*? I make a mess of everything. This is why my relationships fail. This is why I'll always be alone. This is why I'll never move out of my mum's house. I'll be a sad little sixty-year-old still in my old bedroom with *Buffy the Vampire Slayer* posters, and nobody will ever date me because I'm useless and old.'

'Because . . . you shrunk a coat once?' It had escalated quickly, and Neve wasn't quite sure *why*. Yes, Robin could be a little bit . . . scattered. But did that have to be a bad thing? Wasn't everyone just capable of different things? She'd proven to have other talents: baking, making friends, relating to an eighty-year-old man. 'Robin. Your ability to use household appliances does not determine your fate or worth. I promise.'

Robin sniffled, toying with a loose thread on the coat. 'I just . . . I feel useless, sometimes. Like everyone's laughing at me. Like I don't do anything right.'

'Nobody's laughing at you.' Guilt panged through Neve, and she couldn't help it; she reached out again, using the pad of her thumb to draw small circles into Robin's skin. 'I laugh *with* you a lot, but . . . I'm not laughing at you. These things happen. Everybody makes mistakes sometimes. If people use your occasional clumsiness as a reason not to date you, that's their loss.'

Robin worried at her lip and pushed the coat away. It picked up Juniper's moulted fur from the carpet, so it was good that it would probably be thrown away soon.

'It's just a coat.' She said it as though it was an affirmation.

'It's just a coat,' Neve replied with a soft smile. It was perhaps the shortest quarter-life crisis she had ever witnessed, and the only one she had ever resolved. If Robin was good at breaking things, she was a thousand times better at putting them back together again. Still, Neve wondered if this was something more. Had Lexi made Robin feel bad about who she was? Did she blame *herself* for the cheating and the separation?

The thought left a spark of anger in its wake.

'God, sorry.' Robin's face crinkled with shame, and she blew the hair from her face before standing up. 'What are we watching, again?'

'*Home Alone.*'

'Oh yeah.' Robin collapsed onto the couch and stared blankly at the paused frame, swiping a gingerbread man from the plate she'd left out earlier and nibbling on his arm. 'The one where Macaulay Culkin is home alone.'

Slightly disconcerted, Neve shook her head to steady her thoughts and then returned to the couch across from her. 'That's the one.'

As she played the movie again, Robin lounged with her head resting on the arm of the couch, only an empty, sunken cushion between the two of them. It was too quiet, too intimate, and Neve's limbs grew restless and unsure. There was something more than just friendship cloaking them along with the fleece blanket she draped across their laps – for Neve, at least. She just hadn't wanted to face it yet. She shifted slightly closer just to feel her warmth, glancing over at Robin intently – wondering if she felt it, too. Wondering if she knew how easy it would be to close the distance and kiss Neve. Wondering if she knew that Neve would let her.

Maybe she had been lonely without realising. Maybe Robin chased that loneliness away, and Neve wanted more of it. All of it.

But what if Robin didn't feel it? Perhaps Neve should go back to that shield – but when Robin's gaze flickered to her, she didn't want to. Her blue eyes were dull with weariness, and a smear of icing sugar still dusted her chin. Neve fought the urge to reach over and wipe it away with the sleeve of her sweater. Her hand was still warm and empty, left wanting since holding Robin's beneath the dinner table, and she could fix it with just one movement.

She'd never felt this drawn to somebody before. This desperate to reach out and touch someone just because. Because she wanted to be close; wanted to know more, know everything. She'd dated plenty back in her days on the ski team, but that was just for fun. A release after long days on the slopes, usually.

But this. It felt like she might shrivel up if she didn't hold Robin's hand again.

'Thank you for inviting me tonight,' Robin said quietly.

'Thank you for making a mess of my kitchen,' Neve joked in return. They had already cleared the worst of it up together, though remnants of Robin's madness still remained. It had been worth it, though. The treats had turned out perfect. None of Robin's gracelessness had translated into the decorated gingerbread or the orange chocolate brownies. Perhaps baking was just something she'd been born to do. Neve had once felt that way about skiing.

'You know, this is the first time in my twenty-six years that I've actually watched this film.'

'*What?*' Neve gasped, stunned enough to pause the film again – on the iconic moment where Kevin slaps aftershave onto his cheeks and shrieks. '*How?* It's the law to watch this every Christmas.'

A smirk curled at the corners of Robin's mouth. 'It's always so chaotic at my house. The adults want to rant about politics and the kids want to terrorise the dog or play Twister. I don't get a chance to watch films in peace. Besides, I'm not that big on Christmas anymore.'

Neve's jaw fell lower. Robin was one of the bubbliest people Neve had ever met, and she didn't like *Christmas*? 'You're a Grinch?'

'My sister prefers to call me Scrooge.' Robin wrinkled her nose. 'I didn't think *you'd* be so full of Christmas cheer.'

'And why not?' Neve raised her eyebrows in challenge, shifting so that she could face Robin head-on.

'Because . . . you're not that full of normal cheer, for starters.'

Robin did have a point, though Neve resented it. She *had* grown closed off in her not-so-old age, especially since Gran's death. Even before that, Neve's family had always prided themselves on independence and blunt honesty. Gran had been the same, though Grandpa had mellowed her out in his own way. And Mom . . . well, it was hard to open up to people when she couldn't even trust her own parent to stick around. People left, whether by choice or otherwise, and Neve had learned to let them by taking a step back and trying her best not to feel too much.

But maybe all Neve did was distance herself from things she was too afraid to want.

In the end, she tried to take Robin's observation on the chin, playing absently with the choppy edges of her short hair. 'Still. Everyone loves Christmas.'

Gran had. It was the time of year Neve felt closest to her; like it was her responsibility to carry on her Christmas cheer, even if she'd never been able to cook the turkey as perfectly or get her roast potatoes to crisp. Even if Gran had been full of fierce life when Neve felt like the flickering shadow of her guttered flame most days.

'I don't *hate* it. I just . . . find it all very exhausting. Work is always hectic, too. This is the first break I've had over Christmas since I started working at the restaurant five years ago, and that's only because I was supposed to be getting married. I just can't remember how to enjoy it anymore, between covering shifts and having to live up to all these expectations and traditions. I think I'd rather be here. It's peaceful.'

Neve understood that. She remembered all of the Christmases she'd had growing up, when aunts and uncles had come to stay – mostly for a free ski trip, but also to raid their cupboards for chocolate and wine. It hadn't been that way for a long time, though. These days, Neve spent her holidays the way she did every other weekend: enjoying Grandpa, Nick, and Juniper's company with good food and movies.

Juniper's high-pitched yawn broke their conversation. Rising, she stretched out her paws on the rug and then plodded her way over to them. Neve pushed the blanket from her legs, expecting the husky to join her as she usually did – but Juniper, traitorous as she was, crawled onto Robin's end of the couch and curled up by her feet.

'Hello, my little Juni-poo.' With a soft smile, Robin scratched the space between Juniper's pointed ears. And Neve couldn't find it in her to feel betrayed. Their relationship might have started off rocky, too, but it was nice to see them make amends. Nice to see Robin wearing that gleaming adoration for Neve's best friend. Juniper's tail wagged happily at the attention.

'Juni-poo isn't going to be a thing. Her name is Juniper.'

Robin tutted. 'She likes it. Don't you, Juni-poo? Besides, as long as I feed her biscuits when you aren't looking, she doesn't care what I call her.'

Neve scowled. She had pretended not to notice her doing that earlier in the kitchen. 'You can't use treats to bribe my dog.'

'Why not? It worked with your grandpa.'

She snorted at that. Artie *had* enjoyed an extra helping of brownies. 'Hmm. He has warmed to you, hasn't he?'

'Of course he has. I'm a delight. What about you, anyway?' Robin asked.

'Eh,' Neve brushed off, though the heat of Robin's gaze tingled along the side of her face, causing her hands to grow clammy. '"Delight" is a strong word. You're okay, I suppose.'

Robin rolled her eyes. 'I *mean* what are your Christmases like?'

'Oh. Just like this, usually. It's just the four of us.'

'No parents?' Robin worried at her lip, freckled skin golden in the flickering fairy lights. Neve wished she could stop noticing how pretty she was.

'No.' Neve couldn't bring herself to say more about it than that.

'Have you always lived with your grandpa?' There was no judgement there, though the question still made

Neve shift with discomfort. She knew how it looked, for a twenty-five-year-old to live with her grandparent. All of the people she'd gone to school with were getting married or living in big fancy apartments in the city, but she was still here, in the home she'd grown up in, waking up every morning with the same chequered bed sheets and lopsidedly hung ski posters she'd had when she was sixteen. She'd never had to worry about living arrangements when she was travelling all the time, but sleeping in different cities, different hotel rooms every night hadn't been all it was cracked up to be in the end. Had maybe left her even lonelier than she was in Clement Falls. Maybe she wasn't ready to move into an empty place with only Juniper to keep her company. Maybe she was worried that if she did, she might miss the team she'd at least been able to lean on before.

'Mostly. I travelled around when I was on the ski team, but then . . . things happened.'

Robin only nodded in understanding, her cool blue-grey gaze set on Neve too intently, too knowingly. She saw too much of Neve with those round, sparkling eyes, and it made her want to shrink. Or maybe expand. Maybe both. 'I know that feeling. I moved home again after the break-up with Lexi. I thought it would only be a temporary thing. Flash forward eight months, and I'm still there, getting woken up by Cleopawtra slobbering on me every morning.'

'Cleo*paw*tra?' Neve clamped her lips down to keep from laughing.

'My mum's chihuahua.'

'*Ah*.' Was there anything that Robin *didn't* name with puns? 'Doesn't Nick have a spare room at his place?'

He did, and he'd offered it to Neve on many occasions.

'Yes, but . . .' She trailed off hesitantly. Neve seldom opened up to people she barely knew. And yet Robin had never questioned a thing she'd said, instead always seeming to wear a flashing neon sign above her head that said, "I understand." It was refreshing.

So, she sucked in a breath and told her the same thing she'd told Nick. 'I don't feel right leaving Grandpa alone here. My gran only died two years ago. Someone should be here with him, y'know? So he doesn't get lonely.'

Robin softened, and Neve was certain that if Juniper wasn't trapping her legs, she would have moved down the couch. Neve didn't know if she was glad for the big lump of fur in the way or not.

'Neve.' The way Robin said her name almost made her shiver, though with the fire roaring, she was far from cold. 'You can't put your life on hold forever. Your brother lives here. *You* live here—'

'I was going to move to Calgary,' she admitted without thinking, perhaps because the words had been simmering beneath the surface for too long. She hadn't told Artie. Hadn't had time. It had all happened too quickly. She'd found a place, made her deposit, but then Gran had died and moving away from Artie didn't feel right. Besides, wouldn't it just be more of the same? Another group of teammates she didn't really connect with. Another place that wasn't home, just like everywhere else. 'I got accepted into the Olympic ski team right before . . .'

Robin's eyes widened, and she sat forward, still mussing Juniper's fur with her fingers. '*What?* I thought Irina was just exaggerating! Neve, that's insane! You have to do it. You can't miss out on something like that. Calgary's only an hour away.'

'It's too late.' Neve schooled her wavering features into nonchalance as best she could, toying with the TV remote in her hand. 'They gave my place to someone else. My gran had just died when it happened, and there was no way I could go. Now it's too late.'

'So try out again.' Robin said it as though it was the simplest thing in the world. 'Be selfish, Neve. Your grandpa will understand.'

'Is that why you're here? Is this you being selfish, making your own choices?' *Or is it you pining after an ex?* Neve almost added. The thought unsettled her. It was clear that Robin deserved better.

'Yes.' And then, with a sigh: 'Maybe. Not really. I don't know. I suppose this is my one small act of independence. My mum isn't happy with me for leaving her, though, so I'll go home and she'll give me the silent treatment for a while and then I'll go back to the way I was before.'

'Still. You came. That's something.' It was more than what Neve had done. She'd never been afraid to travel, to dream, before Gran's death, because Gran was always the first to encourage her to grab whatever life threw at her. 'When life gives you gold, you take it,' she used to say. Now, Neve couldn't imagine a life where she wasn't here, with Grandpa, making sure he ate enough every day and stayed active.

'I'm glad I did.'

Their eyes locked, Robin's shining wistfully, her rosy cheeks glowing. She stretched her feet past Juniper and tapped Neve on the knee with her toes – the most contact they could manage without disturbing the husky's dreams. That alone was enough to leave electricity sparking through Neve, enough to make her breath hitch.

'I was thinking . . .' Robin yawned and sunk deeper into the couch, Juniper shifting across her hips as though refusing to let her leave '. . . maybe I should give the ski lessons another chance.'

'Yeah?' Fiery hope guttered in Neve. She'd wondered whether this would be their last night spent together, or if one of them would find a way to make more. The fact Robin wanted to see her again . . .

'Yeah. You think you can make time for me?'

'I have a cancellation tomorrow at ten.' A lie. Neve didn't work at all on Thursdays – but she would for Robin.

'Early.' Robin shuddered her disgust. 'But okay, I'll be there. I should get going, anyway. I've probably overstayed my welcome.'

Neve found herself clawing for an excuse to make her

stay. She hadn't felt this comfortable with someone other than family in a long time. It was a nice change. 'I was just going to ask if you wanted hot cocoa. Besides . . . we didn't finish the movie.'

Robin, who was nothing more than a tangle of limbs and dog fur now, grinned her approval and agreed. Neve savoured the sight before pulling herself up and heading into the kitchen.

She took her time making the drinks, lost in thought – and lost in the way her heart wouldn't seem to slow.

The thought of the ski team try-outs played on her mind, too, as she stirred the chocolate and then piled the snowman-patterned mugs high with whipped cream and marshmallows. Maybe it *was* time to start doing things for herself again. Her grandpa was okay, and her brother was always nearby to check on him. Irina had said Lara wanted her back . . .

It was terrifying to even think about it, so she pushed it down. For tonight, she was content here, as she was, with the Christmas lights painting everything a burnished shade of gold and the tinsel glistening across the doorframe, with Robin on her couch.

She returned to the living room and faltered. In the short time it had taken to make hot cocoa, Robin had fallen asleep beneath Juniper. They lay together, completely at ease, Robin's features smoother and younger and angelic, and Juniper dead to the world with her snout tucked into Robin's neck.

Neve trapped a laugh in her throat and placed down the drinks, half-tempted to take a photograph. But she didn't need to. She knew that, as she tugged the blanket across them, making sure Robin's arms were covered so that she wouldn't get cold when the fire ebbed, the image, the memory, would stick in her mind regardless.

It did, at least, as she turned the TV off, drank her hot cocoa, and fell asleep on the opposite side of the couch.

Chapter Eight

Neve woke to a call from an unknown number. With Robin still sleeping soundly on the other side of the couch, she chose to ignore it, but when her phone rang three more times while Neve was making pancakes for breakfast, she sighed, threw down her spatula, and finally picked up. If it was somebody selling triple-glazed glass, they were going to get an earful.

'Hello?'

'Neve, sweetheart!' The sugary-sweet voice was too high-pitched and too familiar at this time in the morning – or any other time of day, for that matter – and Neve winced, dread already fizzing in her gut. 'You finally bothered to pick up your phone!'

That's rich, coming from the queen of no communication.

After the initial unease, her mother's voice brought with it an innate anger that saturated Neve's veins and left red specks floating around her vision. It had been *months*. Months of no contact, months of nothing at all. Neve could have gotten married or died in a ski accident or relocated to the Bermuda Triangle, and Mom would have been none the wiser.

Why the hell was she reaching out *now*? It was a little early for the perfunctory "Merry Christmas" call. A lot early, actually, since Mom didn't usually remember to make it until New Year's Eve, if at all.

'I didn't have your number saved,' Neve remarked coldly, tossing an already burned pancake around the frying pan. Breakfast was, apparently, no longer happening. Neve was too riled up to be allowed near sharp objects and hot surfaces. She turned the stove off and scraped a hand through her knotted hair, though it was caked in pancake mix and ended up making it worse.

'Didn't I text you months ago about my new phone?'

'No.'

'Oh.' Mom clucked her tongue as though it was just bad luck. 'Well, now you have it.'

'What do you want, Mom?' Neve questioned through gritted teeth.

'Well . . .'

Neve didn't like the sound of that, not with the way the syllable rose in pitch at the end, as though she was about to get an hour-long tale about something that probably involved a half-naked man or an accidental, drunken marriage in Las Vegas. Stranger things had happened. 'Look, I don't have time—'

'I've decided to come and stay with you over the holidays!'

Disbelief trickled like a cold drop of rain down her back. She'd heard this before. Many times, actually, in the early days. Until Mom had stopped pretending that she'd show up at all.

'Great. We'll save you a seat at the dinner table.' Sarcasm laced Neve's tone.

Mom tutted. 'I mean it, Neve. I think I may even stay for a couple of months. I've been missing home a lot recently.'

Clement Falls was not Mom's home. Mom's home was probably a beach she couldn't pronounce the name of somewhere, or at the bottom of a Chardonnay bottle. 'Uh-huh. Which one of your boyfriends broke up with you?'

'Oh, that's hardly fair!' Mom had the audacity to sound surprised. 'Honestly, why can't you just be happy to have your mother back for Christmas?'

'Because I'm not,' Neve answered honestly, patience fraying enough that she began to grind her teeth. She glared absently out the kitchen window, hands pressed tightly into the counter as a flurry of snow drifted. It was so fine, she couldn't tell if it was coming from the overcast sky or if it was just the remnants from the day before thawing on the roof. 'I would rather you stayed in Hawaii or Florida or wherever it is you are right now.'

'I'm in *Houston*.' Mom spoke slowly, as though *she* was the one struggling her way through this conversation. As though *Neve* was the awful one. 'I'm waiting for a seat to open up on one of the Alberta flights this weekend. And here I was hoping you might pick me up from the airport.'

Suppressing a snort, Neve turned away from the window and eyed the family portraits along the walls. Most of them were childhood photographs of her and Nick, or ones from Grandpa and Gran's wedding. Mom was in very few of them.

She imagined her mother standing beside her then, warming her manicured hands on a cup of coffee. It was almost impossible. Mom didn't care about any of the things Neve did: skiing, Juniper (she hated to get fur on her expensive clothes), friends and family. Neve didn't know how she had turned out that way; it wasn't Grandpa or Gran's doing, that was for sure. Maybe her personality had just been too big for Clement Falls, or maybe having children and then ending a toxic relationship with Neve's absentee dad had left Mom needing to set herself free. Neve might have understood that if she'd taken off for a few months rather than nigh on fifteen years.

'Have you told Grandpa or Nick about your spontaneous decision?'

'No, not yet. I wanted it to be a surprise.'

'You showing up is *always* a surprise,' Neve quipped bitterly. From the next room, she heard shuffling and suspected Robin was beginning to stir. A bolt of panic shot through Neve. If her mom came home, she wouldn't have time or energy to spend with Robin anymore. Mom would no doubt have some sort of drama or mess for Neve and Nick to clean up, and the idea . . . it triggered fierce doors of protectiveness to close around her. For once, things were good here. She'd actually been *enjoying* getting to know Robin.

In the unlikely event that Mom was genuine in her desire to visit, her return would ruin all of it. Hurricane Stefanie, Grandpa always called her. He was right to.

'Look, I don't know if you're actually serious or doing that thing you do where you tell us you'll come home soon and then miraculously get on the wrong flight and end up in Barbados, but I'd rather not do this with you, Mom. Not right now. Don't come home, okay? Go enjoy the holidays somewhere hot. You hate snow anyway, and there's nothing to do here.' *There's nothing for you here*, is what Neve wanted to say.

A glimpse of blonde hair emerging from the front room distracted Neve from whatever Mom's reply was. 'I have to go now,' she said quietly.

'But—'

'Bye, Mom.'

She hung up just as Robin stumbled through the threshold, squinting into the morning light. Her hair was a nest of frizzy curls on top of her head and Juniper followed at her feet. Neve opened the back door to let the husky out to do her business, pulling the sleeves of her sweater down to protect herself from the chill.

'What time is it?' Robin mumbled, perching on a stool and clawing the sleep from her eyes.

'Early.' Neve checked the clock above the pantry door. She'd always been an early riser, but Robin didn't seem to share the same quality. 'Just after seven.'

'Disgusting. Sorry I fell asleep on your sofa last night.'

'No worries.' She tried to keep her voice nonchalant, though it had felt intimate, somehow, to see Robin sprawled out with Juniper, fast asleep as though she was completely comfortable there. Neve couldn't remember anybody looking so at home, so right, on a decades-old couch. 'Pancake?'

Beside the stove, Neve had managed to salvage two pancakes before her mother's call, but now she glanced at them again, they seemed soggy and colourless on the plate.

Robin must have shared the same impression, because she raised a brow and then rounded the counter to pick up the spatula. 'Maybe *I* should handle breakfast. You put the kettle on.'

That plan sounded much better, and Neve flicked on the kettle before setting out two mugs. 'Tea, I assume?'

'Of course. I'm nothing if not a British cliché.' Robin began measuring out fresh ingredients and whisking them energetically. Baking seemed to wake something up in her that hadn't been there a moment ago. Neve didn't think she'd ever tire of seeing Robin in her element, especially not when she stood in Neve's kitchen so naturally, as though she had lived here forever. It was strange. Nobody new had set foot in this house in years, probably not since Molly, Nick's ex-fiancée, yet Neve hadn't thought twice about inviting Robin in as though she'd always belonged. Why? Why was it so difficult with everybody else and so easy with her?

'So, who were you on the phone to?' Robin asked.

'Hmm?' Neve pretended to be interested in the teabag, the kettle's wafting steam leaving her face tacky. Inside, she was still reeling from the phone call with her mother. No matter how many times history repeated itself, the disappointment and the anger always returned just as intensely as the first time Mom had ever let her down. She'd been eight, then, and Mom had forgotten to pick her up from a friend's house after a sleepover. Neve would never forget the shame she'd felt sitting on her friend's porch, overstaying her welcome while her friend's parents tried to contact Mom for hours. She hadn't answered her phone. In the end, Grandpa had picked Neve up.

'I thought I heard you talking on the phone.' Robin shrugged obliviously, pouring the pancake batter into the pan. 'Or maybe you were talking to yourself. Don't be embarrassed. I do that sometimes, too.'

Neve could certainly imagine it. 'It was just my mom.'

'Oh, okay . . .' She tilted her head hesitantly. 'You didn't really tell me about your parents last night.'

'There's not much to say.' Neve was glad for the distraction when the kettle boiled and she poured the hot water into the mugs, watching, but not really seeing, the teabags steep. She sighed, expelling some of the residual frustration. She hated that, even after all these years, Mom could still have such an impact on her.

'Is everything okay?' Robin's voice had turned honey-soft, and Neve glanced up to find that she had halted over the sizzling frying pan, a line of concern etched between her brows.

Neve forced a reassuring smile onto her face and retrieved the milk from the fridge, pouring a drop into each mug. 'Why wouldn't it be?'

It seemed to do the trick; Robin went back to her pancakes. Still, the silence was stiff, uncomfortable, more of the dynamic Neve was used to. An ache guttered in her stomach, because she realised she didn't want that. Not with Robin. She wanted her wit and curiosity and silly smiles.

As she placed the drinks onto the breakfast bar with some fresh plates and cutlery, she remembered one of the conversations they'd had last night.

'So . . . are you still up for another ski lesson today?'

Robin's eyes brightened. 'Absolutely. I'm going to be a master of the slopes by the time I get home. If nobody else crashes into me, that is.'

Neve couldn't bring herself to dull Robin's determination, so she only sipped her tea quietly.

'All right, I'm going to flip it. Ready?' Clutching the frying pan, Robin backed into the middle of the kitchen, poking out her tongue in concentration.

'Oh, God. Should I take cover?'

'Don't underestimate my pancake-flipping skills!' She flicked her wrist a few times as though warming herself up. 'I'm the best pancake flipper in—'

The pancake launched into the air before Robin

finished – and didn't come back down. Neve lifted her brows with a deadpan expression, craning her neck to search for the missing pancake.

It was stuck to the ceiling beside the lampshade, perfectly round, perfectly flat, and perfectly unsalvageable.

'See?' Robin said. 'I'm so good at it that I defied the laws of gravity. That's talent.'

Laughter spilled out of Neve, and the light sound surprised her as much as it seemed to surprise Robin.

And then Neve realised that that laughter – laughter *Robin* had tugged out of her – was infinitely easier to focus on than anything her unreliable mother had to say that morning. So, Neve tried to push her bitterness aside and just be here, with a pastry chef who didn't seem to realise how brightly she sparkled, in a kitchen of flying pancakes.

And when gravity finally prevailed and the pancake dropped off the ceiling five minutes later, it only meant that Juniper could mop it up off the floor.

'*Oh. My. God.* You *like* her,' Wren's tinny voice accused in Robin's ear as she marched her way through thick snow. Apparently, the only place to get a phone signal today was on the fringe of the resort, where – she soon discovered – a herd of grunting, glaring reindeer resided. She approached them with trepidation, curiosity outweighing fear as she held out her hand . . .

And then she snatched it back when the one closest shifted, looking as though it was about to take a chunk from her fingers.

'Easy, Rudolph.' It was no wonder it hated her, what with its friend, Elk-on John, stuffed on the wall of the lobby. *Probably wondering if it's next.*

'What did you just call me?' her sister asked, growing more high-pitched by the minute.

'I was talking to the reindeer . . .' Robin sighed '. . . and ignoring you. I *don't* like her.'

Naturally, Wren had forced Robin to tell her about every aspect of her trip thus far, and Robin hadn't been able to avoid mentioning the accidental sleepover with Neve. She'd woken this morning on a strange sofa with a vague smell of apple crumble locked into the cushions, Juniper pinning down her torso while Neve's voice drifted from the kitchen. It had been awkward and strange and unexpected, but they'd masked it with their morning tea and terrible attempts at tossing pancakes. And then Neve had dropped Robin off here, agreeing to meet her for the ski lesson she already regretted asking for; the ski lesson she was now running late for. If she was being honest with herself, which she wasn't, she'd only booked it for more time with Neve.

'Oh, you *so* do. You *slept* with her.'

'I slept on the other side of the couch with her *dog*.' Robin rolled her eyes, nudging the snow with the rubber toe of her ski boots. 'With her *grandpa* in the room upstairs, might I add.'

'Maybe you should return the favour and let her spend the night in your cabin. Then you'll have some *real* alone time.'

Robin could practically hear the wicked smirk in Wren's voice. She hated being teased. Hated feeling whatever it was she was beginning to feel for Neve. Hated being so transparent about it that everybody seemed to know. Experience had taught her that it would only bring embarrassment and regret in the end, and Robin had had quite enough of that.

'*Wren.*'

'It's okay, you know. It's *good*. You're allowed to move on.'

'I *have* moved on,' Robin snapped, surprising even herself. 'And not because of some woman I just met – who, by the way, I'll never even *see* again after this holiday.'

'Oh, please—'

But Robin wasn't listening to her sister anymore. She was focused on the dark-haired woman standing in front of her, skis in her hand and her murky eyes narrowed.

Neve.

Oh, God. Dread churned in Robin's gut. How much had she heard?

'I have to go. I'll talk to you later,' she said down the phone.

Before Wren could argue, Robin hung up and slipped her phone safely into the pocket of her coat. She cast Neve an apologetic grimace. 'I . . . If you heard any of that—'

'I didn't.' It didn't sound like a lie, but with the way Neve stood, as stiff and tall as a flower stem tied to a bamboo support, it didn't seem like the truth, either. 'I see you met Santa's helpers.'

'This one doesn't like me.' Robin gestured to the reindeer that had scared her away and then backed away from the fence.

'Don't take it personally. You won't see them again after this trip, right?'

There went any hope that Robin was off the hook.

'*Neve* . . .' Robin began, but Neve was already barging past her towards the ski lift, lowering her goggles over her eyes in the process.

'Come on. You're not paying me to hang out with the caribou.'

No. Robin was paying Neve to spend more time with her. And by the looks of things, that was a privilege she would no longer get to enjoy for free.

She had gone and ruined it all with her big, clumsy mouth, just as she always did.

They walked to the ski lift in silence, Robin's apology lost in her throat. With any luck, she might just fall to her death on the slopes and save herself any more shame.

Neve was trying aggressively hard not to care – but it wasn't easy when she felt like a fool, especially not since she was still putting herself back together after her mother's call this morning. The ski lesson was quiet and uncomfortable, though Robin had at least stayed upright for the most part. It didn't cure Neve of the ache in her chest, brought on by the words she had overheard. She hadn't asked who Robin had been talking to on the phone; hadn't asked about anything at all.

It wasn't as though she'd said something awful. Neve knew well enough that this – whatever *this* was – wouldn't last forever. They were from two different countries, with an ocean between them in more ways than just geographical. But the way Robin had spoken about Neve as though she didn't matter to her at all . . .

It only confirmed that they were on different pages of different books. Neve tried desperately to close hers and throw it as far across the Rockies as she could. Her guards began to rise again like slabs of stone unearthing themselves from overgrown patches of grass. She should never have let herself care in the first place. She wouldn't make the same mistake twice.

'Are your ankles bent?' Neve barely spared Robin a sidelong glance as she fell into her ski stance. She had practised it so often that it was second nature to her now.

'*Can* you bend your ankles? Is that possible?' Robin retorted, her hunched figure sinking lower. A flurry of snow whirled around them, dusting her coat and clinging to her hair. A blizzard had been forecast for later, and the last thing Neve needed was to be stuck up here on the slopes with her.

Neve sighed impatiently. 'For most people, yes. You should be able to feel the tongue of your boot against your foot.'

Robin lowered again, skis slipping ever so slightly in the snow. 'Got it, I think.'

'Knees bent?'

'Yep.'

'Balance in the centre of your feet?'

'Think so.'

'Okay. This is as tall as you should ever get on your skis.' The rules Neve rattled off were an echo of those that had been drilled into her by Irina long ago. 'Don't try to straighten your posture any higher than this. That's how you ended up falling last time. And the time before.'

'So if I stay like this, I'm good to go?'

'Hypothetically.' After the number of falls she'd witnessed in the last week, Neve wasn't quite convinced. 'Keep your feet hip-width apart unless you come to a bump. Then you can narrow them. But *don't* turn your knees in. Move from your toes.'

'You told me all this last time,' Robin reminded her.

'And you ended up needing first-aid treatment.' Beneath her tinted goggles, Neve rolled her eyes and adjusted her grip on the poles. 'If you think you know better, you're welcome to go on without my training.'

'Fine.'

It was the last thing Neve had expected to hear – but Robin had already pushed off down the slope, knees bent and poles flailing only slightly in her hands before she eased into the descent. Neve waited for her to stop at the bottom of the first incline, but Robin kept going on stiffly planted feet, skis leaving parallel tracks in the snow. She screeched only when she neared the bottom.

'You didn't tell me how to stop!'

Neve had definitely told Robin how to stop – at least three times. 'Push through your heels and form the wedge with your skis!'

When Robin still didn't come to a stop, Neve swore. She set off a moment later, the biting wind cutting past her cheeks as she pushed herself through it, down, down, down. Snowflakes clung to her goggles and her stomach swooped with the memory of just how much she had once loved this, with the smooth, powdery snow spraying beneath her feet and her elbows drawing back like wings.

She halted smoothly at the bottom of the slope, where Robin waited – no longer on her feet.

That soon changed, though, when her mouth spread with a wide grin and she hauled herself upright. Before Neve could prepare herself, Robin threw her arms around her. 'I did it! I stayed on my feet! I didn't fall until the very bottom!'

Despite Neve's foul mood, a laugh of surprise tinkled from her, and she let her hands lock against the centre of Robin's back. *Why?* Why could Neve never hold these things in around Robin?

Their helmets clattered together, and Robin had to strain on her tiptoes to meet Neve's height, but Neve didn't want to pull back. No, she wanted this new, unexpected warmth to stay.

And then she remembered what Robin had said this morning and couldn't help but tear herself away, her gloved hands falling to her sides.

'Neve,' Robin began softly, but Neve didn't want to hear whatever it was. Brusquely, she lifted her goggles and freed herself from her skis. The watch on her wrist told her it was almost time to finish up anyway, and she didn't feel like doing this for another moment longer.

'We should get back – unless you want to try again.'

Robin shook her head and peeled her goggles from her face, too. They'd left behind pink lines on her freckled skin. And her eyes . . . while they were behind the tinted visor, Neve had forgotten just how disarming they were. How piercing and marble-like. She looked away before she could lose herself, certain that she'd seen disappointment swirling in them.

'Can't we talk about earlier?'

A traitorous muscle in Neve's jaw feathered, making it harder to feign indifference. It wouldn't stop her from trying. 'There's nothing to talk about.'

'I know how it must have sounded,' Robin continued. 'I didn't mean for it to come out that way. It's just . . . My sister is pushy and when I told her about last night, she got the wrong idea—'

'You don't have to explain, Robin,' Neve interrupted sternly. 'I understand.'

'I don't think that you do.'

Neve rolled her eyes in exasperation and began trudging her way back to the resort.

'*Please.*' Robin's strained plea lassoed her back. 'I didn't mean it. I . . . I like you, Neve. I like spending time with you. In fact, I'd be having a miserable time here without you. I didn't want to tell my sister because she'd ask me a million questions about us, and I don't want that. I like whatever this is too much to worry about what it could be or what other people think it should be. I just . . . I just want to enjoy the rest of the time I have here with you. I don't want to waste it with you mad at me. *Please?*'

Swallowing, Neve couldn't help but soften. *I like whatever this is too much. What it could be. What other people think it should be.* They were things she had wondered, too. Things she had worried about. Maybe she shouldn't have. Robin certainly wasn't. She was just happy to spend the time she had here with Neve.

But Neve wasn't the sort of person who could just enjoy her time. Not anymore. She wished she was. She'd *tried* to be; had thought she *could* be after the disaster pancakes and the ice skating and the way her cheeks had begun to ache from so much smiling and laughing. And yet all of those things confirmed that she'd have something to miss when Robin went home. She knew already how badly it hurt when people left. She wasn't used to feeling so much, wasn't used to caring about someone this way.

It would have been easier if Robin felt like just another fling . . . or maybe it wouldn't. Neve was the one who did the leaving, the breaking things off when they got more serious than planned and she wasn't feeling it. She liked being the one in control, the one who got to walk away so she wasn't the one abandoned instead. She didn't feel in control now. She felt . . . confused.

'Neve,' Robin repeated when Neve didn't reply. 'I hate snow. I hate skiing.'

Neve frowned. 'So? *I* didn't drag you here. You signed up.'

'Exactly. I signed up.' Robin inched closer. 'I don't enjoy falling on my arse all that much, and yet I keep doing it in front of you. To spend time with you. Doesn't that say something?'

'That you have no self-respect, perhaps.' Neve's thinly pressed lips quivered with the beginnings of a grin. She understood. Robin could have been doing a million other things in Clement Falls, but she was here, subjecting herself to this . . . with Neve.

Maybe that meant something. Maybe it meant Neve wasn't the only one out of her comfort zone.

'We already knew that about me,' Robin dismissed with a wave of her hand. 'I think it also says a lot about how I feel about *you*.'

'Hmm,' Neve said without commitment.

'So . . . am I forgiven?'

Neve hesitated. It felt like a trap either way: saying no meant that it would be the end today; saying yes meant it would be the end when she left, anyway.

But it would give you a few more days with her. A few more laughs. You could at least try.

Besides . . . Neve could be casual. She knew now what she was up against. A short connection destined to ebb. She wouldn't have to get any more attached than this, and she was good with short-term.

She was in control again.

'I guess,' she decided finally. 'I'm still charging you for the lesson, though.'

Robin scoffed. 'Fine. You can put me down for another, too. I think I've finally found my snow legs.'

Neve chuckled at that, though it felt forced.

Because when Robin left and went back to her life in England, Neve knew she would still be here, with nothing but memories plaguing her. She needed to find a way to be okay with that.

Chapter Nine

By midday, the supposed hour-long blizzard that had been forecast for later that evening had somehow transformed into five inches of fresh snow, with no signs of stopping. Neve sat at the bar alone, still bundled in her ski coat. Nick wasn't working today, and she had taken the opportunity to ski by herself after the lesson with Robin had finished. She was rusty on the intermediate slope and so out of shape that one round had been more than enough for her, but . . . it was still there. Everything she had learned, everything she had been good at still slumbered in her bones, waiting for its chance to reawaken. It made her wonder if perhaps trying out for the team again wouldn't be such a bad idea.

Juniper lay by the unlit hearth. When Neve was busy, she liked to welcome the guests in the lobby with Helen, the receptionist, but Neve had come back to a mostly empty resort – and an empty bar. She had no idea what Robin had planned for the rest of the day and hadn't dared ask. She wouldn't make the mistake of seeming too keen again.

But it did leave her stuck. With the snow pelting the windows in relentless, thick flakes, she would either have to risk driving through it alone or else stay here, bored and cold, for the rest of the day – or at least until it slowed down, and that didn't seem likely to happen soon.

With a final sigh, she chose the former and whistled for Juniper's attention so she could clip the tartan green leash onto her collar. 'Come on, girl. Let's go home.'

Juniper wagged her tail and followed Neve out of the bar. The snow dampened them immediately, catching in Neve's woolly hat and leaving Juniper's fur slick. They dashed across the resort, where Neve had parked by the main lobby, and she wasted no time in opening the door of her battered pickup truck to let Juniper crawl into the passenger seat. An old blanket waited for her there. Neve climbed into the driver's seat, shivering despite the layers she wore. As she rattled the keys into the ignition, the windscreen wipers came to life, smearing arched streaks across the window. They were barely fast enough to catch the falling flakes.

It wouldn't be the first time Neve had driven in risky weather, but it never seemed to get any easier. Determination gripping her, she clipped on her seatbelt and reversed out of the parking lot, tyres dragging cautiously through the sludge. Though it was still early, fluffy indigo clouds hung low over the pines, concealing the grey Rockies and leaving the afternoon gloomy.

They were barely five minutes down the winding road when the first bout of dread hit. The car's wheels were struggling through the thickening, slippery blanket of snow. Just as Neve was about to make a turn, another set of headlights blinded her. She rounded the corner as slowly as possible, muttering a few expletives for the other driver, though they hadn't really done anything wrong—

It was all forgotten when the tyres slipped and the truck ploughed headfirst into a smothering mound of snow. With a sharp squeal of the brakes, Neve's body was thrown forward against her seatbelt, leaving her ribs tight and aching. Juniper's yelp sliced through her with almost as much force.

Imprisoned by white, Neve's body hummed with panic, her fingers gripping the steering wheel so tightly that her knuckles matched the snow. The pickup creaked beneath the new weight, and Neve imagined the ceiling caving, the windows cracking. She had to get out.

'You okay, Juniper?' As she craned to check on the husky, something in her neck twinged. Still, relief warmed her slightly when she found Juniper still beside her. Her body rose and fell with anxious pants, and Neve soothed her with gentle strokes. 'Good girl. I'm sorry, baby.'

In a daze of shock, Neve unbuckled her seatbelt and carefully opened the driver's side door, thankful when it gave easily. She stepped out onto the road on unsteady feet, searching for help, for headlights.

A mistake.

Without warning, Juniper slid past her and scurried straight into the copse of trees fringing the road, a retreating grey figure vanishing into the blizzard. Her green leash was the only flash of colour as it dragged through the snow behind her, and then that was swallowed by the shadowed woods, too.

'No, Juniper!'

Worse still was that there was no sign of another soul anywhere. The roads were completely dead.

With trembling fingers, Neve fished through her pockets for her phone, cowering away from the vehicle when more snow collapsed from the crags above. Instinct set in, and she scrolled through her contacts until she came to Nick. Waiting agonising seconds for the call to connect, she set off in the same direction as Juniper.

'You again?' Nick jested finally, the phone signal crackly and unclear. She was lucky she had any at all.

'Nick.' It came out a shaky plea as she searched each shadow for a sign of her dog. She knew these woods. She knew the entire resort. But they'd just crashed, and it was snowing so heavily . . . What if Juniper ran out into the road? What if she got lost in the forest?

'What's wrong?' Nick's voice turned grave in an instant. 'Are you okay?'

'I crashed into a wall of snow and lost Juniper. The truck is stuck and I had to leave it to find her, and—'

'Slow down, Neve,' he ordered. 'Where are you?'

'About five minutes down the road from the resort. I was coming home.'

'Jesus Christ. You're an idiot for driving in this weather. There was a warning on the news.'

Neve scowled. She didn't need to be told that now, when fear was pushing acid up her throat and turning her knees to jelly. She almost tripped over a fallen branch, her foot rolling until pain shot through her ankle. With a grunt, she pressed her weight back onto it and found that she could at least still walk through the ache.

'Can you just help me, please?'

'I'll report the accident and see if I can get a tow truck out. How bad was the crash?'

'Not bad,' she said through rasping breaths, speeding up when she found a zigzagged line through the snow. Juniper's leash? Neve could do nothing but follow it and pray it would lead straight to her. 'The truck is just stuck, but I don't think anything's broken. The windshield might crack under—'

'I don't care about the car. Are *you* hurt?' Nick's tut was accompanied by rustling as he sprang into action.

Even if Neve was, she doubted she'd notice in the state she was in. 'No, I don't think so.'

'Good. Just find Juniper and get inside. I'll take care of the rest, okay? Call me when you can.'

'Okay.'

Tears blurred Neve's vision as she hung up and stopped in her tracks to suck in a sharp breath.

'*Juniper!*'

Her call cleaved through the forest, through the snow, through the blizzard.

Only the howling wind replied.

The sound of furious, whistling gales woke Robin from a glorious nap on the couch. Book still open on her chest, she yawned and frowned at the foul weather outside. It was dark and dreary, the windows dappled by thick flakes of snow.

She wasn't quite sure what to do now. Before, she'd been able to go somewhere when she felt lonely: the bar, or the markets, or her ski lesson. Neve hadn't tried to make plans after this morning, and Robin couldn't really blame her. Even if Robin did have something to do, she wouldn't have been able to see past her hand outside in a blizzard like this. Better to be stuck in here, warm and safe.

So this was it then. An afternoon of crushing loneliness. It was never a good idea to leave Robin alone with her brain. She would start *thinking* soon. In fact, the thinking had already started. First about Neve and whether she even liked Robin at all, or was simply tolerating her while she imposed upon Neve's life here. And then there was her mother.

Robin was in a new country, snowed into a cabin, trapped, and her stubborn bloody mum wouldn't call her back. Stretching her legs out, she checked her phone. With the five-hour time zone difference, Wren would be heading home from the office and probably wouldn't pick up. Robin didn't have many friends to call; none close enough to talk to about all of this, anyway. Only her restaurant colleagues knew she'd taken a holiday at all, and the people she'd once been close to she'd met through Lexi, so they'd distanced themselves from her after the break-up.

She scrolled aimlessly for a while to distract herself from the sudden bout of homesickness. It did no good. She couldn't stop imagining lazing in her own bed, in surroundings she'd known all her life. Mum would probably have made awful chicken and mushroom soup that Robin would have to pour down the sink when she wasn't looking, and then Robin would take a long bubble bath with her favourite Lush bath bomb, which would probably be disturbed by Cleopawtra letting herself into the bathroom or Uncle Phil turning up downstairs unannounced with his four raucous sons, claiming he'd been craving a chippy tea from around the corner when really his wife had kicked him out of the house for smoking again.

It was strange how she was beginning to miss the things about home she'd once despised.

Huffing, she finally shoved her pride aside and dialled her mum's number. The tone seemed to drone on for eons, and then the posh Vodafone lady answered the voicemail with her standard 'the person you are calling is currently unavailable' spiel. Only she needn't have bothered. Robin knew her mother. She knew that on any given evening, Mum would be doing a crossword in front of the telly while she watched contestants slagging off each other's meals on a repeat of *Come Dine With Me*.

Tears pricked Robin's eyes, unwelcome but unpreventable. If the silent treatment really *was* about Mum's worries about Robin not coming home the same way that Dad hadn't, she had a funny way of showing it. Robin *could* have slipped on black ice by now, and then what? Mum wouldn't have answered her bloody phone to find out.

A scraping outside began as Robin locked her phone, and she searched for the TV remote to drown out the sound. Even the tree branches had set out to annoy her now. But as it continued, Robin realised it didn't sound like a tree branch at all. And those whines drifting from the front door . . .

She stood on aching legs and dog-eared the open page of her book before setting it down on the coffee table and heading to the door. In her sleep-riddled, mother-stung state, she could only prepare to find two possible things waiting for her: a bear seeking refuge from the wild, or a serial killer *posing* as a bear seeking refuge from the wild. Neither were things she wanted to let into her cabin, so she opened the door cautiously, poking her head out of the tiniest gap she could make.

It wasn't a bear, though Robin had mistaken her for a wolf once before. Now, Robin would have recognised the husky even without the plaid collar around her furry neck.

'Juniper?'

Juniper's tail swayed from side to side happily, and she almost trampled Robin to the ground when she opened the door wide enough to let her in.

'What are you doing here, wolfie?' It was a nickname she used only when Neve wasn't around, to avoid being teased. 'Where's Neve?'

Front paws prancing across the floorboards, Juniper let out an almighty, piercing howl, causing Robin to frown and crouch down to her level.

'What? What are you trying to tell me? Where's your mama?'

The dog's rough tongue left a cold, wet strip of saliva across Robin's cheek, and then she clawed at the door as though ready to leave again. Rising from her haunches, Robin poked her head out to see if Neve was around. But if she was, neither she nor Juniper could see her. The only other visitor waiting for her was the cold.

Still, Juniper loitered patiently at the door, something strange glowing in her one blue eye.

There went Robin's peaceful afternoon.

With a groan, she slipped on her boots, coat, hat, and scarf, making it all of two steps outside before a familiar dark figure emerged from the cluster of pines down the hill.

Juniper barked and ran to Neve, her fur merging with the relentless snowfall. Robin squinted and continued to trudge down the road, her heart racing despite itself. Something wasn't right – but what?

It sounded as though Neve was laughing as she got closer . . . And then, when she reached them, Robin saw that she wasn't laughing at all, but crying as she nuzzled her face into Juniper's fur.

'Is everything okay?' Robin hovered above them uncertainly. It felt as though she was interrupting a moment not made for her. 'Juniper just turned up at my door.'

Neve lifted her gaze only for long enough to take Robin in. 'She came here? To your cabin?'

'Yes.' Robin's teeth began to chatter as the snow dampened the curling ends of her hair. The buffeting winds threatened to blow her over, and she pressed her heels into the ground as though she was back on the slopes. 'What happened?'

'She ran away.' With a firm hand wrapped around Juniper's collar, Neve rose. Her pink nose dripped, and she wiped it with her sleeve unabashedly. 'I was in an accident. I think it spooked her. Or . . . I don't know. Maybe she just knew to come here.'

'An accident?' Robin repeated, hot panic urging her forward. Her hands hovered uncertainly as she scanned Neve's frame, searching for sign of injury. 'Neve . . . are you hurt?'

'I think I'm okay.' Neve didn't look okay. Her fingers trembled, eyes glazed and watery. 'My car, on the other hand, is stuck in a few metres of snow. Nick is sorting it out, though. I just . . . I thought I'd lost Juniper.'

'It's okay. Juniper's here.' Desperate to comfort her, Robin curled her arms gently around Neve's taller frame, drawing soothing circles on her back – though with such a thick coat, she probably barely felt it. 'Come on. Let's get you both warm and dry.'

Neve's only answer was a subtle nod into the crook of Robin's shoulder.

Chapter Ten

Robin's hands shook as she poured the boiling water into two mugs, the teabags floating on the surface. Watching the colour of the leaves bleed into the water calmed her slightly, as did the burning heat against her cold palms when she picked them up. She'd stolen the English breakfast teabags from Neve's house this morning, shoving a handful into her pocket when Neve had been getting dressed.

Neve didn't need to know that, though.

'I'd offer you hot chocolate, but I drank it all,' she said apologetically, turning from the small kitchen to find both Neve and Juniper wrapped snugly in a duvet in front of the log fire. 'I don't have any milk, either. I hope you like black tea.'

'Anything will do,' Neve replied with a weak smile. 'Thanks, Robin. I don't know what I'd do without you.'

Robin's heart stammered in her chest. She tried to ignore it as she collapsed into the armchair, though heat had already begun to bloom beneath her skin. It was perhaps the nicest thing Neve had ever said to her.

'What did Nick say?' Neve had just gotten off the phone with him, but her words had been hushed and Robin hadn't been able to glean anything above the sound of the bubbling kettle.

'That I'm an idiot and I'm never allowed to drive again.' Neve sipped her tea and winced. 'And they towed my car. It's at the repair shop now. He'll pick me up as soon as the roads are safe.'

'There's no rush. You can both stay here as long as you like. I don't have any food for Juniper, though . . .'

'Don't worry. I fed her before we set off.'

The duvet sagged as Juniper settled into it, much calmer than she had been when Neve had brought her in. She'd clung to her owner like a child, then, as though knowing that Neve had been in danger. And the fact she'd come here after the accident, having navigated her way through the forests fringing the resort . . . Robin couldn't quite understand how that had happened. She could only put it down to sheer luck.

Neve stretched – and then flinched, massaging her neck with a groan.

'Are you hurt? Should we find someone to help?' Robin placed her mug down in an instant, already pulling out her phone, though she had no idea who to call.

'No.' A surprising laugh fell from Neve, and then her icy hands were in Robin's, stopping her from dialling. 'I'm fine. Really. It's just whiplash.'

Though worry still gnawed at her, Robin nodded. She didn't dare let go of Neve's hand, instead kneeling in front of her. The lick of flames warmed her back as Neve's hazel eyes locked on hers.

Neve's unfallen tears gleamed against the guttering light, though her cheeks were at least flushed with a reassuring amount of colour. Not as they had been earlier. Robin couldn't stop watching her, couldn't stop worrying and wishing she could find a way to make it better. If the roles were reversed, she'd bet that Neve would have known what to do. That's what she did; she took care of people. Her grandpa, her brother, Robin when she'd drunk one too many of Nick's eggnogs or fallen on the slopes.

Who took care of Neve?

Robin would. It was a silent vow she made to herself, and then to seal it, reached out a hand. The soft curve of Neve's cheek was already feverish from the fire. Warily, Robin waited for her to pull away, but Neve didn't. Instead, her eyes fluttered shut, throat bobbing with a gulp.

'I'm glad you're okay,' Robin whispered, the raw honesty scraping her throat.

'I'm glad she came to you. She was my grandmother's dog before she was mine.' Neve opened her eyes slowly, a tear making its solitary journey down her splotchy face, past her nose – to her lips. When she didn't lick it away, Robin pressed the pad of her thumb to it, trying desperately to chase away the sadness. She tried not to think about Neve's chapped lips touching other parts of her skin, though the idea left her gut twisting with want all the same. Robin hadn't felt desire in so long, she barely recognised it at first.

The words surprised her. Robin couldn't imagine Neve without Juniper, or vice versa. She let her hand fall, bowing her head against the embarrassment that came with it. There was no natural way to stop touching somebody. What was she *doing*? 'Your grandpa didn't want her after . . . ?'

'He always wanted a cat.' Neve shrugged with a watery smile that left Robin's chest even heavier. 'I have a feeling that he's just waiting for me to move out so he can finally get one.'

With a laugh, Robin crossed her legs and swiped her still-damp hair from her face. Neve's had matted to her neck, the tips curling so that her edges seemed younger, less frayed than usual. Robin had forced her to take off her hat and scarf, her wet clothes, so that she could warm up, and now Neve wore a pair of Robin's plaid pyjama bottoms and a knitted jumper, both of which were just slightly too short in the hem and far too large around the chest and waist for her.

'I don't know what I would have done if I'd lost her.' Neve's voice thickened with fresh tears, and Robin shushed her gently and pulled her closer, letting her rest her head in the crook of her shoulder. 'She feels like the only real thing I have left of my gran.'

'You don't have to think about that now, love,' she whispered, her fingers tracing absent spirals into Neve's shoulder. 'She's here. Safe and sound. You both are. And I'm sure your gran knows how much you love her.'

As though proving it, Juniper let out a content sigh and rolled onto her back, legs akimbo and long, furry belly exposed. They both giggled, Neve stretching out to rub her chest.

Only then did the random thought of Robin's tea going cold pop into her brain. She sat up onto her knees, making to reach for it—

Neve tugged her back, her dainty fingers lacing delicately around Robin's wrist. Before Robin could even ask why, her lips met with Neve's, soft and hungry and so completely unexpected that Robin gasped into her.

She couldn't pull away. Wouldn't pull away. Her stomach had been set on fire, and she would let it burn as brightly as the hearth that smouldered behind them. The earthy, sweet taste of tea lingered on Neve's tongue as the kiss deepened to breathless explorations, and then Robin's fingers curled around Neve's damp, knotted waves as though her life depended on it.

When they finally parted, Neve blinked and clenched her jaw, her features smoothing back to that blank, unreadable stare that Robin always struggled to see through. Robin's fingers rose to trace the ghost of Neve's lips as her heart thundered.

'Sorry,' Neve murmured weakly.

'I'm not.' It was the same candour that had only ever ended with Robin's heart getting broken before.

'It was a mistake.'

The words left Robin feeling as chipped as old ceramic. Neve had been through something traumatic. She'd been seeking comfort, and Robin had been all too willing to give it to her.

Robin swallowed down the pain and shifted away. 'Oh. Okay.'

'You're leaving soon,' Neve explained as though Robin didn't know. A troubled crease had formed between her dark brows.

'I am.' It was all Robin could say as she pulled herself back onto the armchair, nursing the mug of tea in her palms. She couldn't bring herself to drink it, not with nausea swirling in her gut. What had she been *thinking*?

'Robin . . .'

'But what if I wasn't?' Robin couldn't help but blurt.

'You are.'

'But if I wasn't. Would this still have been a mistake? Is this about me leaving, or about you not . . .' *Wanting me*, Robin stopped herself from saying. *The way I want you.*

Because she did want Neve. She wanted to kiss her again, hold her again, wanted to wrap her up in blankets when things were bad, wanted to eat takeout and gingerbread men as she laughed with her family. She wanted . . . *too much*. Too much, too soon. It was enough to make her want to yank out her hair, or else her heart.

She had been on dates after Lexi and felt nothing. Nothing until Neve. And she didn't even have to try.

'Not what?' Neve asked finally.

'Nothing. Never mind.' Robin rose to throw away her tea. Juniper stirred at the movement, one pointed ear rising from where she lay beside Neve. 'Are you hungry?'

'No,' Neve said, throwing off the duvet so that she could stand, too. Robin thought she was answering her last question, the one about being hungry, and she scoured the cupboards as though it might change her mind. But then Neve continued: 'No. If you weren't leaving, maybe it wouldn't have been a mistake.'

Robin inhaled sharply, daring to look at Neve again. And for once, everything that Neve felt was written on her face clear as day – the mirror image of what simmered in Robin. Longing. Uncertainty. Conflict. *Want.* 'Can't we just . . . pretend for a few days that I don't live so far away?'

Neve muttered, 'I don't know how. I like you, Robin, but I don't want to care this much about somebody who won't even be here at Christmas.'

'You say it like I'm dying.'

Neve's face scrunched. 'I don't know what else you want me to say. I've never . . .' She trailed off as though she couldn't finish that sentence. Robin desperately wanted to know how it ended. She waited for agonising seconds before realising she'd never find out. Neve had clamped her lips shut.

'I don't want you to say anything,' Robin replied. 'You're right. This makes no sense. But it seems like we'd be wasting just as much time pretending there's nothing between us as we would if we started something we won't have time to finish. Doesn't it?'

Neve hesitated, her fingers twirling around a stray thread from Robin's jumper. 'Maybe.'

'It's okay.' To hide her pained expression, Robin returned to the kitchen in the hopes of finding her cupboards were not as empty as the last time she searched them. 'I understand. I'm jumping the gun, and you've just been through h—'

Neve swallowed Robin's words, pulling her back and kissing her more desperately this time. Fingers furling in Neve's jumper, Robin let her, a coil of heat pressing low in her stomach. It threatened to snap when Neve's hands travelled along her spine. Lower.

'I changed my mind,' Neve whispered when they finally drew away, breathless and flushed and bristling with need. 'You're right. Forget everything I just said.'

'Gladly,' Robin breathed, and then kissed her again.

A knock at the door set Juniper barking hours later. Neve had just dozed off in Robin's arms, safe and warm and happy enough that she'd forgotten anything else existed. It felt surreal that only a few hours ago, she'd been ripped apart by anxiety and shock, and then they'd been kissing and lying together as though they had all the time in the world. Neve kept telling herself they did. She wasn't ready to think about what it would be like when Robin left.

She groaned when Robin slid out from under her, grabbing Juniper's collar to keep her from running off again as Robin padded to the door. 'It will probably be Nick.'

It was. Neve had been expecting him for hours, since the weather had calmed and night had fallen over the fresh snow – but he'd claimed he'd been busy.

'Where have you been?' she asked now, straightening up on the couch as Nick stamped his boots on the welcome mat.

'Picking *your* truck up from the mechanic.' Just as much accusation laced his own words as he crouched to greet Juniper. Robin shut the cold out behind him. 'Hello, Juniper,' he said in the high-pitched voice he reserved for animals and the occasional baby. 'I heard you went on an adventure. My sister's a silly goose, isn't she? Yes.'

Juniper revelled in the attention, tail wagging as she licked Nick's face in agreement.

Neve rolled her eyes. 'I'm okay, by the way. Thanks for asking.'

'Physically, perhaps.' Nick pursed his lips and straightened up. 'Thanks for taking care of them both for me,' he said to Robin.

'Not a problem. Would you like something to drink?'

Silently, Neve cursed Robin for being so damn kind. The last thing she needed was for her brother to stay and have him find out what was going on between them; that they'd *kissed*. Several times. Neve's lips still tingled with the memory.

'We should head off before it starts to snow again.' Nick twirled his car keys around his finger and waggled his eyebrows. 'Unless you two want a little more alone time, that is. I could always come back in the morning . . .'

Neve glared. Robin turned a furious shade of beetroot red. Juniper grinned, tongue lolling over her canines.

'Meaning?'

'Oh, nothing. Grandpa tells me you two had a little sleepover last night is all.'

'Well—' Robin began, but Neve cut her off before she gave anything away.

'Oh, shut up. It was late. I saved us both the drive back here because that's what *friends* do. You don't have any, so you wouldn't know.' She rose on exhausted legs and slid on her boots, tying the laces haphazardly without daring to gauge Robin's reaction.

Nick let out an unconvinced hum and rattled his keys again. '*Robin's* my friend. Aren't you, Robin?'

'I'm your *best* friend, Nick.'

Ignoring them, Neve clipped on Juniper's leash before she shucked her coat over the too-small-slash-big clothes Robin had loaned her. 'Thanks again for . . . everything, Robin.'

'No worries,' Robin said – too quietly. Neve didn't have time to think about what it meant. She cast Robin a wave, wishing her brother wasn't here so that she could have snuck in a final kiss before leaving. She already knew she'd spend the rest of the night thinking about Robin: her lips and her laugh and the way she'd called Neve "love" with all the delicateness in the world.

Robin only smiled at them both. 'See you tomorrow?'

They'd already arranged a trip into town tomorrow morning before Neve's lessons; Neve had a few last-minute gifts to buy for Nick and Grandpa. She nodded, silent confirmation, and then let Juniper drag her into the icy night.

'Tomorrow, huh?' Beneath his stubble, a wry grin spread across Nick's lips as the door fell shut behind them. 'Hot date?'

'Can you give it up?' If she had the energy, Neve would have shoved him into the snow. Her neck still twinged, though, and any adrenaline had long since worn off, leaving her drained and aching. She trudged down the steps with slumped shoulders and wobbly legs.

'Come on, Neve. I've seen how you are around her. It's been a long time since you last smiled this much.'

Neve hoped her brother wouldn't notice the heat smattering her cheeks in the darkness. Was she that transparent? She hoped not, though perhaps she had been a little . . . lighter recently. It was impossible not to laugh around Robin, impossible not to be swallowed up by that golden warmth she seemed to emit everywhere she went. Neve wouldn't tell her brother that, though. She'd like to keep at least one thing in her life private, hers. That, and she felt too vulnerable tonight. Too raw.

'I don't know what you're talking about.'

With a roll of his eyes, Nick unlocked the car door. Neve let Juniper into the back and then sat in the passenger seat, eyes narrowed and arms crossed. Nick sank into the driver's side a moment later, a smirk playing at the corner of his mouth. The smell of the cold outside clung to his coat.

'I know you too well, Neve.'

Neve scoffed. 'So you think.'

'You don't have to hide it from me. You know I like her a lot and I think she's good for you.'

'She leaves soon. Long-distance never works.' She didn't know if she was reminding him or herself. Either way, the knowledge left an ever-festering hole in her chest, and she wasn't sure how she would fill it when Robin was gone. But she refused to waste the time they had by acknowledging it. Besides, having an expiration date . . . perhaps it was better than getting too attached – or letting *Robin* get too attached. They both knew where they stood this way. No confusion, no expectations.

She hoped.

'So you *do* like her. So much you're already thinking about the future. That's not like you.'

'Quit playing Cupid and drive, please.' Neve tutted in exasperation and slapped the back of his head lightly. She thought about telling him about Mom's call just to change the subject, but then thought better of it. She shouldn't get his hopes up. Besides, if he knew that Neve had told Mom not to come at all, she'd get another lecture. He would always be too patient and forgiving when it came to their mom.

'I suppose now is as good a time as any to mention that I picked your truck up hours ago.' Casually, Nick put the keys in the ignition. The radio crackled to life automatically with an old, repetitive Christmas song Neve would usually turn off.

But she was frozen now.

'What are you talking about?'

He gave a smug shrug as he reversed onto the main road. 'I didn't want to take away from your time with Robin.'

If Nick hadn't been driving, Neve would have kicked him or slammed his head into the dashboard. As it was, she glowered and shuffled as far away from him as she could get in the small space, though she wasn't all that angry when she weighed it up. Her afternoon had been full of tender, comforting touches in front of the fire, ones she wished would be branded on her skin forever.

But Nick didn't know that. He didn't know anything, much as he pretended otherwise, nor did he need to.

'You're a dick.'

Nick chuckled. 'You're welcome.'

Chapter Eleven

It was far too early to shop. After visiting only one store, where Neve had picked up a bottle of aftershave for her brother, a gift she got him every year for a lack of any better ideas, she was quite happy to let Robin drag her to Clement's Cakes for breakfast.

The sweet smell of cake and coffee woke Neve up – and woke her stomach up, too. It grumbled as soon as she set foot in the door. Though Robin claimed not to be a fan of the holidays, her features brightened all the same. Then again, that might have been down to the desserts rather than the ridiculous number of decorations. It might as well have been Santa's grotto – and would be in a few days when kids piled in to see the bearded man himself, just as they did every year in Clement Falls.

Nick and Neve had made it a tradition long ago to visit the bakery each time they ventured into town together, and even after years, it still warmed Neve's heart just to be here.

In the calm before the morning rush, Neve took the opportunity to peruse the menu properly. Though she adored the red velvet cakes, she couldn't even think about eating something so tooth-rotting so early, especially not when she had ski lessons later. The cream cheese frosting would surely make a reappearance halfway down the slopes in front of her clients. Neve had learned that the hard way.

Robin, on the other hand, seemed not to share that worry.

'Ooh! I want to try them all.' She licked her lips as she peered into the display of goods by the counter. And then, a gasp. 'Oh my God. Crushed candy cane cheesecake?'

'It's eight a.m.' Neve winced and wandered to her side, both awed and entertained by Robin's iron stomach – so much so that she couldn't help but slip her fingers into Robin's free hand.

Almost immediately, Robin pulled away to point at something else. 'The clementine cake looks to die for.'

Neve tried to swallow down the icy disappointment settling through her. They had kissed only yesterday, but today, it felt as though Neve had imagined all of it. Robin hadn't acted any differently around her than before, though Neve had tried her best to show that she wanted to be around her, *closer* to her, by making sure they brushed elbows as they wandered the aisles of the store and smiling more than she probably ever had before.

'That's our signature cake.' Hazel popped up seemingly from nowhere behind the counter, beaming. 'I'd also recommend our maple and cinnamon buns for a breakfast treat. You two are here early this morning!'

Robin startled and hopped back. 'Jesus bloody Christ on a bike! Where did you come from?'

Hazel laughed. 'Sorry. I spilled some milk on the floor. So, cinnamon buns?'

Neve grimaced, stroking her stomach regretfully. 'I have a ski lesson to get to soon. Better keep it light.'

'Well *I* don't.' Eyes falling to the cinnamon buns, Robin moaned her approval. 'Go on. I'll take you up on one of those cinnamon bun thingies! And then the clementine cake and the cheesecake boxed up for later, please. *Ooh*, and hot chocolate with extra cream and marshmallows! The last one was so yummy.'

Hazel set to work, tarnishing the neatly decorated cakes by taking the first slices of the day and placing them carefully in a takeout box. 'Neve?'

'I'll take the cranberry granola bar and a latte.' Neve doubted it came as much of a surprise – she ordered the granola bar almost as often as she ordered coffee – but her desire for adventure had dwindled faster than an Albertan summer. Something was off with Robin, and Neve needed to know what.

'No Nick today?' Hazel enquired with a failed attempt at nonchalance as she noted the orders in a pad and rang them up at the register.

The baker had harboured a not-so-subtle crush on Neve's brother since the age of seventeen, when Hazel had studied at Neve's house for a group project and Nick had decided to wander the house in just a towel, post-shower. She'd thought it a teenage crush, but every time Neve brought Nick into the bakery, Hazel's cheeks still pinkened and she miraculously forgot how to count five-dollar bills – and she *always* gave Nick the largest, chocolatiest slice of mud pie. Obviously back then she'd been too young, but for some reason, Nick continued to remain oblivious to the jolly, curly-haired woman and her Pavlovian attempts to get his attention, and it had gone no further. She knew it wasn't because of Molly; as much as Nick disliked being single again and wondered if he'd made mistakes in letting her go, he had no problem flirting with other women and going on the occasional date. It might have been the age difference, but Nick had surely noticed that Hazel wasn't a teenager anymore, even if she had been when they'd met. Maybe he was just more like Neve than he knew. Pushing away the good things before they could touch him.

'Not today.' Neve smiled knowingly. 'I'm sure he will be tomorrow, though.'

Hazel's shoulders slumped as she announced their total, and Robin scrambled for her purse. Neve lifted a hand to stop her. 'It's on me.'

'Are you sure? I don't mind . . .'

The fact Neve couldn't even pay for Robin's breakfast said more than enough about where they were. Clearly, nothing had changed between them. They were just friends who had kissed yesterday. This wasn't a date. They weren't *dating*. Neve had gotten it all very, very wrong. 'I got it.'

She paid Hazel before Robin put up more of a fight, and then they wandered to one of the empty tables by the window, their breakfasts set in front of them.

Robin didn't waste any time. She speared her fork straight through the cinnamon bun, eyes fluttering closed in delight as she took her first bite. Neve could only nibble her granola bar warily. She had no idea what to say, what to do, how to act. She was no good at trying to guess where she stood with someone, which was another reason why she always made sure that everybody stood a decent distance from *her*.

'Is everything okay, Robin?'

'Everything is absolutely delightful.' Crumbs sprayed from Robin's mouth as she slid the plate towards Neve. 'Want to try some?'

'I mean with you. Us.'

She frowned. 'What do you mean?'

'It's just . . . I feel like nothing's changed. Which is fine. It was only a kiss. I just . . .' Neve struggled to find the words, scraping her hair back from her eyes and turning her gaze to the window.

Everything seemed easier out there. A world away. The lights of the markets, rousing slowly from their slumber, blurred into orbs against the snow-spattered glass as the dark shapes of early morning shoppers drifted by. In here, everything was too still, too tense.

Mustering any dregs of courage she could find, Neve pulled the sleeves of her sweater over her cold fingers. 'I guess I'm just confused about where it leaves us.'

Robin worried at her sugar-frosted lip and placed her fork down carefully. This must have been serious. 'Well . . . I'm confused, too. I thought you didn't want anybody to know about us.'

'Why would you think that?'

'You told your brother we were just friends. I thought maybe you wanted to keep us a secret. I thought maybe . . . you were embarrassed by me.'

Neve softened at the heart-wrenching honesty in Robin's hoarse voice, unable to keep from reaching across the table to grab her hand. She didn't care if Hazel saw, or anyone else for that matter. 'That's definitely not true.'

'No?' Robin's eyes danced with an uncertainty Neve wanted nothing more than to ease.

'No, not at all. Why would I be embarrassed by you?'

'Because I'm me.' Her lips quirked into a watery smile. 'I embarrass *myself*. I'm bound to embarrass whoever I'm with, too.'

'Well, you don't embarrass me.' Neve meant it. All of Robin's quirks and goofy jokes and puns, all the messes she got herself into . . . they were all of the reasons Neve had been drawn to her so quickly, even if she had been reluctant to show it at first. Robin brought sunshine to her dreary days in the snow. It was an adventure, not knowing what she would say next, how she would next tug a laugh straight from Neve's belly. She'd never met anyone so unapologetically themselves, even if there were a few cracks in her confidence now and then. It hurt to think that Robin didn't see herself that way.

But something else still lay heavy on Neve. 'You did sort of do the same thing to me the other day. Y'know, with your sister.'

Robin scratched her cheek sheepishly. 'Yeah. You're right. I'm sorry. I suppose I didn't really know if you liked me then. It's difficult being vulnerable again, especially around people who saw the way Lexi hurt me. I got . . . defensive, I suppose.'

'I get that,' Neve murmured softly. She'd never had her heart broken, and she was still guarded. Of course Robin struggled to open up after cancelling an entire wedding. 'The only reason I played things down to Nick is because he loves to tease me – but that was stupid because he already knows there's something between us and wouldn't shut up about it last night.'

'How?'

'I guess I'm not that good at hiding it.' Neve chuckled, squeezing Robin's fingers gently. 'Don't worry. He's rooting for you.'

'Is he?' A flicker of pride sparked across her features.

Neve nodded, eyes locking on Robin's. They would tell her more than Neve's mouth ever could; would tell her things she couldn't bring herself to say aloud. *I'm rooting for you. For us. Even if it can't last.*

A sharp wave of panic spiked through her suddenly, and Neve almost gasped. She was sinking. In too deep.

She pushed all of that away, though, when Robin rose to place a gentle kiss on Neve's nose. 'Sorry for being so daft.'

'Ditto.'

Neve was left cold when Robin pulled her hand away to open the takeout box Hazel had just given her. 'I can't wait. I have to try the cakes,' she said. Her appetite was certainly something to behold.

'Do all pastry chefs eat this much sugar for breakfast?'

'It's our God-given right,' she confirmed through a mouthful of frosting. '*Mmm. Yum.* Although I would have put almonds in this. Ooh, and maybe yoghurt in the frosting.'

It just so happened that Hazel was approaching as Robin gave out her critique, their drinks wobbling a dangerous amount on the round tray she clutched. She halted upon hearing their conversation, and Neve could only wince apologetically.

'You bake?' Hazel set down first Neve's latte and then Robin's hot chocolate, towered with whipped cream and embellished with a candy cane on the saucer.

'Sorry.' Robin grimaced. 'You weren't supposed to hear that. It's delicious, really. I just have a bad habit of sticking my nose in where it's not needed.'

'No, no,' Hazel dismissed with a wave of her hand, pressing the empty tray into her hip. 'Honestly, I'm a little lost right now. Our best baker, Lou, just went on maternity leave. She left me the recipes, but I can barely make out her handwriting, and you saw how chaotic it was in here the other night. If you can help, I'm all ears.'

Robin shook her head. 'Oh, no. The cakes are great, Hazel. You don't need my help.'

'But they're missing something. It's okay. You can say it. Stanley over there certainly does – every day.' Hazel motioned over to Stanley, who obliviously sipped his coffee and completed a newspaper puzzle with a plate of crumbs at his side. 'All my regular customers are so used to Lou's recipes, and I keep messing them up. Between that and managing the Christmas rush, I'm one bad shift away from having no cakes to sell at all.'

'Have you looked into hiring new staff?' Neve questioned.

Hazel cast her a look that clearly meant "*duh!*" and motioned to the noticeboard hanging by the chalkboard menu at the front. In bold letters, it read: **"New staff needed NOW! (please) Ask Hazel (the flustered lady crying at the counter) for details (please)."**

'A very effective advertisement. I can't imagine why you haven't had any enquiries.' Neve checked her wristwatch absently. 'Anyway, I'd love to help out, but I have lessons in half an hour.'

'I wouldn't trust you with my cakes anyway.' Hazel sniffed in jest and turned to Robin. 'What about you? Be my little British Christmas angel? Please?'

Robin hesitated, her focus flitting to Neve in question – and though Neve knew it was wrong, she prayed Robin would say no. If Robin took on work here, they'd have even less time together. Neve just wanted to soak up every bit of Robin she could before she left.

But she could see in Robin's twinkling eyes that she wanted this, and Neve wouldn't be the one to hold her back from it. So when Robin caved with a grin, Neve could only smile with her, even if it left her chest tight. 'I suppose I *do* have time to kill while Neve's working. Only today, though.'

With a peal of applause, Hazel squealed and pulled Robin up from her chair. 'Yes! Thank you so much. I'm going to print out a picture of your face and stick it at the top of my Christmas tree. *Thankyouthankyouthankyou*. Let me show you the kitchen.'

Robin mouthed, 'I'll see you later,' as Hazel lured her away. The cakes were left abandoned on the table, and Neve along with them. She waved, forcing a reassuring nod as she watched Robin disappear into the kitchen.

'I don't think I've ever tasted anything this good before.'

Hazel's praise was muffled by the two gooey bites of salted caramel blondies she'd hungrily piled into her mouth without giving them time to cool. They'd used any spare time they could squeeze in between customers for Robin to help out with Lou's recipes – which may as well have been written in hieroglyphs for how well Robin could read them. Her own input eventually led to her showing off her talents and offering new ideas.

It was nice to be back in a kitchen. The restaurant was always so hectic that Robin had little time to stand back and appreciate her creations. It didn't help that said creations had been the same four dessert dishes for about three years now. No matter how she begged, the new executive chef of the restaurant refused to think about a new menu. *Why change a winning formula?* he loved to ask. It had been a long time since Robin had last gotten free rein like this.

Despite the small town and the excessive holiday cheer, she enjoyed working in the bakery. It was nice to return to something familiar: a home away from home. She no longer had to long for normality because it was here, in the way her hands moved deftly around the kitchen. For the first time, she realised she didn't have to remain stagnant to be comfortable. She didn't feel lost or wandering. More so, since she wasn't sweating in a chef's hat while a million different people yelled at her to hurry up. Everything she loved had followed her to Canada. It left her wondering if she had outgrown her old restaurant job. Maybe it was time to branch out to new things. Not here, obviously, but there must be a cosy bakery in Manchester *somewhere* that would appreciate her recipes as much as Hazel did.

'I'm glad you like them.' Robin beamed, cutting the tray of blondies into symmetrical squares. Another busy spell had rolled around out front, and with it being mid-afternoon, this one probably wouldn't end anytime soon.

Behind her, Hazel blew out a breath and tightened the scrunchie fastened around her brown curls. 'Here we go again.'

They fell into their respective duties with an ease Robin had never found before. Hazel assisted the customers and Robin served the orders. The coffee machine hissed at her every time she made a cappuccino, and she had no idea how to froth the milk properly in the steamer, but she hadn't received any complaints yet.

In fact, nothing bothered her. She had no time to think or worry, and the flow was rhythmic and pleasant and . . . fun. Locals complimented her baking, leaving tips in the tinsel-wrapped mason jar by the cash register. Other than having to listen to the same five cheery Christmas songs playing from the old-fashioned jukebox by the slightly wonky Christmas tree, she could have seen herself enjoying working here – in another life, at least.

'You're a natural at this, you know,' Hazel praised once the queue of customers shortened again. 'You said you were a pastry chef?'

Robin nodded, wiping the crumbs from the counter with a damp cloth. 'At a restaurant.'

'In England?'

'Yep. Good ol' Manchester.'

'Too bad you live so far away. We could really use you here.'

She wasn't sure what to say to that. Though Robin had found something special here, she couldn't imagine uprooting her entire life for it. She wasn't that brave, for starters, and her entire family, everything she knew, lived an ocean away. Her mother would never talk to her again if she moved so much as ten miles away, let alone thousands. She was ready for change; just perhaps not that much of it.

Still, though it wasn't something she'd ever dreamed about before, she could suddenly imagine owning a place like this herself one day: maybe in the Northern Quarter where all the cool, indie shops were. She would walk in every morning to the smell of cinnamon and spend her days piping out colourful frosting.

Those hippie-type people in their early twenties would banter with her across the counter until they became regulars, or maybe a social media influencer with millions of Instagram followers would post a picture of one of Robin's pretty cakes and the place would take off overnight. Fancy folk who "brunched" would find her, too – footballers and successful business types who never had to be in the office, perhaps – and parents who would sit and gossip over iced coffees for hours while their babies gurgled happily in their prams. And she could paint the walls pastel, or maybe hire a local artist to create some murals to make it unique. And in summer, she could make some of her sorbets and have a little ice cream cart . . .

She was getting a bit too ahead of herself there, though. Running a business required money, and Robin didn't have many savings. Half of them had been blown on this bloody trip, the other half on the wedding that never was – most of which had been non-refundable. Besides, the bank wouldn't give her a loan, would they? She had no idea how to start a business. She wouldn't even know who to call about trying. And Britain didn't get reliable enough weather to shell out on an ice-cream cart, so that proved she wasn't clever enough to make good business decisions.

Deflated by her plunge back into reality, Robin shrugged apologetically. 'If they invent teleportation devices soon, I'll think about it.'

'Well, we just opened another branch in Calgary. I'm sure my manager would love to have you on board if you *did* decide you'd like to stay in Canada.'

Calgary. Other than the airport, Robin had never seen the city properly and had no real idea of how she'd like it. She could check it out on the way home if she wanted. Which she didn't. At all. Not even a little bit. 'Maybe. I can't see myself moving across the Atlantic anytime soon, though.'

'Not even for cakes and a pretty skier who is clearly smitten with you?'

Heat flushed across Robin's cheeks – and didn't stop there. She was sweating all over a second later.

'Sorry. You can tell me to shut my big mouth,' Hazel continued, grinning wryly. 'I just think . . . well, you shine here. Do you shine in Manchester?'

Robin wasn't even sure what Hazel meant by "shine". She didn't think she'd ever *shone* anywhere, Manchester or otherwise, unless it was the shine of perspiration and humiliation. No, she fit in quite well with the dingy grey streets and the one-legged pigeons of Piccadilly Gardens. 'No. In Manchester I stand in a packed kitchen, sweating my arse off and praying my soufflés don't sink.'

Hazel snorted. 'Do you enjoy it?'

'Not as much as I used to,' she admitted. 'Working in a bakery is a lot more fun than I expected, though. Maybe it *is* time for a change. Not a transatlantic move, mind, but . . . a change.'

'So you'll do it again tomorrow?'

'Maybe.' If not for the fact that she only had a week with Neve, she might have jumped at the chance.

'And the day after? I'll give you a gigantic Christmas bonus.'

'We'll see.' A bit of extra money wouldn't be the worst

thing in the world, especially since she was actually enjoying the work. Hazel had already insisted that Robin would be paid the bakery's full wage with tips, and it was almost the same hourly rate she was paid at the restaurant.

'I'm taking that as a "yes", so you can keep the apron,' Hazel teased. 'I hope Neve won't mind that I'm stealing you away.'

Before Robin could reply, they were interrupted by another customer, who ordered two cups of hot chocolate to go. While Hazel tended to them, Robin took a tray and began clearing some of the empty tables. Hazel startled her, appearing seemingly from nowhere, not long after.

'So, what *is* going on with you and Neve? Is it a holiday thing? 'Cos I have to admit, I haven't seen Neve dating in a very, very long time. She's a little bit of a lone wolf.'

'*Jesus.* Do you do that a lot?' Robin pressed a dramatic hand to her chest and took a moment to steady her breathing. 'It's . . . a long story. We're just taking things as they come, I suppose.'

Not that long, since Robin had known the woman for about a week, but she didn't know how to explain their connection aloud without sounding a little bit bonkers and far too whipped. Still, curiosity niggled at her. She didn't know anything about Neve's love life, despite the fact Neve knew everything about Robin's.

'Have you hung out with her brother much?'

'I met Nick at the bar before I met Neve.' Upon noticing Hazel's violent blush, Robin raised an amused eyebrow. 'Why? Want me to put in a good word?'

'*No.*' Hazel distracted herself by straightening up one of the poinsettia centrepieces. Even so, she wasn't playing it nearly as cool as she thought. Robin could see it written all over her face. 'I don't even know what you mean. I was only making conversation about our mutual friends.'

'*Wow.* You are not subtle at all.'

'What?' A timid, innocent smile danced on Hazel's lips.

'You're practically in love with the guy. I saw how you looked at him at the concert the other night.'

'All right, fine.' Hazel huffed and rolled her eyes, tying and untying the strings of her apron nervously. 'I'm not *in love* with him, though. I just . . . well, you know. I'm only human and he's . . . you know.'

Robin did know – or could at least see how anyone that way inclined might take a liking to the ruggedly handsome bartender. Both he and Neve shared chiselled, interesting features, but to the outward eye, Nick was softer, friendlier, warmer. The sort of person you knew you could trust with any secret just by looking at them. Easy to get along with.

'Have you never asked him out?'

Hazel pressed her lips together and blew out a *pfft*. 'No. I see the women he flirts with. He brings half of them in here.'

'And?'

'And I am just the flustered, simpering idiot who spills hot drinks on him and talks in monosyllables to avoid saying something embarrassing.'

Oh, Hazel had it *bad*. Robin knew that feeling. She'd had it with almost everyone, whether she was attracted to them or not. The only problem was that she never did seem to avoid embarrassing herself.

Sympathy softened her, and she eyed Hazel again. Her beauty might have been more subtle than the blonde woman Nick had been flirting with on the rink, but it was there all the same . . . and looks aside, Robin wasn't sure anyone could *not* love the baker. After only two meetings, Robin already felt comfortable with her. Hazel had a unique ability to lift spirits – like sunshine after a summer of non-stop rain. A bit like Nick in that department.

'You're selling yourself short,' Robin scolded. 'You're wonderful, and Nick would be lucky to have you. How long has this been going on?'

'Oh, I don't know . . . I was a teenager when I met him, which I suppose immediately put me in the weird "sister's friend" zone.' At Robin's slack jaw, Hazel defended herself quickly. 'Don't! I'm more the admire from afar type . . . in a completely non-creepy way. And he had a girlfriend for a while. Some things aren't meant to happen, even if you'd like them to. Besides, I have my hands full with this place and Margo right now. There's no way anything will ever happen, even if Nick paid any attention to me.'

Robin had tuned out halfway through the excuses, having already decided that a little bit of meddling was long overdue. Had Neve honestly sat in this bakery for years, watching while Hazel struggled and Nick remained clueless? She almost tutted at the idea. They clearly needed help.

'Oh, come on. It'll only take one taste of your cake.'

'He's already tasted my . . .' Hazel trailed off, face glowing even redder. 'Oh. That was a euphemism.'

Robin waggled her brows suggestively. 'I am an excellent wing woman. I'll have you wed by the time I leave.'

'No, Robin—'

But Robin wasn't listening. She sauntered back into the kitchen, where a tall pile of dirty dishes awaited her, and began to scheme.

Chapter Twelve

'What are you doing?' Neve asked.

Robin had doubled in height. Mostly because she had stepped onto one of the benches outside the bar and now held her phone at an odd angle, her tongue stuck out.

'Your face will freeze that way if you're not careful, you know.' So Gran had always told Neve whenever she was particularly moody, at least.

'I'm taking a selfie!' explained Robin. 'Get in with me!'

'No.' Neve wasn't in the mood to have her photograph taken – but then, that was nothing new. She wasn't in the mood for much at all. Her day on the slopes had been tedious to say the least, and all she really wanted was to crawl into bed and watch a movie. But instead, she had met Robin for a drink at the resort's bar after her third shift at the bakery – which Robin hadn't shut up about for even a second since starting out. They'd been squeezing their ski lessons in first thing, though they at least got their evenings together.

'Grumpy. You sound like my mum.' Robin pouted and lowered her phone before hopping down from the bench. 'I haven't posted anything to my Instagram yet. I needed to make sure I get at least one decent picture.'

'God forbid you go on vacation without posting it all over social media.' With a grumble, Neve pushed open the door to the bar, treading snow into the old floorboards as she made her way to the stools. Nick gave her a nod, though he was too busy with a group of customers to approach.

Behind her, Robin sighed. 'Is something wrong?'

'No.' Neve took a seat, scraping her hair back. Her scalp

itched from her ski helmet, and she felt grimy and wrong somehow, like she wanted to crawl out of her skin.

'Are you hungry?'

'I don't know.'

'We can find somewhere to get tea. Sorry, dinner. Keep forgetting I'm in Canada.'

'I think I'm just going to wait for Nick to finish his shift and take me home.' Neve barely cast Robin a sidelong glance as she sat down beside her. Neve was afraid that if she did, she'd never stop looking at her. Or worse, she'd realise that she was being silly and pushing Robin away. It wasn't as though they didn't have time, still. Robin didn't leave for another five days yet. The days were just passing too quickly.

'Fine,' Robin muttered. 'I'll leave you to it.'

Maybe Neve should have let her go. It would have been easier for them both if she did. But she was selfish, and the moment Robin slid off the bar stool, her heart wrenched, and she couldn't keep from catching her wrist before it was too late. 'No. Don't go.'

Robin's forehead wrinkled with confusion. 'Then *talk* to me. Tell me what you want. We can go back to my cabin if you want. Order pizza. Get in the hot tub.' Her brows lifted suggestively at that.

All of those things sounded better than wallowing in bed. Neve nodded weakly and let Robin pull her back out of the bar by the hand. Nick still had an hour left of his shift, and Neve could always get a cab home later. She'd left Juniper with Grandpa today. He'd been quiet and glassy-eyed this morning and Neve suspected he needed the company. Neve had days like that, too, where missing Gran was all she could do. She wondered if it would ever get easier.

'If you need to talk about anything, I'm here,' Robin said gently as they traipsed their boots through the thick snow.

Robin's patience and gentle tone made Neve feel awful in comparison, especially with the white-hot jealousy coiling around her gut. 'It's nothing. I'm being silly.'

'Well, that makes a change. Usually, I'm the silly one.'

That at least left Neve smirking. 'True.'

'You're not supposed to agree.' Robin nudged her playfully and then shuffled closer so that their arms brushed together, steps syncing, as they made their way to the cabin. It was so easy when it was like this.

Or it would have been if Neve could shut her brain up for long enough.

'What's wrong, Neve?' Robin asked again. 'Please tell me. I can see the cogs in your brain going. I get enough silent treatment from my bloody mum. I can't stand it from you, too.'

Neve gulped down a deep breath. She hadn't meant to give the silent treatment. She just didn't know how to open her mouth without letting all of her worries spill out. 'Nothing's wrong. I just . . . I don't know if I should go home to check on Grandpa. I think he was a little sad this morning.'

'We can go together. I can cheer him up with cake.'

Neve kicked up the snow, thrusting her hands in her pockets and humming an absent agreement.

''Kay, well, you're going to have to help me out here.' Robin's words sharpened with impatience, and Neve couldn't blame her. 'What aren't you telling me? Is this really about Artie?'

'Yes . . . No . . .' Shoulders sagging, Neve caved. 'I guess it just sucks that you'll be busy working now. It leaves us with less time together.'

'Well, you work all day, too.' Robin frowned.

'I know.'

'Do you want me to stop working at the bakery?'

'Of course I don't. I want you to do whatever it is that makes you happy. It's your vacation.' It was the truth. If the bakery made Robin happy, Neve didn't want to stop her from going. It was her own selfish want, need, that was upsetting her, not Robin's new interest. Everything always seemed to get in the way of their limited time, and she couldn't stop

162

noticing the seconds ticking by, a pendulum clock locked behind her ribs, each swing reverberating through her bones.

'It's no different than it was before. We still have ski lessons and our evenings together. Nothing's changed.'

She peeled her gloved hand from Robin's, chewing on the inside of her cheek. 'Right. You're right. I told you I was being silly.' She shouldn't have said anything. She *wished* she hadn't said anything. But something else niggled at her. 'What did you mean about your mom giving you the silent treatment? Is she still not talking to you?'

Robin blew out a breath, seeming to relax. Her hand slipped back into Neve's as they continued towards the cabin. 'No. She won't answer my calls or texts.'

'Why?' Anger fizzled in Neve on Robin's behalf. The sadness written across her features . . . she didn't deserve it, whatever had caused it. 'I mean, I get why you travelling might make her anxious, but . . . this is extreme.'

Her throat bobbed. 'My dad died in a car accident on the way home from one of his trips. It was really sudden and unexpected. Now, every time anyone leaves the house, she worries. Because Wren moved in with her boyfriend, I usually bear the brunt of it. But it doesn't feel fair. If she's so worried, why doesn't she pick up the phone?'

Neve shook her head, speechless. It seemed like Robin's mom was the opposite of Neve's: overbearing to the point of cruelty. And yet it left them both in that same, uncomfortable space where they had to question how loved they were. Robin's mom should have been proud of her. She was a good, bright person doing her best. Living her life. That wasn't a crime worthy of punishment.

'I'm sorry.' Neve stopped again, tugging Robin closer and placing her hand on her round hip. 'You don't deserve to feel bad for doing something for yourself. And making you feel the same way is the last thing I want. It's your vacation, Robin. You deserve to enjoy every minute of it. And I'm glad that you are. You were so sad when you got here and now . . .'

It was true. Robin had shed old skin these last few days. No more crying over shrunken coats or getting too drunk to stand. She was still a terrible skier, of course, but aside from that . . . she seemed happy. Neve could only hope she'd had something to do with it.

'Now you just sparkle,' Neve finished quietly, bashfully.

'I do feel very sparkly.' Robin's lips spread into a sad smile, their visible breaths mingling as she leaned closer. 'And I am enjoying every minute of it. Especially the ones I spend with you.' She cupped Neve's jaw, placing a careful kiss on the tip of her nose. Neve almost melted. 'Anyway, I pinched some of the leftovers from the bakery. Want to pig out on cake in the cabin?'

She chuckled. 'Yes. Absolutely.'

Robin made to pull away, but Neve held her back, desperate for one last moment – and all the ones that would come after. They had time, still. Robin was here. Neve would appreciate whatever they had left, as long as it made her happy.

As long as she could kiss her for a little bit longer.

'Is everything okay with you and Robin? You seemed tense earlier.'

Neve had been sitting at the bar for a grand total of two seconds when Nick asked the question, eyeing her warily as he finished polishing off the pint glasses.

'Not that it's any of your business, but everything is fine.' She glared, resting her chin in her hands. 'Can we just drop it and go home, please?' She slid off the stool and tucked her hat back onto her head, looking anywhere but at her brother. She didn't want to see sympathy or judgement or whatever else swam in his eyes. 'You should come round for a bit tonight. Grandpa's been all distant and lonely again recently.'

'Yeah, sure. You know, if you're as miserable as you look, it's probably a sign,' Nick pointed out, but drew on his coat all the same.

'A sign of *what*?'

'That you give a damn. Don't ruin it, Neve. If you care about her, don't push her away. You'll regret it when she's gone. Believe me, I should know.'

The words surprised Neve enough to still. She hadn't known Nick felt that way – and why should he? Molly had been awful. She'd expected him to uproot his life for her and left him without hesitation when he couldn't. 'Do you regret not going to New York with Molly?'

'*No*, I'm not saying that.' He tightened his scarf around his neck like a coat of armour. His eyes were narrowed: defensive. They were too alike sometimes.

'Then what *are* you saying?'

'I just . . .' He shifted and stamped his shoe into the wood floors, looking anywhere but at Neve. 'I wonder sometimes if I made the right decision. I mean, look at me. I'm a thirty-four-year-old bartender, and that's about all I have to show for my life. I might never find a real purpose or another person.'

Neve sighed, softened. She'd had no idea he thought that way. Bartending was all he'd ever done, and she just assumed he enjoyed it. But maybe he didn't. Maybe he'd been trapped by it because he'd had no choice. Because he'd had a sister to take care of when Mom was away, and that meant he'd had no time to explore other options. They'd needed food on the table. He'd provided it. 'Molly wasn't right for you. You know that.'

'Maybe there is no right and wrong.' He shook his head, a muscle in his jaw ticking. 'I loved her, Neve. For a while there, I loved her. I know she had her flaws, and, hell, I had mine, but . . . I want to feel that way again. I want to at least know I *could* feel that way for somebody again. So, yes, maybe I regret not giving us more of a chance. And so will you if you don't let Robin in.'

She and Robin were nothing like Nick and Molly. Still, Nick's words left her stomach uneasy for more than one reason. That Nick would have been willing to settle for a woman who only ever treated him like dirt, yes, but also because . . . well. Neve, in her paradoxical fashion, was preparing for it to end when she should have been enjoying the little time they had left together.

'Are you unhappy?' she forced herself to ask.

'No,' he murmured softly. 'No, I'm not unhappy. It's not that I wish things were different with Molly, not really. I just have to wonder why I didn't go with her sometimes. New York is full of opportunities. I'm worried I'm too comfortable in the same routine, the same damn bar. But I don't know what else could come next anymore, and that's scary.'

Neve could barely remember the conversations they'd had when Molly gave him the ultimatum. She'd been locked away in her own grief and she hadn't liked Molly enough to push Nick. But maybe that had been selfish.

'Why *did* you choose not to go with her?' she asked.

He scratched the back of his head as though he didn't know himself. 'Honestly? I don't know. I've just spent so long feeling as though . . .' He struggled for the words, and guilt wormed its way into Neve's gut.

'Say it. Feeling as though what?'

'Feeling as though everybody needed me to be stable. Steady. The opposite of Mom. I worried that if I moved away, you would think I was like her, and so would Grandpa and Gran.'

A part of her had worried that would be the answer, because it was also part of the reason she'd quit the team. She'd hated Mom for travelling for so long that it felt hypocritical to do the same, especially when it meant leaving Grandpa to grieve alone. But to think she was the reason Nick had held back . . .

It was the last thing she wanted. It made her feel as selfish as she had when Robin had told her about the bakery. Like she was trying to cling on to her entire world to keep it from ever going away or growing. This fear of abandonment . . . she'd had no idea how rooted it was in her and Nick until now.

'I didn't know,' she breathed, her brows drawing together. 'Nick . . . you did so much for me as a kid. You took care of me. You were always there.'

His eyes fluttered closed, his hand finding hers. She squeezed, knowing then that he wasn't just a brother. He'd been a replacement mom and a best friend, and after Gran died, he'd been the one to hold them all together, cooking her favourite meals and organising the funeral and making sure Grandpa was okay. All this time, he'd had to be everything to other people. Neve couldn't imagine how exhausting it was.

'You have to start doing things for yourself now,' she continued. 'I love you and of course I always want you here, but if you think there's something else out there . . .'

'That's the thing. I just don't know. Clement Falls is home, and I don't want to leave. I just don't know where to go from here. I don't have any plans. I was never supposed to be a bartender for the rest of my life, but . . . what else is there?'

'I don't know. But we'll figure it out,' Neve vowed. 'You'll find what's right for you. Just don't feel like you have to hide it. I want to take care of you, too, even if you are a pain in the ass.'

He scoffed, nudging her, but appreciation widened his smile. 'Thanks. Shall we get going?'

She nodded. She remained silent as they prised themselves away from the warmth of the dimly lit bar. As her feet sank in the snow and, after getting into Nick's car, the resort fell away in the rear-view mirror, her brother's words niggled at her like a repetitive Christmas carol.

Because she *did* give a damn about Robin, and she didn't want to keep making the same mistakes. She couldn't be afraid for the rest of her life. 'Could we make a stop at Irina's on the way home?' she asked, mind already milling over ideas. 'I need to ask her for a favour.'

* * *

It had been years since Neve had walked the narrow, well-gritted path up to Irina's cabin. She lived on the outskirts of the woods not far from the resort in a secluded, small house that made Neve restless with nostalgia. So many memories teemed around this place. Irina hadn't just been her instructor, but, in many ways, like a substitute mother. Neve would come here for dinner after lessons or help weed her garden for extra pocket money in the summer.

It made her feel sick to think she'd been avoiding somebody so important to her all this time. Almost like she was no better than Mom.

She gave a weary knock on the wooden door, frozen icicles shaking on the portico in the mild breeze. The sound of approaching footsteps followed, and then the door opened and Irina poked her head out.

Surprise crinkled across her features. 'Neve?'

'Hi.' Neve shifted from foot to foot, wondering if she'd made a mistake. Irina had every right to tell her to get lost.

But she didn't. She stepped aside. 'Come in, stranger.'

Neve did, greeted by warmth and the smell of Irina's pine-scented reed diffuser. The house looked exactly as it used to: pictures of Irina's students littered the small corridor below those of Irina herself, grinning in ski gear while proudly holding all sorts of medals. Neve was in one of them, from her first ever competition in Calgary. She'd come third, and Gran had been so excited when she got to stand on the podium to receive her bronze trophy.

'What can I do for you? Finally changed your mind about the team?' Irina led her into the living room, where two flattened old couches drooped around a table with a steaming mug of coffee on a coaster. She motioned for Neve to sit, so she did.

'No. I was actually hoping for a favour.'

'I'll do you any favour,' Irina said as she sank back on the couch opposite Neve with a steady gaze, 'if you talk to me about skiing first.'

Neve narrowed her eyes. She'd known it wouldn't be easy. Irina was stubborn, not one to drop anything as long as she felt strongly about it. Probably the reason Neve had turned out similar. 'There's not much to say.'

'Exactly. You just keep throwing it all away. All that potential, all the things you could do.'

She clenched her hands together tightly in her lap. 'That's my choice.'

'I invested enough time and energy into your training to deserve to know why. You were one of the best students I've ever had, Neve. It eats at me at night, knowing you gave it up. So give me some peace. Tell me why.'

Frustration surged through her. She definitely shouldn't have come. 'I can't travel the way I used to. My grandpa needs me.'

Irina rolled her eyes. 'Bullshit. I've seen Artie out and about all over town. He's not a frail old man you have to coddle.'

'He's still grieving,' Neve replied, firmer now.

'That won't ever change. Are you going to put your life on hold forever?' A tilt of her head that made Neve want to shrink. Even now, Irina was impossibly intimidating. It was a good quality for an instructor, but not during a conversation like this one. Neve was sick of having to explain herself, her choices. Everybody else quit things all the time and the world kept turning. Mom had quit being a mom. Her friends quit college or their jobs. Nick had quit his relationship. Why couldn't she have the same luxury?

'I didn't come here to debate this with you.' She prepared to get up. 'I came for a favour. As a *friend*. Not an old student.'

Irina weighed her up for a moment. Neve had to look away. She couldn't stand the disappointment glistening in her dark eyes.

'Friends?' Irina scoffed. 'You've avoided me since the moment you came home.'

'Because our conversations go in circles. Like this one.' But Neve had hoped it could be different if she just put in the effort, extended the olive branch. She should have known better. 'So forget it.'

She stood up, tugging her hat over her ears. As she made to leave, Irina's voice stopped her. 'I see you on the slopes sometimes after lessons. It's still inside of you. Don't you regret it at all, Neve?'

Neve's heart sank, with her own pain and with Irina's. Perhaps some part of Irina had wanted to live out her success with her. After all, she had earned it just as much.

She turned around, her eyes stinging. All of her stinging. 'Yes.' She wasn't sure if she was talking about quitting, or the other thing, the thing she still couldn't face.

Irina opened her mouth, and Neve cut her off with a firm hand. 'Don't ask me why again. I already told you.'

'It'll never make sense to me.'

'It doesn't have to.' She let out an uncomfortable puff of breath. 'For what it's worth, I'm sorry that I broke our friendship. You meant a lot to me. You were like a *mother* to me. I just . . . I couldn't face you afterwards. You act like I don't know what I've given up, but I do. I know. I live with it. It's just not as easy to fix as you make it out to be.'

Irina lowered her gaze, dusting non-existent crumbs off her knees. 'I only ever pushed you so hard because I know, deep down, you're meant to be a skier. Not an instructor, Neve. That comes later, when you're old like me. You belong at the Olympics, and you were *so* close. I just want you to have the success you deserve.'

'I know.' Neve bit her lip. 'I appreciate everything you've done for me. I guess I really don't have a right to come here and ask you for more.'

She pondered that, standing up and stepping closer. 'No, you don't.' A sigh. 'But I suppose I can hear you out. What exactly does this favour entail?'

Neve grinned, gratitude bubbling in her. She almost wanted to hug her. Instead, she sat back down and explained exactly what she wanted.

Chapter Thirteen

Neve knew that something was wrong as soon as she stepped into the house. Juniper didn't greet her at the door as she usually did when Neve left her at home for the day, for starters, and then there was the fact that she could smell something burning.

If she hadn't been so concerned for Grandpa's wellbeing, she might have taken a moment to wonder why she had tripped over a neon pink suitcase on her way to the kitchen. As it was, the pieces only fell together when she barged in to find a tall, dark-haired woman hovering over their stove while Grandpa sat stiff-spined at the dining table.

Mom.

With the car accident and the fear of losing Juniper and the kiss with Robin and everything that had happened since, Neve had forgotten all about the conversation she'd had with her mother over the phone the other day. And even if she hadn't, she wouldn't have expected Mom to *actually* come home. With her long, sun-kissed legs and skyscraper-high Louboutins, she belonged in this kitchen about as much as Gran's old gemstones and tarot cards did. And yet, here they all were: Mom, the gemstones, and the tarot cards. The latter had been left out on the kitchen countertop since Gran's death, much like a lot of the things she'd owned. She had always insisted on doing her readings over a plate of scrambled eggs. Something to do with balancing chakras with breakfast food.

Maybe Neve should have listened to those damned cards and transferred some positive energy into them, the sort that would keep certain *negative* presences from entering the house.

She felt Nick's warmth at her back a moment later, and a wave of dread drowned her. She hadn't told him about the call when she'd had the chance. Would he hate her for it?

'*Mom?*' he asked, voice raspy with bewilderment.

'Oh!' Mom turned around with a wooden spoon in her hand and a bright, white-toothed grin on her face. 'You're both finally home! We've been waiting all day.'

'Yes,' Grandpa said, peering disapprovingly over his glasses. 'We have.' And then, to Neve, because they were the only two people who had stopped putting up with Mom and her bullshit, he mouthed, '*Save me.*'

Neve's main concern was her missing husky, though, and she glanced around, half-expecting to find her cowering under a table. 'Where's Juniper?'

'That *dog*!' Mom clucked her tongue, flicking her curls over her shoulder. 'She got her muddy paws all over my favourite dress, so I let her outside until she learns to behave. You really should start training her, Neve.'

Clenching her jaw, Neve marched over to the door and let Juniper in. She had been trained by Gran from being a pup. *All dogs* got a little excited when someone new entered the house.

Sopping wet, Juniper wandered in with her ears back and her tail between her legs. Still, she perked up when Neve crouched to her level.

'I know, baby,' she cooed sympathetically. 'What did that mean lady do to you?'

'I just . . . I can't believe you're here.' Nick blinked, stunned, and then hugged Mom tightly. Mom chuckled into his shoulder, keeping the embrace brief. She wasn't one for affection, unless it was for the wealthy businessmen she liked to seduce in hotels. 'Why didn't you tell us you were coming?'

'I wanted it to be a surprise!'

'And a surprise it was,' Grandpa grumbled. Neve stopped

fussing over Juniper to put a reassuring hand on his shoulder. Mom hadn't just abandoned her kids, but her dad, too. Even when Gran had died, she'd only come home for two days to attend the funeral before disappearing again.

'How long are you staying?' Nick quizzed. 'Will you be here for the holidays?'

'That's the plan!' She was too animated, too . . . false. The red-lipstick-painted smile on her face was so taut that it looked as though it might crack open her cheeks. 'Maybe even longer!'

Neve's brows knitted together as she tried to work out why. Regardless, her main concern wasn't Mom's strange change of heart. It was Nick. His face gleamed with joy, and it left nausea writhing in Neve's gut.

'Amazing.' He beamed, keeping hold of Mom's shoulders as though she might run away otherwise. Neve wouldn't put it past her. 'It's so great to have you home.'

'Well, I'm just glad that *someone* is happy to see me.' Mom's green eyes flashed over to Neve sharply.

Neve couldn't help but scowl at the less-than-subtle jab. 'Do you expect anything less?'

'*Neve*,' Nick scolded.

Grandpa only lifted his hand to Neve's, tracing his coarse thumb in soothing circles across her skin. He understood her in a way nobody else could. She didn't know why – he was patient where she wasn't, kind where she never had been – but it was a comfort that not everybody in this kitchen made her out to be the enemy merely for being apprehensive. Hell, she deserved to be apprehensive. Furious, even. This was the first woman who had broken her heart; the first person who had made her realise that the people who brought her into this world wouldn't always make her feel loved and safe or even important. And on the rare occasion Mom decided to show up, Neve was expected to pretend otherwise for the sake of a couple of days of forced conversation and false happy families? She wasn't *that* good at acting.

'Enough of that, anyway. I've made us all dinner!' Mom beamed.

'Don't eat it,' Grandpa warned in Neve's ear, and then mimicked himself gagging with his fingers down his throat.

Strangely enough, Neve had never intended to – especially since whatever it was had made her kitchen reek of charred fish. 'I'm not hungry,' she said. 'I'm going to catch an early night.'

Mom tutted and began ladling out something thick and goopy into the bowls set out on place mats on the kitchen table. 'No, you'll sit and eat with us. I learned this recipe in Barcelona, you know. It has prawns: your favourite.'

That at least accounted for the odour.

'I'm allergic to shellfish.' It didn't surprise Neve in the slightest that Mom hadn't remembered.

'Nonsense. I used to make lobster casserole for you all the time!'

Speechless for a moment, Neve parted her lips and then closed them before choking out, 'In which parallel universe?'

'Well, you can have the rice.' Mom shovelled a heap of plain white rice onto Neve's plate. Her eyes set firmly on Neve's as she ordered, 'Sit.'

Neve did, if only to find out why Mom was here, slumping into the chair beside Grandpa and tickling Juniper's chin beneath the table. For a moment, she was tempted to eat the prawns in the ominous thick soup. Anaphylactic shock would surely be a good enough reason to get out of this house, wouldn't it?

Nick cleared his throat and cast Neve a warning glance as he sat down, too, chair legs screeching against the tiles. Mom sat last, wiping her hands on a frilly apron – Robin's, she realised. She'd left it here the other night.

'So. This is nice, isn't it?'

Neve choked down a scoff. Mom might have paid the occasional visit, but she had never tried *this* hard, with a home-cooked meal and false pleasantries. Neve was surprised she even know how to use the oven – though judging from the smell, it hadn't turned out too successfully. Still, the fact she wasn't already boasting about a new boyfriend or a scuba diving trip in the Maldives was suspicious enough. 'What are you doing here, Mom?'

'I told you. I wanted to see you all.'

'Right. But *really*. You hate the cold and you never stay for the holidays. What's going on? Bad break-up? Low on cash?'

'*Neve*—' Nick began again, but Mom's low, shaky words soon cut him off.

'I've been made redundant.' She clasped her hands together at the table as though about to say grace. Her perfect composure wobbled just slightly.

Of course. Why else would Mom have been here if not because there was nowhere else *to* be? Perhaps Neve should have felt sympathy, but Mom's sombre expression only seemed to leave acid burning on her tongue.

'That explains it, then.' She hated that even now, disappointment still bled into her voice. It would always feel like the first time, the first let-down, the first realisation that she wasn't a good enough reason for Mom to stick around.

Brows drawn together sympathetically, Nick reached out for Mom's hand across the table. Always the better person. The *best* person.

And Neve would always be the worst, because instead of pushing her personal feelings aside, instead of supporting her mother through a tough time, she stood up and glared. 'Is that it, then? We can stop pretending that you're happy to see us and we're happy to see you, now?'

She didn't wait for a reply or a scolding from Nick, instead heading straight up the stairs to her room with Juniper following at her heels. She had no interest in spending time with a woman who would leave again as soon as she was able to. No interest in investing her heart into someone who had never wanted it. She didn't care what kind of person that made her.

A knock sounded at her bedroom door before she even had the time to shrug off her coat. She knew who it would be – or at least, who it wouldn't.

'Yep?'

The handle turned, the door creaking open again on rusted hinges. Nick stood in the threshold, wreathed in the buttery light from the hallway. Concern left his face full of shadows.

'I don't want to hear it, Nick.' Neve shook her head and turned her back to him, frustration brimming from her chest and clogging her throat. She stepped out of her boots and pretended to be interested in the buttons of her cardigan. 'I *told* her not to come.'

'You *knew*?'

Neve bowed her head, ashamed. Not because of Mom, but because she'd kept a secret from Nick. 'She called me the other morning.'

'And you didn't think to tell me?'

'I stopped believing anything she says a long time ago, and so should you,' Neve snapped, and then instantly regretted it. It wasn't Nick's fault that he was *good*. He didn't deserve to bear the brunt of Neve's anger.

A sigh filled the room, and then she heard Nick's boots tread closer. 'I get it, Neve. You know I do. She caused us both a lot of pain growing up. But can't you just *try* while she's here?'

'So she can go back to comfortably ignoring our existence when she leaves again?' Neve mustered the courage to turn around, glad when her eyes remained dry. 'I tried for long enough. I'm done. I don't need her anymore. You can go downstairs and pretend everything's fine, but I can't, and I'm tired of you making me feel bad because of it.'

'I'm not *trying* to make you feel bad. I just wish it could be different. Maybe this time it *could* be different.' He scraped a hand through his hair in frustration, collapsing onto the corner of her bed. The sheets were still bunched and tangled from the night before. Neve was always too exhausted to make her bed in the morning, especially when she got up at the ass-crack of dawn.

She sniffed defiantly, keeping her eyes locked on a solitary rip in her pale blue wallpaper. 'I won't hold my breath.'

Silence fell, uncomfortable and suffocating. Mom was the only reason things were ever awkward between them, and Neve hated the rift slicing them apart. She hated Mom for causing it. She hated herself for making it worse.

Finally, Nick's shoulders heaved with a huff and he stood. Relief filled Neve. She thought he was going to leave, drop it, and she could go to bed without having to keep doing this.

But Nick didn't leave. Instead, he pulled her to his chest, the musky, bitter scent of the ski resort's bar embedded in his shirt. 'I don't want you to feel like I'm on her side.'

Neve nodded her head, but traitorous tears pricked her eyes – because she did. She felt as though she lost a piece of her brother whenever Mom was so much as mentioned in conversation, and it shouldn't *be* that way.

'I get it,' she said, though she didn't. Not really. 'You think she'll change.'

'I do.'

But nothing would change the days when Neve had just needed her mom: the day she'd started her first period and had to ask Gran, red-faced, what the hell she was supposed to do with a sanitary towel; the day she'd been injured in a ski competition, and a seventeen-year-old Nick had had to sit with her in the emergency room for hours on end when he should have been at a party with his friends; when Gran had died and Neve had had to hold Grandpa together while no one held her.

Mom could make all the exotic prawn soups in the world, but it wouldn't make up for the things Neve had lost, and looking at her, seeing her downstairs in the kitchen, in Neve's *home* . . . it was just a reminder of that heartache. Neve didn't need it. She didn't want it. She would rather have nothing at all than an occasional, fleeting visit just because Mom had nothing better to do.

At least for now, Neve had other things to focus on. Robin, for instance.

Just so that she can leave in the end, too, Neve reminded herself. But she didn't want to think about that again tonight. She would cross that bridge when she came to it.

And between England and Canada, it would have to be one hell of a long bridge.

Chapter Fourteen

The thick haze of sleep had barely left Robin when she was startled by a rap at the door. Her hair was still damp from showering and she had to rush to pull on her jumper. She hoped to God it was the cleaner – her damp towels and old clothes were strewn all over the place, not to mention the brownie crumbs that had accidentally melted into the ribbed material of the armchair. The brown stain was sure to look suspiciously like something else.

It wasn't the cleaner. It was Neve who greeted her with the frosty cold. Neve, and Juniper by her side.

The husky stepped forward to lick Robin's hand in greeting, her tail wagging impatiently as she waited for attention.

'Hello, Juni-poo,' Robin cooed, kneeling down to hug her properly.

'Still not a thing,' Neve deadpanned, though her lips twitched with a smile.

'Juni-poo disagrees.' The morning air began to bite at Robin's toes, and she folded one socked foot over the other to shield them. Looking down at the pyjama bottoms she still wore, she grimaced. 'Sorry. I'm running late. Give me a minute to change.'

'Jeans will be fine today.'

'Oh?' She frowned in confusion, and then realised that Neve, too, wore black jeans and casual combat boots rather than the thermal snowsuit she usually conquered the slopes with.

A cunning grin curled across Neve's lips, puzzling Robin even more – and sending a hot lick of fire through her. 'Don't ask questions.' She revealed a bag that she'd been hiding behind her back, and it rustled in the breeze. 'You can wear your new coat. Shoes are usually a good idea, too.'

Robin raised her eyebrows. 'You bought me a new coat?'

'A replacement for Cara, may she rest in peace.'

Robin took the bag and peered inside, a swell of emotions rushing over her. The coat was the same powder blue as Cara, only a smooth wool blend rather than the teddy style, with fleece lining the inside that would keep her twice as warm. She tried to fight the tears stinging her eyes as she lifted her gaze to Neve. 'It's so lovely. Thank you, Neve. You really didn't have to.'

Neve shrugged as though it meant nothing. As though everybody was this kind, this thoughtful. Robin couldn't help but remember last winter, when Lexi had thrown on a denim jacket for Manchester's Christmas light switch-on. Robin had swapped Cara the coat with the too-small jacket when Lexi had gotten too cold halfway through, ever the good fiancée. She'd spent the rest of the night freezing while it poured down with rain, her teeth chattering, but Lexi didn't mind. She was warm, and that was all that mattered.

Neve couldn't have known how much it meant to be thought of like this.

'Go and try it on,' she nudged.

With a new spring in her step, Robin ran into her bedroom, slipping on her jeans, snow boots, and the new coat. It fit her perfectly, double-breasted and reaching her knees. She didn't dare look at the label to see how much it had cost.

Outside the window, the promise of snow lingered with the swollen white clouds draped like garlands across the mountain, and the wind was sharp as bullets even inside the cabin, so she made sure to wrap herself in her thickest scarf before plonking her bobble hat onto her head and, finally, her gloves.

She wandered back into the living room, where Neve and Juniper waited by the couch. She twirled for her audience and then struck a pose that was somewhere between a broken-winged penguin and a flamingo. 'Do you like it?'

Neve smiled, all dimples and glistening eyes. 'It matches your eyes. Does it fit okay?'

'It's perfect. Really. And so warm.' She snuggled into the fleece collar to prove it, and then hugged Neve tightly. 'Thank you.'

Neve chuckled, her breath brushing the shell of Robin's ear. 'You're welcome.' She pulled away only to place a soft kiss on Robin's nose. 'Shall we go?'

She extended her free hand to Robin, and Robin took it eagerly. Her heart floated with joy, excitement, as she locked up the cabin with one hand and the two – three, if they counted Juniper – set off in the complete opposite direction to the slopes.

'You're not going to push me into a lake or something, are you?'

'Nah. I'll save that for tomorrow,' teased Neve.

'Anything to keep me in Canada for longer.' When Neve didn't laugh, Robin frowned. 'Are you okay?' She seemed distracted, more distant than usual, and a hint of panic sliced through Robin.

Neve squeezed her hand and pecked her on the cheek, and it was all the reassurance Robin needed. 'I'm perfect.'

Yes, you are, Robin almost replied.

She expected them to slip into the bar when they reached it, but it was closed at this hour and Neve continued to tug her along without so much as a second glance. And then the furthest rows of cabins appeared and disappeared, too, and the resort was left behind them.

Finally, just when Robin began to worry that they were lost in the vast, snowy tundra completely, a cluster of furry, four-legged figures appeared against the infinite white. 'Oh my God.'

'Don't worry. They're not wolves.' Neve stopped to untether Juniper from her lead, and the husky sprinted off to meet her canine friends lined up in front of a sledge. A dark-haired woman – the one from the first-aid room, Robin realised – greeted Juniper as though she was an old friend before hooking her up to the long reins connecting each of the dogs in turn.

'Are we going sledding?' Unbridled excitement and perhaps a little bit of anxiety bubbled in Robin's question, her grip on Neve's hand growing tighter with each step.

'Maybe.' The soft lines bracketing Neve's mouth deepened with pride, though, and Robin knew she was right. They were sledding. With dogs. While the sun began to rise. Robin might not have liked snow all that much, but the idea still sent shivers fluttering through her. Neve had done this for her. Neve had planned something special to make her happy.

It had worked.

'Juniper's raring to go today,' Irina observed when they finally reached her, amusement softening her gravelly, lilting voice.

'Always is,' Neve replied – and somehow, her voice seemed free of the rough stoniness it usually carried.

'How's the wrist?' Irina asked. The instructor couldn't have been much older than her mid-forties, with shoulder-length hair divided into two braids. Still, youthfulness twinkled in her brown eyes, the same way it did in Neve's when she'd just glided weightlessly across the mountains.

'Oh . . .' She'd almost forgotten about the disaster at all. While it sometimes throbbed a little, Robin had had far worse strains and certainly worse oven burns.

Considering she'd witnessed a hostile conversation between Irina and Neve not too long ago, she couldn't help but be wary as she replied, 'Much better. Thanks.'

Irina beamed, flashing a set of overlapping teeth. 'You must be a special one, for Neve to turn up on my doorstep after all this time.'

'*Irina.*' Neve rolled her eyes, but she didn't pull her hand away from Robin's, even when Robin's gaze flicked back to her in surprise.

'You set all this up?'

Neve shrugged modestly. 'You hate skiing. I thought this

might make a nice change – and hopefully pose less risk of injury.'

'I can't believe you did this for me,' Robin breathed, wonderstruck eyes glittering as they fell to each dog in turn. There were seven in total, with Juniper panting happily at the very front.

'All right.' Irina clapped her hands. 'Who's getting in first?'

The sledge barely looked big enough to fit both of them, but Neve climbed in with ease, setting her legs straight and motioning to the gap in the middle.

'Ready?' she asked when Robin's feet remained planted firmly where they were.

'Won't I squish you in there?'

Neve wrinkled her nose as though the question was absurd. 'It'll be fine. Cosy. Come on.'

Absently, Robin nodded, a prickle of heat creeping up her neck as she tried not to trip over Neve's legs. She'd fallen on her arse in front of her, for God's sake. She could sit between her legs without melting into a puddle of humiliation.

Neve's warmth was a roaring hearth against her back, their thighs brushing, breaths mingling. Robin had missed that unbreakable sense of closeness ever since last night, when they'd wandered around Clement Falls while Neve did some more Christmas shopping. She must have snuck the coat in while Robin had been picking up two cups of hot chocolate from the bakery.

If Neve was uncomfortable, she didn't show it, instead leaning into Robin as though it was the most natural thing in the world.

'Let's do this,' said Irina, stepping onto the back of the sledge. Robin could no longer crane her neck far enough to see her. The dogs in front barked eagerly, and then, spurred by Irina's bellowed orders, they were off.

The huskies dragged the sledge with ease, and all self-consciousness fell away as the powdery snow sprayed Robin's side and the world passed her by in flashes of white.

Ahead of her, the pink, rising sun bled through the trees, casting elongated shadows across the planes: fingers that were never quite able to grab them. They could outrun everything here. Nothing would ever catch them again.

It was magical. Every bit of it.

Robin sank further into Neve, something between a laugh and a sob building in her chest. Neve's arms wrapped around her, caging her in, her chin resting on Robin's padded shoulder. Robin could only shake her head as tears filled her eyes, wondering how this corner of the world, where so much warmth and wonder lived, had been kept hidden from her for so long. When their hands clasped, she wished she wasn't wearing gloves. Robin would gladly suffer frostbite if it meant feeling their fingers lacing, their skin brushing; if it meant feeling Neve with her. She wished she could see her face, her smile, her eyes drinking this in.

The sky flooded with amber as they sped further away from reality, from anything that had once tied Robin down. It was like a dream – one she never wanted to wake from.

She relaxed into Neve's chest and let the cool wind kiss her smile-swollen cheeks. 'This is the most perfect thing ever. Thank you.'

Neve's soft lips brushed against Robin's jaw and then fell to her neck: the only places she could reach in the confines of the sledge, swathed in winter clothes as they were. 'I'm sorry for being moody yesterday.'

'You're always moody. It's part of your charm.' The last time she had felt this strange blooming in her chest, it had almost broken her. It was terrifying, having wandered upon this unexpected thing without ever intending to. That Robin couldn't take Neve home, smuggle her into her suitcase with the souvenirs and gifts she'd bought, was a depressing thought, and one she'd been trying not to linger on for too long.

'I want to make the most of any time we have left,' mumbled Neve in her ear. 'Just you and me.'

'Please,' Robin begged, because she wanted nothing more.

'I just want this, now. I just want to pretend for a little while that I can keep you.'

'Deal.' Neve's kisses fell lower, to the side of her throat. She nudged Robin's hair out of the way to reach, and Robin's stomach turned to a fire ferocious enough to thaw the Albertan winter. They'd been taking it slow, and this was why. Robin was afraid she'd crumble under Neve's touch.

When Irina cleared her throat from behind, reminding them of her presence, they giggled and sat back again in the sledge; held one another and pretended. And with the wind melding them back together again and their bodies entangled, it was enough.

'So . . .' Irina began with a wry smirk, shredding the thick snow with her ski pole. 'You must tell me everything.'

Neve had come to the slopes to squeeze in some practice before her lessons started, and Irina had followed her, claiming to have lessons of her own. Robin hadn't been able to join – which Neve suspected she'd been glad about – since Hazel expected her at the bakery bright and early again. Juniper would be napping for the rest of the morning at the resort's front desk, probably while Helen complained of dog hairs moulting all over the rugs.

Neve was trying not to notice that the seconds ticked by much quicker when she and Robin weren't together. *I want to make the most of any time we have left*, she had begged on the sled. It hadn't been a lie. It was just easier said than done.

It didn't help that when Robin wasn't around, Neve had more time to think about her mother. Luckily, she'd been out the door too early to see her both today and yesterday morning, and it wouldn't be a surprise if she was gone by tonight. It was rare that Mom visited and even rarer she stayed. *Here's hoping she finds a new job before the New Year.*

'About what?' Neve shielded her eyes from the rising sun with her gloved hand. She was beginning to suspect that they wouldn't be doing much skiing at all.

'You know.' Irina fluttered her eyelashes and sang, '*Robin*.'

The flush that rose to Neve's cheeks at the mere mention of Robin was an inconvenience to say the least, and she looked away in an attempt to hide it, feigning interest in a couple stumbling disastrously off the rotating ski lift. 'I told you last night.'

'You told me that there was a girl you liked. You didn't tell me she was *British* and *cute*.'

'I didn't realise those things were pivotal pieces of information.'

Irina scoffed. 'Come on. In all the years I've known you, you've never made an effort like this for anyone.'

And it *had* been a lot of years. Neve had started skiing when she was eight, the same year Mom started working as a flight attendant and disappearing frequently. Nick had discovered a love of skating, and Gran wanted Neve to have something too. It was easy to convince her when they spent that winter watching the Winter Olympics in Torino together. Neve had been awed by the speed of the race and the way the skiers seemed to fly through the air without any tethers. Irina was the first and last instructor Neve had ever gotten, minus her team trainer, but it was Gran who had pushed in the first place.

She tried not to think about what Gran would think if she'd known Neve had quit – because of her death, no less. She'd probably be even more disappointed than Irina was.

'Well . . .' Neve shrugged, forcing nonchalance. 'I like her. Of course I like her. But that's all it is. She leaves in a few days, and I suppose I just wanted to make the most of it. Anyway, thanks again for helping me out so last-minute. Shall we ski?'

'No.' Irina placed a hand on Neve's shoulder before she could put on her goggles, a knowing look sparkling across her dark features. 'What are you going to do when she goes home?'

Neve sighed. She didn't want to have this conversation again, even with Irina. 'Nothing. It will be over. I guess it's a holiday fling.'

'I've had *plenty* of holiday flings. They usually don't involve anything that takes place outside of the bedroom.'

'That's too much information,' she groused, wrinkling her nose and fighting the urge to cover her ears. Still, Neve knew herself that this was more than just a little bit of fun. She and Robin had found an instant connection, and not just physically. In fact, they hadn't even explored *that* facet yet. They were so different, and it shouldn't have worked . . . but it just *did*.

Irina lifted her hands in surrender. 'I'm just saying. I know you. I know when you're in deep.'

Neve could only shake her head and try to unclench her jaw. But it had seized up, as tense as the rest of her, and she steeled herself against another barrage of apprehension. *Don't ruin this by overthinking*, she told herself. *It is what it is.*

Her discomfort must have been as palpable as it felt, because Irina changed the subject quickly. 'Other than *Robin*, what's the latest in the land of Neve, anyway? Any updates?'

Neve pushed down any thought of her mom. 'Nope, no updates. I'm just focusing on teaching.'

Irina pursed her lips. Like Nick, she was too good at seeing right through her. '*Neve*.'

'*Irina*,' Neve mimicked, kicking her skis through the snow defiantly. Strange how one moment, Irina was a friend ready to discuss holiday flings, and the next she was a mother scolding her child.

'You're hiding something. What? *Another* girlfriend?'

She snorted. 'No.'

'Then what?'

'Nothing.'

'Fine. Then I'll pester you about the ski team again instead.'

Neve puffed her cheeks out in frustration. 'I've been waiting for that.'

'Look, I know you've had a lot on your plate these last couple of years, but I'd hate to see you turn into a bitter old athlete who never took their shot. It feels like I need to put a rocket up your ass for you to see it. You've gotten complacent, and you'll live to regret it.'

Was that what Neve was? Complacent? It didn't feel that way. She'd just . . . lost something vital when Gran had died. Perhaps, with the death of one of the only consistent parental figures in her life, and seeing how it had affected Grandpa, too, she'd realised that everything she loved could be lost too easily. She had to cling to what little she had left.

'I'll think about trying for the team again. But *only* think about it,' she decided finally. It wasn't a lie. Neve *had* been thinking about the team since she'd talked about it with Robin. It would make her a hypocrite if she told Nick to find his dreams when she was still pushing away hers. She just didn't know if she was strong enough to try again now. It had been so long, and yet not long enough.

'That's your problem.' Irina rapped on Neve's helmet. 'Always thinking.'

Neve scowled without meaning to. Maybe she was tired of everybody telling her what her problem was. How she should open up more, be more forgiving and understanding, how she should just go for things as though it wasn't putting everything on the line. Was it so bad to protect herself? Not everything was as easy as people liked to make out.

'*Ooh*, don't give me that look, missus,' Irina crooned, gesturing with her ski pole.

'Shall we ski or are we going to stand here all day?' Neve dismissed, though her words came out harsher than she'd meant.

'Nope, that's my line.' Irina's pink, runny nose jutted into the air stubbornly. 'Something else is bothering you. Tell me. I don't like it when you're even moodier than usual.'

'I'm not moody,' Neve ground out impatiently. 'I'm just . . .'

Neve clamped her lips together, debating. But there was no keeping secrets from Irina. Once, Irina had made Neve stay out on the slopes for over an hour when Neve had shown up to her lesson tear-stricken. She'd only let up when Neve had finally admitted that she was upset because her best friend had stopped talking to her after a stupid argument about concert tickets. She'd been sixteen then, but she didn't doubt that Irina would still try to enforce the same authority now if she needed to.

'My mom is back in town, so I suppose I'm a little on edge,' she admitted finally.

Irina whistled through her teeth, though the sound was lost on the wind. As a frequent step-in, she was well aware of Mom's poor parenting skills over the years. 'Isn't she usually on a sun lounger somewhere exotic at this time of year?'

'Apparently the airline she works for made her redundant.'

'Ah, of course. She has nowhere else to go, so she comes back with her tail between her legs.'

'And prawn soup in her hand,' Neve agreed absently. She'd still been able to smell the burned, fishy concoction this morning – mostly because Mom hadn't bothered to clean out the pots and pans. They'd been left piled in the sink, still filthy, the smell strong enough that Neve had been one breath away from becoming a puffy-eyed chipmunk.

'Huh?'

'Nothing.' She shook her head and slid her goggles on. If they didn't start moving soon, she might start turning blue, and Neve still had four lessons to teach later. 'I'm just trying to stay clear of her until she finds somewhere better.'

'I don't blame you,' Irina agreed – and Mom was about the only thing they ever *did* agree upon. 'You don't owe that woman a thing. You know that, don't you?'

It was everything Neve had needed to hear, and she smiled softly as she readied herself at the top of the slope. She'd missed having somebody to talk to, regardless of how irritatingly persistent Irina was. 'I know. Thanks, Irina.'

'All right.' Irina adjusted her gloves, the Velcro crackling, and then got into position a few metres from Neve. 'No more chit-chat. Let's ski.'

And finally, they did.

Chapter Fifteen

Robin's peppermint-glazed cheesecake went down a treat that afternoon. Clement's Cakes brimmed with school children celebrating the final day of term with sugar, sugar, and more sugar, and there seemed to be even *more* holiday decorations up now than there had been before. At least, Robin didn't remember garrotting herself on quite so many pieces of tinsel as she paced between the kitchen and the front counters yesterday.

She was so rushed off her feet that she didn't even notice Neve and Nick arrive until she heard the familiar, gruff voice of the latter. She lifted her focus from the frothing milk she was steaming to find them both standing by the counter beside a bored-looking Margo, who had been waiting for her aunt to finish her shift all day – and would be, it seemed, for a good few hours yet.

Seeing the new arrivals, Hazel turned a violent shade of pink at the counter. Nick seemed not to notice, instead offering them both a quick wave. Neve followed, her cheeks still flushed from another day on the slopes. Though Robin had only seen her that morning, her stomach fluttered and she had to wipe down her suddenly clammy palms on her apron before she dropped the mugs and plates.

'I didn't know you two were coming today.'

'Oh, we never miss this,' Nick said.

Robin frowned, but Neve remained as elusive as ever. 'You'll see.'

'You and your surprises.' Robin would have kissed her had they not had an audience. As it was, she cast Neve a soft smile and then shifted her attention to the blushing woman at her side. 'You should try Hazel's special today. Spiced pear tarts. *Very* yummy.'

'Oh, no.' Stray curls fell across Hazel's face as she shook her head. 'Everyone's here for Robin's black forest cake.'

Robin nudged Hazel lightly in the ribs: a subtle attempt at scolding. No wonder nothing had ever happened between her and Nick. She deflected any attention she got. Neve eyed Robin sceptically, the only other person wise enough to see Robin's unsubtle attempts at matchmaking.

'I had to taste-test them both,' Margo grumbled, as though sitting at the counter all day, eating cake and playing on her Nintendo Switch, had been a great hardship.

'And what's the verdict?' Nick sidled up to Margo and peered over her shoulder. Last time Robin had looked, she'd been catching fish on Animal Crossing.

Margo's underwhelming feedback was a mere shrug. Apparently, she'd reached adolescence a little earlier than most.

'Margo, put that game away,' Hazel huffed. 'It's rude to stare at a screen when people are talking to you.'

'You do it all the time when you go on Instagram to stalk Gerard Butler!'

'I do not stalk him! I'm merely . . . appreciating his face.'

'We'll try both cakes,' decided Nick finally, putting an end to what otherwise might have become a domestic dispute.

With a pleased grin, Robin prepared the desserts. She was glad to find that the queue had died down when she straightened up – and almost lost an eye to a sprig of mistletoe dangling above the displays. Instinct left her glowering at the white berries and green leaves. She despised every bit of the old-fashioned tradition of forcing two people to kiss beneath it as it was, never mind the fact that she'd already knocked into it five times today . . .

But then an idea popped into her head. She narrowed her

eyes, finding Hazel wiping down the counter beside her and Nick seating himself in the corner with Neve. With as much stealth as she could muster, she unhooked the mistletoe from where it hung and carefully tucked the ribboned bunch into the pocket of her apron.

A mistletoe kiss was just what was needed to make Nick notice Hazel.

'What are you doing?' Margo questioned, lifting her gaze from her games console for long enough to look at Robin as though she had grown a third arm.

'Oh . . . I just think it might look better somewhere else.' *Dangled over Nick and Hazel's heads, for example.*

But her plans came to a dishearteningly swift halt when a round-bellied man dwarfed by a red suit made an energetic entrance into the bakery.

'Ho, ho, ho!' Santa's impersonator chuffed, dragging a sack of presents over his shoulder. It spurred an explosion of cheers from the children.

Robin bit back her grin as she made her way to Neve's table and placed down the desserts. 'You came for Father Christmas?'

Neve gestured to him again. 'Doesn't he look familiar?'

Frowning, Robin watched closely as Santa began to hand out gifts wrapped in golden foil. It was difficult to make him out beneath the round glasses and fake beard, but . . . that bulbous nose and crooked grin could belong to none other than Neve's grandpa. 'Oh my God.'

'He does it every year.' Pride shimmered in Neve's voice. 'That's so sweet!'

Robin almost melted when one of the little girls gave Artie a big hug. The bakery had become a sea of smiling, glowing faces. People who still believed in magic. Even the parents looked ecstatic as they sipped their hot cocoa and snapped photographs on their phones.

But she hadn't forgotten the more pressing matters she had to attend to.

'Nicholas.' She pinched him on the arm as though that might make him see sense.

'Ow!' Nick groaned, slapping her away. 'What was that for?'

'For being a fool!'

'Do you have any idea what she's talking about?' he asked Neve.

His sister only shook her head innocently. 'I'm sure there's something you did to deserve it. You *are* a fool.'

'You know that pretty woman over there handing out free biscuits?' Robin motioned over to Hazel, who crouched with a plate of the decorated shortbread they'd made earlier today, feeding a group of fighting toddlers.

'That's Hazel, Robin. Haven't you been working with her all week?'

'Oh, good, you know her name!' She clapped, feigning excitement. 'Now go and learn her phone number.'

Amused understanding smoothed Neve's features as she speared her tart, but Nick remained as baffled as he had been before. '*What?*'

'Would it be easier if I wrote it down?'

'Her phone number?' Nick blinked. 'Well, yeah, but why do I need it?'

Robin huffed and turned to Neve for backup. 'Neve, tell him.'

'Oh no.' Neve shook her head. 'Don't involve me in this. I don't meddle.'

So Robin was on her own, then.

'Nick.' She sighed. 'Let me make it easy for you. Hazel is a gorgeous, talented woman, who is single. You are a . . .' she grimaced '. . . somewhat decent-looking man, I suppose, who is also single. Put the two together and . . .' She could only finish the sentence by demonstrating with her hands, clasping them together until her fingers laced tightly. If there weren't kids around, she might have made another, less savoury gesture.

Nick's face remained blank. Clueless. *Men.*

193

Patience fraying, Robin slapped her hands to her sides. 'Go and talk to her,' she ordered.

'*Robin*—'

'Oh, for fuck's sake. What's *she* doing here?' Neve's outburst was enough to make Robin forget all about her Cupid duties. She had only ever heard Neve curse under her breath before, and not with nearly as much ire as she did now.

Shadows had darkened her face, a muscle in her jaw straining at the hinge. Robin followed her unwavering, steely gaze and saw only children gathered around Artie – and then a glossy-haired brunette woman who had just slipped into the bakery and now lingered uncertainly by the door. With bright crimson lipstick and legs for days tucked into black skinny jeans, she didn't look as though she belonged in a small-town bakery at all. But she did look familiar, somehow . . .

'Who is it?' Robin questioned.

'*Neve.*' Nick spoke lowly. A warning? Why?

For a brief second, Robin found herself wondering if she might have been an ex, but she bore the faint wrinkles of a woman nearing middle age. Then again, Robin would have dropped everything for Jennifer Aniston given the chance.

She knew those high cheekbones, though. She knew them from the flight here. It was the attendant who had helped Robin through a complete meltdown.

'Did you know she was coming?' Neve's eyes sliced into Nick like daggers, accusation blazing there.

Nick lifted his hands in defence. 'No. I mean . . . not really. It may have been mentioned at dinner last night, but I didn't think she'd *actually* show up.'

At dinner last night? Did that make her a member of Neve's family? Had Robin met Neve's mother or aunt before she'd met *Neve*?

Though Robin didn't want to interrupt, she had to know – especially as they'd just begun to open up to one another. Well, Neve had. Robin had been a drunken, oversharing mess from the start. 'Er, I've met that lady before.'

Neve's focus snapped back to Robin. 'You have?'

'She was the attendant on my flight here. But who is she and why aren't we happy to see her?' She'd been so lovely to Robin, after all. Robin might not have made it through the flight without her.

Neve's chest rose and fell with a deep, jagged breath. 'Our mother. She decided to show up out of the blue, and now she's staying with us for Christmas.'

'I mean, she did call to warn you,' Nick interjected, leaving Neve's glare to intensify.

Robin remembered the way Neve's face had fallen just slightly after that phone call the other morning; how she'd evaded Robin's questions and then quickly changed the subject when she'd mentioned her mum. If Neve's mother–daughter relationship was anything like Robin's was at the moment, Robin could only imagine. Still, it didn't add up. There'd been something so maternal about the way Stefanie had comforted Robin.

Perhaps she was just a better flight attendant than she was a mother.

'I'm going to go and say hi, anyway.' Nick left his seat to approach the tall woman – she most certainly answered for Nick and Neve's chiselled, tall, dark, attractive genes – and Robin took his seat. And his cake. She hadn't eaten since this morning, and she hadn't realised just how long she'd been standing until her feet began to throb. Thankfully, now that Santa was here and the cakes and biscuits were being offered out for free, the queues at the counter had all but vanished, and Hazel looked to be handling everything fine. Well, she had time to try to snatch Margo's Nintendo from her between coffee orders, anyway.

'Are you okay?' Robin frowned, unsure whether she should reach out or let Neve process whatever she felt alone for a moment. With the noise and the drama, Robin didn't want to make things any worse.

Neve licked her lips and thrust her fork into her tart until the buttery crust began to crumble. Robin suspected that she might have been imagining it as a certain someone's head. 'Fine. Just . . . Things have always been tense with my mom. Sorry. We're supposed to be having fun, and now I'm . . .'

'Murdering a tart?' Robin finished for her, mustering the courage to stop her from leaving the entire plate to dissolve into shards and crumbs. She dragged Neve's hand away, waiting until she'd dropped the fork to squeeze reassuringly. 'Don't apologise for something you can't control. Mums can be a pain in the arse sometimes. I get it.'

'Yeah.' A chuckle of agreement fell from Neve, and she softened. 'That's an understatement. I can't believe she was on your flight, though. What are the chances?'

'It's a small world.' Robin smiled tightly, thinking it better not to mention *how* she had come to meet Stefanie. 'You know you can talk to me about it, though?'

'Maybe later.'

'Okay.' Robin fiddled with the ties of her apron, wishing there was something more she could say or do. She cast her focus back to Stefanie, who had sat in the corner with Nick. Nick must have told her to stay away for the time being: a wise decision, unless Neve's mother wanted to end up in the same state as the spiced pear tart. 'Well, since Nick has rudely abandoned my cake, I'm going to eat it.'

She stole two more forkfuls of cake and shovelled them in greedily. It *was* good, if she did say so herself. The dark cherries and subtle notes of ginger laced it with the richest flavours of Christmas, and the sponge itself was so moist it seemed to melt in her mouth. She'd proposed adding this very recipe to the restaurant's seasonal menu last year, but her boss hadn't even tasted it before shrugging her off.

'Does Hazel know she has a Cupid in her midst?' Neve watched Robin eat with an arched brow. 'That matchmaking attempt was certainly . . . something.'

'I'm simply speeding things up for them both.' Robin

placed down her fork to pull out the stolen mistletoe from her apron. 'I'm waiting for the right time to strike again.' Preferably when they weren't standing on opposite sides of the room with Father Christmas, dozens of hyperactive kids, and a mother Neve wasn't too fond of between them.

Neve sputtered out a laugh, and it left Robin relieved. 'Where did you even get that?'

'It was hanging by the counter.'

'*Robin*,' she scolded lightly. 'Let them work it out themselves. You don't want to push them into it. They might pull away.'

'Ugh.' Robin groaned. 'You're so logical.'

'You know what else I am?' Brows rising in challenge, Neve tugged the mistletoe from Robin's hands and dangled it above her head. 'I'm standing under some mistletoe.'

'Sitting, you mean.'

'I am *sitting* under some mistletoe,' she amended. 'Stop being pedantic and kiss me.'

A grin split across Robin's face as she leaned across the table to meet Neve's lips. With Neve's entire family and the kids around, she tried not to get too lost in it, though it was difficult with the warmth that spread through her whenever they so much as touched. Even more so now. Robin didn't have to worry about Neve being embarrassed anymore. She was kissing her in public, in front of everyone. It made Robin feel special. Chosen. She didn't know what had changed to help Neve open up, but she was glad for it. Proud to be the one who got to experience this side of her.

When they finally pulled away, Neve's foot brushed Robin's shin lightly. She planted the mistletoe in the poinsettia centrepiece, and Robin wondered if it would still count that way. Maybe she could trick Hazel and Nick to sit down here together later. On second thoughts, Robin tucked it back into her pocket.

'Do you have plans tonight?' Neve asked.

Robin shrugged, tracing slow circles into Neve's knuckle

with the pad of her thumb as she pondered the question. She was somehow both exhausted from so much excitement and chaos and more alive, more invigorated, than ever. 'Bath. Sleep. More sleep. My thrilling schedule can be changed, though, for the right person.'

'Good. I'll pick you up after your shift.'

'For?'

'You'll see.'

'*Another* surprise?' Robin's voice rose in disbelief. 'You at least have to tell me what to wear. Just tell me there's not too much walking involved, though, because my feet are *barking* and I already told Hazel I'd help out again tomorrow. And the next day. And the next. In fact, I don't even think I'm on holiday anymore.'

Neve wrinkled her nose in amusement. 'As long as you're enjoying yourself. That's all that matters.'

Robin's lips parted to tell her just how much she was enjoying every moment, but Artie's gleeful, 'Ho, ho, ho!' interrupted her. He waddled over to them, fake belly jiggling and his trousers slipping down dangerously low at his waist. Robin was certain that she caught a glimpse of rubber-duck-patterned boxers.

'I *told* you Father Christmas was real,' she jested before getting up to hug Artie. 'Hey, Grandpa Artie.'

'Shh. The name's Grandpa Claus today, miss,' Artie chastised before pulling away. 'Let's see if Santa has gifts for the two of you.'

He rifled around his sack with a gummy grin and pulled out two wonkily wrapped gifts. The rectangular one was handed to Robin, her name scrawled in marker in the corner, and Neve was given a smaller box.

'You shouldn't have!' Robin gushed, her heart softening with warmth. She would miss Artie almost as much as Neve when she left. 'Thank you, Artie.'

'Well, what are you waiting for? Open them!'

They did, exchanging appreciative looks with one another

before they tore into the penguin-printed foil. Whatever it was rattled, and Robin soon understood why. It was a jigsaw – of Clement Falls' town square, lit up by the towering Christmas tree they had all stood around at the concert.

'You have plenty of pieces of us to take home with you now,' Artie said.

Robin could barely see through the tears blurring her eyes. She'd been shown so much generosity these past few days that she could no longer find enough words to express just how grateful she was. For Neve and her family. For a holiday she'd never forget – and one that should have been the most miserable, lonely experience of her life yet had turned out the complete opposite. 'This is so much better than a pillow girlfriend. Thank you, Artie. I love it. Thank you so much.'

Neve opened her box and pulled out a small nutcracker. It was beautiful. Hand-painted with golden buttons and pink cheeks, a royal blue uniform and a velvet top hat. Its age showed in the fades and chips, but they only added to its magic.

She seemed to still. 'This was Gran's.'

'It was the first Christmas present I ever bought her.' Artie nodded. 'I want you to have it. I always said it brought us luck – we got married that next year.'

She softened and pulled Artie into a gentle hug, the almost empty sack of gifts rustling between them. 'Thank you. I thought she got rid of this years ago.'

'Nope. She was going to give it to you that Christmas before . . .' He swallowed as though he still couldn't say it, and something tugged tightly around Robin's stomach. Homesickness. Grief. She missed her mum and Wren. She wished more than anything their Christmases were like this, full of love and close-knit family rather than the terrible Christmas Eve countdown meals and the billion different aunts and cousins running around all over the place.

She wished she had a piece of Dad to hold, too. Travelling made her feel closer to him than ever, but it wasn't something she could touch.

'Isn't that fancy?' A clipped voice emerged from the din of merriness. It belonged to Stefanie, and Nick hovered uncomfortably at her side. 'Anything in there for me, Dad?'

'Plane tickets, perhaps,' Artie muttered under his breath. The other children called for Santa again, and he rushed off. Saved by his festive duties.

Robin tried to ignore Stefanie, though it was difficult when they'd already met. Did Stefanie recognise her? Should Robin mention it? Lacing her fingers through Neve's, she shifted uncomfortably and decided against it. This was Neve's moment. It shouldn't have been ruined.

'I hate to interrupt, ladies, but I was hoping to have a word with my daughter,' Stefanie said, looking for all the world like she *loved* to interrupt.

'Oh . . .' Robin pulled away – but Neve tugged her back firmly, placing the nutcracker on the table.

'I'm busy, Mom.'

'Yes, I see that.' Stefanie's pale green eyes flickered to Robin, recognition passing across her preened features. 'Wait. I know you, don't I?'

'Er, yes.' Robin extended the hand that wasn't clutching Neve's. 'I'm Robin. I'm . . .' She didn't finish; didn't know how to. 'Robin?' she settled on when the sentence had been left trailing for too long. 'I'm the girl you found blubbering to *Bridget Jones's Diary* on the flight here last week.'

'Oh, of course!' Stefanie replied, the handshake almost as fleeting as British summertime. She glanced between Robin and Neve. 'And . . . you two met, too?'

'Neve ended up being my ski instructor and . . .' Their entwined hands probably said enough about what had followed. Robin gulped nervously, waiting for some sort of reprimand, though she'd done nothing wrong.

'Incredible. Isn't it a small world?' Light laughter burbled from Stefanie. 'Isn't that crazy, Neve?'

'Crazy,' Neve deadpanned. 'Anyway, I want more hot

chocolate. Come on, Robin.' She was already tugging Robin away, stopping only when Stefanie called her back.

'Oh, Neve. Does it have to be like this?'

Neve spoke through gritted teeth. 'I'm not doing this here. Not now. I'm trying to enjoy my afternoon.'

'Then when? Are you going to keep pretending as though you don't know me until it suits you?'

Robin wondered if mistletoe would also be effective for dissolving tension between mothers and daughters, or perhaps there was a non-romantic equivalent Christmas plant she could use. She would have to experiment on her own mum when she got home before risking it now.

'You've done that to me plenty.' Neve's voice was colder than Robin had ever heard it – and considering the way they'd met, that was saying something. 'You can be on the receiving end for a change.'

Stefanie's face began to glow the same shade of red as the tinsel draped from the ceiling, but Neve was already turning around and pulling Robin along with her to the counter.

'Are you okay?' Robin frowned, hooking her fingers in Neve's jumper.

With a beleaguered sigh, Neve twirled a finger into Robin's sweaty, knotted hair. Her dark brows knitted together, casting a shadow across her face, but she nodded all the same and left a small peck on the tip of Robin's nose. 'Later,' she repeated. And then: 'You were crying on the flight?'

'I, er, may have had a bit of a freak-out, yes. In my defence, though, I was watching *Bridget Jones's Diary* and trying to come to terms with the fact that I was thousands of miles from home, on my honeymoon alone. Plus . . . Colin Firth.'

'Should I even try to unpack that?'

Robin smiled, tracing a finger through the cropped hair behind Neve's ear gently. 'No. Better you don't.'

'Thought so.'

* * *

Anticipation jittered through Neve as she retrieved her coat from the stand and folded it over her arms. They hadn't escaped the bakery yet, but she'd planned to take Robin to her favourite Canadian restaurant and introduce her to more traditional Albertan dishes. She hovered by the door now, a soft smile unravelling itself across her face as she watched Robin tidy up the last of the cakes. Grandpa and Mom had left not long ago, Artie whispering a quiet 'God help me' as Neve bid them goodbye. Apparently, Mom was cooking again tonight – part of the reason Neve had been so hellbent on plans with Robin instead.

The family drama was easier to deal with when Robin was here. She liked to watch Robin in her element as she bagged up the leftover cakes and cleaned the coffee machine. The world around her seemed to mould itself to her shape, the Christmas lights twinkling around her soft frame like silver doves flocking to her. Even the bakery's pastel walls were brighter than Neve remembered, and Robin's vibrant, striped sweater blended in as though she'd always worked here, as though she and Clement's Cakes were made from the same ingredients, the same colours.

In another world, maybe, this would be their everyday. Neve finishing up on the slopes and finding Robin here, both of them working in places they loved, only a few miles between them rather than thousands. With ease smoothing down Robin's features, Neve could believe it for a moment. She could pretend.

And then Hazel emerged from the kitchen, her face sickly pale, cell phone clutched in one hand and a tea towel in the other. Nobody else seemed to have noticed, not until she started with a wavering voice: 'I just got off the phone with my mom. My dad . . . he had a heart attack. He's in the hospital.'

Margo was the first to lift her head, which only proved the urgency of the matter. Neve hadn't seen her put her games console down once all afternoon. Robin straightened next, and then Nick, who had been mopping the floors.

'Oh, Hazel . . .' Neve began, at a loss. She knew from experience the sort of anxiety Hazel must have felt; knew there was never anything to say that would help. That feeling of panic, helplessness, fear, eddied in her chest as though she was reliving it again for the first time.

'What can we do?' Nick asked. 'Is he close by?'

'In Calgary.' Hazel's eyes darted unseeingly, and she pushed back her wiry curls. 'I have to go, but . . .'

'We can take care of Margo,' Robin offered.

'And I can drive you there,' Nick added, propping the mop against the wall.

'Why can't I come?' Margo asked.

With a sigh, Hazel leaned across the counter to squeeze her niece's shoulder gently. 'Oh, honey. You don't want to spend the evening in a hospital waiting room. I'm sure Grandad's fine. I just want to check up on him, okay?'

Margo's shoulders slumped in resignation. By the coat stand, Neve searched quickly for Hazel's deep green coat and scarf, handing it to her as she rushed over. Nick followed, plucking his jacket and scarf from the hook.

'Thank you.' Flustered, Hazel buttoned her coat up wrong, leaving it lopsided. 'Are you sure you don't mind?'

'Of course not,' Neve said. 'Keep us updated.'

Hazel offered a shaky, appreciative smile and then bid Margo a quick goodbye before she and Nick slipped out the door together. An eerie silence blanketed the bakery when the door fell shut, and Neve wasn't quite sure what to do with it. She hung her coat up again, locking eyes with Robin across the empty tables and chairs.

Robin only raised her brows as though asking, *What now?* Neve wished she had an answer. As it was, she could only perch back on a stool at the counter and give Margo a reassuring nudge. 'You okay, kiddo?'

'I'm not a kid,' Margo muttered. 'I'm eleven. And I don't need to be watched.'

A smirk tugged at the corner of Robin's mouth, hidden

quickly by the clearing of her throat. 'Well, I'm certain everything will be okay with your grandad, and Hazel will be back before you know it.'

'Uh-huh,' Margo replied doubtfully, balancing her chin in her hands. 'Whatever. Adults always leave or die, anyway.'

The words took Neve aback. This kid was even more cynical than *her*. 'That's a . . . healthy way to look at it.'

'It's true.'

'It's not *always* true. Look at your Aunt Hazel. She's going to be around for a long time yet, I bet.'

'Only because my mom isn't.'

Frowning, Neve leaned closer. She knew that feeling. 'Where *is* your mom right now?'

Margo pursed her lips as though refusing to reply, leaving Neve to wonder. It was Robin who kept another uncomfortable silence from descending. She balled up the rag she'd been cleaning the counters with and abandoned it on the side.

'You know what? It's absolutely criminal that I've been here for almost a week and I haven't made a snowman yet.'

'I'm *eleven*,' Margo repeated, attitude sharpening her tone.

'And *I'm* twenty-six,' Robin retorted. 'But we never get snow as thick as this in Manchester, so I'm going to make the most of it. Neve?'

The last thing Neve had planned for the evening was building snowmen, but she knew what Robin was trying to do – and perhaps she admired her for it. Margo needed a distraction, even if she thought she was too old for this one in particular. 'Beats sitting in here, I guess.'

'Margo?' Robin asked. 'You coming?'

'No.' Margo picked up her Nintendo Switch again and stared glumly at the screen.

'*Boring!*' Robin sang, skipping over to the coat rack. She must have forgotten that the tiles had just been mopped by Nick, and before Neve could warn her, she skidded into one of the tables closest, causing a shrill clatter. Somehow, she managed not to fall on her ass – again – but her arms did end up sprawled across the table and the poinsettia centrepiece toppled sadly onto the floor.

Neve shook her head, stifling her chuckle. 'I don't know how you've survived life for so long. I really don't.'

After peeling both herself and the crimson flowers up, Robin was sensible enough to walk the rest of the way with cautious steps. 'I'm a miracle.'

'That's one word for it.' Neve followed her and they shrugged on their coats, exchanging looks that ended up back on Margo's hunched figure. 'You sure you're not coming, Margo?'

'Nope.'

It didn't feel right to leave her on her own. Neve's lips parted to say as much, but Robin tapped her nose and scrunched her eyes in what must have been an attempted wink.

'Trust me,' she whispered. 'I have cousins. I'm a child whisperer.' And then, louder: 'Well, I'm going to make the biggest snowman out there and name him . . . Stollen. Bye, Margo.'

'You're really weird,' Margo called, which wasn't necessarily untrue. Wasn't Stollen a type of *bread*?

'We'll be just outside if you need us,' Neve reminded her. 'I won't.'

Neve decided then that she didn't want kids.

She followed Robin out onto the street, where it looked as though a snowplough had attempted to clear the roads and then given up halfway. The closer it got to Christmas, the less everybody in town wanted to work. It at least meant that Robin had enough snow to build her beloved Stollen, though Neve personally didn't feel like sticking her hands in it in the middle of the street. Anything could be hidden in there.

Robin didn't seem to share the same worries, bending to begin patting the snow into a small ball. 'Give her five minutes. Kids don't like sitting alone, and the Nintendo has to die sometime. She'll get bored and come out soon enough.'

Neve only hummed, unconvinced, as she peered into the bakery. The Christmas lights strung around each lamp post and across every street were reflected, and she had to press her forehead to the cool glass to see anything. Margo hadn't moved, though she didn't seem to be playing on her games console anymore. Maybe Robin had been right about that.

Sympathy welled in Neve. Margo was probably terrified and confused and completely lost, and Neve didn't know how to talk to her, how to show her that she understood.

Robin's voice pulled her focus away eventually. 'Why didn't you tell me about your mum?' she questioned softly, scooping up more snow to pat onto the ball.

Shrugging, Neve thrust her hands into her pockets, her breath visible in the twilit night. It would be dark soon, and Neve couldn't help but feel disappointed at the fact that they might not have time for dinner together. 'She's always coming and going from my life. I didn't want to waste any of our time on her. I'll deal with her when . . .' *When you're gone*, Neve almost said, but she didn't want to talk about Robin not being here yet. She settled on: 'Later.'

'You know that you *can* talk to me, though? I know technically we haven't known each other that long, and . . . well, you know . . . I'll be off soon. But I don't want you to feel that you can't just because of all that. I'd like to know more about you. And your family welcomed me into your home so easily. It just felt a bit weird that you didn't mention anything.'

'I'm sorry.' Neve softened in understanding. 'I suppose I'm just used to handling Mom stuff on my own. Nick . . . Nick is a little more optimistic than me and I feel like it's better to keep it to myself.'

'Well, you don't have to anymore. Not with me.' Robin met her eyes, watery from the cold. Sincerity clouded in them, rendering Neve speechless. She'd never had someone who wanted to hear about all the worst parts of her, too. Someone who would accept her even when she was angry or sad. But Robin looked like that was exactly what she wanted to do.

'Thank you,' Neve whispered.

Robin smiled and then put her hands on her hips, her eyes falling to her snowball. 'Do you think this is big enough to roll now?'

It wasn't all that big, or circular either, but Neve nodded all the same. Absently, she swiped a heap of snow from the windowsill of the bakery and rolled it into a ball of her own. It ended up just as uneven and lumpy as Robin's – but left her with an idea. With her back turned to Robin, Neve moulded the snow with her palms to curve and point where she wanted it to. It wasn't as easy as it should have been, but the shape of a heart began to emerge. It was as good a way to say "thank you for being here" as any, wasn't it?

A flutter of embarrassment soared through Neve, and she thought about throwing the snow heart away before Robin saw. But she quelled the instinct, perhaps for the first time putting aside her pride and fears for the sake of something much more important.

'I made you something.' Neve turned around and opened her cupped hands to reveal the heart, bashfulness leaving her cheeks feeling feverish.

Breathless from rolling the ball through the snow, Robin slapped her hands together and straightened to inspect Neve's creation. Neve watched her face carefully, heart somersaulting when her eyes shimmered with surprise, and then something else, something Neve hoped she wasn't just imagining.

'You made me a heart.' The words were quieter than the light trickle of snowfall that had just begun. A gradual, wonderful grin spilled across Robin's face. It reminded Neve of the first day of spring, when the clouds finally unveiled the sun. 'You big ball of cheese. I love it. Do you think Hazel would mind if I put it in her freezer so I can keep it forever?'

Neve laughed, but inside, all she could think was that it was more realistic this way. The heart would melt soon. So would they. The thought made the space behind her ribs ache, and she forgot for a moment how to breathe.

'Stay for Christmas.' The words seemed to tumble from Neve's lips all at once, well and truly severed from her brain, her logic, the sensible part of her that already knew it was a silly, unrealistic, unfair request. But they were out there now, drifting between them with the snowflakes.

Robin's lips parted in surprise. 'Pardon?'

'You said you hate Christmas at home. So spend it here, with me. Stay.'

'I . . . I can't.' Robin blinked, shock dissolving into sadness. The corners of her mouth turned down, golden lashes fluttering against round cheeks. 'I wish I could . . .'

Something painful and serrated twisted in Neve's stomach, though she had expected it. Had known it would come.

A silly idea. Even if Robin could stay, it would only make things hurt more in the end, wouldn't it? The more time Neve spent with Robin, the more she would have to let go of when the time came. It was a double-edged sword, and Neve wished she couldn't feel both points burying themselves through the slats in her ribs. 'No. Of course. I don't know what I was thinking. Ignore me.'

'Neve—'

'Forget it, Robin,' Neve begged. 'I shouldn't have asked. It wasn't fair of me.'

She dropped the heart into the snow. It felt as though heavy boots were trampling over her own.

Robin opened her mouth to say something more, but the bakery door creaking open, pouring light onto the shadows, stopped her.

Margo stood in the threshold, her dimpled chin dipped into her scarf and a brooding, solemn expression on her face. 'Fine,' she said. 'I'll help.'

Neve was impressed that Robin had been right, to say the

least. Still, she tried not to make a big deal of it as Margo stepped out. 'Want to help me make Stollen's head?'

A nod was all Neve received, but it was better than nothing. Margo gathered a heap of snow and began to work while Robin smirked proudly. Then she picked up the heart, giving Neve a meaningful look before she hunched back over her own ball and continued to roll it around the corner, leaving them outside of the bakery alone.

Uncertainly, Neve glanced at Margo. They shared none of the same features, but somehow, Neve felt as though she was looking at a younger version of herself. The one who had just learned that adults were human, too, and just as unreliable as everybody else.

'You know, I used to be a lot like you,' she confessed finally. 'The adults in my life sucked when I was growing up.'

'That's because adults suck,' Margo deadpanned without dragging her focus from the snow.

'Yeah, we do,' Neve agreed. 'Some of us, at least. My mom was *never* around when I was growing up, and I always blamed myself for it. But you're right. She sucked. She was the one in the wrong. And now I'm older, I'm sort of glad she came and went. It meant I got to live with my grandparents and my brother, and they loved and looked out for me enough for five moms. Kind of like Hazel looks out for you.'

Margo seemed to shrink, her wobbling lip tucking between gapped front teeth. Neve hoped she wasn't overstepping. Most of what she'd heard about Margo's mom was from Hazel: the sister who was always in and out of Clement Falls, always shirking responsibilities, including her own kid. She'd had Margo young, still in college, and whenever Neve had seen Margo as a kid, she'd always been either with Hazel or Hazel's parents. Never with Catherine herself. It seemed some people just weren't meant for full-time parenthood.

'She doesn't get a choice,' Margo said. 'She has to look after me because nobody else will.'

'She gets a choice, Margo. Everybody who surrounds you

chooses you. It took me a really long time to see that. And it really, *really* hurts when somebody *doesn't* choose you. But for as many people who go away, I bet you have just as many who choose to stay. If your Aunt Hazel is taking care of you right now, it's because she wants to.'

She sighed, her lids shuttering for just a moment. When they opened again, Neve saw that her eyes were glossy with tears. 'My mom moved away without me. She got a new boyfriend – a horrible doctor who doesn't like kids. I didn't want to go . . . so she told me I could stay with Aunt Hazel. I asked her to come see me play in the concert last week, and she didn't. She was busy. And now they're engaged, and I don't think she's ever coming home.'

Neve sucked in a breath, feeling the ache, the loss, as though it was her own again. She'd never understood why parents abandoned their responsibilities the second something shinier came through the door. She'd never understood how a person like Margo's mom could sleep at night knowing that her child was somewhere else, missing her, relying on her. But for Margo, she had to pretend she did, so she squeezed her shoulder gently. 'I'm sorry. I'm *so* sorry. But you know what? We all watched you play the flute. You were amazing, and Hazel was so, so proud of you.'

She'd expected tears, but Margo surprised her with a sad smile. And it was enough for Neve. Hopefully enough for Margo. They continued to build the snowman in silence, while the occasional late-night shopper walked past, stares full of interest, and Christmas music and laughter floated from the markets across the road.

'All right. I have a snowman here who needs a head,' Robin said finally, stepping back from the large mound. It was speckled with dirt and more oval than round, but Neve didn't dare point it out. It was getting late, and she didn't feel like standing here all night.

Sheepishly, Margo placed her own somewhat triangular pile of snow onto the body. 'What about the face?'

Robin smirked conspiratorially. 'You shall see.' Without another word, she stepped into the bakery. Neve rolled her eyes and jigged up and down to keep warm. Finally, Robin returned with a box of Smarties.

Neve couldn't pretend as though the big reveal wasn't a little bit underwhelming. With impatience and a chill making a home in her bones, she said, 'Okay, well, I'm going to go check that my brother or Hazel haven't called. You two have fun.'

Maybe it was selfish, but all Neve wanted was tonight with Robin, and waiting around made her antsy. Judging from the lack of updates she found when she got inside, though, tonight's date was becoming more unlikely each minute.

Time and circumstance just didn't seem to be their friend.

'Who is the very fine fellow standing outside?' were the first words to leave Nick's mouth when he and Hazel burst into Clement's hours later.

'That is Stollen the Snowman,' Robin replied, hopping up from her chair. After Neve had retreated back to warmth, she and Margo had searched through the bakery's lost property box for some more decorations, and now Stollen was indeed a stylish gentleman with a trilby hat, a woman's summer scarf, an abandoned walking stick, and one infant-sized Paw Patrol mitten.

Though she was childishly proud of her creation – *their* creation, Neve had corrected – Robin's concern lay with Hazel, now, and she gathered the pink-nosed, watery-eyed woman into a tight hug. 'How is he? How are *you*?'

'He's okay.' A small chuckle fell from Hazel. 'He said he thought it was indigestion. He should make a full recovery. My mom's with him, anyway, and we can visit him tomorrow if you'd like, Margo.'

'That's great news,' Neve said as Margo, much to Robin's surprise, let Hazel pull her into a hug once Robin had prised herself away.

'Thank you so much for taking care of everything here,' Hazel gushed between sniffles. 'And thank you, Nick, for taking me. I don't think I would have made it there alone in one piece.'

'No problem.' Nick smiled, dimpled and charming if not slightly tired. 'I'm glad I could help.'

Slowly, Robin inched her hand into her pocket and searched for the sprig of mistletoe she'd stolen earlier. Before she pulled it out, though, Neve slapped her hand away and shook her head in warning. *Ugh*. Robin supposed it wasn't the *best* time to trap Nick and Hazel in a kiss, but still. When opportunity struck . . .

'Anyway, you guys should go,' Hazel said to Neve and Robin. 'I've eaten up so much of Robin's time already.'

Robin didn't need the reminder. She was exhausted, as much as she'd like to stick around and make sure Hazel really *was* okay. It was already going on nine p.m. – way past her necessary feeding and pyjama time. 'Are you sure? If you need anything, we're here.'

'Oh, we're fine. You guys go. The night is young and all that. Thank you again.'

They were practically shoved out the door, Nick lingering behind – much to Robin's satisfaction. 'There's hope for them yet,' she observed as she and Neve passed the bakery window, Robin throwing on her hat haphazardly. It was another bitter night, cold enough to keep Stollen in one piece for the time being. 'Bye, Stollen!'

Neve choked on a laugh and looped her arm through Robin's so that they could share warmth. In front of them, their breaths curled together. Robin wished she could just be here, enjoy it, but she couldn't stop thinking about what Neve had asked earlier. She'd wanted Robin to stay over *Christmas*.

And maybe . . . maybe Robin wanted that too.

It had certainly taken everything in her to decline. Neve made Robin feel as though she were floating, and she didn't want to crash back down to earth anytime soon. There was nothing more Robin wanted than extra time to learn about her and all of her little quirks; the food she didn't like and the things she loved; whether she woke up in the morning with messy hair or whether it was short enough that it never really moved. But her mother would never talk to Robin again if she didn't go home before Christmas.

Then again, Mum wasn't talking to her anyway.

'So . . .' Robin sighed and rested her head on Neve's shoulder. At this rate, they wouldn't make it to the truck without her collapsing. 'Want to come back to the cabin with me tonight? I'm wiped, but . . .'

'I was wondering if you wanted to get dinner first. But if you're too tired . . .'

If Robin were at home, she would have said no. She *was* tired, her feet throbbing, eyelids drooping. But Neve had planned something for them, and Robin wanted to make the most of every second. The only thing better than a good night's sleep was spending more time with her. She would soak up whatever she could get. 'Then let's do it.'

'Really?' Neve brightened in the silvery moonlight, and it was all the confirmation Robin needed.

'Really. I'm starving. Where are we going?'

Neve grinned. 'I guess you'll see.'

Chapter Sixteen

Robin didn't know why, instead of taking the much-needed nap she'd planned after another bustling day at the bakery, she spent the two hours she had to spare before Neve picked her up for another "surprise" date browsing job listings in Calgary. Last night's had been an all-you-can-eat restaurant – Robin's favourite type of restaurant – serving traditional Albertan dishes, including cute mini bison burgers, yummy ginger fried beef, and heavenly butter tarts with Saskatoon berries. Robin had come home with a glorious meat and carbohydrate-induced bloat that still lingered now, and she regretted nothing.

Excitement surged through her when she found a Clement's Cakes advertisement for pastry chefs at the new city branch, just as Hazel had said. Her thumb hovered over the "Apply Now" button on her phone for longer than it should have.

Wren saved her from having to wonder why. Her sister's caller ID lit up the screen – a picture of the two of them wearing green top hats in an Irish bar on St Patrick's Day. Those were the things she would miss if she moved to Calgary. The things she would miss if she spent a Christmas here. Her sister. Her mum. Cleopawtra. Home. They would all be a fifteen-hour flight away.

But she'd found home here, too, somewhere in the snow. A different home, but one that was quickly beginning to mean just as much. Clearly, if she was thinking about uprooting her entire bloody life for it. Not that she was. That would be silly.

After the fourth shrill ring, Robin realised that she might actually have to answer or else leave her family to panic and send out a search party. She accepted the call and pressed the phone to her ear. 'Hello?'

'Oh no. What's wrong now?' asked Wren immediately.

'Nothing's wrong.' Robin couldn't help but set free a sigh as she stood and slipped on her boots. She'd told Neve she'd meet her in the lobby tonight rather than make her drive to the other side of the resort.

'Liar.'

It was time Robin gave up even trying to hide things from Wren. 'It's just . . . do you think Mum would hate me if I stayed here over Christmas?'

A shuffle sounded down the line. Robin winced when she heard her mother's voice, stern and hoarse, shout, 'Robin Louise Ellis! Tell me I did *not* just hear you say what I *think* I heard you say.'

'You could have told me you were with Mum!' huffed Robin, pinning the phone against her shoulder with her cheek so that she could slip on her coat. It was so typical that her mother had decided to cease the silent treatment *now*.

She heard Wren's faint reply in the background. 'Sorry!'

'The answer is yes. Your mother *would* hate you if you missed Christmas with your family,' Mum scolded. 'And so would Cleopawtra. And Wren.'

'Don't bring me into this,' Wren muttered.

'Oh hello, Mum. How are you? Lovely to hear your voice, too. I suppose you're talking to me now, are you?' Bitterness seeped into Robin's tone. She could no longer pretend as though her mum's cold shoulder hadn't hurt her. Weren't parents supposed to *want* their child to get out in the world? To travel and find new things – perhaps even people – to love? Didn't Robin deserve even an ounce of support for finding her independence and sense of adventure? She was proud of herself for doing this. She wished everyone else would be, too.

'I was upset – and rightly so.' Mum tutted. 'As if it's not bad enough that you won't be home until Christmas Eve, you want to miss the entire thing now!'

'You've had twenty-five other Christmases with me. You don't think you and Cleopawtra could do without me for just one year?'

It was a mistake to have even asked. Mum was so set in her ways that nothing would ever change: they'd had the same turkey dinner since she and Wren had had enough teeth to chew through the tough old meat, and the same shabby decorations that hung around the house had been saved from Mum's childhood, stored in a soggy cardboard box that still smelled of Grandad's cigars.

'*Twenty-four*,' Mum corrected. 'You missed 2007 to have your appendix out.'

'Well excuse me for needing emergency surgery!'

'You're not missing Christmas. It's not an option, Robin. I've already brought down the extra chairs from the attic.'

The extra chairs were usually designated for the youngest in the family. Without Robin, one would go spare. She knew that hassle first-hand – she was usually the one to brave the cobwebs and bring them down. 'Cleopawtra can sit on mine.'

Robin heard Mum whisking something furiously and imagined her seething in the kitchen as she made her Christmas Eve Eve Eve Eve Eve omelette, which came with a rather disgusting concoction of turkey, stuffing, and Brussel sprouts.

'*Honestly*,' Mum said. 'I can't believe you'd even suggest such a thing. Don't you want to be a part of this family anymore, Robin? Aren't we good enough for you?'

Ah, yes. The guilt trip. 'Don't be silly. I'm just enjoying myself here. It would be nice to stay a little bit longer.'

'Nonsense. You hate snow, and you're on your honeymoon *alone*. What could you possibly be enjoying about that?'

So Wren hadn't told her about Neve. Good. It was nice to have something that wasn't yet tarnished, something that was only Robin's and nobody else's.

'You're already missing Christmas Eve Eve Eve, Christmas Eve Eve, *and* half of Christmas Eve,' Mum continued. 'That's not enough?'

'Forget it, Mum,' Robin hissed through her teeth, her own irritation surging through her. 'I'll see you when I get back. Christmas Eve.'

'Robin Lou—'

Robin hung up before Mum could use her full name again, thrusting on her hat and scarf and then stomping her way through heavy snow, to the lobby. Helen stood as stiff-spined as always at the front desk, looking less than pleased to see Robin there. It was a good thing Robin was too annoyed to make moose puns, though she did wish Elk-on John a good evening on her way past.

'You haven't seen Neve yet, have you?'

'Nope. I don't think she does ski lessons at ten p.m.,' Helen answered, and then went back to tapping something out on her keyboard. Robin could have explained that she wasn't waiting for a ski lesson, but it was unlikely Helen would care either way. If only Mum was so laid-back.

To kill time, Robin browsed the rack of pamphlets displayed at the desk. She probably should have read a few more of them when she'd arrived; there were all sorts of activities listed that she wouldn't have time to try now.

Wouldn't have time to try with Neve.

Not unless she stayed.

Her fingers froze over one in particular, shelved on the front row as though it had just been added. A skier covered the front page, but it wasn't one of Neve's leaflets advertising lessons. She plucked it out and fanned through it, brows rising in curiosity.

She halted on the third page in.

Trials for athletes hoping to get on the national ski team were being held in Calgary soon, advertised in bold letters.

All of the dates and details were listed here. If Neve knew . . .

Robin folded it and put it in her pocket, remembering their conversation on the couch a few nights ago. She had to at least try. If all Neve needed was a little push, Robin would be happy to give it to her.

'Robin.' Her name was called across the lobby, and Robin whirled to find Neve stood by the door, snow melting from her boots onto the welcome mat and her nose pink from the cold. 'Ready?'

She was. Wherever Neve was taking her, Robin was ready.

She hadn't been ready, after all. Not for this.

Neve had driven them through the pine-tree-lined outskirts of Clement Falls, along quiet, sludgy roads that wended beneath the star-speckled night . . . to a lake.

'Lake Serissa,' Neve named it as she shut off the ignition. The low, wistful notes of an acoustic Christmas song ebbed with it. 'The best place in Alberta to see the Northern Lights.'

'Wait.' Robin's eyes widened as the words sunk in. She snapped her gaze to Neve, who grinned like a proud Cheshire cat as she unclipped her seatbelt. 'The Northern Lights? Really?'

'Go take a look,' Neve urged.

Robin didn't need to be told twice. Bubbling with excitement, she struggled with her own seatbelt until Neve had to help, and then hopped out of the pickup so quickly that her ankle almost buckled.

And then she gasped, frozen.

The rippling lights of the aurora borealis sifted through the velvet night, their green glow reflected in the black, still surface of the lake. The lights haloed the snow-capped mountains, jewelled crowns bestowed upon craggy, white-haired queens. Robin had never seen anything like it. It was otherworldly enough that she forgot how to breathe, how to think. She hadn't even noticed Neve get out of the truck until their arms brushed, and she turned to find her smiling with none of the shields she usually hid behind. Her cheeks swelled with joy, dimpled and rosy, and Robin couldn't remember ever seeing anybody look so *alive*.

This was what raw, unbridled happiness looked like. She was certain it was mirrored on her own features, just as the lake mirrored the lights.

'This isn't real,' Robin whispered. She wasn't talking about the Northern Lights anymore, ethereal as they were. She was talking about Neve: about the connection they'd somehow found, a cord tethering them by the wrists. Robin had felt more in these past few days with her than she had in almost a year. Maybe longer, if she was honest with herself. Maybe ever.

'It's real,' Neve replied softly, and Robin wondered if she meant the lights, too, or this. It *felt* real. It felt the most real thing she'd ever had. Maybe this wouldn't have been half as special if they weren't steadily reeling towards their expiration date.

She'd never know. She was okay with that for tonight.

A few other cars had parked across the opposite shore of the lake. Photographers with their tripods who would probably be here for hours. But in this corner, on this side, there was no one but them.

With ice and stone crunching beneath her boots, Neve went back to the pickup. Robin frowned, panicked – it was too soon to leave, too soon for it to be over – but she realised that Neve wasn't getting ready to go. She was pulling something out of the back seat. Blankets and pillows and sleeping bags.

'Are we staying?' Excitement glittered unabashedly in Robin's words.

'As long as it stays clear, the lights will be visible for a few hours, at least. May as well make the most of it.'

It was freezing enough that her bones began to shudder, but Robin didn't care. Neve had brought more than enough to warm them up, and Robin would have happily caught hypothermia if it meant staying.

Luckily, Neve also pulled out two flasks. 'Hot cocoa,' she said, handing one to Robin.

'You thought of everything.' Tears pricked Robin's eyes as she unscrewed the lid. They fell freely when Neve pulled out a pack of mini marshmallows from her pocket and tipped some into her drink.

'No whipped cream though, I'm afraid.'

'Almost everything.' After wiping her damp cheeks with

her sleeve, Robin couldn't keep from reaching out with her free hand and cupping Neve's strong jaw in her palm. Her face was cold, soft, framed by a loose, woolly, tree-patterned hat and scarf to match. 'It's perfect. Thank you. Nobody's ever done anything like this for me before.'

'This was where Gran brought Grandpa. When he was telling us about how they met, when Gran showed him the best place to see the lights. It was here.'

The words . . . Robin couldn't comprehend how special, groundbreaking, they were. Neve had brought Robin to the place where Artie had fallen in love so many decades ago. As though she was as special, as deserving, as Artie had been with her grandmother. She felt like she was going to burst out of her own skin as she imagined it. This was where it had all started. Neve and Robin wouldn't be here now if her grandparents hadn't chosen each other under these same lights, by this same lake, all those years ago. Robin couldn't bear to think of a world where that didn't happen. Where Neve didn't exist and Robin never met her.

'It's no wonder they fell in love here,' Robin whispered.

Neve's eyes glistened in the dim light, and their noses brushed as though wanting to savour not just the kiss, but also what came before it. The closing in. The pulling away. Every touch and graze and dreg of proximity they could drink up, they did. And when their lips met, heat that sparked in Robin's gut flamed like a log fire. She wanted to let it burn her to ash and dust. Let that ash and dust blow away, into the lake, and stay there forever.

She wanted her atoms to be knitted into Lake Serissa, into Neve. She wanted everything. For the first time in her life, she wasn't wandering, always in the wrong place at the wrong time. This was where she was supposed to be, where she wanted to be.

Tonight, she had everything.

Neve didn't spend much time admiring the aurora rippling

across the sky. No, she spent it looking at Robin. She wanted to remember every held breath and shed tear, every smile and every shiver. They ended up curled together in the back of Neve's pickup, her arm around Robin's shoulder as they snuggled into a dozen blankets to keep warm and sipped their hot – warm, now – chocolate. It was perfect. A night she wanted to stay locked in and never escape, even if Juniper *had* shot her daggers when she'd left her at home earlier with Mom.

'I have something for you,' Robin said after what felt like hours. Neve hadn't felt the pressing need to restart the conversation when it had dulled, and it was the most peace she'd ever felt with another person.

Robin wiggled out of Neve's embrace to dig through her coat pockets now. A folded, glossy flyer was handed to Neve a moment later. It was difficult to make out the writing in the darkness, but the silhouetted skier thrusting forward down a clear slope and Alpine Canada's shielded red maple leaf logo at the top said enough. Neve's heart stuttered.

'Trials are in March, in Calgary,' Robin said. 'It's worth a shot, isn't it?'

Neve sighed hesitantly, worrying at her lip. 'I don't know, Rob. That's so soon. I'm not even in shape anymore.'

'You're on the slopes every day.'

'It would change everything I have here,' she breathed, hiding the leaflet with her blanket so that she no longer had to look at it. 'My grandpa—'

'I know.' Robin tucked a short strand of hair from Neve's eyes with delicate, gloved fingers. 'I know. You don't want to leave him. But this is only a try-out. You don't have to have it all figured out yet. Just . . . *try* it *out*.'

Neve held back a chuckle at that. 'You should write ad slogans.'

'I know.' Shuffling closer, Robin nudged her elbow lightly in Neve's ribs, and then the hinges of their hips touching mustn't have been enough, because she looped a leg over Neve's, their hands tangling. The pressure left Neve wanting more, and she wet her lips hungrily. 'Promise me you'll at least think about it.'

Neve swallowed down her arguments and let herself be here again, where she was free of worry. What harm would a trial be, anyway? She'd done one before. It didn't mean anything would change right away. With Robin here, curled around her, she would agree to anything – because Robin made Neve feel as though she was *capable* of anything. 'I promise.'

'Good. I'll hold you to that.'

Still, the truth weighed on her, dying to be set free. She clenched her jaw and bowed her head. How much longer could she let this lie like lead in her heart?

'There's another reason I haven't wanted to get back on the team.' Her voice shook.

Robin frowned. 'Yeah?'

She steeled herself against the cold wind. 'When . . . when Gran died, I wasn't there. I didn't get to say goodbye. I was in Italy with the team. Partying because we won a competition.'

Robin squeezed her arm gently, urging her to continue.

So she did. 'That was the worst part. When I left, she was there. When I came back, she was just . . . gone. And I couldn't bear it happening again. Grandpa is all I have left, and I know he can't be around forever, but at least this way, I'd be here if something did . . .' She couldn't finish that sentence. It hurt too much. 'If I get back on the team, it means leaving him. It means I'm not here if something happens. If he needs me. It means having to go through it all over again.'

'Neve . . .' Robin's forehead wrinkled with concern, understanding, and that was why. That was why Neve could open up. That was why it was different to anything she'd ever had before. She'd only ever been able to trust three people and one dog in her life and only because they were family. But Robin had come from halfway across the world and just . . . got her. Without even trying. Like she could see every part of Neve, or maybe like somewhere beneath all their differences, they were made of the same things. It made

Neve feel raw, but she couldn't seem to cover up, hide, the way she might have once.

She *wanted* Robin to see her.

'Losing somebody you love is the worst thing in the world,' Robin continued finally. 'And not getting to say goodbye . . . I know. I didn't, either, when my dad went. But Artie could have ten or even twenty good years in him yet, and then you've wasted a decade not doing the thing you love because you're afraid. What happens when he does go? What will you have left if you haven't chosen anything for yourself? You need to make sure you still have a life when he . . .'

'When he doesn't,' Neve finished for her. Robin was right. Of course she was. Logically, Neve could have figured that out for herself. But it was so much easier to imagine pushing away the fear than actually doing it. And it was so much easier to stay home, knowing Grandpa was okay and so was Nick, than having to pack up and leave again only to find out she might not be as good as she once was.

'I think it's why my mum is so mad at me.' Robin pressed her back to the edge of the truck, watching the lights. The glow turned her eyes a sea-green. 'She's afraid too. Because we lost my dad so suddenly, she's afraid that something will happen as soon as we leave her sight. I lived with it for three years, but . . . I had to stop. We can't control every single thing, and God, I wouldn't want to. Look at this. Us.' She smiled softly, nudging Neve's knee. 'I wouldn't be here if I'd listened to all that fear. I wouldn't have met you.

'Bad things can happen unexpectedly, Neve,' she whispered. 'But good things can, too. You just have to give them a chance.'

It was true. Too true. Neve was so desperate to control everything all the time, but if she'd given in to it, she wouldn't have gotten here. If she could push the fear aside for Robin, why couldn't she do it for skiing? For her future?

She had to at least try. At least contemplate that she could really return to the team, maybe even get picked for the Olympics again. She would always be filled with anxiety after Gran, but wasn't she anyway? Didn't she wake up every morning desperate to avoid Irina or any talk of the ski team? 'I hate it when you make sense,' Neve admitted.

'Make the most of it. It happens rarely.'

She snorted. 'Thank you, Robin. I think I needed to hear that from someone who really understands. I could never bring myself to talk to anyone else about it.'

'Of course. You can tell me anything.'

They stayed like that a little bit longer, finally peaceful, until Robin nuzzled into Neve's hood, the cold tip of her nose brushing against Neve's neck and making her breath hitch.

'You're freezing.' The words were stuttered and mangled. Neve wasn't concentrating on what she was saying anymore. She was concentrating on Robin's lips running across her flesh, leaving goose bumps in their wake, and the heat coiling low in her belly in response. Neve tucked her chin further down to find Robin's lips.

'Then maybe you should warm me up,' Robin responded between kisses.

Neve was glad, then, for the privacy they had on this side of the lake. She let her kisses get greedier, let herself be lost to the scent of Robin's coconut shampoo and the light spritz of peachy perfume on the hollow of her neck. Beneath that, she could still smell the bakery: cocoa powder and vanilla extract, flour and peppermint. So very Robin.

She flipped Robin over, straddling her legs, but it wasn't enough. Too many layers of clothing separated them, and Neve wanted to feel her, wanted to touch her. She pulled off her gloves, her fingers – warmed from the hot flask – dancing across the constellations of Robin's freckled cheeks. The Northern Lights paled in comparison, though they twirled above still, their glowing green ribbons as entangled as she and Robin were.

Robin did the same, peeling off one glove while Neve took the other. Her hands were freezing enough to stun Neve.

'Jesus. You need new gloves.'

She giggled as Neve cupped them in her own, blowing on

them to warm them up. Their gazes locked, and the cold fell away again, and Neve felt like something vital had slotted into her chest, never to leave. She couldn't stop looking at Robin, couldn't stop feeling and wanting and needing. Robin must have sensed it, because she reached for her again, expression tender enough that Neve wanted to cry. Nobody had ever looked at her that way, as though Neve was made of moonlight – and if they had, it wouldn't have mattered. Not if they weren't Robin.

Robin tugged on Neve's bottom lip with her teeth. Neve's hands meandered to Robin's hips, squeezing lightly until she swallowed Robin's gasp. And then she found the hem of her sweater beneath her thick coat and crawled up soft flesh, wishing she could see it, too. Wishing she could see her.

She stopped when she found the lace of Robin's bra, wondering if she should cross that line; wondering if Robin wanted her to. But Robin unzipped Neve's coat urgently, breathlessly. 'Don't. Don't stop.'

It was all the permission Neve needed. Robin arched her spine so that Neve could unhook her bra, and then her fingers nudged the fabric away and returned to the swells of her breasts, brushing tenderly across her pebbled nipples. She heard Robin's breath catch in her throat, felt her roll her hips in reaction, and it made her want more, want all of her. Robin's fingers on Neve's stomach surprised her, and then they fell from her hips to the uneven, jagged staircase of her spine. She let herself fall so that they lay facing one another, hands entangled, legs knotted, hearts racing, lips swollen, buried in blankets and too many clothes.

After a few moments of drinking her in, letting herself be here with Robin – beautiful, funny, soft-edged Robin – Neve was too desperate to wait. She had never wanted to touch this way before, and be touched this way. Not for a quick release, but an exploration. To make Robin feel good; to show her what she meant to her. Hot pulses of need shot through her, until her own hips rocked against Robin's thigh, placed between her own, searching for friction. Robin's fingers dipped to the waistband of her jeans; lower.

'Neve,' she rasped out as they found what they'd been seeking through the cotton of Neve's underwear. Neve burrowed her face into the warm, furry crook of Robin's neck, the only place she could muffle the moan that arose when Robin began tracing light circles across the most sensitive part of her. But she didn't want to do this alone. She wanted Robin to feel it, too. So she grazed her breast a final time and then slid her hand into Robin's trousers, past her underwear, where bare, prickly skin lay. The moan that fell out of Robin almost drove Neve to release, and she searched, inching the tip of her finger inside of her as Robin's own hand moved faster.

'I can't believe it's you,' Neve whispered in her own haze of pleasure, a laugh burbling from her as tension began to build in her stomach. She used the heel of her palm to bring more pleasure to Robin, until she was writhing to meet her touch, writhing to go deeper, to have more of her. 'The girl who thought my dog was a wolf.'

Robin's laugh was light as snowfall. 'The girl who hated me and my puns.'

'Never.' Neve kissed her again, and again, as she teetered on the edge of climax. It drew an honesty from her she could no longer hide. 'I never hated you. I never could.'

Beneath the blankets and the glow of the Northern Lights, they rocked against one another – and let that warm wash of bliss drown them at the same time, through muffled moans and trembling legs and hot, heaving breaths.

And it was enough to forget.

Enough to fall.

Enough for Neve to feel alive and loved and herself for the first time in perhaps ever. They stayed that way long after the last threads of light knitted back into the clouds. Together – both unravelled and completely intertwined.

'Come to Manchester for New Year's.'

Robin had been working up the nerve to ask for hours, and when the aurora disappeared and the cloudy sky turned a mottled pink, she finally did. They had stayed up most of the night, moving back into the truck when it got too cold. Now, they were wrapped in blankets and layers together, the gearstick nudging into Robin's hip as she leaned into Neve's warmth across the seats. The heater whistled, the radio emitting a crackly, melancholy Christmas song.

The night had made Robin feel . . . free. As though something wrong and heavy had been building in her muscles for years, and Neve had chased whatever it had been away. Nothing pinned her bones down anymore. She was happy. And she wanted more happiness with Neve. Ending it . . . It didn't feel like an option anymore. She would even stay for Christmas. It would be worth the earache from Mum. More time with Neve was worth everything.

'What?' Neve's voice was thick with sleep. From this angle, with her head pressed against Neve's chest, listening to her heartbeat, Robin couldn't glimpse what Neve felt.

'My mum throws this New Year's Eve party at our house every year. Come. I want you to come.'

The silence went on for moments, its only filler Neve's laboured breaths beneath Robin's ear. 'I don't know, Rob.'

'I could stay here with you for Christmas like you asked, and then you could come back with me for a couple of weeks. That way we still have so much time, and you can meet my family. Not that I'd wish that upon you, mind, but . . . it could be fun. It could work.'

Her only response was an unconvinced hum that vibrated against Robin's cheek.

Something panged in Robin's chest, and she pulled away, propping herself up with a pillow to gauge Neve's expression. It was unreadable, if not a little wrinkled with . . . with what? It occurred to Robin then that maybe she didn't know Neve well enough to identify what she did and did not feel. She didn't know her well enough for a lot of things – asking her to fly to England and spend New Year's with her, for example. But Neve had done the same. She'd asked her to stay.

'Why?' she asked in a small voice.

'Because . . . it's so far away, and I should really spend New Year's with my grandpa. It's . . .' Neve struggled, pursing her lips.

'It's what?'

'Is it a good idea?' She sat up, too, so that they were facing one another with the blankets pooled around their waists and their coats askew from a night of zipping and unzipping coats. 'Dragging this out until New Year's?'

Dragging it out. As though this were a burden for Neve. As though she were forced here against her will. As though it hadn't been *her* idea to bring Robin here, to touch her and make her feel as though maybe they could work this out as long as they were together.

Robin tried not to show her hurt, though she had never been any good at hiding what she felt. *Weak*, she scolded herself. *This is exactly how you got hurt last time.* 'Okay. Fine. If that's how you feel.'

'I thought it was how we both felt.' A crease formed between Neve's brows, seeping into the hem of her woolly hat. 'Don't be mad at me. Don't ruin this.'

With a scoff, Robin kicked the blankets off her legs. *Her* ruin this? She'd been playing by Neve's rules from the beginning: forgiving her when she got upset, agreeing to the pretence that this mattered when really all it seemed to have become was a holiday fling, thinking about missing out on time with her own family to stay here. 'I'm not ruining it. I'm stopping you from having to drag it out.'

'That's not how I meant it.' Neve caught her wrist, pulling her closer, into her warmth. If Robin wasn't so weak, she might have pulled back – but she couldn't stop wanting, wishing, even now. 'I just mean that it will hurt more if we try to make something of this once you're gone. Long-distance never ends well. I don't want us to end up losing what we have here because we're trying to make it into something more. And the longer we see each other, the more it will hurt when it ends.'

'You *asked me* to stay here for you, Neve.'

Neve bowed her head as though the fact embarrassed her. 'I know.'

'And I . . . I was *going* to,' Robin continued through her stutters. 'I was going to *stay*.'

Surprise flickered in Neve. 'You were?'

'Yes, I bloody well was! *God*, Neve. Would it be so bad if we did try? Or is asking you to do that a step too far? Is this only good for you on *your* terms?'

'You know that's not fair. I wouldn't be here, doing this, if I didn't care. If I didn't want to try. But it's just not realistic to carry this on. I'm sorry, Robin. It's just not. You live in England, for God's sake.'

'I know where I live,' Robin snapped. Neve said it as though it was so far away, but Robin . . . Robin had been looking through job listings in Calgary. She'd been imagining seeing in the new year with Neve – with a person who gave up on her so easily, who drew the line at getting on a plane but still expected Robin to stay. A person who didn't even want to try. Tears burned in her eyes, and in her attempt to blink them away, they only spilled onto her frostbitten cheeks. 'You've done all these things for me. You brought me *here*. You asked me to stay. I thought . . .'

'I told you I was wrong to ask you that. I should never have put that pressure on us. This was only supposed to be a . . .' Neve trailed off as though she didn't know herself. Maybe that was the problem. They'd never really decided what they were – not out loud. Not since the kiss. They'd been moving so quickly since then, Robin had just assumed it was more. More than a holiday fling. After all, Neve had gotten upset when that's what she'd watered it down as to Wren. She'd put in all this effort, all these romantic dates and surprises. They hadn't even been intimate until last night. That wasn't a fling, was it? That was dating. That was caring. What was Robin supposed to think?

'A what?'

'It was only supposed to be temporary.'

'Do you bring all of your dates here for a casual hook-up? Because I thought this place was important.' It hurt to even think about. Hurt more when she thought about the words she couldn't say: *I thought* I *was important.* And maybe it wasn't fair or rational, because even Hazel had called Neve a lone wolf, but what else was she supposed to think when everything that had mattered last night was being dismissed?

Neve flinched. 'Of course not. This was for you.'

Robin couldn't look at Neve anymore, so she turned her gaze to the lake as she pulled her hat over her ears. 'Okay. Then I suppose it was just a perfect goodbye, wasn't it?'

'It doesn't have to be goodbye. You don't leave for another couple of days,' Neve countered, her frown deepening and her grip on Robin's hand tightening. Robin finally found the courage to snatch it away, winding her scarf tighter around her neck.

But why drag it out? Robin thought but didn't say aloud. Her silence must have been clear enough because Neve said nothing as she packed away the blankets. And maybe Neve was right. Robin didn't want to keep doing this, knowing that they were just biding time until she left. She wanted to feel wanted. Special. The way she'd felt last night when Neve had brought her to look at the lights and touched her like they were both made of magic. But the problem with Neve was that she changed too quickly. Robin would never really know what she wanted, probably because Neve didn't know herself. Whatever it was, it wasn't her. Not past the next few days, anyway. That was clear now.

They drove home without another word, disappointment and something far worse that Robin wasn't willing to acknowledge lying like jagged-edged stones in her gut.

It's over. It's over. It's over.

She repeated it in her head until it felt like the truth.

Chapter Seventeen

Neve felt stripped bare as she wandered into the kitchen that morning, having dropped Robin back at the resort. They'd barely talked on the way home, and Neve still felt that hollow silence echoing through her now, as though she was the one carrying it, causing it. As though she *was* the silence.

Juniper was the only one to break it. She bounded down the stairs upon Neve's arrival, as happy to see her as though she'd been gone for years.

'Hey, girl,' Neve whispered, a twinge of sadness in her voice as she crouched and petted the husky. 'I missed you.'

When Juniper had gotten her fair share of attention, Neve gathered the blankets she'd dropped at her feet and rose from her haunches. Something colourful floated from them, crumpled and torn, when she threw them onto the couch lazily. The Alpine Canada flyer for the team trials that Robin had given her. With a sigh, she picked it up off the floor and skimmed through it. The page she was looking for was the first one she opened. A popular alpine skier who Neve had once idolised was pictured between boxes of information.

The Calgary trials were in March, just like Robin had said. She could apply online to get her place, but really, it would be easier to contact Lara directly.

Frustrated and confused and *aching*, Neve snatched her hat off her head and threw it on the couch. The leaflet soon followed.

'Now what did that hat ever do to you?'

Grandpa stood in the doorway, bushy eyebrows raised. He still wore his pinstripe pyjamas. Sleep crusted his glassy eyes and he had his slippers on the wrong feet.

She couldn't help but give him a small smile as she smoothed down her mussed hair. 'Sorry. I didn't know you were up.'

Grandpa shrugged. 'Heard you come in. It must have been one heck of a date.'

That was one way to describe it. She perched on the armchair as Grandpa hobbled in on arthritic ankles and collapsed onto the couch. He found the leaflet wedged into the cracks of the cushions. 'Another of your victims?'

Panicked, Neve tried to snatch it away, but for all his bad joints, Grandpa was still quick when he needed to be. *Had to be*, he'd told her once. *Your gran pinched all the food off my plate otherwise. I'd have to go hungry.*

'And what's this?' He whistled through his teeth, sifting through the pamphlet with a lopsided smile. 'Ski trials, huh?'

'It's just something Robin picked up from the resort,' Neve brushed off, though curiosity – and perhaps a little hope – gnawed at her. She knew that if she told Grandpa, he'd support her; urge her to do it, even. Maybe that was half the problem. 'It's nothing.'

'Are you finally getting back on the team?'

'No.'

His face crumpled in confusion. 'Why not?'

'*Because* . . .' she reasoned, shucking off her coat. She kept her scarf on, too cosy to let it go yet.

'Oh.' Grandpa's smile twisted with sarcasm. 'Well, in that case . . .'

Neve huffed. 'It would mean a lot of change.'

'And?' He waited expectantly, those pale eyes turning stern; judgemental.

'I like my life how it is. Here. Teaching. It's simple and uncomplicated.' Minus the woman who had managed to turn everything upside down in a matter of days – and Mom's return, of course. 'Travelling all the time . . . I don't want to go back to that.'

'You're running away in case it doesn't go the way you want it to,' he stated as though it was a fact.

'No.' Neve couldn't help but pout at the accusation.

'*Neve.*' Her grandfather gave her a pointed look, his mouth pursed into a crinkled, thin line as he placed the pamphlet down. 'It's okay to be afraid. But you can't let it stop you from chasing your dreams. You loved being on the team. You can't fool me into thinking otherwise.'

Tears gathered in Neve's eyes without invitation, and she couldn't stop them from falling – for her grandpa, who had always been so kind and loving, and for her future, which was so uncertain, and for the unspoken things she had lost today because she was too afraid, and for herself, for being the reason that she always found a way to mess things up before they could ever really start.

She was afraid. She was afraid of setting her heart on something, someone, only to lose it. To try out for the team again and find out she'd lost her talent. To try out a long-distance relationship and find out she wasn't good enough. It felt as though she didn't have a grasp on anything. Everything she had ever wanted could slip so easily through her fingers, just like it always had before. God, the first person she'd ever relied on had left her over and over and over again. What did that say about her?

Juniper crawled into her lap, grounding her. She buried her face into the dog's fur, smelling the earth and the cold and the subtle cinnamon shampoo the groomer had washed her with last week. Grandpa shuffled, and then his hand was on hers, and it was the least alone she'd felt in a long time.

'You kept me going on some of my darkest days, sweetheart,' he said delicately. 'But it's time to do something for yourself again. It's time to show everybody what you're made of.'

Neve clenched her jaw, a moment away from crumbling. 'You wouldn't be lonely here without me?'

He scoffed. 'Are you kidding? I'd have a blast. I could

walk around naked like one of those nudists, and live off microwave meals and takeout. No more hair in my drain, either . . . I might even get a cat. Not that I'm trying to get rid of you, of course. Mind you, that's only if your mother skedaddles again soon, too.'

Neve couldn't help laughing at that, even as her tears flowed steadily into Juniper's grey fur. 'She's good at that.'

'Well, maybe you should take a leaf from her book. Try.' He squeezed her hands, and she lifted her gaze to find his own eyes watery, too. 'Try for me, Neve. Your gran would have wanted it. In fact, she would have forced you not to give up your dream, because it was hers, too: to see you at the Olympics one day. You can't do that if you don't try.'

Neve sucked in a ragged breath and wiped her face with her sleeve. She no longer had any excuses, and she wouldn't have wanted them anyway. Everybody believed in her – Irina, Grandpa, Robin, Nick. Gran had, too. Maybe it was time she believed in herself.

'Okay,' she vowed. 'I'll try. For you.'

Robin had been moping all morning and she had no intention of stopping anytime soon. The unsolicited plate of "poutine" placed in front of her by Nick – to Robin, it was just chips and gravy with the cheese in curd form instead of grated – when she relocated her sulking to the bar did little to cheer her up. That was saying something, too. Robin loved comfort food.

'I didn't order this,' she pointed out, barely bothering to lift her gaze as she rested her chin glumly in her palm.

Nick placed a fork beside the plate and then pressed his palms into the bar. 'Gravy and cheese fix everything.'

Wrinkling her nose, Robin stabbed the fork into the soggy fried potatoes and nibbled on the crisp corner. The gravy was rich and salty, the cheese melting into it deliciously. It wasn't tasty enough to fix what had been broken, though.

'Are you going to tell me what happened?' asked Nick. 'No.'

She didn't even know why she'd come here, to the one place she knew Neve's brother would be. But the bar had become a shelter when she was feeling icky, and not just because of the alcoholic eggnogs and terrible karaoke – which, thankfully, was not happening this early in the day. No, she'd come to like Nick's company, which was unusual, since she rarely found friendship in rugged, older men like him. But he'd been kind to her, and she didn't think she had to talk to him for him to know how she felt, or what drink it was she needed. He seemed to understand her, sometimes even better than Neve did. And the siblings shared that strange sense of steadiness, as though they were rocks Robin could lean all her weight against without budging.

But maybe she'd been wrong about that when it came to Neve. Maybe Neve was the slipperiest type of rock Robin had ever found – the seaweed-covered sort she tried to avoid in the ocean. Robin would never be able to rest her weight on her without falling and cutting open her soles.

'Wrong answer.' Nick sniffed and wiped the bar down with a damp cloth, slipping beneath Robin's elbows to catch the drips of gravy she'd already spilled. 'Talk to me.'

'I don't think I should,' she admitted. 'I don't want to put you in an uncomfortable position.'

'I love my sister, but I know as well as anyone else that she can be a stubborn pain in the ass.'

Robin shook her head. 'She's not a pain in the arse – though she is stubborn. She's done nothing wrong. Maybe *I'm* the problem.'

Nick lifted an eyebrow expectantly, and Robin knew she had no chance of avoiding the subject now.

'I get too attached,' she elaborated. 'I . . . I care too much.' Her voice cracked with the last word, and she hated herself for it; hated herself for only proving the fact that she did care. She *always* cared.

Nick sighed and poured an undiluted shot of whiskey into a tumbler, sliding it across the table for Robin. She took it gratefully, throwing it down in one and relishing the burn licking down her throat. 'Don't fool yourself into thinking you're the only one who cares, Robin. I've known my sister her whole life, and I've never known her to . . . *glow* like this before.'

'*Glow?*' Neve didn't glow. Not because of Robin, anyway. Maybe she'd shimmered a little bit under the aurora last night, but that was just the magical green lights and the moonlight. Not Robin. Robin would never hold that much power over somebody as guarded as Neve. Would she?

'When your family's a little bit broken and messy, it weighs on you. Neve has spent a long time protecting herself from getting hurt again, from being abandoned. She likes to think it makes her strong, makes her unbreakable. But she isn't like that with you. She's opening up to you, slowly. She lets herself be happy with you.'

Despite the flutter in Robin's stomach, Nick's words made no sense to her. Neve *wasn't* opening up. She was pushing Robin away, shutting her down, refusing to entertain anything more than the last few days they had together unless it was on her terms. 'Because of your mum, you mean?'

Nick gave a solemn nod. 'We could never rely on her, and I think Neve took that personally. I think it makes her scared to trust. But that doesn't mean she won't, in time. She cares about you. Maybe more than she's ever cared about anyone.'

Robin understood the fear that came with trusting. People were unreliable, ever-changing, and every connection she made would be a gamble – one she'd always broach with caution after what Lexi did to her. But when it came down to it, Robin would always try.

'She has a funny way of showing it.' There was no bitterness in Robin's words. She couldn't blame Neve, not really. Maybe she still blamed herself for not being better. Prettier. More extraordinary. She was just a girl from Manchester who had an insatiable sweet tooth and embarrassed herself often. Just the girl Lexi had cheated on.

'She does,' agreed Nick. 'But that doesn't mean it's not true. You wear your heart on your sleeve, Robin. Neve keeps hers a little closer, a little more hidden. You have to accept that. You have to keep trying with her.'

'But she doesn't *want* to try. I can't force her to.' Robin's eyes blurred with tears, and she pushed her plate away as words she'd only ever thought before spilled out of her. 'Besides, it shouldn't be this hard, should it? We've known each other for less than two weeks, and we're already on completely different pages. Maybe I don't want to have to keep *trying*, Nick. Maybe I just want someone who wants me back, plain and simple. Maybe I just want it to be easy for a change. I've been hurt, too. I'm on my bloody honeymoon alone, for God's sake. So why? Why is it always me who has to care and love and forgive? Why can't someone try for *me* for a change? Why can't I just be *enough*?'

Nick sucked in a breath, hazel eyes softening with sympathy until Robin no longer wanted to let him see all of the awful, needy, desperate things inside of her. But it was too late, and it was all true. She'd always been the one to try more. With Lexi, with her family, and now with Neve. All it ever brought her was pain and silent treatments and betrayals. Why was she here, trying to fix something she hadn't been the one to break?

How much more of herself could she give?

For the first time since she'd gotten here, Robin wanted to go home. She wanted to see her sister and her mum and Cleopawtra. She wanted to sleep in her own bed and eat a colossal chippy tea – instead of bloody poutine – while she watched *The Chase* on telly. She was done. Completely, utterly done. She needed normality back. She needed something familiar.

'Robin,' Nick began, his voice tender. But Robin didn't want to hear it. She wanted to get on the next plane to Manchester.

She stood from the stool on numb legs and dragged her

heavy coat on. The coat Neve had given her. 'Thanks for the food. I'm going to go.'

'To see Neve?'

'No. No, I'm going home. It was really nice to meet you, Nick.'

Concern flickered across Nick's dark features, and he wiped his hands down on his towel, shifting on his feet as he watched Robin loop her scarf around her neck. 'No, Robin. Please don't go yet. Just talk to her first. Please.'

'I can't,' Robin refused, throat aching with sadness. 'I just . . . I can't do it again. Bye, Nick. Say goodbye to Hazel and Margo and your grandpa for me, too, won't you?'

'*Robin*,' Nick pleaded – but Robin couldn't listen anymore. For once, she was choosing to do the right thing for herself. She wouldn't let anyone stop her. Not even if a small part of her still wanted to stay, to try.

She was done trying and done staying for people who didn't want her. It was time to move on. Time to let go. Time to walk away for good.

Chapter Eighteen

Being back in the cabin made Robin want to cry. It held too many memories of Neve and the day they had kissed for the first time. They'd been lying to each other, themselves, by pretending they could fall into something without consequences. Or Robin had, at least. She should have known she wasn't built for short-term. When she cared, she cared with everything she had. A million miles away from home, on her honeymoon alone, and that still hadn't changed. She still hadn't learned.

Or maybe she had, and she just didn't care. Maybe she'd rather throw her heart into something completely than not at all, because as much as her separation from Lexi had hurt, and as much as this hurt now, the months spent feeling hollow and without purpose after the grief had ended had been far worse.

And it wasn't a bad thing to care. A part of her even knew Neve did, too. For all her guardedness, she'd still taken care of Robin and surprised her with all sorts of nice things. It just wasn't enough in the end. She wasn't on the same page as Robin. She wasn't willing to keep going. Robin couldn't force Neve to want her any more than she could turn back time and un-propose to Lexi.

Still, she had to pack her things, book a flight, get the hell out of here, and pull herself together once and for all. She gathered her suitcase at the foot of the bed, heaving it up as she sniffled. She could wait it out if she wanted to. She still had the bakery and Hazel, even Nick. But she felt ready to go. She'd gotten everything she needed to out of her time away. She'd learned to love being on her own again, had realised she wanted more from life than a dull job with a boss who didn't listen to her and a mother who couldn't support her when she needed it. She was going home with a clear head . . . mostly. A Neve-infested head and heart, perhaps, but she'd manage.

Robin left her romance books on the table, half-tempted to throw them in the log fire altogether. All they'd ever done was make her believe in something that didn't exist, first with Lexi and then with Neve. Maybe that was her problem. She expected people to act like characters did in books, where love conquered all. It didn't. People had different hearts. Robin couldn't keep hurting herself by waiting for people to love her.

She marched into the bathroom for her toiletries, leaving wet puddles of snow in her wake, and threw them into any bags she could find. It would be a pain at customs, but she just wanted to go before she changed her mind. Seeing Neve again after this, when Robin had asked her to fly to England, to try for a real relationship . . . it was too humiliating. She couldn't cope if Neve offered her pity. Couldn't cope with going back to being strangers after what they'd had together.

Once the bathroom was cleared, she searched for her purse, finding it hidden beneath the four-poster bed. Her passport and plane tickets were all tucked in there. God help her if she couldn't get on an earlier flight now. She checked her phone app just to be sure and found there was a flight to Leeds tonight with seats still available. It would do.

Her throat ached as she zipped up her suitcase and cast a final glance around the room. The log fire was nothing but ash, and a blanket on the couch had been left by Neve the last time she was here, with blondie and biscuit crumbs scattered across it.

Robin couldn't help herself. If this was the last, only, bit of Neve she could keep, she wanted to soak it in. She lifted it to her nose, nostrils tickled by the fuzzy material as she inhaled. It still smelled like her: like fresh snow and pine, and that sea-salt-scented deodorant she always freshened up with after a day on the slopes.

Tears rolled down Robin's cheeks. She really thought she'd found something special for a moment. Something worth moving to Calgary for. She'd hoped for something new for the first time in so long, but that had all been stamped out. Again.

Closure was a myth. She'd never gotten it with Lexi, and she wouldn't get it with Neve. But that didn't mean she couldn't move on, keep going. After nine months, Robin had figured out that she'd never been the one who hadn't been good enough for Lexi. It had never been about her at all. Just like Neve's commitment issues weren't Robin's fault or a measure of how well she deserved to be loved. People were just . . . messy. And Robin had to find a way to be okay with it, to stop using it as a way to make it about her, to put herself down.

She put the blanket in her suitcase as a reminder of that – and a reminder that just because it couldn't last, didn't mean it wasn't good. Because it had been good, and she had crawled out of her shell with Neve. Trusted again, even. She wouldn't forget the good experiences she'd had in Clement Falls.

And that was it. Apart from the worn paperbacks, everything Robin owned was piled back into her suitcase. The cabin wasn't hers anymore. It never had been. Just like everything else.

Robin was relieved to be out in the fresh air, closing the door on the emptiness. She trudged towards the lobby, the gleaming snow blindingly bright against the midday sun and her suitcase impossible to navigate in a straight line. Helen waited behind the front desk when she stepped in, her expression as blank as ever.

'Hello, Helen.' Robin forced a watery smile, swiping her hair from her flushed face as she set down her luggage. 'I was wondering if you'd be able to book me a taxi to the airport.'

'Leaving early?' Helen sounded not to care much either way as she dialled a number on an old-fashioned telephone.

'Yep.'

'What a terrible shame.'

Robin rolled her eyes, any retort cut off as Helen began to request a cab in clipped syllables that surely must have frightened whoever sat on the receiving end. She was one person Robin wouldn't miss. Elk-on John on the other hand . . .

She wandered over to him, patting his stiff snout. 'Bye, old friend.'

Elk-on only looked at her out of hollow, beady eyes, and it was about the warmest anyone had been to her all day.

'Tell her I said bye,' she whispered, quieter now. 'Juniper, too.'

Elk-on looked as though he planned on telling Neve no such thing, but it still brought Robin some comfort to know she had at least said it aloud, even if Neve wasn't here to hear it.

It would have to be enough. Helen placed down her receiver not a moment after to tell Robin that a cab was on its way.

The honeymoon was well and truly over.

Neve practically sped her way back to the resort when she'd gotten the text from Nick that Robin was planning on leaving early. Her chest had throbbed with guilt and sadness and desperation as she put her foot on the gas. The truck groaned in complaint as they crawled uphill towards the resort, but Neve had no time to worry. She had to stop Robin, had to tell her that she wanted more time. That she wanted so much more than she'd let on this morning, when she'd been overwhelmed and afraid, because nothing had ever felt this good before. Nothing. Not even winning the gold in her last competition before she'd quit, or finding out she'd been chosen for the Olympic ski team. If it meant going to England for New Year and navigating some kind of long-distance thing, she'd do it. She'd do anything. Robin needed to know that.

She gritted her teeth and tried to accelerate again as she rounded the same bend she'd crashed on just a few days ago. Flakes of snow drifted across her windshield, somehow seeming to move faster than she was. She was slowing down.

'Come on,' she begged. Her tyres seemed to resist, the truck screeching now – and then stopping completely. The engine cut out without permission, leaving her in a soul-crushing silence.

'No.' She slapped the steering wheel as though that might revive it, then tried to turn the key in the ignition again with tremoring fingers. The engine sputtered slightly and then ebbed again. Gone. 'No, please.'

With a vehement curse, Neve pocketed her keys and hopped out of the truck. The resort was only a few minutes away. She would just have to run.

So she did, the vicious wind stealing her breath and her muscles burning. She took a shortcut through the woods, almost collapsing with relief when Robin's solitary cabin came into view. Breathless, she raced up the steps and knocked on the door, teeth chattering.

But she was greeted only by silence.

'Robin?' she shouted. 'Are you in there?'

Nothing. Neve peered through the window and found the cabin in darkness, empty. She was too late.

Her heart sank, but she wasn't ready to give up yet. She almost tumbled back down the stairs and headed for the main lobby, taking the shortcut through brambles and leafless shrubs until her hands were scratched and clothes tattered. No. Neve wouldn't let Robin leave her. She would catch her in time.

Only when she reached the old building, the taillights of a cab winked at her before retreating into the pines, onto the winding road away from the resort.

She could guess who might be in it. She could feel it in

the way her heart deflated and knees buckled, as though her absence had sucked away Neve's life. Robin.

Neve gulped down her tears and, after watching the cab disappear completely, checked the lobby just to be sure. She had to be sure.

Hope was the only thing that kept her feet stumbling forward. She skidded to a stop in the mostly empty lobby, almost impaling herself on the taxidermied moose head as she reached out for something to clutch on to. Helen stood at the desk, blowing a pink bubble of gum from her permanently pouty lips.

'Robin,' Neve gasped out. 'Have you seen her?'

'The British woman who talks to the moose?' Helen asked, though Neve was certain she already knew who Robin was. 'Sure. She just left.'

'Where? Where did she go?' *Not the airport. Please, not the airport.*

Helen's pencilled brows knitted together. 'The airport?' She said it as though it was a question, or else an obvious answer.

Neve's heart collapsed into her stomach.

Robin was really gone – and Neve had a feeling that even if she somehow miraculously found her before her flight took off, it wouldn't make a difference. She had already well and truly blown it. That little bit of hope she'd held on to dwindled, leaving her in darkness.

She couldn't be abandoned again. She couldn't go to the airport and beg for Robin to stay, only to have to watch her leave anyway, whether today or this weekend or in four weeks' time. She'd learned long ago never to cling to somebody impermanent, and she just . . . couldn't do it again. Couldn't feel that pain. Not with Robin. It was why she was better off alone. It was why she should never have gotten attached.

She stared at the moose – Elk-on John, she'd heard Robin call him more than a few times – as though he might have the answers she needed. But the lifeless, stuffed head wouldn't bring Robin back, Neve knew. Nothing would now.

When Neve stepped back out into the cold, she seemed to feel it in a way she never had before. It burrowed into her skin and bones and made a home there. Neve could only kick at the tyre-packed snow and wonder what would have happened if she'd realised her own stupidity sooner.

She had a feeling she'd be wondering "what if?" for a long time to come.

Feeling hollow, Neve went to the bar if only to slap Nick around the head for making her come here and face this. It would have been easier if she hadn't tried. If she hadn't seen that cab taking Robin away.

'*Ow!*' he shouted, clutching his skull as though she'd used a cricket bat and not a weak, trembling hand. 'What was that for?'

'What was *that* for?' Neve repeated incredulously. 'Why am I here, Nick?'

'I was doing you a favour! Robin said she was leaving. Why aren't you stopping her?'

'I tried!' she snapped. 'I fucking tried, Nick. My car broke down, and I couldn't get here on time.' And then, quietly: 'She's gone.'

Sorrow leached the colour from Nick's face, and he stopped cleaning down the bar to look at Neve properly. She could only scowl at him, though she knew deep down it wasn't his fault. It was hers, for being a stubborn, emotionally unavailable idiot with trust issues.

'There's still a chance. Have you checked flight times?'

'It doesn't matter.' Neve sniffed, the garland-sheathed fairy lights blurring in her bleary eyes. She prayed to God she wouldn't cry. Not here. 'It's over.'

Nick's chest heaved with a heavy sigh, and he slammed down the pint glass he'd been polishing with so much force that Neve expected it to shatter.

'Is that what you want?' The question was aggressive, too loud, so that the few couples who had come in for midday drinks turned to look at them. Neve scowled at every one of them – even the one she'd taught on the slopes yesterday.

'It doesn't matter what I want,' she hissed, voice low: a warning. 'I tried. It didn't work. It's over.'

Her brother scoffed in disbelief. 'You tried, did you? So you told Robin how you really felt?'

'Did you not hear me? She's gone!'

'She's not gone. She's heading to the airport, where she will probably be waiting for hours yet before she gets on a flight home. And when that happens, she's going to think you didn't care enough to stop her. Only you can change that.'

Neve shook her head. 'I'm not going to chase her down and pour my heart out like this is some rom-com. It isn't, and we barely even know each other, and she chose to leave without a goodbye. You're *my* brother. You're supposed to be on my side.'

'No. It doesn't work like that. As your brother, it's my duty to tell you that you're a fool.' He narrowed his eyes, leaning across the bar to meet her eye. 'I spoke to Robin. She told me that all she wanted was someone to try for her. Someone to fight for her. Hell, she deserves that. Everyone does. You're not going to get her back by sitting on your ass. I wish I would have fought harder for my last relationship. I wish I would have compromised when Molly asked instead of throwing in the towel as soon as it got tough. You and me, we're too set in our ways, too content with letting people leave us – and as long as we stay that way, we're going to end up alone. Do you understand?'

'What am I supposed to do?' Her voice came out mangled, broken. 'She lives in England; I live here. How can that ever work?'

'If you want it to work, it will work.' He softened and curled his hand around hers. 'I know that you like her. I know that she makes you happy. You're running out of time to make sure *she* knows that, too. And if you want her to stick around, she *needs* to know – and you need to be willing to work for it.'

'It shouldn't be this hard.'

The corner of his mouth rose with a soft, solemn smile. 'She said the same thing to me.'

Lost for words, Neve blinked the tears from her lashes and traced crescent moons into the old, rough wood beneath her fingertips. It *shouldn't* be this hard. But was she making it harder? She should have been more willing to try. Should have said yes when Robin had asked her to go to Manchester for New Year's. She didn't even know why she hadn't; only that it had filled her with the same fear that crept in on her every time she thought about Robin leaving.

But now she *had* left. They had run out of time. And the pain she felt was all the confirmation she needed that she wasn't ready to give her heart away to someone who might break it – or worse, abandon it. If she went to the airport and had to watch Robin get on that plane anyway . . .

Neve couldn't keep standing by and watching people walk out of her life. She couldn't do it to herself again.

'I'm going home.'

Nick's jaw ticked with tension. 'You're making a mistake.'

Neve sighed, too exhausted to argue. 'I guess that's nothing new, then.'

Chapter Nineteen

The last thing Neve wanted to do when she got home was face her mom. And yet, lo and behold, her mom sat on the couch, watching *How the Grinch Stole Christmas*, with Juniper on her lap. An interesting development.

Traitor. Neve fed and walked the husky every damn day, and after one morning left at home, Juniper was fraternising with the enemy. The very woman who had locked her outside in the snow a couple of days ago.

They both turned around when Neve kicked off her boots, the movie left paused.

'Where have you been?' Mom asked. 'We've barely seen you since yesterday.'

'That was the point.' Neve shucked off her coat, slapping it down in annoyance when it clung to the thick sleeves of her sweater. She felt . . . hollow. Hopeless. Robin was gone. Neve had to keep repeating it to herself otherwise she might forget. All of the sparkle she'd found so suddenly, so unexpectedly, had been leached away, and it was no one's fault but her own.

'Are you okay, sweetie?'

Neve almost gagged at the pet name. 'Wonderful. I'm going upstairs.'

Juniper hopped down from the couch to allow Mom to do the same, and Neve gritted her teeth when Mom's footsteps padded behind her own. 'Has something happened? You look all sad . . .'

'I *am* sad!' Neve erupted, surprising even herself. She clutched the staircase banister for support, her knuckles turning white. 'I'm sad that I got so used to being let down by you that I expected the same thing from everyone else. I'm sad that I push people away and I'm sad that now Robin is gone because of me.' The words came out choked, clogged by the sob building in her throat. 'I'm sad, Mom, all right? I'm sad.'

And I'm scared, she wanted to add. Scared that she'd never be brave enough to let anybody in. That she'd be alone for the rest of her life, just like Nick had warned.

Mom's lips parted, her green, eyeliner-ringed eyes widening in confusion. 'Slow down, Neve. Please.'

'Just forget it, okay? You stopped being my mother years ago, and you're the last person I want to talk to about this.'

'I . . .' Mom inched forward cautiously, fingers curling at her sides as though she was stopping herself from reaching out. 'Don't say that, please. I never stopped being your mother.'

'But you did. And I stopped expecting you to. So let's not pretend. I . . . I don't have the energy to pretend today.' She was so tired. Drained. Her skin was sagging from her bones, shoulders slumped, one step away from falling apart – if she could just get some privacy. If her mom would just let her go upstairs and deal with it alone like she always did. But as she made to leave, Mom's hand caught her wrist.

'I'd like to talk about this.'

Neve shook her head, at a loss. They'd had *years* to talk about this. Years of nothing. 'It's too late.'

'Look, I know I haven't always been . . .' Mom hesitated, chewing on her glossy pink bottom lip. Neve almost snorted. Even now, Mom couldn't just admit the ways she'd let her down. 'I know our relationship is frayed, and I know a lot of it is because of me. But you can talk to me, Neve. You can *always* talk to me.'

'It's too late,' Neve repeated, ripping her hand from Mom's grasp. Tears pricked her eyes. Any moment, she'd fall apart. Any moment. 'You weren't there for me. Now I don't need you.'

'That's not fair. You haven't been there for me either.'

Disbelief left Neve's lungs tightening, her breaths jagged. 'I was a *kid*!'

'I mean recently,' Mom snapped. 'You never call. When *I* call, you don't pick up the phone or you're short with me. You didn't want me here over Christmas. You couldn't care less about me.'

'Because you stopped caring about me when I was *eight*.' The first hot trickle of dampness rolled down Neve's cheek, her chest aching with so much more than she could say. 'How can you not see that? You missed out on half of my childhood, Mom. Nick and Grandpa and Gran raised me. They came to my ski competitions and my graduation and my school shows. You weren't there. You were gone.'

'I had a busy schedule, Neve. For heaven's sake, *somebody* needed to bring an income into this house.'

But Neve would have been happier living in a cardboard box than dealing with the fact that her mom just didn't care. Because she hadn't just stayed away for work. She'd stayed away for oily men in Magaluf or mansion parties in LA. She'd road-tripped with her single, younger friends all summer and made a home out of airport hotel rooms. It had all been a choice: her children or her social life. Being a parent or being a rootless, fun party girl. The fact was that Neve just hadn't fit into the things Mom had wanted, and Neve had blamed herself for too long. That ended now.

'I'm done with this conversation,' Neve hissed out now. 'I'm done with feeling bad about this. You made your choice, Mom. You let me down. You can deny it all you want. You'll be gone again soon anyway, and we can go back to biannual phone calls. How's that?'

She didn't wait for a reply, instead marching up the stairs. Juniper must have seen sense, because she followed her up, into her room. And only there could Neve finally admit to herself that she had to change. She might not have been a sun-kissed, Chardonnay-sipping jetsetter like Mom, but she was about as emotionally unavailable as her.

Neve didn't want to end up alone. She didn't want to end up surrounded by a house full of people who resented her for being cold and uncaring and self-absorbed.

Most of all, though, she just wanted Robin back. She wanted a chance to turn back the clock and say yes when Robin asked her to go to Manchester for New Year.

And now, like everything else in her life, it was too late.

Chapter Twenty

Robin's mum almost dropped the family's beloved stack of china plates when she answered the door the following afternoon, juggling half of the kitchen's contents in her hands. The warm, slightly charred smell of her nut roast followed her out of the door and wrapped itself around Robin like a fluffy cardigan.

After seven hours of waiting on standby in Calgary Airport yesterday, they'd managed to squeeze Robin onto the cramped flight to Leeds Bradford, with brief, albeit chaotic, layovers in Toronto and Dublin. It was a relief, being back. The dreary English rain and motorways – normality – had embraced her with open arms, and she'd let herself fall into them as soon as she'd gotten into the taxi with a very chatty Yorkshireman.

Beneath all that, though, she couldn't help but feel disappointed, unfulfilled. This wasn't how it was supposed to end. It didn't feel like it really *had* ended yet. Knowing Robin would never see Neve again, or Juniper, or Nick, or even Artie and Hazel . . .

And she hadn't said goodbye to anybody but Nick.

She couldn't ignore how much it hurt, right to the very pit of her stomach. But it was for the best, she told herself. She was home, and she would move on, and it would be for the best in the end.

It was easier to pretend that it was the truth when her mother's shrill voice distracted her from her internal pity party. 'Robin! Bloody hell! You're home!'

'I'm home.' Robin forced a taut grin and walked into Mum's arms. The plates dug into her ribs, but Mum's grip dug harder.

'Thank goodness you've seen sense. Christmas wouldn't be Christmas without you! You could have warned me, though! I don't know if there'll be enough of my nut roast now!'

'Robin?' another soft voice echoed from the hallway. Robin lifted her gaze from the floral apron ties across her mother's shoulder and found her sister standing at the foot of the stairs, her blue eyes wide and her arms drowned by an old knitted reindeer jumper gifted to her by Nanna Bessie four years ago. 'What the hell are you doing back here so early?'

Robin stepped away from Mum, willing her eyes not to fill with tears as she smiled solemnly at Wren. 'I was ready to come home.'

Wren seemed to understand – she *always* seemed to understand – and opened her arms out, waiting. Robin abandoned her suitcase on the welcome mat, Mum shifting out of her way so she could stumble inside and fall into her sister's familiar arms. There were a lot of things she wished she could change about her family, but this wasn't one of them.

At the end of the day, she would always feel that comforting, tingly feeling in her chest when she came home. Maybe she was better off here. Maybe, in the end, this was just how it was meant to be, and Canada had just been a reminder of that, a punishment for that crazy, fleeting moment Robin had spent letting herself believe otherwise.

'What happened?' Wren whispered into her hair and then pulled away to get a real look at Robin, squishing her cheeks together until she laughed.

'Nothing.'

Cleopawtra, delayed as ever, bumbled in from the kitchen before Wren could respond. The chihuahua yapped at Robin's feet until she picked her up, wincing as her sandpaper-like tongue swiped across her cheek. Her breath reeked of tuna. No doubt she had been the one to eat Robin's helping of the Christmas Eve Eve Eve fish pie yesterday. 'Hello, Cleo.'

'Nanna Bessie will be so chuffed to see you!' Mum said, brushing past them to return to the kitchen.

'Yay.'

Wren smirked at Robin's lacklustre response, but then her brows knitted together again. 'You sure you're okay?'

'I'm sure. I'll tell you about it later.'

'Come on!' Mum bellowed again from the kitchen. 'The food is getting cold!'

Robin rolled her eyes and let Wren drag her into the kitchen, Cleopawtra still in her arms. Besides Nanna Bessie sitting at the table with a large tablecloth tucked into her collar like an adult bib, everything was how she had left it two weeks ago, and she kept trying to convince herself that it was a good thing. Wren's boyfriend, Tom, had joined them, too, eyeing his helping of nut roast warily.

She forced a shaky smile, exhaustion weighing her down. 'Hello, Nanna. Hello, Tom.'

Nanna Bessie's milky eyes fell to Robin in surprise. 'Oh hello, love! Where have you been? Work?'

'No, Nanna. I was in Canada.' Robin took a seat beside Nanna. Mum shoved a plate of food in her face, and Robin had missed home so much that she actually risked eating it. It was at least a smaller helping than usual.

The huge bite she took was a mistake, but a bitter-sweet one – or bitter-savoury. The charred, crusty edges of the roast were vile, but they were home, and Robin had missed it.

'Canada,' Tom remarked, nudging his thick-rimmed glasses back onto the bridge of his nose. The lenses were fogged up from his steaming plate of food. 'The land of maple syrup. Did you know that they're one of the world's leading countries in uranium mining?'

'God.' Tears prickled in Robin's plane-dry eyes. 'I've even missed your boring facts, Tom.'

'*Robin*,' Wren scolded, but then patted Tom's hand and said: 'That *was* a bit boring, babe.'

Tom shrugged, defeated, and then there was no more

putting off pretending to eat the nut roast. The table dissolved into intermittent conversations, Mum skilfully avoiding any more talk of Robin's holiday. Apparently, she still didn't want to acknowledge it.

It was so normal, so familiar, as though Robin had never been away at all – and yet she had to keep reminding herself that the canine at her feet wasn't Juniper, that it never would be again, and the dry loaf of spiced nuts began to clog her throat and lie heavy on her stomach. Not long ago, she'd woken bathed in a rosy sunrise, her usual four walls replaced by Neve's pickup truck, with the snow-capped Rockies and tall pines outside and a yawning Neve curled into her side. And now Robin was here again. Now it was over.

'So . . . is it Christmas Eve stir-fry for tea tomorrow, Mum?' she asked in an attempt to lighten her own mood. If she picked around the fish, she quite enjoyed the claggy noodles.

But Mum batted her hand. 'We decided to try something different this year. Bit sick of fish, and Cleopawtra ate the leftovers from the pie, anyway.'

This was a surprise. The Christmas Eve stir-fry was a decade-old tradition. Robin lifted her head from her plate, catching Wren's wry smirk and frowning. 'Eh?' was all she could stutter out. 'Have I walked into the wrong house?'

'Me and Mum were just talking about how we could make a few *new* traditions this year. Besides, I'm trying to cut back on fish. Watched an awful documentary about the environmental impact of fishing last week, and I'll never look at a tin of tuna the same again.' Wren shuddered. 'Anyway, I learned this recipe for spinach and carrot risotto—'

Robin groaned. She hated spinach, and Wren would probably use vegan cheese that tasted of cardboard. Still, stepping out of old, fishy tradition was a feat for Mum. Maybe things had changed after all. Maybe Mum was finally waking up again.

'Can't we just get a takeaway?' Robin asked.

Mum rolled her eyes. 'Don't push your luck, love.'

* * *

'All right. Tell me everything.' Wren thrust a mug of hot chocolate and Baileys into Robin's hands and sidled up to her on the sunken-in couch. Mum snored in the worn armchair beside the Christmas tree, Nanna Bessie had gone for a bath hours ago and never returned, and Tom was politely pretending to be interested in the film flickering on the flat-screen TV. Of course, the channel he'd chosen was the one currently playing *Home Alone*; a nice little reminder of Neve that Robin had to force her eyes away from. She didn't have time to be sad, not really. Tomorrow, the extended family would start rolling in and any semblance of peace would be shattered.

'There's nothing to tell.' Robin played with Cleopawtra's paws gently. The chihuahua must have missed her, because she'd sprawled out on her lap and now snored, tongue lolling with each exhalation.

'Liar. You sounded happy on the phone the other day.'

'Well, things changed.' She sighed. Neve and Robin's relationship had been so unsteady that she still felt the residual unease now. Or maybe that was just the what-ifs, the regret, the not knowing what was real and whether Robin should have left early. Had she been too impulsive? Given up too quickly? 'I shouldn't have gone in the first place anyway. It was a terrible idea.'

Wren poked Robin in the arm with enough force that she winced in pain.

'*Ow!*'

'Tell me,' Wren ordered. '*Now.*'

'*Fine.*' With a huff, Robin placed her snowman mug on the coffee table and made herself comfortable beneath the fluffy blanket. At least she could hide behind it should she need to. 'It just . . . all got very complicated.'

'With that ski instructor woman?' Wren arched a neatly plucked eyebrow.

Robin nodded, picking at her chipped, glittery nail polish to distract herself. It still didn't feel real. It didn't even feel as though their last conversation had only happened yesterday. It felt more like a hallucination or one of those vivid dreams Robin sometimes had when she ate cheese before bed, where everything felt hazy and far away.

'What happened?'

Creases etched themselves into Robin's freckled forehead. She could only shrug, though a million thoughts of Neve still spun around her mind, making her chest feel as heavy as the full-fat whipped cream floating in her Baileys. 'It didn't work.'

'Why?'

'Because she didn't want to do long-distance.'

'She *what*? After all that time she spent with you? What a b—'

Robin shushed her sister, glancing apprehensively at their snoring mother not too far away. Even Tom lifted his brows at his girlfriend's outburst, ever the polite, well-mannered gentleman. Wren cast him a saccharine smile before turning her attention back to Robin.

'*Ugh*,' she whispered. 'What a coward. She didn't even bloody try.'

'Maybe,' Robin murmured without conviction. She knew Neve wasn't a coward. She knew that she was only protective of her heart, and Robin couldn't blame her for that. In fact, she envied her. Maybe if Robin had the same guardedness, the same aloof defences, she wouldn't be here now, miserable. 'Suppose it was just a holiday fling thing. All the young people are having those now, aren't they?'

'Ay up,' Tom interrupted, peeling back the curtain. Strips of amber light from the streetlamps outside flooded into the living room. 'It's snowing.'

Robin frowned and pushed back the blanket – and Cleopawtra – to get up. The glass was cool against her forehead when she pressed her face to the window, searching for evidence of snow. Indeed, swollen, fluffy flakes drifted down onto the road, made more visible under the streetlights lining the cul-de-sac. 'It never snows at Christmas here.'

She didn't know why her voice cracked; why, for the first time, the snow didn't make her scowl in disdain.

'Maybe it followed you home,' Wren suggested. 'Gross. Take it back.'

But Robin didn't think it had followed her. She didn't think it was the same snow at all. It was a weak imitation of what she'd experienced in Clement Falls. Still, it reminded her of how the flakes had dripped into her coat and down her back when she'd found Neve emerging from that forest, searching desperately for Juniper. And Juniper had come to Robin that day; had come to find her after running away from Neve, as though she'd known. Neve had kissed her for the first time not long after. Robin's lips still tingled with the memory.

When she blinked, Robin found her eyes damp. She drew away from the window and forced herself back onto the sofa. She could feel Wren's eyes following her every move carefully and didn't have the energy to school her features, to hide her pain.

'I'm worried I'll never feel that way again,' she finally admitted, as much to herself as to her sister. 'I'm worried I'll never find the right person or the right job or the right place.'

Warmth wrapped around Robin's hand. Wren had taken it in her own, and she squeezed reassuringly. 'You will. Of course you will. If she didn't want to hold on to you, she didn't deserve you to begin with. But there's someone out there who'll do anything to be with you. I promise.'

Robin let the tears fall, then, and she let her sister wrap her arms around her as though she was trying to hold all of her broken pieces together. Because for just a moment, Robin had thought she'd found that. For just a moment, she'd thought Clement Falls had been the right place, and Neve the right person. For just a moment, she hadn't felt lost; she'd felt hope. Daring, daunting hope.

But that was gone now, and Robin wasn't sure she could ever get it back.

Chapter Twenty-One

Neve spent her Christmas Day as she always did: at home, with Grandpa, Nick, and Juniper, her belly swollen from good food and a few too many glasses of brandy in her system. But it all felt . . . wrong, and not just because Mom was still hanging around.

First off, she'd somehow burned dessert – a pre-made pumpkin pie from the store that had only needed warming in the oven. It had made her think of Robin and how, if she were here, nothing would be burned or missing. She longed for that day they'd had together, when Robin had baked gingerbread and they'd watched a movie on the couch until it had lulled them to sleep. It was too quiet without her. Too . . . everything.

Things were only more miserable because Mom still wasn't talking to her, and Neve didn't want her to. They'd left their final, bellowed words out in the open and not acknowledged one another since. Nick and Grandpa were pretending not to notice, but it still made Neve's chest feel heavy. All she'd wanted was an apology. Some sign that Mom knew she'd been shitty and flaky and distant. But maybe it was time to accept that Neve would never get it. Maybe all she'd get was the woman sitting in front of her now, tapping a fork against her flute of cheap sparkling wine bought last minute from the corner store. A sure downgrade from Chardonnay.

Everybody stopped stuffing themselves with burned pie to listen, forks clattering back onto plates.

'Here we go,' Grandpa murmured into his brandy.

'I just want to say thank you to you all for welcoming

me home.' Mom grinned, her red lipstick patchy. The silver paper crown won from a pulled Christmas cracker with Nick was perched wonkily on her head. 'It's been a long time since I've spent the holidays with family, and I've had the best time. Honestly, I was devastated when the news came that I was let go from work, but I think everything happens for a reason, and now, I can't help but be glad, because it's given me the opportunity to come home and be here with you all.'

Neve bit back a retort and rolled her eyes, lifting her glass as Mom said, 'Cheers. Here's to family back together again.'

'Cheers, Mom.' Nick's rosy cheeks swelled with a big grin, the only person in the house who wasn't bitter or tired.

'Yeah, yeah, cheers,' Artie muttered.

Neve didn't say anything, instead gulping down her shandy and going back to stabbing her pie with her fork.

When Grandpa started singing "Auld Lang Syne" six brandies in an hour later and a headache began to pulse its way into Neve's temples, she slipped outside for some fresh air. Snow drifted down in timid, insubstantial flakes, but she didn't have the energy to get her coat, instead wrapping her arms across her torso and glancing up at the cloud-stained sky. Peaceful, but still not enough to make her feel as though she wasn't constantly sinking in an icy lake.

What was Robin doing now? Did she miss her the way Neve missed Robin? Did Neve even *deserve* to be missed after the way she'd left things?

'You'll catch your death out here without a coat.' Nick's boots crunched in the snow as he stepped out. He draped a blanket around Neve's shoulders and then rubbed his hands together to create friction, shivering.

Neve pulled the coat closer, though she barely seemed to feel the cold anymore. 'Thanks.'

'What are you doing?'

She shrugged, watching Juniper chase a squirrel that darted across the fence. The tree branches sectioning off their small garden hung low, heavy and splintered from years worth of snowfall. Even the bird table her grandmother had bought a few months before she'd passed was on its last legs. Nothing was permanent in this house. Nothing ever had been. 'Just getting some fresh air.'

'No you're not.' Nick smirked, his breath puffing out in front of him. 'You're moping.'

She glared at that, though it was perhaps a little bit true. She'd been moping for two days now. Before she could lie and tell him she wasn't, though, Juniper barked again. A bird had fluttered down from one of the trees, red-breasted and grey-winged. It left its triangular footprints in the untouched snow as Juniper watched warily.

A robin, Neve realised, heart somehow sinking and soaring at the same time. Was the world determined to remind her of Robin every chance it got?

'Hey, look.' Nick pointed to the bird. 'Maybe it's a sign.'

Neve scoffed. 'A sign of what?'

'That you're miserable and should talk to her.'

'*No.*' She clenched her chattering teeth, glad when Juniper sent the bird flying away. Just like Neve had chased away Robin.

'You know' – Nick sighed, flakes beginning to dust his dark hair – 'I'm really tired of being the voice of reason, so if you could just figure this out on your own, I'd be endlessly grateful.'

'I never asked for your advice.'

'She left Hazel her address, you know,' he said anyway. 'I'm sure she'd be happy to give it to you.'

'And then what?' Neve snapped, turning to land her frosty eyes on him. 'I get on a fifteen-hour flight to knock on her door? I tell her I'm sorry?'

'What a great idea!' Nick flashed an annoyingly straight set of teeth. 'You start packing, I'll go get the car running.'

She scoffed at the absurdity of it. Nick's fairy-tale stories of how it should be weren't helping. 'I'm done having this conversation. I couldn't afford a plane ticket even if I wanted to.'

'Hmm.' Nick pondered this, rocking on his heels smugly. 'That's true. If only somebody bought you a plane ticket for Christmas this year . . .'

Neve whipped around, a spike of anxiety rushing through her. She waited for Nick to grin and say he was joking, but his dark features were swathed in seriousness as he rooted through the pocket of his coat. He pulled out an envelope, unsealed, with Neve's name written on the front in slanting black letters.

'No,' she whispered. 'No, you didn't.'

'We all chipped in. Even Mom. But we thought that if we ambushed you earlier with it, you probably would have destroyed the house. You're stubborn like that.' He extended the envelope. Neve glanced down at it. She didn't want to take it. She didn't want to open it. If she saw the ticket, she would have no more excuses, no more reasons why she couldn't do this. She'd have to try. She'd have to give her heart away to someone who lived halfway across the world.

'Take it,' Nick urged.

'No.' Tears filled Neve's eyes. She shook her head, trying to blink them away, but it only made them fall harder. 'You shouldn't have done this.'

'It's your last chance, Neve.'

'*No.*'

Nick's arms slapped his sides in frustration. 'Then I'm done helping you.'

'Good.' She hissed out a breath, trying desperately to relieve the pressure building in her lungs.

'Because you're beyond it,' he continued. 'You're too damn stubborn, and it'll end with you being miserable.'

'Fuck you.' The venom bubbling inside her set her teeth on edge, though she knew she was only so angry because he was right. Everything felt hollow and colourless without

Robin, yet even now, with nothing but an ocean standing in her way, Neve couldn't bring herself to get her back.

'Is this honestly what you want?' He threw his hands out again, motioning to the small, crooked little house. 'To live with Grandpa all your life?'

'No.'

'Then do something about it!'

'I have!' she shouted finally, so high that her voice cracked and Juniper stopped digging a hole in the snow to look at her.

It hadn't meant to fall out. She wasn't going to tell them until she'd done it. But it was too late to go back now. She knew that when Nick's thick brows furrowed.

'What? What have you done?' He didn't sound as though he believed her.

Neve glared at an old, rusted watering can so she wouldn't have to look at him. 'I signed up for the Alpine Canada trials in Calgary. I'm going to try to get back on the team. I . . . I was going to tell Robin,' she admitted weakly. 'She was the one who encouraged me, and I wanted so badly to tell her. I would have gone to see her even if you hadn't texted me she was leaving. But then . . . I let her go.'

It was the truth. Neve had already planned to visit Robin, not just to apologise, but also because she'd made her decision after her grandfather's pep talk. The first person Neve had wanted to tell was Robin. But she'd never had the chance, and she hadn't felt like telling anyone else. Not until she knew if she'd got in or not.

Nick remained quiet for a few moments, his lips pursed into a thin line. 'Grandpa doesn't know?'

'No. I mean, he knows I was thinking about it, but I haven't told him I signed up.'

'Why?'

'Because I don't want to come home and tell him I didn't make it a few months from now.'

He nodded as though he understood, and then pinched her elbow and pulled her into his chest. 'You're a fool.'

'So you keep telling me.' She nestled into his warmth all the same. It wasn't often they hugged anymore. Wasn't often Neve let anyone close enough to – anyone but Robin.

'I'm proud of you,' he murmured, his stubbly chin digging into her scalp. 'And if you don't want to tell him, I won't, either. But you have to know we both only want what's best for you. I think sometimes you're scared to want it for yourself.'

'I know.'

His grip tightened, chest heaving beneath her cheek as she sighed. And then, because she couldn't see his face and everything was muffled and far away beneath the blanket and her brother's arms, she finally confessed, 'Robin invited me to Manchester for New Year's. She was going to stay here over Christmas and then take me back with her. That's why we fought that day. That's why she left. Because I said no. I pushed her away, Nick, and now she's gone.'

'She's not gone,' he said softly. 'She's in Manchester, where she invited you to go, too. So go. Take the damn plane ticket and make it right.'

'I think the invitation has been well and truly revoked.'

'No, you don't. You know Robin would welcome you back with open arms. You're just scared.'

Neve hated him for always being right. She *did* want Robin back. Now, she had no reason not to try. No reason but her own fears.

In signing up for the ski trials, she'd conquered some of them – but could she keep going? Could she get on a plane and turn up at Robin's door? It felt stupid to even think about, something a corny hero of a bad rom-com would do. But what was the alternative? Never knowing if they could have made it? Never seeing Robin again, never hearing her laugh, never kissing her?

There would be other people eventually, but they wouldn't be Robin. She wouldn't feel the same, because everything with Robin had been so spectacularly different from the beginning, with the first damn moose pun.

Neve pulled away and chewed on her lip nervously. 'When's the flight?'

Nick's grin was toothy and unbridled and proud. 'Thank God.'

As it happened, the flight was booked for the day before New Year's Eve. Neve would get into Manchester the following evening, and then it was just a matter of finding Robin with the address Hazel had texted her earlier. They would visit the bakery tomorrow anyway, and Neve had bargained with Nick by asking him to take Hazel on a date while Neve was away. Whether he would or not was another story.

Neve didn't want to think about the trip too much yet. If she thought about it, she'd back out, and she was tired of backing out. So, to distract herself, she washed all of the plates by hand while Grandpa, Nick, and Mom played a game of charades in the living room. It was easy this way, to stand on the edge of it all looking in – or listening in, since she couldn't see them from here. Laughter echoed through the house, but Neve couldn't help notice that none of it belonged to Grandpa. Whether it was because he was missing Gran or still uncomfortable around Mom, she didn't know.

'Dad?' she heard Mom ask now. 'Aren't you playing?'

A moment's pause, and then Grandpa replied, 'No, Stef. I'm not playing.' The words were thick, heavy, as though he meant more than just charades.

'Don't tell me you're upset with me, too,' Mom said.

Neve bowed her head, expecting Grandpa to brush her off. He always had before, never one for conflict. It had always been Gran's job to say it like it was.

But apparently not today. 'I am upset with you. Thank you for finally noticing.'

Neve stilled with her hands in the soapy washing-up bowl as she waited for Mom's response. Her heart began to pound.

'Why? Because I had a job?'

'If you truly have to ask after all this time . . .' A pause, and then the clearing of his throat. 'Look. I can't make you visit your old man, but I'm tired of seeing the effects your absence has had on my granddaughter. June and I practically raised her, and we were happy to, but you can't just come back and expect her to be okay with it.'

'Grandpa . . .' Nick's poor attempt at an interjection.

'No, son,' Artie said. 'You made your kids feel disposable, and it's about time they got an apology for that. Neve is going through a lot. She needs her mom. If you want to come back, it's time you started being there for her. Otherwise, don't bother.'

Tears burned Neve's eyes. She pulled her hands out of the bowl slowly and shook off the suds, a strange relief rushing through her. She'd only ever wanted someone else to acknowledge the pain Mom had caused. To have her back. To make Mom see. Finally, she'd gotten that.

'She doesn't want anything to do with me.' Mom's voice shook. 'You've seen that.'

'I wonder why that may be,' Artie retorted.

Another awkward silence followed. Neve was afraid to so much as move just in case they realised she'd been listening.

'It does hurt.' Much to her surprise, the words belonged to Nick. 'With Dad not around and everything . . . it's been hard to deal with you always being away. I know you love your job, but I guess we wish you would have loved us just a little more when we needed you as kids. I spent a really long time hoping you'd come back and stick around, but you missed out on so much. You were never there.'

'I didn't know . . .' Mom said quietly. 'I didn't realise.'

And maybe that was the worst part. She hadn't stopped for a moment to think about Nick and Neve.

'I'm sorry, sweetie,' she whispered now. 'I really am.'

Neve shook her head. It just wasn't enough. It would never be enough.

And she realised then that she didn't want to be the

woman who ran away from things. She didn't want to have to apologise for not being there long after the damage had been done. She wanted to be better than that.

There was nowhere else she would have rather been than on her way to Robin to fix things. Because if she left it too late, this is what would happen. She'd never face up to her mistakes. She'd never even notice she was making them.

It was time to change the pattern.

Nick left not long after. After saying her goodbyes, Mom sashayed over to the breakfast bar and slipped onto a stool, looking at Neve expectantly.

'So,' she said.

'So.' Neve narrowed her eyes on the plate she was polishing dry. She'd purposely remained in the kitchen, drying off the plates as slowly as possible to avoid everybody.

'Nick tells me that you liked our gift.'

'Right. Yes. Thank you.'

'What was she called again? Robin? She seemed really nice.' Mom tucked her hands under her chin, her voice softer than Neve ever remembered it being before. 'I remember being drawn to her on that flight. I can just tell that some people are special, y'know? Anyway, I caught her crying. Panicking and heartbroken, bless her heart. I could hardly believe she was the same woman I met in the bakery. She was so at ease, so happy, standing next to you.'

The words were enough of a surprise to make Neve's spine stiffen, and she clutched her fingers tighter around the plate to make sure she didn't drop it. She had no way of responding, no idea how to even try. This was foreign territory, and to avoid another screaming match by pointing out the fact, she remained silent.

'I'm so sorry, Neve,' Mom whispered after a few more moments. 'You were right. I wasn't there for you growing up, and it's my fault that we don't have a close relationship. How could we when I'm always away?'

A lump built in Neve's throat, and she tried to clear it away. It was everything she'd ever wanted to hear. An admission; an apology. What now? 'It's okay.'

'No, it's not. I let you down. I let you both down, and Grandpa, too.'

'Why?' Neve's voice cracked as she threw the plate back in the sink. Both of them were polite enough to ignore it. 'Why weren't you here more? Were we so bad . . . ?'

'No, sweetie. God, no. It wasn't you at all.' Mom's eyes sparkled with tears, and she reached out for Neve's hand. Neve let her take it. 'It was me. I . . . I guess I just never felt at home here. After your dad left, I just . . . needed to feel free. Figure out who I was. I've spent my whole life searching for somewhere I belong, but I've been looking in all the wrong places. Home isn't a place, not really. It's family. It's you, Nick, and Grandpa. I'm sorry it took me so long to realise that.'

Neve understood that if nothing else. She hadn't known it, but she'd been searching, too. Settled to a life of making sure Grandpa wasn't lonely, she'd been searching for something to love again; had tried to find it on the slopes, teaching, because that's where it had always been before. But it was different now. Home wasn't a white mountain and a set of skis. Home felt like Robin's arms; looked like her freckles; smelled like citrusy soap and cinnamon; tasted like baked gingerbread and creamy frosting. Home was across the ocean, in Manchester, a city she'd never even been. Neve was just too afraid to admit it.

'If you'd told me that years ago, I would have understood,' Neve admitted. She wasn't sure if it was true, but at least she would have stopped blaming herself for her mother's absence.

'I know. I guess it took me a long time to figure myself out. I was selfish. But I do want to make things right, Neve. I don't want to spend the rest of my life with you hating me.'

'I don't hate you.' That had always been the problem. She

couldn't hate her mom, so her not being here, not choosing Neve, had always hurt more. 'I just . . . Sometimes, I just needed my mom.'

'Oh, honey.' Mom softened and rounded the counter, pulling Neve into a bruising, perfume-laced embrace. It was the first time they had hugged in years, and Neve almost collapsed with sobs of relief. She didn't have to be angry anymore. She could let go. 'I'm here now. I know it's late, but I'm here.'

Neve let herself cling on to her like a child, just for a while longer. It didn't take away all the pain she'd struggled with over the years, but it was a start. For now, that was enough.

Chapter Twenty-Two

Robin got home on New Year's Eve stinking of the frying pan oil the new sous-chef had spilled all over her on his way to the dishwasher. It had been the last straw. Enough was enough. Since getting back from Canada, she'd been miserable at work, spending her evenings longing to make new recipes the way Hazel had let her at Clement's Cakes – and ones that consisted of more than a tiny pot of crème brûlée or a stingy spoonful of sorbet for an extortionate price. She might have been able to see the positives before, but not now. Now, she knew that a restaurant with a rigidly set menu with prices she wouldn't even be able to afford wasn't where she was supposed to be.

The party had already started for everyone else. Her house was crowded with relatives, most of whom she made a point to avoid for the rest of the year. They were busy stuffing their faces with pigs in blankets and Pringles while Robin shrugged off her coat.

'Oh, Jesus. Rough night?' Wren whistled through her teeth as she eyed the yellow stain covering Robin's white chef's uniform. Her sister was iridescent in a black, sparkling cocktail dress that caught the lights when she moved. Always so annoyingly beautiful. Had they really come out of the same womb?

'I'm quitting,' Robin vowed wearily. 'Please tell me you saved me lots of food and alcohol.'

'Oh, there's plenty. Don't go into the kitchen yet, though. Mum will have a fit if she sees you dressed like that in front of the guests, and Uncle Gordon has already stripped off his shirt to dance to ABBA.'

'Ugh.' The last thing Robin wanted was to change into even more uncomfortable clothes just so that she could look her best for drunk, dancing relatives, but rebelling in stained work uniform – or, even better, pyjamas – wasn't worth the hassle. She traipsed up the stairs with Cleopawtra following at her feet, almost tripping over the loose carpet halfway up.

The harrowing patchwork girlfriend that Nanna Bessie had indeed sewn together from pillows and old throws for Robin's Christmas gift greeted her in her bedroom.

'Hello, Cate Blanket.' Robin eyed the lopsided creation on the bed warily. She was missing an eye – Cleopawtra's doing – and held no resemblance to Robin's long-time celebrity crush, Cate Blanchett, but it had been the only name she could think of. These days, she was the only thing Robin had to come home to – and perhaps she *did* make for a good big spoon when Robin was particularly lonely. Which was every night. 'Has Cleopawtra been trying to steal you away from me again?'

As though confirming it, Cleo went straight for Cate, her tail wagging happily. She was at least getting more use out of it than Robin had.

Robin dressed quickly, caring little for the fact that she still reeked of grease. With any luck, a few spritzes of perfume would be enough for Mum to lay off. The only decent thing she had to wear was a plaid jumpsuit Wren had gifted her for Christmas, but it would do. It wasn't as though she was leaving the house anyway, for God's sake.

A knock on the door disturbed her from twisting her knotted hair into a bun.

'Come in,' she sang, and then winced when Mum stepped into the bedroom.

'Okay, I know I look awful but I don't have time for a shower and the new bloke spilled oil all over me at work and it's been an absolutely awful day – an awful week, actually,' she blurted, tucking a hair grip between her teeth so that she could pin back any stray tendrils. 'This will have to do, and no I won't change.'

Mum said nothing, which somehow felt worse than her usual scolding. Instead, she wandered over to the bed and perched on the corner, smoothing down the poppy-patterned sheets as she did.

'Oh, God, what have I done?' Robin's mind instantly assumed the worst. Had she left a few puddles on the floor after her shower this morning? Had she not washed her cereal bowl? Had she forgotten to feed Cleopawtra again?

'Nothing, sweetheart. You've done nothing.'

Sweetheart? Mum never called her sweetheart. "Pain in the neck" perhaps, and "the demon who forced me to have a C-section against my will" sometimes, but never "sweetheart". Though the silent treatments had stopped, they were from the north of England. That meant no signs of love. Ever. Unless for strangers in the street, in which case, a simple awkward smile would do.

'Are you drunk already?' Robin questioned tentatively.

'No.' Mum patted the space beside her. 'Come sit.'

Robin made sure to take very slow, very cautious steps towards the bed, trying not to rile a wild beast. 'What's up, Mum?'

'You haven't been very happy recently, have you?'

She frowned at that. 'What do you mean?'

Mum sighed and tried again, her throat bobbing with a swallow. 'It's just that you seem to have lost your sparkle a little bit. I don't think you're happy, Robbie.'

'I'm happy,' Robin said slowly. It felt like a lie. She wasn't miserable. She wasn't crying herself to sleep every night. She was just . . . lost. And for a minute, somewhere at the foot of the Rockies, she thought she'd found herself. Now, she was searching again. 'I'm fine. What are you on about?'

'I suppose I've been feeling a little bit guilty, is all. I forced you to come home when you wanted to stay. I . . .' Mum seemed to blink back tears, and it was enough for Robin's blood to run cold. What was this about? 'I've been selfish with you, Robin. You're the baby of the family and I wanted to keep you here, where I know you're safe, but it was wrong of me. I see that now. You've been sad since you got back, and it's my fault.'

'It's not your fault.' Robin's voice was hoarse, her palms sweaty. She had no idea Mum had ever felt that way about her. She'd always thought her overbearing, not . . . caring. 'I came back for my own reasons.'

'What happened while you were away?'

It was the first time Mum had asked about the holiday. Because of that, Robin hadn't spoken to her about any of it. It was Wren she could confide in; Wren who had always been easy to talk to.

'A lot of things,' Robin evaded now, playing with her sleeve nervously. 'It doesn't matter now.'

'I don't want you to feel as though you can't talk to me.'

But Robin *couldn't* talk to her. If she told Mum that she wanted to quit her job and find a new place to work; if she told her that she'd been considering applying for a job in Calgary; if she told her any of it . . . Mum wouldn't just sit and listen and accept it. She wouldn't be happy or proud. She'd argue. Tell Robin that she couldn't move away. She couldn't let go of a nice, decent-paying job. She couldn't leave her family. She had other people to think about.

But she couldn't say any of this, so she rose, straightened out her jumpsuit and then dabbed a wand of lip gloss across her lips. 'Where is this coming from?'

'I just worry, that's all. I hope you know that I only ever want you to be happy.'

'Even if it meant moving out?' Robin couldn't keep from asking, her stomach twisting with nerves, and she regretted asking the question immediately.

Mum pursed her lips as she considered the question. 'Of course. If that's what you feel is right.'

In other words, it wasn't the right answer. 'Moving away? Getting a new job?'

'Is that what you want?'

'Maybe,' Robin admitted for the first time aloud. 'I don't know. I don't think the restaurant is where I should be anymore. I was . . . I was looking at job listings in Calgary. Not that I want to move there, or anything, but just . . . Maybe change would be nice. I don't know where, but . . . well, there are bakeries everywhere.'

Mum's eyes shone with tears, and Robin knew she had gone too far.

'Mum,' she whispered helplessly.

'I only get upset because the idea of not having you here every day . . . I'd miss you. Your sister's all grown up now. She and Tom are solid. You're the only one I have here with me, and now your dad . . .' Mum's words were thick with grief, and she swallowed them down to replace them. 'It was difficult being here all alone while you were away, that's all. The house gets quiet. But you're right, Robin.' Mum reached out her hand, and Robin took it uncertainly. 'If change is what you need, you have my support. It's what your dad would have wanted.'

After the way Mum had reacted to a two-week holiday, Robin wasn't certain that she meant it, but it was enough just to hear it for now. She had her blessing. She could branch out, find something new. At least she was trying. 'Thank you. I miss him, too, you know.'

A soft, solemn smile flickered across Mum's lips, and she placed a gentle kiss on Robin's forehead before wiping her eyes with a handkerchief that had been tucked up her sleeve. 'I know, love. We all do. But he's with us. Bet he's bloody proud of you and all your adventures. Maybe it's time I started having a few of my own, eh?'

He would have been proud. In fact, Robin had visited his grave on Boxing Day just to tell him all about Canada. He loved taking the family on holidays, though Mum talked him out of them the older they got. Robin didn't want to be that way. She didn't want to talk herself out of anything anymore or let anyone else do it, either. Maybe Mum finally felt the same.

'I think that's a really good idea,' Robin said.

'Anyway, I better get back to the guests. Don't take too much longer, okay?'

'I'm ready,' Robin said, though she was barefoot and had no intention of putting shoes on. The only options were high heels, which would probably have her breaking her neck before she'd even reached the stairs, or scuffed tennis shoes.

She followed Mum down the stairs, checking the clock on the wall as she did. Ten-thirty. Only an hour and a half until midnight. She couldn't help but wonder what Neve was doing now in Clement Falls; sat on the couch with Artie, maybe, or at the bar with Nick. Maybe she'd even made amends with her mum. And maybe, just for a second, Robin let herself wish she was there, too.

And then she continued down, into the sea of overbearing and quirky relatives who wanted to know if she was still single, still a lesbian, still a pastry chef, as though any of these things changed on a regular basis. She stuffed herself with Doritos and greeted them all half-heartedly, searching for her sister as she mingled. But Wren was nowhere to be seen. Only Tom idled by the collection of drinks in the kitchen.

She thought nothing of it until she made her way back into the hallway and found Wren at the door, her brows furrowed. She must have sensed Robin coming because she lifted her gaze. Robin didn't like the way her eyes glittered with warning.

'There's someone here for you.' Wren's words were barely audible above the din of rowdy relatives and awful pop music.

Robin frowned and placed down her sharing bag of crisps, clapping her fingers free of the cheesy dust before she approached the door. 'If it's a Jehovah's witness again, I swear—'

But it wasn't a Jehovah's witness – not unless Neve had taken up unsolicited door-to-door evangelism.

That wasn't right, though. How could Neve be here, in England, on Robin's dreary cul-de-sac, her boots buried in sludge from the brief and pathetic bouts of snowfall they'd been getting? It didn't make sense, didn't compute, like those photos of cats wearing suits and ties on the internet. Cats weren't supposed to wear suits and ties. Neve wasn't supposed to be in Manchester.

'Hi,' Neve greeted gingerly, a crooked smile gracing her lips. And Robin's heart almost racketed out of her chest, because God, she had missed her, even if she was a potential hallucination.

But it still hurt. Robin thought of all the ways they'd made a mess of things together, and couldn't help but wonder why the woman she thought she'd never see again was now standing on her doorstep.

'I'll leave you to it,' Wren whispered in Robin's ear, giving her shoulder a reassuring squeeze before she did. Robin barely felt it. She felt nothing, saw nothing but Neve, and had to cling on to the doorjamb for dear life or else risk her knees buckling from beneath her.

'What are you doing here?' Robin swallowed in a desperate attempt to ease her dry throat, but it did nothing. 'Are you . . . Are you real? Have I gone mad?'

'I'm real. I was hoping that maybe the New Year's invite still stood.'

Robin sucked in a breath and stepped out into the cold, the stone rough and wet against her bare soles. The door swung shut behind her, leaving the music and the laughter a dull muffle that could no longer reach her. 'You came all the way here?'

Neve nodded. 'Looks that way.'

'Why?'

'Because . . .' Neve chewed on her bottom lip, eyes sparkling like twin lakes in the silvery moonlight. 'I missed you. And because Nick bought me a ticket for Christmas. But mostly because I miss you.'

Robin let the words sink in. They'd been all she'd wanted to hear a week ago. Now, they held little weight. 'It was your choice to end this.'

'It was the wrong choice.' Neve's voice shook. 'I'm sorry. I'm so sorry, Robin. I don't want this to be over. I never wanted it to be over, and I thought that by pushing you away I was protecting myself from that. But I wasn't. And you leaving . . . It hurt all the same.'

Robin had no idea what to say. Nothing she felt seemed enough to put into words. She only knew that she had dreamed of this. But she had vowed not to let herself love too easily again, not after all of the heartache. So she remained frozen, wondering if Neve might disappear in a moment.

But she didn't.

'I went after you,' Neve continued. 'After I heard you were leaving, I went back to the cabin. You weren't there. I was too late. But I went after you, Robin, because I was ready to fight, ready to try. I still am.'

'The distance—' Robin's argument was cut short.

'We'll find a way to deal with the distance. I don't care. They gave me one of those yummy cheesecake pots on the plane, so the flight didn't turn out so bad. I'd do it again. I just don't want to spend the rest of my life wondering what would have happened if I wasn't a complete idiot. I like you. I can't *stop* liking you, and when you're not with me, I miss you like crazy. It has to mean something. It has to be worth trying for.'

Tears clogged Robin's throat, her teeth chattering against the biting cold. And for all the promises she'd made to herself, that cord still tugged her towards Neve.

'I couldn't stop thinking about you,' Neve whispered, and her own tears spilled down her cheeks. 'I just wanted you to come back. I've never begged for anybody to come back before but . . . please, Robin. Please, let's just try again.'

'You really mean it?' Robin asked.

'I wouldn't be here if I didn't.'

She dared to take a step forward, though her toes were numb and might have fallen off at any moment. This was all she'd wanted. For someone to try. And Neve had tried. She'd come all this way, had done the one thing she didn't want to for her. How could Robin walk away now?

She couldn't, so instead she rested her hands on Neve's cheeks, their eyes locking. Robin saw the pleas and the apologies and the want there, felt it mirrored in herself – and something in her knew that it was right and real. They were where they needed to be, even with the uncertainty trying to topple them from beneath. With Neve's hands snaking around her elbows, it didn't matter. Robin felt steady. It was enough.

She leaned into her, their lips meeting as though they'd never separated, and it was easy to believe they hadn't for all the ways Robin's body seemed to settle in and make her home in Neve again.

'It's not midnight yet,' she whispered without knowing why. 'Shouldn't we wait?'

'We've waited long enough.'

Neve's nose grazed against Robin's. They kissed again, hungrily now, Robin's body thrumming with fireworks – and for them, it was midnight. For them, it was a New Year's kiss. While everyone else waited for the countdown, Robin and Neve started fresh then and there, with time racing to catch up with them.

Her toes, on the other hand . . . 'I think I have severe frostbite,' she murmured against Neve's lips. 'My feet are frozen.'

'Where are your *shoes*?' Neve questioned.

'Oh, I'm sorry. I wasn't expecting a grand gesture on my doorstep tonight.' She pushed the door open and collapsed back into the noisy warmth of her house. Neve followed inside and shut the cold out, their hands still intertwined. Robin dragged her under the stairs where no one would see them, hidden among coats and shoes. She wasn't ready to share her with her family yet.

Oh, God. Her family.

'I hope you know that my family is absolutely bonkers. Like, if you walked out again now and saved yourself, I'd understand.'

'I'm not going anywhere.' Neve's cheek dimpled as she leaned in close, her breath fanning across Robin's face.

'*Ow!*' A prick of pain in Robin's torso caused her to jump away, searching for the source. 'Why are you all spiky? Are you carrying a cactus?'

'Oh, I forgot!' Neve rooted through her pocket and pulled out . . . a branch of *holly*. Puzzled, Robin could only stare at it. Was it supposed to mean something? 'They wouldn't let me take the mistletoe through customs, and the best I could do was the holly bush outside your house. Sorry.'

Giggling, Robin sank into her again. 'I taught you well.'

Neve pinched the holly above their heads as they kissed in the shadows. Everything in Robin pulsated to life again. The loss she'd been feeling disappeared. Her heart stitched itself back together. The blood in her veins turned to fire again.

Neve is here. Neve is here. Neve is here.

Her heart thumped along to the reminder, a mantra Robin couldn't stop repeating in her head.

She pulled away just to make sure, trying to blink the Neve-induced haze from her eyes – but it stayed. Neve stayed. 'Hello.' She felt like an idiot, especially when she grinned toothily.

'Hi.' Neve sparkled just as she had that night beneath the Northern Lights – brighter, maybe.

'I missed you.'

'Me, too,' she said, her feather-light fingers dancing along Robin's jaw. 'And I've been wanting to tell you something.'

'Something good?' It was practically a plea. No more bad news. No more fighting.

'I think so.' Neve pulled off her hat and smoothed down

her short hair quickly. Her face was flushed, lips pink from Robin's kisses. 'I signed up for the ski trials in Calgary.'

Robin had to swallow down a squeal of excitement, instead flinging her arms around Neve so tightly that they both almost stumbled to the floor. 'I'm so proud.'

'I wouldn't have done it if you weren't there, Robin.' Neve's hands crawled up to the nape of Robin's neck, burying themselves in her hair.

'So what you're saying is that it pays to be annoying?'

A giggle fell from her, and Robin wished she could hear it again and again. Neve happy. Neve laughing. Neve in her arms. 'It certainly seems to have gotten you a long way.'

'*Yoohoo!*' The shrill call interrupted them.

It came from Wren, who stood at the foot of the stairs with her hands cupped around her mouth. Thankfully, nobody else was with her. 'Are you going to hide under the stairs all night or are you going to introduce us properly?'

Robin laced her fingers through Neve's. 'Are you sure—?'

Her question was cut off before Robin could even ask it. Neve stepped out into the hallway, pulling Robin with her. 'Hi. I'm Neve.'

'Oh, I know who you are.' Wren glanced coldly between Neve and Robin, crossing her arms over her chest. 'What are your intentions with my sister?'

'*Wren!*' Robin scolded.

'*What?*' Wren replied innocently. 'I've always wanted to say it, and last time I didn't, look what happened!'

Lexi happened. But Neve wasn't Lexi. Neve was like nobody Robin had ever met before, and Robin could only hope that she could trust her. She'd felt so solid, so reliable, since the moment Robin had met her. Maybe even then, in the woods, Robin had known.

'I suppose my intentions are something we have to figure out together,' Neve said. 'But they're only good, I promise. Also, it's really nice to meet you.'

'You too! Welcome to Manchester!' Wren's stern features

softened, and she pulled Neve into a bruising hug. Neve's arms flitted in the air for a few moments as though she didn't quite know what to do with them, and then they settled around Wren's shoulders.

Over Neve's shoulder, Wren mouthed, 'She's hot.' And then, to them both as she pulled away: 'Come on. Let's introduce you to the rest of the family. Also, please don't make direct eye contact with the topless man in the kitchen. That's Uncle Gordon and we all agree he's very strange.'

Neve wrinkled her nose. 'Noted.'

They ambled into the kitchen together, passing Aunty Caroline, who was ranting about the current state of the Tory government, and Cousin Teagan, a three-year-old who was painting her sleeping dad's face with glittery makeup on the couch.

The kitchen was even worse. Uncle Gordon had stripped off his trousers now, too, and was carting his wife around the kitchen to "Knowing Me, Knowing You" in Christmas-pudding-patterned boxers. Aunty Joan had taken out her teeth and was scaring the kids by making them appear to talk with her hand. Cousin Heather sported a remarkably teenagery frown through crimped, dyed black hair, very deep into her goth phase along with the heavily pierced boyfriend standing next to her. Robin glanced at them all warily, wondering what Neve thought, but if she was intimidated, she didn't show it.

Wren marched them straight up to Mum in the corner, whose eyes were already bleary from a few too many sherries.

'All right, Wren.' Robin slapped her sister's hands away from Neve's shoulder possessively. 'I'll do the introduction part, thanks.'

Wren took a step back and went to join Tom, who was too polite to tell Alice, Uncle Gordon's toddler, to stop pulling on his earlobe while he shoved a chicken skewer into his mouth. Complete mayhem.

'Mum, this is Neve,' Robin introduced. 'I met her in Calgary when I was away, and she came to join the party!'

'Oh, heavens!' Mum hopped up from her seat as though she'd just received an electric shock, wiping down her hands on her dress and almost spilling her drink in the process. 'Why didn't you say you'd invited your own guests? I would have made more egg mayonnaise!'

'It's just one guest, Mum – Neve.'

'It's a pleasure to meet you, Ms Ellis.' Neve extended her hand politely.

'Oh my golly-gosh, you're Canadian!' Mum gasped, gathering her into a hug. 'Did you fly here?'

'Nah,' Robin said. 'She walked.'

'Oh, Robin. Sarcasm is the lowest form of wit.' She pulled back to look at Neve properly, gripping her tightly by the shoulders. 'How did you two meet? Robin didn't tell me she'd made friends!'

That was because Robin hadn't told Mum anything about the trip.

She felt a presence sidling up to her, the unmistakable old-lady smell of potpourri and clementines filling her nostrils. Apparently, Nanna Bessie was very interested in Robin's new guest. She pointed an arthritic finger and said, very predictably, 'You know, my neighbour is one of those bisexuals. I think it's just marvellous.'

Neve bit down on an amused smile as Mum's attention darted between all three of them.

'*Oh!*' Robin could almost see the light bulb go on above her head. It was quick for Mum. She'd thought that Robin and Lexi had just been best friends for about six months, and had almost had a heart attack the first time they'd kissed in front of her at Robin's birthday dinner. 'Oh, I see! You two are . . .'

'*Anyway!*' Robin pulled Neve away quickly, cringing. 'Neve will be staying with us while she's here, and you're not going to be weird around her. I'm going to go and get her a drink now. Ba-bye!'

The drink in question was a bottle of wine she pinched

off the side before dragging Neve back out into the living room. Compared to the kitchen, anywhere was quiet, and Robin's ears hummed with the change. Still, she wanted to be with Neve. Only Neve. Just like they'd been in Calgary. It had been so peaceful, so easy, especially when Neve had introduced her to Artie and they'd spent the night asleep on the couch together.

'Shall we go upstairs?' Robin wiggled the wine bottle around suggestively.

'Are you sure? I don't want to drag you away from your family.'

'My family has had me for twenty-six very long years.' Robin was already pushing her way back to the stairs, hauling Neve with her. '*You* can have me tonight.'

Neve whistled through her teeth. 'You don't waste any time, do you? You haven't even bought me dinner yet.'

'Oh, you know what I mean.' Still, Robin couldn't hide her blush as she tucked them both away in her bedroom, the music and raucous laughter ebbing to muffles. It was the first time they'd shared a bedroom. The first time they'd done a lot of things, actually. 'How long are you staying?'

'Nick got me an open return, but I need to get back to skiing next week if I want to be ready for the trials in March.'

A week. A week was enough. Robin would soak up every moment of it. Placing down the wine bottle, she turned around from the vanity – and winced. Neve had found Nanna Bessie's pillow girlfriend and hovered over it with a concerned frown.

'What's this?' She twisted the one googly eye around curiously.

'That's Cate Blanket, my other girlfriend.' The word spilled out before Robin could stop it, leaving her face blazing with heat. *Girlfriend*. Typical that Robin would jump the gun when they'd only actually known each other for a bloody fortnight. Neve had only just gotten through the door, for God's sake.

'Oh, your *other* girlfriend?' Neve's brow arched, a crooked smirk curling across her lips. Robin waited for her to run for the hills, but she didn't. For some reason.

'I didn't mean that . . .' Robin stuttered. 'Obviously, we're not . . . I mean, I wasn't suggesting . . .'

Neve silenced Robin's verbal diarrhoea with a kiss, her arms looping around Robin's neck. 'I don't think you need your other girlfriend anymore. You have me.'

'Maybe I can have Nanna Bessie make one for you, too, for when you go back to Calgary,' Robin suggested, breathless and certain that at any moment, she might explode. Would it always feel like the first time with Neve? 'I can stick my face on it.'

'No, thank you. The googly eye is following me, and it's creeping me out.'

They smiled into another kiss, and heat snaked through Robin's gut. Without meaning to, her hands began to search: Neve's jacket, the dips and swells of her body beneath it. She unzipped the coat, greedy, uncaring. Neve was here and she was hers and Robin had never wanted somebody so much before.

Neve's nimble fingers knotted in Robin's hair.

'Sorry.' Robin grimaced, wishing now that she'd bothered to have a shower after work. 'I smell like frying pan oil.'

'You smell like cakes. You always smell like cakes.'

Did she? Robin had never noticed, but her heart soared at the fact all the same, and then panged when Neve searched her hips, her spine, the crook of her neck.

'Where the hell does this end? How do you take it off?' She huffed in frustration, pulling away to get a better look at Robin's playsuit.

'Oh, there's a button . . .' Robin brushed her hair off her shoulder. Neve unbuttoned it before Robin shimmied it off her shoulders.

And then she was pushed back to the bed, her weightless

body flopping down onto the mattress when the edge hit the back of her knees sooner than expected. Neve straddled her, still kissing, but now behind her ear, her jaw, her collarbone, her bare shoulders. All over her, just like Robin had wanted the night of the Northern Lights.

'Sorry, Cate Blanket, but you need to move.' Neve yanked her away and threw her to the floor. Then she was kissing her and touching her, her knuckles tracing a line down the valley of Robin's breasts. Lower. Her mouth followed like a second carriage on a train track, roving across slatted ribs and soft flesh, to her belly button. Robin stifled a moan when Neve's lips found the waistband of her underwear, tugging on the delicate pink ribbon there.

Her breath fanned across Robin's lower stomach for a moment as though in asking. As though she needed to ask. Robin's toes were already curling with want, need, and she threaded her fingers through Neve's short hair desperately.

'I missed you,' Robin whispered again: a prayer; an answer; a raw, honest-to-God truth.

The corner of her mouth dimpling, Neve tugged off her jumper, and Robin finally saw her for the first time. Not all of her, but enough to know that there was no going back, no reversing what they'd found together. She was all sinewy muscle and delicate hollows, pale skin against dark hair, and Robin wanted to kiss every inch of her; wanted to memorise the crests and the dips and the flesh in between. Robin had never felt at home in her own body before, but she could do with Neve, with that contrast of Neve's honed leanness and Robin's dozens of curves. She could feel at home with Neve's body, too, and so their legs forged together to prove it, to make a start.

Neve's mouth returned to Robin's belly, placing delicate kisses across the lowest ridge of her soft, stretch-mark-dimpled skin before tugging at her underwear again. Robin lifted her hips, watching as Neve's head dipped between her legs to slip her underwear away. And then she was bare. Uncovered.

Neve's eyes sparkled just like they had when they'd watched the Northern Lights together.

A lick of heat surged through Robin when Neve's nose brushed against her, and she gasped out for more, tugging her hair again. She'd never been so in tune with her own body before.

So Neve gave her more; just by being here, by proving that she wanted to be, it was more than Robin had ever gotten before, but it kept going, the flames spreading, Neve's fingers clutching Robin's thighs until her mouth finally drove her to an aching, dizzying release. Robin whispered her name over and over again as they moved together; as bliss trickled through her; as she realised that nothing in the world had ever felt this good, this right, and it hadn't mattered where they were: Calgary or Manchester, Canada or England, snow or sleet or rain, Christmas or New Year's.

Together or apart, Robin would fight for it. And she would let it hurt if it had to, as long as it meant moments like this. As long as it meant loving Neve, tasting her, melding with her. And that's what they did.

Neve didn't know where she was when she woke in the darkness not long after. When she caught the blonde tendrils of Robin's hair pouring across the pillow beside her, the panic ebbed as soon as it had started. She checked her phone on the bedside table, the movement eliciting a groan from Robin that sounded a little bit like the moans Neve had drawn from her earlier; a reminder, sending an echo of those sparks through her again.

'Time is it?' Robin mumbled into her pillow.

Neve squinted against the phone screen's brightness. 'Midnight.' The realisation only dawned on her after she said it. 'New Year.'

As though confirming it, a cacophony of cheers floated from downstairs, the first keening fireworks swirling through the velvet night outside.

Robin lifted her head, adorable bewilderment crossing her features for a moment. It was quickly replaced with a smile, one that Neve couldn't possibly deserve. Nobody could. It swathed her in warmth, left her floating with the embers outside: her welcome into a year of brand-new possibilities and experiences. With Robin. There couldn't have been anything better.

'Happy New Year, Robin,' Neve whispered, brushing Robin's hair from her face and peppering a delicate kiss on her nose. She wouldn't bother to make any resolutions this year. She knew what she wanted. It was here, with her now.

She would keep it as long as it stayed.

Robin's eyes fluttered closed, and she shuffled closer, their legs knotting together, her warmth a steady pulse against Neve's chest. 'Happy New Year, love.'

If it continued as well as it had started, it was going to be the best one yet.

Epilogue

As it happened, Robin was warming up to the snow – as best she could, anyway. She could manage it until it turned to sludge, at least, which is what it had done on a Saturday morning in March in Calgary, Alberta. She stamped it off her shoes on the welcome mat of Clement's Cakes and then shrugged off her parka, exchanging it for the apron behind the counter, where her name tag was pinned.

In the end, it hadn't been that difficult a decision. There were no bakeries in Manchester that could ever come close to the magic of Clement's and the joy she'd felt there this Christmas, so she'd had Hazel ask her boss about the city branch, applied for her visa, and found a one-bedroom apartment to rent not long after. Mum had been surprisingly supportive of the whole thing; the silent treatment had only lasted a week this time round, and now she called every day. She'd even planned to visit over summer.

Robin looked forward to the warmer months, when she hopefully wouldn't have to mop up her own footprints every time she walked through the door. Well, unless Canadian summers were as rainy as British ones – in which case, she might be due a relocation to somewhere like Greece instead.

'Good morning!' sang Robin's co-worker, Sunny, whose name suited her personality. Whether rain – or rather, snow – or shine, she walked into the bakery each morning with a smile on her face and some form of colourful hat, and Robin enjoyed her job all the more because of it.

'Morning, Sunny,' greeted Robin happily.

With her pastry chef experience, the manager had soon

put Robin in charge of the dessert menus, and she went over today's now before the baking began. Plenty had been prepped last night. All that was left to make were the banana split blondies and lavender blueberry muffins. With spring supposedly on its way, she'd strayed from the heavy, spiced chocolate pastries of Christmas. Raspberry and white chocolate was her new favourite flavour combo, and it showed in the row of delicate cheesecakes in the fridge.

As soon as Clement's doors opened at nine a.m., Robin was rushed off her feet. Apparently, people still needed coffee at the weekend, even if they had nowhere to commute to. It stayed that way well beyond lunch, too, until Robin barely noticed that the woman requesting a granola bar and hot cocoa was, in fact, her girlfriend.

'Oh!' she gasped, finding Neve staring expectantly at her as she handed over the order. 'Hello!'

'Honestly.' Neve shook her head in despair and shimmied out of the queue so that they could talk without the customers growing impatient. 'I'm beginning to think you love this job more than me.'

Robin hadn't actually claimed to love Neve at all, yet, though she'd come close a few times – and she did. It was too soon to throw out the word, though they both knew it was waiting patiently on their tongues. For the moment, Neve still lived with Artie and Stefanie in Clement Falls, but the trials were tomorrow. Whether they went successfully or not, she planned to move in with Robin at the end of the month, and had already gotten a job offer as a ski instructor at a leisure centre closer to the city. Juniper, of course, would be joining her, and Robin had made sure to get a pet-friendly place for that reason alone.

'So dramatic.' Robin scoffed and pecked her on the nose before glancing around. Sunny and the new trainee, May, seemed to have everything under control for now. 'Anyway, I'm glad you came. I have something to show you.'

Neve looked worried. 'Oh no. What now?'

With a roll of her eyes, Robin scurried into the kitchen, where a handmade poster had been propped against the wall last night. She'd stayed here until ten p.m. to finish the thing, and it had taken everything in her not to send a picture to Neve right away. She displayed it proudly when she emerged now, giving Neve a moment to read the lettering she'd shaded in with blue and green markers.

"*Neve-r Give Up!*" it read, with Neve's name contained in a slightly lopsided heart. Beneath, Robin had written: "*I Snow You Can Do It!*"

Neve lifted her hand to her mouth to suppress a chuckle, her eyes dancing over the words quickly. 'What *is* this?'

'It's your sign for tomorrow,' said Robin. 'I'm going to be cheering you on!'

'You're ridiculous.' Even as she said it, Neve's lips spread into a wide grin, and she leaned forward for a kiss. Robin made it as work-friendly as she could, but still lingered when Neve's warmth, her smell, *her*, wrapped around her.

'Are you nervous?'

'A little.' Neve shrugged. 'But I'm okay. If it doesn't work out, it doesn't work out. I have other things to look forward to.'

'Like our trip to Manchester next month?' Robin reminded her. It was Mum's birthday, and Mum, though slowly learning to accept Robin's absence, refused to let her miss it. Not that Robin would. 'It *will* work out. And if it doesn't, it's because there's something better waiting.'

Neve smiled softly and tucked a loose, slightly sweaty strand of hair behind Robin's ear. 'I know.'

She'd come so far from being afraid to even try that it made Robin's heart burst with warmth. Neve deserved every bit of goodness in the world, and Robin prayed she would get it tomorrow.

'All right, lovebirds,' Sunny teased from the cash register. 'Wrap it up. We've got customers.'

Robin groaned, though getting back to work wasn't a

bad thing at all. She left a final, delicate kiss on Neve's lips. 'See you tonight?'

'I'll be here.' Neve grinned. She would go to the leisure centre for her final practice now, and then they'd planned for Neve to stay with Robin tonight so she didn't have to get up too early only to drive back to the city for the trials again tomorrow. She pushed off the counter, casting Robin a final wave. 'Love you.'

The world stopped, time with it. Neve paled, her eyes widening as though she couldn't believe she'd said it, either.

But she had, and it made Robin's stomach flutter with an army of sharp-winged butterflies. She beamed, and then before Neve could take it back, said: 'Good, because I love you, too.'

Neve's features relaxed in an instant. She waved a final time and left the bakery with her granola bar and hot cocoa still in hand. Robin watched her drift past the window and couldn't staunch the smile on her face.

Because she *did* love Neve, and she was more certain of it than she'd been of anything before. And now Neve knew it, too.

Adjusting her ski goggles a final time, Neve sucked in a deep breath and readied herself at the top of the slope. She was surrounded on both sides by the crowd, who lingered behind the barriers and cheered when warranted. Robin's sign stuck out like a sore thumb towards the back, causing Neve to chuckle again at the terrible puns. If Robin hadn't been here, Neve wasn't sure she'd have made it to Calgary at all. Her nerves were an unsteady current of electricity, zapping through her veins and sending her internal organs fluttering erratically.

But Robin was here. So were Grandpa and Nick and Hazel, hand in hand, Mom and Irina, and Margo. And they all believed in her. So Neve owed it to them to believe in herself.

She tightened her grip around the ski poles determinedly,

bending her knees and sinking low. And then a horn sounded, and Neve pushed off the powdery snow, all thoughts, all worries, drifting behind her with the crowd. Robin's sign slipped past Neve in a blur of colour. She made her first jump gracefully, and then a second, a third, swerving down the slope as though the skis were part of her anatomy; as though she did this every day.

She did. She had done for years, and now it was second nature.

The crowd cheered as Neve reached the finish line what felt like mere nanoseconds later, skis burying themselves into the snow on a diagonal. She was breathless, dizzy, weightless, floating, and only an announcement over the speakers surrounding the slopes brought her back to earth.

It was her time – and not only was it her personal best, but also one of the quickest and smoothest they'd seen today. Tears welled in Neve's eyes as she pulled off her helmet, receiving pats on the back from old teammates who had been delighted to see her return – but her attention slipped straight back to her family. Robin was at the centre of them, cheering and jumping, her biggest supporter.

Neve smiled, tears of joy filling her eyes. She'd done it. Now there was only waiting to see if it was enough.

Acknowledgements

I firstly must thank my wonderful agent, Clare Coombes at Liverpool Literary Agency. *Honeymoon for One* wouldn't be half the book it is without you (literally, since it was once only a novella), and I can't express how grateful I am that I found you to champion my stories and make this one a smidge more British. Somewhere along the way, I forgot that I was allowed to write characters with a northern background like mine, and you reminded me the minute you introduced yourself. You work magic for us northern writers every day, and it's such a pleasure to be part of the journey. Thank you for laughing at my moose puns, too.

Thank you to the Embla team for choosing Robin and Neve's story and welcoming me to the family. I'm so lucky that my books found a home with you. Special thanks to Hannah Smith, my lovely editor, who has always been so enthusiastic, warm, and supportive of this book and also has thousands of handy facts up her sleeve, spanning from Canadian Alpine skiing to the British peerage system (but that's a story for another time).

To my best friends and soul mates, Leah and Ivy. Thank you for always meeting me on Google docs. You are always the first to read my first drafts, and there's no one I'd trust more with my half-formed ideas and typos. You have no idea how much it means to me to be able to share this journey with you. Thank you for believing in me even when the imposter syndrome kicks in and proudly collecting my books on your "Rachel shelves". Writing would be such a lonely experience without you both. I love you endlessly. Also to

Mahlina, the milk to my honey. Thank you for sending me those random midnight memes. I'll cherish your friendship always. To Fi and Beth, who I don't get to see often enough but who still support me nonetheless. To Katie and India, my first uni friends, who made sure I didn't drop out when I really, really wanted to and made my first year at Chester bearable. I'll always be thankful for the memories we shared in Astbury House.

To the Bryant Street Babes: Wendy, Emma, and Melissa. We started our little writing adventure together, and you'll forever be the first people I want to squeal with when an exciting email lands in my inbox. When people ask me who my favourite authors are, you're always the first to come to mind. Not that I'm biased. Thank you for the beta reads and the long Discord rants. We didn't choose an easy job, but it'll be worth it in the end.

To Rebecca, otherwise known as Indie Book Spotlight. I'll always be in awe of the way you put so much time and effort into championing the indie community. You make Twitter a better place, which is no easy feat. Thank you for the RTs, reviews, and just being a wonderful person.

To my mum, nanna, and auntie, for encouraging me to read when it mattered. My love of books got me here, and I have you to thank for that. For also saying "you liked that one set by the sea" when vaguely talking about my books and nodding to my rants when expected. To my sister, Isabelle, who claims she wants to be a writer like her big sister despite never reading the books I buy (force onto) her and instead makes a lot of noise when I'm working. I'll pay you back when you're older.

To Enzo, my very own Juni-poo, who is always by my side or else sitting on my feet. I'll always spend my writing breaks rubbing your tummy.

To the creative writing department at the University of Salford. My lecturer asked me on my graduation day, "You'll keep writing, won't you?" and I didn't quite know the answer yet. But I did, and I'm grateful for the encouragement. Your feedback has stayed with me.

Lastly, to the readers who have picked up one of my books or still have yet to; particularly to those who support queer fiction, as well as those who have read my novellas, left reviews, and supported my work. There are already so many more of you than I could have dreamed of and it's because of you that this book is out in the world. You taught me there will always be an audience for my little sapphic kissing books, and I thank you for letting me be part of such a friendly community. Also, to fellow sapphic authors, who make the publishing world a little bit brighter. Nothing is more wonderful than seeing yourself in a character, and if Robin and Neve resonate with even one person, I'll be happy. Like the characters in this book, I hope you find love, family, and hope in these pages. After all, that's what it's all for in the end, and we need a little bit of light – now more than ever.

Rachel Bowdler grew up and still lives just outside of Manchester, on the edge of West Yorkshire. After graduating from the University of Salford with a degree in English and Creative Writing, she became a freelance romance author, focusing on queer, plus-size, and working-class characters. Her only wish is that her words make readers feel warm and fuzzy inside. When she isn't assaulting her computer keyboard or daydreaming about fictional people in her pyjamas, you can find her cuddling and walking her talkative dog, Enzo, venturing out with her camera, wishing it was time to put up her Christmas tree, and painting with watercolours (but not very well!).

About Embla Books

Embla Books is a digital-first publisher of standout commercial adult fiction. Passionate about storytelling, the team at Embla publish books that will make you 'laugh, love, look over your shoulder and lose sleep'. Launched by Bonnier Books UK in 2021, the imprint is named after the first woman from the creation myth in Norse mythology, who was carved by the gods from a tree trunk found on the seashore – an image of the kind of creative work and crafting that writers do, and a symbol of how stories shape our lives.

Find out about some of our other books and stay in touch:

Twitter, Facebook, Instagram: @emblabooks
Newsletter: https://bit.ly/emblanewsletter

www.ingramcontent.com/pod-product-compliance
Lightning Source LLC
Chambersburg PA
CBHW020229260626
47156CB00002B/600